CHANCE

Sue Ryland

P en Press

Copyright © Sue Ryland 2009

All rights reserved

No part of this publication may be reproduced, stored in a retrieval system, or transmitted in any form or by any means, without the prior permission in writing of the publisher, nor be otherwise circulated in any form of binding or cover other than that in which it is published and without a similar condition including this condition being imposed on the subsequent purchaser.

First published in Great Britain by Pen Press

All paper used in the printing of this book has been made from wood grown in managed, sustainable forests.

ISBN13: 978-1-906710-02-6

Printed and bound in UK by Cpod, Trowbridge, Wiltshire
Pen Press is an imprint of Indepenpress Publishing Limited
25 Eastern Place
Brighton
BN2 1GJ

A catalogue record of this book is available from
the British Library

Cover design by Jacqueline Abromeit

CHANCE

CHANCE

She sat on a rock overlooking the farm. Aunt Jane's rock, that's what they called it now. She had finished reading the Day Books and she knew she ought to burn them. That's what Jane intended, so that's what she ought to do. Only it wasn't that easy. It would be like destroying a life, destroying history.

Oh yes, all the events that had happened here would be documented somewhere: the births, the marriages, the deaths... particularly the deaths. In registrars' offices, solicitors' vaults, police records. Typed in cold words, in storage files, or on computer discs. All the facts. No feelings.

Aunt Jane hadn't wanted anyone to know those feelings, but they were as important as the facts, weren't they? Weren't they the reason for the facts?

No, it wasn't that easy.

Chance.

Chance and Jane.

She looked across to Halfpenny Hill. Then nearer to Cap Hill and downwards to the farmhouse below her.

The yards were busy with people, horses and machinery. Jane would have liked that. It would have reminded her of the beginning of it all. Not the beginning of Chance, of course, just the beginning of Jane's part in it.

The beginning.

Jane had believed in plays and scripts and actors knowing their lines. The trouble was, you see, everyone wanted to murder

Jeff. Jane had a list before it ever happened, and Chance was the reason for everything…

Maybe she would go back to the beginning and read them all again. Then she would decide.

She ought to burn them.

It just wasn't that easy.

* * * * *

A FLEETING CHANCE

She watched the mare's heaving flanks and willed it to push.

"Go on, gal... Go on..."

Her mind and body did a gentler imitation of the muscular strain needed to give birth, as though she could speed up the process by some sort of telepathy. She couldn't help it. She always did this, echoing the forcing down and out with every contraction. She wondered if it was something to do with hormones calling to hormones. Once you had done it yourself, you joined the sisterhood of sympathy. Like it or not, you relived the feeling every time you saw, or heard, the action. Yes, maybe that was it, because she had been there... done that...

She closed her eyes, head resting on the top of the stable door, forcing the thought from her mind. No, she couldn't think about that now. She would think later. Not now. Do her usual Scarlett O'Hara trick. Think tomorrow.

The mare snickered quietly as she breathed out. A low, juddering sound.

"Come on, gal, or they'll find you. Come on, Florrie," she muttered.

It was Jane's turn on watch and she hated it when they had to help the foals into the world. It seemed to her that so many needed help and she sometimes thought it was more for the owner's sake than the mare's. They wanted it over and done with. Oh, not because they didn't want to waste time. No, not that. But because they couldn't stand the suspense…couldn't wait to see what she had…even couldn't bear to watch her pain.

I'm probably wrong anyway, she thought. Usually am. They know best and I'm just being daft. They have to be careful.

The mare brought her head up, eyes withdrawn, feeling, as she stared back at her own body.

Jane stood on the step outside the bottom door of the stable. She ought to get the boss up, but was reluctant to leave the mare. She didn't want to wake Shirley and she didn't want to miss the birth if she left, but Eva was next on watch. She would be here soon, so why wait to get the boss? Eva wouldn't wait.

Jane shuddered. God, it was nippy.

Her eyes never left the mare as she fastened the top toggle of her duffel coat, eyes that just reached above the half door. Short, stocky, blonde-haired – she called it mousy – big, blue eyes, straight features and cold. Yes, very cold, she thought.

The mare stretched out again, hooves kicking the floor in another contraction.

Now… Come on, Florrie… Now.

"How's it going then?" Eva's muffled voice said in her ear. "Oh, she's started. Have you told the boss?"

"Just going to."

"She been going long?"

Eva stood on the concrete step to peer over the door. On tiptoe, head thrown forwards, breasts hooked over the door top, she spoke quietly sideways, back and down, to Jane.

"She looks well on to me."

Jane felt the accusation in her tone.

"Yes, well I was just going," she said, and got down from the step to plod along the path to the house, followed by two of her dogs. Hope she's not so well on, she thought, they'll blame me for not watching. Ah well…

She knew she would probably miss the birth now. It wasn't her job to be there. She only joined in foaling watches to ease the load for the others, give them more time to rest, but she was sad she would miss it.

"Least I'll have missed Jeff and his comments though," she muttered to herself. She was glad of that.

Anything vaguely to do with sex and, if his nasty side was on display, Jeff would start the dirty talk. Foaling time was one of the worst. It really set him off.

She cringed badly enough at his words, but for the young grooms it was torture. And he didn't stop at words. Not given half a chance he didn't.

Dirty devil.

She screwed up her face and shook her head as she thought of some of his comments last time.

She detested him.

She lifted the latch and went into the cold tack room. Boots off and in her socks, she padded through on the red, quarry-tiled floor into the large kitchen, where the heat from the stove hit her, making her eyes and nose run after the cold outside.

The boss was dozing on the settee in the breakfast room. She was there every night throughout the foaling season. Jane was sorry to have to wake her again.

"Shirley," she said, shaking her shoulder. "Shirley."

The figure moved, throwing back the quilt and standing up, ready to go.

"Thanks, Janie. Get the cocoa on, will you, love?" she said as she left.

No staggering steps or eye rubbing. No stretching and yawning, as Jane would have done. Just instant action. Instant efficiency.

That's our boss, Jane thought. That's our Shirley.

Shirley Hensham. Mid-twenties. Tall, dark, thin, but muscular. Pretty in a soft way that belied her toughness. Long, dark eyelashes against a skin that seemed to feel the sun and wind rarely, instead of seven days a week, fifty-two weeks a year. But, squinting against that weather had caused fine lines around the eyes, lines that would be deeply etched by the time she was in her forties, Jane knew. Jane had the same pale skin, but she was indoors so much of her time that, even several years older, the lines had not etched in as Shirley's would do.

They were cousins of sorts. Just how 'second' or 'removed' no one had ever had time to find out. But they were 'family' and that was all that mattered.

Jane was the 'domestic' one, people said.

Jane saw to the farmhouse, the food and the family. Enough 'F's to give Jeff a chance to air his wit with, "She's a lot of f***ing good," or, "She's a right f***er," On and on...ad nauseum.

That was something Jane couldn't understand. Shirley could reduce an employee to tears with one sentence...freeze out an exuberant rep with one look, so he shuffled and stammered as though being interviewed for his first job...and, as far as animals were concerned, she was fearless, so why did she put up with Jeff?

Jeff was the man around the place...least he thought he was. Tall, barrel-chested, beer-belly. Short legs for his height. Blondered hair, curly or matted, probably both. He looked the part he played. Jane was never sure whether he created the character to match his image, or the other way round. Perhaps, if he was born nasty, the rest just followed naturally.

He had been at Chance before Jane arrived. Maybe if she had known about him, she would have thought twice about coming.

No, that was daft, she admitted to herself. Where else do you go when you've reached the end? To family. She would have come here, Jeff or not.

Her marriage in tatters. Her nerves the same. Aunt Ruth had phoned Great Uncle William and Jane came to Chance.

And that's what it's all about for me, she thought. Chance.

Chance Farm. The family home for four centuries.

It stood on a rocky outcrop, deep in rural Worcestershire.

It was big, but not like stately homes are big. Not a patterned structure. Not an Elizabethan or Georgian mansion. Full stop. Chance was a bit of everything, all stuck together at odd angles.

The Elizabethan part was now used as what they called the kitchen side.

That comprised pantries – each fifteen foot long and ten foot wide – the large kitchen itself, the dairy, the pots room and other small rooms, each with its allotted purpose. All beams and low ceilings, small doors with latches and red flagstone floors.

There was more to this part of the house, but it had burnt down in seventeen-hundred-and-something. Jane wasn't sure when.

The largest part of the house was the main Georgian section. Here was the breakfast room, the dining room, the lounge, the morning room. Names for rooms whose use no longer matched them.

"Who has time to sit in the morning?" as Great Uncle William used to say.

All of the Georgian block had higher ceilings, which meant that halls and landings' ceilings suddenly sloped up or down where they joined ceilings of other ages and different levels, but it too was full of beams and flagstones. It was straighter in its main design though, without the little nooks and crannies of the older house. It had larger windows and symmetrical patterns. It was the 'posh' bit.

Of course, no one really knew any certain dates. Parts were just called 'Georgian' or 'Elizabethan', which seemed to be confirmed by interested historians, who called in occasionally, asking to look at this or that. They enthused about the boxes of information in the County Archives, all about the house, and they said the family should really go and read it all.

Yes, they answered, they certainly would sometime…but there never was time.

Although the two blocks standing at right angles formed the largest part of the house, they were not the entire of it.

In early Victorian times, a kitchen had been built on one side. It had a huge bread oven, disappearing back into the walls, a washing copper, a cooking range and stone sink. There were fire holes underneath the range, the copper and the bread oven. They used it as a sort of scullery now.

Jane imagined with all the fires going it must have been heaven in the winter, but in the summer…?

Other rooms had been added too, stuck on the sides or ends of the two blocks, with no apparent attempt at maintaining, or creating, any attractive architectural features. Need another room downstairs and an extra bedroom? Right. Stick it on there and bash another doorway through into wherever it's attached.

A purely functional procedure, repeated many times over the centuries.

And the result of all this was a hodgepodge of buildings, doorways, chimneys and levels known as Chance.

Jane loved it.

She opened the wheel on the bottom of the range with her foot, then leaned over to pull out the slide of the top vent. The range obediently started its low hum as the air was drawn up through the opening at the bottom, and rushed through the coke to go up the black chimney pipe.

"Good girl," she said.

The big kitchen range was her friend and her enemy. She spent hours every week tending to its need for more coke, poking and riddling it to get rid of the accumulation of ash, or the larger lumps of clinker.

She fought to keep it alive on days when the wind was in the wrong direction and the up-draught too slight to be effective.

She swore at it when the wind was in the north, and no amount of damping down would stop it roaring like a furnace and burning everything she cooked.

It took a week to go out when she needed it cold for the annual cleaning of chimneys and flues. Yet, to re-light it could take two days worth of attempts unless the wind was in the right direction. So, if it burned itself out because one of the dogs knocked the bottom catch up, or the wind changed to the north when she was asleep, the sight of the lifeless fire in the morning would bring frantic attempts to rekindle the slightest spark she thought she had seen.

"Haven't you got it going yet, Janie?"

"God, it's cold in here."

"You haven't let that go out, have you?"

The comments went on and on until she got it going again. She pleaded with it. She threatened it. She hated it.

But when she came down at four-thirty in the morning to a warm kitchen and hot kettles ready for her coffee…when it responded immediately to open wheels and vents…when it provided all the hot water, all the food, just as she needed… when it fulfilled all the functions of a farm range, from burning everything burnable, to bringing to life abandoned chicks and kittens in its cavernous warming oven…then she loved it.

"Good girl," she said and put a pan of milk on the hottest part of the top plate. She made herself a coffee while she laid out the mugs for cocoa. She took a sip from her mug and stood it at the back of the range, furthest from the fire.

All day long she had a cup of tea or coffee standing there, to be sipped each time she passed.

Sometimes she was still sipping from the same mug hours after it was made. The range kept it just warm and she didn't mind how stewed it tasted. It was wet and it was a comforting habit.

The milk quickly formed a skin, ready to boil up, and she moved it off the plate to keep warm by the side of her coffee.

"Move, Monny," she said quietly to the dog, which was lying in such a way as to prevent her pulling a chair from under the scrubbed, wooden table.

Monny stood up and walked a few steps, then flopped down again with a sigh, head resting on the heap of dogs lying by the range.

Jane sat and stared at the range, debating whether to close it down again, or get it ready for action at four-thirty.

The kitchen clock said two-thirty now.

She decided to give them ten minutes, then she would shut the wheel and vents again. If they were in before that, she might as well riddle it out and get the day going.

She sipped her coffee and leaned back in her chair to stretch her legs under the table. A movement at the edge of her vision made her turn, only to find it was her own movement reflected in the long mirror on the far wall. She realised she was sort of smiling. She stopped smiling straight away and looked puzzled. Why was she smiling? People didn't just smile for nothing, did they? Well, some people did, but she hadn't got that sort of face. She wasn't smiling because the range was behaving itself, was she?

Hell's bells! Is that what my life has come to? It's okay folks, the fire's going so we have no problems!

Now she really smiled at the thought.

"Thinking about what you're not getting?" Jeff's voice came from the door.

She didn't move, didn't react. She wouldn't give him the satisfaction.

She wouldn't give him any satisfaction, she thought, and smiled again inside her head.

He moved to the range, looking at the milk.

"Any chance of a cocoa?" he asked.

"That's for the others," she said. "Get some more on if you want."

"Florrie's on then, is she?"

Jane nodded.

"Do they want any help?"

"They didn't say so."

"No, she'll be all right. Built like the Mersey tunnel that one."

He moved back to the table, standing behind her chair.

Jane knew what they meant about feeling your skin crawl, but she wasn't frightened. Uneasy, but not frightened. She knew he was looking down at her.

"Yeah," he said quietly, "built like the Mersey tunnel."

She could feel his breath moving her hair. She knew his hands would be in his pockets again. Dirty devil.

She sipped her coffee and pretended to ignore him.

It was because she didn't react like the others, that was what made him unsure. She was calm and strong and could outwit him. There was some aura of power about her that threw him off-balance.

Of course, he didn't think like that, he just called her names in his head – insulting names, mocking names – but he kept his hands to himself...in his own pockets.

He moved round the table to sit in the chair opposite.

"Get us a coffee," he said.

"Get it yourself," she answered.

"It ain't my job," he snarled.

She sipped her coffee again.

"Come on, you frustrated bitch, get us a coffee. I might even be nice to you if you do." He smiled at her meaningfully.

She just glanced at him, smiled back and went on drinking.

She was doing it again. Not reacting in the right way. She should be scared of him. She should have tried to leave the room when he came in. She should be running away now. He knew how to handle that. He knew how to handle all those frightened, trembling bodies. He liked handling them. He didn't understand her.

His fist crashed onto the table, giving physical force to his uncertainty, his lack of power.

"Get us a bloody coffee!"

The dogs jumped to their feet, the four older ones in front, the three younger ones behind, watching her and the older dogs.

She clicked a sound at them and they stood, waiting.

That was the other thing, he thought, her and her bloody dogs. He knew she could order them to attack him with one hand movement, one sound. He had seen it before, seen her training them. She could get them to do whatever she wanted. She was a witch, that's what! No, he thought, she was a bitch. No wonder the dogs understood her. Just another bitch.

He sneered at her. Just another bitch.

She got up and he thought he had won. She was going to get him a drink. He was relieved, because he didn't know what to do next, if she didn't. He couldn't lose face by getting it himself, so he leaned back in his chair, relieved.

She went to the sink and swilled out her mug, then returned to sit at the table.

Bitch! Bitch! She had done it again.

He jerked to his feet. He wanted to walk out, to ignore her, to show he didn't care. Above all, he wanted to humiliate her, like he felt she humiliated him.

"Idle little cow," he said. "I suppose some of us had better work, so I'll go and check they're doing okay. Don't you move your fat backside, you idle cow. No, don't you move."

"Tell them the cocoa's ready," she said calmly.

He wanted to kill her.

* * * * *

She breathed out in small jerks as she heard the tack room door shut and she relaxed. She got up to make herself another cup of coffee, telling the dogs to lie down again as she did so.

Why did Shirley put up with him? She knew what he was like. So why? It didn't make sense.

Jane had thought of every possible scenario that she had ever heard of, or read, in paperback novels.

He was her lover, her secret husband? No chance. She had seen that Shirley could be as disgusted by him as she was. His words. His actions.

A fleeting chance

Not a lover. No chance.

Her husband? No. When would she have married him? Her life was an open book to everyone in the house, so when would she have gone off to get married?

No, not her husband. Anyway, Jeff had been part of Chance as long as anyone could remember.

Her father then? Her real father. That would mean he would have to have had sex with Auntie Doris!

Auntie Doris and Jeff?!!

It was a miracle to Jane that Auntie Doris had had Shirley. She sometimes wondered if they should be worshipping Shirley with gold, frankincense and myrrh, because for the life of her, she couldn't think of any other way Auntie Doris would conceive a child. She even averted her eyes when the blacksmith rolled up his sleeves, for crying out loud! But, maybe that was it, thought Jane, maybe she was a secret nympho', likely to explode with passion at the sight of old Eddie Arbour's forearms.

A spurt of laughter shot out in the silence of the kitchen as she imagined Auntie Doris as a nymphomaniac.

The dogs looked up to check if she was all right, then sighed back down again.

No, Auntie Doris had to be out of the frame. So, what about Jeff being Shirley's brother? The result of a liaison between Uncle Paul and some ripe village wench? She had read a lot about that in bodice-ripping paperbacks, only the bodice-ripper never sounded like Uncle Paul.

Uncle Paul, pottering round the garden with his secateurs and straw hat; so vague, so gentle, that butterflies would land on him. That was the way he had always been. Jane couldn't remember him any other way. When she had been brought on visits as a very small child, he had looked and acted just as he did now. He must have been in his twenties then, but lusty young man certainly didn't fit his description. She could remember his father bawling at him about something on one of those visits. She remembered because it had frightened her. Great Uncle William was his father

13

and he had frightened her. But Uncle Paul didn't even seem to hear, he just went on pottering around the garden.

No, definitely not your bodice-ripping type, Jane decided.

She was just reworking her ideas on whether Jeff could be a cousin when the dogs raised their heads.

She hastened to the range to check the milk, pulling the skin to one side and adding more milk as she moved it to the hot plate.

The tack room door opened and Eva's head appeared around the kitchen door.

"A filly," she said. "Bloody hell, it's cold out there."

Her head disappeared again as her voice called, "Pour the cocoa, Janie."

Jane laid out another mug for Jeff, putting in cocoa and sugar. Then she poured out the steaming milk and stirred each mug carefully, squashing any lumps of cocoa against the side to disperse them. She left the spoon in the last mug and added a spoon to each of the two others. It was one of the rituals on cold days and nights, one of the many traditions that abounded at Chance. People liked stirring their cocoa in between sips. It was comforting, as most traditions are.

She put the mugs in front of them as they flopped at the table, then went to stand in her usual place, leaning against the range at the cool end.

"Okay, then?" she asked.

"No problems," Shirley said, "you needn't have bothered to come out, Jeff."

He didn't answer.

"Well, I'm to bed," she said. "You're on now, Eva, aren't you? Call me if there's any action."

She took her cocoa and went to the door, turning to say, "You had better get some sleep too, Janie. Thanks for this." She lifted her mug and left for the breakfast room settee.

Jane felt, rather than saw, the nervous stiffening in Eva's back as she glanced across to Jeff. She held out her mug to Jane.

"Could I have some more cocoa, Janie?"

Jane knew, without having to look at her pleading eyes, that this was an attempt to keep her in the room.

"She only makes drinks when it's part of her job," Jeff's sarcasm was thickly laid on. "No extras. You have to get it yourself if you want it. She's an idle little cow is our Janie."

Clever, thought Jane. Untrue, which they all well knew, but clever. Now what could she do? She didn't want to make a drink for Eva and so give Jeff more ammunition to fire at her, which, at the same time, would make it clear that she was concerned enough to treat him differently. But, if she told Eva to help herself, what excuse would she have for hanging around? And she would have to ignore Eva's pleading eyes. Clever, she thought.

She felt annoyed at being put in this position. Eva didn't like her. She treated Jane with superior contempt most of the time and, even though Jane helped her out of many predicaments like this, Eva never acknowledged it afterwards. In fact, she always resented Jane's help, seemed more contemptuous after the moment had passed. No, let Eva fend for herself. She wasn't a teenager. She should know how to sort Jeff out. What the hell is it to do with me? she thought. Let Eva get on with it. It wasn't her problem...

She looked at Eva's frightened eyes...

Ah, well, her gran always said she was too soft...

"Tell you what, I could do with a cocoa too. How about you make some more for us all?" She smiled at Eva and went to sit by Jeff at the table.

Eva readily acceded to this idea and moved to the stove.

Jeff just glowered and got up to leave without saying a word.

Hopefully, now he would take some more potent drink in his room and be out like a light for the rest of the night.

Eva said nothing when he left, just banged around more than was necessary for washing two mugs and making two cocoas. It took a lot longer and was a lot louder than if Jane had done it.

Jane thought of telling Eva not to bother as soon as Jeff left, but she knew Eva would be just as angry as she was now. Her anger was obvious in every move. Jane knew what was coming next. Eva was angry with herself for her fear and that wasn't tenable, so it got translated to Jane.

She slammed Jane's mug on the table, cocoa slopping over the side.

"Okay?" she said, sarcastically. "And you didn't have to move a muscle."

She shook her head, blinking her eyes slowly, to show what she thought of Jane's 'idleness'.

"Thanks a lot," Jane said, brightly, and thought, yes, thanks a lot, Jane, for saving me from Jeff.

Well, she might as well thank herself. No one else would.

She went to bed.

* * * * *

"Did you say it was lunch?" Uncle Paul's mild voice said in her left ear.

"It's still on the table, Uncle Paul," she said, without looking up from the mixture she was beating for teatime scotch pancakes.

He looked around, as though he couldn't remember where the table was, then pottered towards it.

Lunch and the other five meals – or breaks – of the day, were always laid out at strictly set times and then left out for about an hour, before Jane cleared them off. It was a system that worked well, because the activities of the farm and stables meant that people could not rely on a set knocking-off time and meals were taken as and when possible. For much of the day, food was available on the large kitchen table. Breakfast, elevenses, lunch and tea were spread there throughout the day.

A fleeting chance

Jane put dinner on the dining table at seven and supper on the lounge table at nine.

Yes, food was always available, or just a short time away, and that meant someone had to plan, and prepare it. It was a major part of Jane's day, around which all other tasks were arranged. After all, she was the 'domestic' one, wasn't she?

Just how she came to be so, still occupied some of her thinking time. No one who knew her at eighteen would have believed that this was the way she would end. And, she thought, she probably would end this way…found, stone-cold, sitting at the kitchen table, in front of her endless lists…one of which would be instructions on what to do in the event of her being found, stone-cold, sitting at the kitchen table, no doubt.

She decided to leave everything she owned to the kitchen range, on the grounds that it had already taken most of her life, so it might as well have the rest!

* * * * *

As a young woman, Jane had the world at her feet, they said.

She excelled at her office job during the day, and attracted a growing crowd when she appeared singing with a local group, or acting with an amateur company at night. It never bothered her being in front of so many people. She had never been frightened of people, never worried if she made a fool of herself. She was self-sufficient as a child and adult. Even in her early teens she never dressed to be one of the crowd, or needed to pose to hide her feelings of insecurity. She really didn't care what others thought of her, laughing harder at herself than others did. The mockery of her peers was wasted by her self-mockery.

She would go far, people said, when they first saw her at work, or on the stage, but she didn't fit the stereotype her confidence seemed to suggest and they couldn't understand it.

She didn't understand it herself for many years.

Her gran told her not to worry, it would come with time.

It was a puzzle because she wasn't the brash, outgoing leader she ought to have been…that her confident stereotype would have been. If she led, it was because she was the only one who could do so, the only one who would speak fearlessly at meetings, or who would take an unattractive acting role that others would shun. And she did these things instinctively, feeling the discomfort of her colleagues and not wanting to feel it. And, when it was done, she quickly tried to drop into the background again.

At work she would credit others with her ideas and even manage to convince them they were their own ideas in the first place.

She was completely non-competitive, taking more pleasure in her ability to manipulate others to success, enjoying seeing her ideas work under other leadership.

On stage she would perform, then want to get off before the plaudits began.

No, she didn't understand it, either, until the day she was due to go for an audition for a new radio series. It was to be a weekly show called *Café*. A sort of regular cabaret. The audition was a formality, they said. She would be one of the resident performers.

Her family was excited. She didn't feel anything.

It was on the way to the studio in a taxi that she realised, at last, what was wrong. She didn't want to be a company director either. She wanted to be left alone. Fame was what she dreaded. Fame was her fear. She loved organising, singing and acting, but she would prefer that no one noticed!

It didn't make sense, she knew. Since she wasn't frightened of people, or their criticism, why be frightened of fame? But there it was. That was the answer. She wanted to be anonymous.

Her family tried to understand, particularly her mother, but they all thought she was throwing her life away. A waste of all that talent, they said. Her father virtually ordered her to succeed in business. He had always been uneasy about the stage, so that didn't bother him, but work...well, she should go to the top in that. Her brothers and sisters thought she was mad. 'Nerves' they could understand, but she didn't have any!

They shook their heads in disbelief, but she knew now what she wanted – or did not want – and from then on, she only aspired to attain her own standards...little things, unimportant things... of no interest to anyone but herself. It really didn't matter what others thought.

Her gran understood. Her gran was her best friend.

Terry was one of those weak – or insecure – people who always hone in on someone to carry them through.

From childhood, Jane's strength had attracted those in need of a shoulder. She could make sense and order of their disorder. They could find purpose and direction by allowing her to lead. Jane let them lean on her and understood that their devotion would turn to rejection if they ever recovered their balance.

Her gran said she let them kick her until their legs were strong enough to walk away. They laughed about it together. Jane loved her gran.

Terry wasn't one of those who walked away. He stayed around and made her laugh. His quicksilver wit and charm confused her usual sense of judgement. Or, maybe, she thought later, she had just reached a time when she needed to lean too.

Her gran had died and she felt that now there was no one to talk to...no one she could sit with and not talk to.

Terry was around on one of his frequent incursions into her life, so, somehow, she tried to lean on him.

It was a mistake. She had forgotten he was there to lean on her.

Such an unstable structure had to crash to the ground.

She closed her mind to his insecurity, to his drinking, to his lies. She laughed and closed her mind.

It surprised her when she became pregnant, within three months of her gran's death. They married immediately, because in her world illegitimate children were unthinkable. It was a shoddy, little ceremony in a registry office. Only her mother came from the family. The instant it was over, her mother picked up her shopping bags and left and Jane went back to work in her office.

One did not celebrate mistakes.

She worked until she began to show and then she hid in her bedsitting room in the slum district of the town. Terry said it was cheap, so she sat there and waited.

From the moment they married, Terry assumed the role of husband, patterning his behaviour on what he had learned from his own upbringing. No more the wit, the laughing, the conversation now he was the breadwinner. He became like his father and grandfather. The life and soul of the party at the pub and at work, surly silence at home.

"Pass the salt," and "Where's the sauce?" were the limits of communication.

Now Jane really was alone.

Her family acknowledged her for she was safely married, but she had disappointed them, so they kept a careful distance.

Her mother's visits were conducted with an air of furtiveness, as though she would be in trouble if her father discovered that they had any contact.

Her brothers and sisters said hello when she visited her old home on rare occasions, but they asked no questions, displayed no interest.

Her father nodded to her.

She wasn't lonely, but she was alone…until Elizabeth was born.

Elizabeth Jane Warren. Six pounds, four ounces. After a protracted labour, the light of Jane's life appeared.

She was nearly two years old when she died. Killed one Christmas Eve as Terry drove them home from a party at his family's house. He was drunk. He survived without a scratch and Jane, too, was little hurt…at least not where it showed.

She left him and returned home to become the family drudge.

Two social crimes. A baby started before marriage and a marriage deserted. Being a drudge was all that was left and she became good at it. So good that Aunt Ruth had sorted Great Uncle William's problems by getting Jane shipped out to Chance.

Sorting out the domestic chaos that was Chance, then, helped Jane sort herself out. All that strength and self-sufficiency came into play again, helping her to survive and adapt. She ended up, as so many survivors had before her, stronger for having walked through the fire.

Her gran would have understood.

When Jane first came to Chance, it wasn't the same place as it was now. The house was pretty much the same structurally, of course, but the atmosphere was different. Great Uncle William still ruled. He was about seventy years old and worked as though no one had told him that. He was well respected in a community that, as so many rural communities did, judged a person by the amount of work they could achieve. To be a 'worker' was to be worthwhile.

Great Uncle William worked.

It seemed to Jane that was all he did. She never saw him relax, or do anything that could be vaguely termed as fun.

He was the oldest of several brothers and sisters, all of whom had married and produced the large number of children that was expected in a family of large families. Future Henshams. Future workers.

Great Uncle William only had Paul. His wife died very young and he never remarried. Jane wondered if that was because her death had soured his outlook on life, or whether he simply never had the time. She had never known her Great Aunt May and so did not know if he was a different, more carefree personality when she was alive.

She did know that his son, Paul, was a total disappointment to him.

By the time Jane moved to Chance, Great Uncle William had almost ceased to acknowledge Paul's existence. Paul was a person out of place, someone who lived as though he was on a different planet.

"He wants to get his feet down here on the muck heap with the rest of us," she had heard a neighbouring farmer say.

That more or less summed it up.

As far as the local community was concerned, Paul had a 'free ride'. He was not a worker. He was even exempted from army service because of a weak something-or-other. Their sympathies lay with his father and they pursed their mouths and shook their heads at the mention of Paul's name.

If he had been simple, not quite all there, they would have sympathised and accepted, but he wasn't simple. He wrote books about historical figures. He wrote articles about flowers. And that would have been okay, too, if he could have joined in when needed. Well, Roger Bailey in Yelton village wrote books, didn't he? But he could still turn a ton of hay at harvesting, or help birth a calf…

Paul couldn't. Hay and straw scratches made him hurt so much that he would go to the doctor and he felt sick at any birthing.

"A free ride," they said. "Useless."

Jane felt sorry for him most of the time, but even she could get irritated by his vagueness, his dependence, his need for constant direction. How he had managed to marry Aunt Doris, she couldn't imagine, but local gossip said it was Great Uncle William that married her really.

Oh, not in the sexual sense, there was no hint of that, but in the sense of arranging the marriage with her family.

Jane thought there must have been quite a lot of arranging, quite a lot given away, or promised, to Aunt Doris' family of smallholders, for Doris was seen as a 'likely lass' when she was young. Full of fun and robust health. Industrious and determined. A likely lass.

* * * * *

Young Doris Hensham.

A likely lass.

After the birth of Shirley, all that bustling activity stopped. It wasn't just a case of a young mother obsessed with her first child, shutting out the world as she tended to the needs of the baby; it was what would be easily recognised now as post-natal depression. In those days not many old, country midwives could name it, let alone recognise it, and even less, would new mothers know how to seek help.

She responded. She smiled. She was polite. She seemed to be quieter, but she was okay and, after all, motherhood did settle women down, didn't it? Everyone knew that.

But she cried a lot, hidden in her room, and didn't understand why she felt so bad. She couldn't talk to anyone about it because she was frightened she wasn't normal.

Normal women loved their babies. She didn't. The demands of the baby filled her with despair, anger and fear. She could not cope and she felt guilty. Guilty for failing. Guilty for not loving it.

No, she must not talk to anyone about it. They would think she was mad. So she kept up as good a face as she could and cried a lot in private.

Paul did not notice anything was wrong. She doubted he would have noticed she was pregnant in the first place if she hadn't told him.

The advent of Shirley never seemed to affect him at all. He did not play with her, waggling his fingers and making nonsense sounds, rocking her cradle, or picking her up. He said, "That's nice," when the midwife said it was a girl, and went off to plant some more crocus bulbs.

Doris had tried to talk to him when they had first married. She was aware he was a 'catch'. Her family had made sure she had understood that. Heir to a thriving farm. Heir to land and house.

She didn't fancy him, of course, not in the sense she fancied Cliff Finlay. She would feel her face flush if Cliff smiled or winked at her when she walked past. She dreamed of Cliff Finlay. His twinkling eyes. His brown, strong hands and arms. His smile. Oh, yes, she dreamed of Cliff Finlay…hot, exciting dreams…but he was heir to nothing. Just a farm labourer from a family of farm labourers. She could do better, her mother said. And she did.

Paul Hensham was as far above her in social status as Cliff Finlay was below. She did well to marry Paul, but it wasn't the stuff of dreams. There was no exciting courtship, no shared future plans…no shared anything really. The whole thing was arranged between the families.

Doris could not recall Paul ever actually asking her to marry him. It was somehow assumed.

He arrived at her house and had tea, but spent more time talking to her younger sister than her.

He walked with Doris in the fields and accompanied her to church on Sundays.

He listened to her chattering and said polite things.

He kissed her swiftly on parting.

She couldn't remember him ever telling her that he loved her.

She couldn't remember ever feeling excited by him and excitement was what most girls thrived on.

Buying her trousseau was exciting. Standing, whilst her white, crinoline dress was constructed around her, was exciting too. Her mother and sister were excited by it all, so she caught their mood. The day of the wedding was exciting. The centre of all attention. Feeling good. Looking good. Excited. That was about as far as it went. That was when all the excitement stopped.

A fleeting chance

She wasn't nervous of her first night. She knew what would happen. Well, she had been brought up on a farm. She'd had friends to whisper and giggle with about things like that since she was thirteen. She was confident in her youth and attractiveness.

It had been clear from the start that she had been chosen to continue the Hensham line because of her robust health, her assumed ability to provide heirs. Her friends said old man Hensham had chosen her like a heifer at market. She laughed with them about it. Yes, she was confident. She hadn't been with a man yet, but it was natural, wasn't it? She knew what to expect.

The silent fumbling wasn't exciting. It wasn't even painful.

His embarrassment communicated itself to her and she was left feeling sorry for him. She chattered away to cover the shame she thought he must be feeling. It would get better, she thought.

She supposed she was lucky to get pregnant so quickly. She had endured four months of nightly fumbling before she was certain her periods had stopped.

It never did get any better. If anything, it got worse. After the first week, she had felt emboldened enough to try to make love to him, to teach him by example, but when she stroked his chest, he said, "No, please...no," and removed her hand.

Once, after he had completed his quick ejaculation into her body and turned away from her onto his side to sleep, she slid her hand over his hip to his groin, trying to rouse him to a second, perhaps more prolonged contact. He got quickly out of bed and did not return that night.

Her confidence slowly seeped away, like the sticky results of his unwilling efforts, seeping from her body onto the sheets every night. Wasted.

As soon as she was pregnant, all contact ceased.

He said he had to get on with his book and took to sleeping on the small bed in his study. He did not want to disturb her, he said. She said nothing.

She immersed herself in running the house, in planning for the baby. She was still the Doris people knew...full of bustling activity and fun on the outside, but she didn't think of Cliff Finlay any more. She tried not to think of anything like that too much and, if some such thought came into her mind, she crushed it down and felt shame. It was 'dirty' to think of such things. It wasn't natural at all, except for animals, so she would not think about it. Four months of marriage had taught her a lot.

A few months after Shirley's birth, Paul returned to her bed and she refused him. Now it was she that said, "No, please... no." Now it was her fear, revulsion and embarrassment that communicated to him. He went back to his study and never returned again.

Years passed. The Aunt Doris that Jane knew was still industrious and cheerful as she passed through the house. A bustling figure in smart suits and chiffon scarves, always off to this committee meeting, or that fete. She had a few good words for everyone and was unfailingly, unthinkingly cheerful. A 'do-gooder'. A pillar of village society. Yes, she was very busy indeed. Too busy to see to the running of the house... "But I'm sure you can manage, dear." Too busy to tend to Shirley's cut knee... "Oh, what a shame. Go and ask someone to clean it for you." Too busy. Just too busy.

Jane recognised it as a survival technique. She had been there too. She was sure, though, that Aunt Doris wouldn't know what she was talking about if she suggested that to her.

She wondered if it was Uncle Paul she was surviving.

* * * * *

Jane's first look at Chance confirmed all her childhood memories.

A black and white building, full of odd angles, doors and windows.

She had arrived late one autumn afternoon and, as the Land Rover turned a corner, there it was.

Golden in the low sunlight. A breathtakingly beautiful, timeless scene.

Trees and shrubs obscured parts of the house leaving small, individual snapshots, each of which held its own fascination and then hinted at the whole picture. Every turn of the lane brought a different part of the house into view. Roofs of many levels, with dark brown tiles, which curved and buckled rather than sat flat, as they did on newer houses. Black, or brown doors, wide or narrow, oval-topped or straight, with latches or ring handles or knobs. Windows, mullioned, barred or quartered, black-edged, and all sizes, from a tiny hearth window to the large Georgian bowfronts. And chimneys. So many chimneys. Tall or short. Rectangular or round.

Every view seemed to have her eyes lingering back to it, but was forgotten in the delight of the next snapshot.

Aunt Ruth had said, "Now, don't forget, dear, it will take a lot of sorting out. Poor Uncle William works far too hard outside to arrange inside matters and Doris doesn't have the time, you know."

The magic of the outside disappeared as Jane stood in the hallway and surveyed the grubby tip in front of her. She thought, Ah well, after the Lord Mayor's show... Now she knew what Aunt Ruth was getting at.

She wandered around, passing – or being passed – by several people who barely acknowledged her, they were so intent on their own business. No one seemed curious as to who she was or what she was doing.

She went into rooms that were thick with dust and sheet-covered furniture. Other rooms seemed to be used for storing anything from old corn sacks to broken chairs. She found plates on settees, cups on stairs and boots just about everywhere.

The red flag floors had more straw and dried mud than the yard outside. The whitewashed walls were not white any more, being light brown at the top and murky, streaked grey at the bottom where people and animals had knocked against them in passing.

She stood in the large kitchen doorway and thought about leaving.

"It's grim, isn't it?"

The voice was too low to make her jump, but she turned quickly to look up at the pretty teenager. She had to look up at her. The girl's lips were on the same level as Jane's ear.

"Sorry," she said and smiled ruefully at Jane. "I expect you don't recognise me. I'm Shirley. Grumps sent me to find you."

"Grumps?"

"Your Great Uncle William. My grandfather. I call him Grumps."

Jane soon realised that Shirley was the only one who would dare to call him anything like Grumps. She was as fearless with him as she was with any plunging, snorting animal on the farm. That he pinned his hopes for the future on her was clear, but he didn't treat her with any special consideration. He was as gruff and tough with her as he was with any of the farm workers.

Shirley smiled at him when he glowered and threatened because something hadn't gone right. She took the brunt of his tongue and smiled. She pretended agreement and exaggerated the failure to ridiculous proportions with a solemn face and laughing eyes.

"You're right, Grumps. We've all had it now. If we have to buy one more chain for that tractor, we had better put the farm on the market. Shall I go and tell Dave he's sacked?"

"Less of your cheek, Miss Clever Clogs," he grumbled, but his mouth twitched and he bit his lip.

She would intercede for others when he made their lives miserable, but those who thought her a soft touch soon realised that such intercessions would only happen if she considered their case to be just. She would dismiss the free riders as harshly and rapidly as he would. In fact, her cold calmness was somehow more fearful than his angry shouting.

A fleeting chance

Shirley was a teenager when Jane came to Chance. She was in her early twenties when Great Uncle William died. The farm now belonged to Paul, but he barely acknowledged the fact and left all the running to Shirley. She had worked up the horse side of the business over the preceding years, until it had become one of the top livery stables in the county. The war was long over. People were coming back to their lives. The stables flourished, keeping Shirley very busy. The farm side of the business she left to Jeff, appointing him manager.

Jane had spent many years wondering why.

* * * * *

Uncle Paul got up from the table, leaving a circle of crumbs and other debris around his chair. He wandered out, still holding his knife, then returned a few seconds later to give it to Jane.

"That's yours, I think," he said. "What time is tea?"

"The usual time," she said, not looking up from the sink.

She said that to him after every meal. It didn't irritate her any more. It was just part of the day.

She looked through the window, over the sink, and saw the other Jane. Young Jane. 'Jay' they called her. She was backed against the barn side, trying to get under the two arms each side of her. Jeff was at it again.

She saw him drop his one hand down as Jay tried to duck under his arm, saw Jay jerk back upright as his hand cupped her breast.

Jane clenched her teeth in response to the surge of anger she felt. She reached forward to open the window and shout at him, but, before she could, she saw him turn his head away to one side, giving Jay a chance to duck under his arm on the other side and run off.

Harvey had appeared around the barn corner and said something to him. It had distracted Jeff long enough for Jay to escape.

She saw Jeff glance around looking for his victim, then vent his frustration on Harvey. Jane couldn't hear what he was saying, but she could guess it wasn't exactly a Bible class lecture. Harvey was walking away, back around the barn corner, while Jeff's mouth was still working.

Good lad, thought Jane. Ignore the little sod.

She liked Harvey Bateman. Almost everyone did. He was twenty-one, the son of Dave, who had worked for the Henshams since leaving school, as had Dave's father before him. The Batemans were a part of Chance. The cottage they lived in, on the farm, had been called Bateman's cottage for as long as anyone could remember, acknowledging the long connection between them and Chance.

Jane watched as Jeff stood glowering after Harvey, then kicked his frustration at a hen that was carefully, slowly walking past, clucking to encourage her brood to keep up. Five little balls of fluff with legs. One yellow, two brown and two black. As his boot caught her underneath, the hen flew up in the air, partly from the kick, partly from her own efforts to escape. She loudly crowed her protests and fear, tipping sideways as she landed a few yards away. Her wings beat the air as she regained her balance and smoothed her feathers.

Three of the chicks scattered, running in different directions. Two of them froze, folding themselves down to the ground, legs underneath, heads tucked back. Tiny lumps on the stones, like moss balls on roof tiles.

Jeff stamped on the yellow one and walked off.

Jane decided she was going to kill him.

"Shirley, can I have a word?"

Jane didn't know why she was trying again really. She had tried for the last umpteen years and never got anywhere.

"Yes, love, what's up?"

"It's Jeff…"

She watched the shield come down over Shirley's smiling face, before she turned away to continue brushing the gelding, standing quietly for his daily grooming.

"What's he done now?" Shirley's voice came from the other side of the horse.

Jane was standing in the stable doorway and could only see the top of Shirley's head, but she knew she wouldn't be smiling now.

"He's been having a go at Jay again."

"Has Jay complained to you then?"

"No. I saw him from the window. He was holding her against the barn wall."

There was silence, except for the swish of the brush on the gelding's shining flanks.

"Shirley?"

"I'll have a word with him," she said.

There was another silence as Jane tried to think of a way to get more than this usual response…and tried to decide if it was worth trying anyway.

Then she thought of the little flattened body lying on the stones.

"But, Shirley…"

Shirley's head appeared from the back of the horse. The expression was closed and cold.

"Jay hasn't complained," she said. "She is nearly eighteen and can speak for herself."

"She's frightened. You must see that, Shirley. Everyone knows you won't hear anything against Jeff and she's frightened of him."

Shirley looked away, her head resting momentarily against the horse, as she drooped the hand holding the brush across his back.

"Why, Shirl', why?" Jane pleaded yet again. "He's a real nasty piece of work and you know it. So why?"

"I said I'll speak to him," the voice answered quietly and she bent out of sight again to resume brushing.

Jane gave up.

She found Jay mucking out in the four-stall block.

As Jane's shadow crossed the floor of the second stall, Jay swung round, pitchfork in hand. Before she smiled in recognition, Jane saw the determination on her face.

Jeff would not have got past the pitchfork this time.

Jane remembered when Jay had applied for a job as a groom at Chance. It was that same determination that decided them to choose her.

There were always loads of applicants for any job that offered work with horses. Choosing someone was a task that Shirley and Jane did together. It seemed to work well, with Shirley judging their ability with horses and Jane guessing how they would cope and fit in with the rest of the 'family'.

Advertising for a trainee groom seemed to give hope to the horse-besotted dreams of every young girl in the county who owned a pair of jodhpurs and a riding hat. The phone would ring incessantly and Jane would talk to many young, excited, tremulous voices. From the following CVs, they would whittle it down to five, or six, and invite them, and their parents, for an interview.

It was rare to get anyone to apply for this lowly position who had actual experience of working with corned-up hunters, or temperamental thoroughbreds sent for schooling. No, they were used to riding school ponies, or, if they were lucky, their own bombproof pet. Thoroughbreds – raised, fed and trained to keep them at the peak of performance – were a different kettle of fish...or horses. So, the nervous applicants usually came straight from riding school and 'Black Beauty', full of love and devotion to all the equine race and convinced they understood everything the intelligent creatures were trying to convey. It was only wicked humans that made horses nasty, wasn't it?

If employed, within three months they realised that was only partially true and you could hear them cursing to themselves out in the yard at five o'clock on a cold morning, as some bolshy sixteen-foot-two hunter decided to have a bad day. It made Jane smile. 'Black Beauty' didn't come into it any more.

A fleeting chance

Shirley would put them up on Freddie first. Freddie was her own thoroughbred gelding and his patience was renowned, but he was beautifully schooled and responsive, needing only the lightest touch to perform the rider's wishes.

Young girls, used to the solid iron flanks and steel mouths of riding school ponies, knew that, most of the time, you really had to kick them on to get them moving at all.

The better ones would respond to some gentle heel-nudging, it was true, but most needed it to prove that you were more determined to move, than they were to stand still.

You only had to twitch a nerve for Freddie to canter off. So, while the results of some candidates' enthusiastic heel movements were amusing to watch, whether they stayed on or not, and whether they listened to Shirley's called instructions, certainly sorted out the potentials from the no-hopers.

Jay had got up on Freddie and pulled his rein to turn him away from the hitching post as she kicked him on. Freddie obediently pranced around in small circles on the spot, and kept going round, waiting for someone to tell him to stop. Shirley always swore he did it for pure devilment, enjoying playing up to these silly riders and their daft instructions.

As Jay bobbed up and down, trying to stop Freddie turning, Shirley called calm orders and they watched her response.

"At least she's still up there," Jane said, "and she's listening."

They had both liked the determination on her face then. It was the same determination that Jane had just seen at the end of a pitchfork.

"Okay?" Jane nodded at the pitchfork. "I saw what Jeff was up to."

"He won't catch me that easily again," Jay said, shaking her head to emphasise the point. "God, I hate him. Dirty old man."

Then, suddenly, she began to cry. The defiance collapsed and she was just a frightened young girl. The pitchfork fell, as she collapsed to her knees. Jane knelt beside her.

"He hasn't done anything else, has he? Anything more than that, I mean?"

Jay shook her head and fought to control her shuddering breath.

"Come on, come in the kitchen and have a talk." Jane pulled her up.

"No. No, I've got to finish this," she said. She got to her feet, brushing straw off her jeans. As her breathing calmed, she added, "It's what he says, you know. He says I'm old enough to start enjoying myself, what he wants to do to me and how I'll like it, and…" She dropped her head again. "Harvey says he's going to kill him."

"That's him and me both," Jane smiled. "Tell you what, you join in as well and we can share the pleasure."

Jay looked up and smiled a little as Jane went on, "You can stab him with the pitchfork. Harvey can shoot him. But I want to be the one who kicks him to death. Much more satisfying, don't you think?"

Jay smiled wider at this and picked up her pitchfork again. "Why…?" she said, as she started turning the straw.

"Why what?"

"Oh, nothing," she said.

"Why does the boss put up with him?" Jane asked for her.

Jay looked round, waiting for an answer.

"God knows," Jane said.

"You doing anything?" Eva asked, coming into the kitchen and opening a drawer. Jane didn't bother to say she was peeling potatoes. She figured it might have been obvious.

"What do you want?"

"A skewer. What have you done with the skewers?"

Given the accusatory tone, Jane thought what she would like to have done with the skewers…

She dried her hands on her overall and reached past Eva to

give her a skewer from the drawer. Eva used it to widen the hole in the leather of a head collar she was holding.

"Well, are you doing anything?" Eva looked up and demanded an answer.

"What do you want?"

"Can you just go and start the Thomas boy's lesson? We're having a bit of trouble catching the new mare."

Jane took off her overall and started for the door. "Yep. Okay. What's he doing now?"

"Rising trot," Eva said, without looking up.

Jane slid off her mules, leaving them on the tack room ledge, and she pulled on her boots. She called two of the dogs and went out, heading for the five-acre field.

"Well, thank you, Janie. That's very kind of you," she muttered, praising herself under her breath. "I'll help you with the cooking sometime."

Ha, and pigs will fly, she thought.

She was used to helping out with various tasks on the farm, or in the stables, when they were pushed for time, and she didn't mind. It made a change. Nevertheless, it always seemed unfair to her that, if she had been working outside half the day, some of them still moaned like mad if she wasn't exactly on time with lunch, or dinner, or whatever. How she was supposed to do both things at once, she didn't know.

Eva was one of the moaners. But then, Eva didn't like her. It was Shirley. Eva and Shirley had been at school together. They were the same age and had known each other since their first day at primary school. As far as Eva was concerned, Jane had stolen Shirley's friendship.

It was not true. But from the first time Jane had shared a joke with Shirley, Eva had resented her.

Jane had thought then Eva would grow out of it, thought it was just the usual possessiveness seen in so many children.

"She's my friend, not yours!"

But years passed and she didn't grow out of it. If anything, she got more bitter. A working rapport had developed between Jane and Shirley. They had meetings with prospective workers, made arrangements about working rotas, and so on, and all of this excluded Eva, so she had more to resent.

Perhaps if she had more life outside work it would be better, Jane thought.

Eva was good at her job and deserved to be head groom, but, in all the years she had lived at Chance, Jane had never heard her talk about anything but work. She didn't take holidays as such. She might have the odd day off to go shopping, or visit someone, but that was about it. When they worked out the holiday rota, she just said she would take it in days over the year, as and when convenient. That may be good for the stables, but it didn't point to much of a life outside.

Hang on, though, thought Jane, you could say that about me too. She didn't take holidays at all. Well, she didn't really 'work', did she? Not according to the likes of Eva and Jeff. Anyway, not taking holidays was her choice. Where would she go? She didn't want to see any other counties, or countries, and her family had long ago distanced themselves from her.

Perhaps Eva was in the same position. Perhaps she had family problems.

* * * * *

"…And don't come back until the fat hand is on six, pointing straight down. See?"

Eva learned to tell the time before she learned to use the lavatory properly.

Her mother would give her the big, copper alarm clock with green numbers and show her which number to wait for, then she would shut the door.

She was a bright three-year-old, and soon learned she would get into more trouble for coming back before the black clock hand with the green middle got to its right place, than she would for coming back with wet or soiled pants.

Off she would go, down two garden steps, holding on to the little side wall with one hand, fingers tightly closed around the copper handle. She went through the bushes at the other side of the small lawn and into her house. It had 'Eva's House' painted over the door in wobbly black letters. Her mother had made her the house from an old door and some wooden pallets. She had pinned a big, green piece of tarpaulin over the roof to keep it dry and put four bricks under the base to hold it off the ground. Inside there was a box to sit on and lots of Eva's stuffed animals. Cats, dogs, bears; all sorts of animals. Her mother got most of them at jumble sales. The house was just big enough to stand up inside.

On cold, wet days she spent most of her time playing with an old, crock child's tea set. She had one cup and three saucers and a teapot without a lid. She collected water from the garden puddles and poured tea for her toys.

On hot days she sat under the bushes and made holes with an old teaspoon. She found if she wet on the ground, she could make mud shapes with her cup.

Everywhere she went, whatever she did, she carried her clock. When the hand got to the right number, she would go back across the lawn and climb the steps to wait by the door.

She liked it when her mother opened the door and laughed and hugged her and swung her round. She called her a "good girl" and gave her biscuits. She liked that. Usually, though, it didn't happen. Usually her mother wasn't that happy.

By the time she was four, she could not stand up properly in the house any more. By the time she was four, her mother was never happy any more.

One day, when she was climbing a bush by her house, she fell and crashed right through the roof. It hurt and the blood was going all over her toys. It didn't stop like blood usually did. Eva got frightened. She was frightened because the blood kept coming out and she was frightened of her mother's anger if she went to the house. So she cried herself to sleep, curled in the ruins of her house.

She never saw her mother again.

When she woke up she was in hospital and there was a lady sitting by her bed. Every time she woke up the lady was there. The lady said she was her aunt and Eva was going to live with her in the country.

Eva wanted to ask where her mother was…she wanted to ask where she, herself, was…but she had learned long ago to keep quiet. She wished she had her house to go into and was sad when she remembered it was broken.

Her aunt's garden had lots of bushes and big trees. It did not have a house. Eva missed that…and her toys…and her mother.

Her aunt had two boys aged eleven and thirteen. They soon realised that Eva said nothing and did exactly what she was told.

They told her to take her knickers down first and they giggled a lot. Then it was walking around with no pants on, then lying down, then other stranger things, of which she must never tell.

By the time she went to school, her life was full of secrets and threats.

Her first year's school report said she was quite a solitary child who worked diligently on her own, but contributed little to any class activity or discussion.

Shirley was her only friend, although they were not friends in the usual sense. They didn't huddle in the corners to exchange secrets, or play games of 'let's pretend'. They just stood close together and sat together in class when possible. There was little conversation. No holding hands and running round. No giggling. No animation. The teachers thought Shirley was a loner, too, and remarked how like attracted like. But when Shirley was about seven years old, she began to change. She had always been one of the brighter children academically, but now, as she grew in confidence, that intelligence blossomed. She contributed more in class and out of it. She had natural leadership qualities and other children began to seek her out.

When Eva was about seven years old, her aunt walked into the garden shed where her sons were sitting on a bench, trouserless and spread-legged, with Eva in front of them, trying to bring both to a climax at the same time.

Her aunt said she was just like her mother. Dirty.

Her aunt said she had spent half her life getting her mother out of one scrape or another and how was she repaid? Her filthy little daughter came and corrupted her two sons!

Her aunt was angry.

Her aunt cried.

Her aunt was in despair.

Eva learned more about her mother in those few moments than she had ever known. She knew now why her mother built her a little house. Her mother went with men, sending Eva out to play in the house, getting her out of the way. Her mother was a bad mother who didn't care about her.

Eva started to scream. She screamed for a long time, alone in the shed, until she fell asleep under the bench. Over the next eight years, she was isolated within the family and told frequently how lucky she was that her aunt had taken her in. If she hadn't done that, Eva would have been sent to a foster home.

Eva grew up and realised she would have been better off if she had been sent to a foster home.

Her two cousins avoided her from the moment of discovery. They had let her take all the blame, going along with their mother's opinion of her inherited promiscuity. Their mother still adored them so it wasn't their fault, they said to each other.

But their mother talked to her sister of the child's behaviour, and the sister talked to the other sister, and they both talked to their husbands. The boys' uncles were not so willing to believe in the boys' innocence and the resulting thrashing, the threats to tell everyone what they had done, and the fear of further retribution ensured they kept well away from Eva for the next eight years…physically that is, but they did ensure she remembered everything was her own fault.

Eva stayed by Shirley all through school. She followed Shirley's lead, taking on all her interests and concerns. So, she was good with horses. As that was Shirley's main love, she had to be good with horses.

Eva didn't have any boyfriends. Young boys were frightened off by her glaring eyes and sharp tongue. Older boys frightened her off.

She didn't have any other girlfriends. She treated other girls with contempt and any overtures of friendship quickly subsided after the first few sarcastic retorts.

She didn't have a lot of time for females of any age. Teachers who tried to get through to her gave up. She just stared at them and gave monosyllabic answers.

Her final school report said little different from her first one.

She went straight from school to Chance and never went back to her aunt's house.

Her aunt tried to maintain contact, tried to do the right thing. She sent birthday cards and bought her a small gift at Christmas. She used to invite her 'home' for Christmas dinner, but Eva never came, so she would arrange to meet her for "coffee and a chat" once a year. Eva would turn up sometimes. When she did, it was the most uncomfortable thirty minutes of the year for her aunt, but she felt she had to do it.

Occasionally, Eva saw her cousins. She passed them in the street, or at a local agricultural show, on a day out with their families. She would nod. They would nod back and lower their eyes under her direct stare. Their faces would flush as they looked from her to their own little daughters. Now they understood what they had done and it was too awful to think about, so they usually managed not to think about it.

Eva dreamed of her mother sometimes. Laughing and swinging her around and giving her biscuits. Mostly, though, she didn't dream at all.

* * * * *

"Janie! Janie!" Eva's voice called after her.

She stopped and turned.

"Patch is already tacked up in the middle stall."

Jane lifted her hand in response.

"I'll send Alice as soon as we've got this blasted mare."

"Okay," Jane smiled.

Eva looked as though she couldn't decide about something.

Jane waited.

"Thanks," Eva said and walked off quickly.

Jane stared after her as she disappeared round the stable front block.

What was all that about? Eva didn't thank her for anything. She didn't thank anyone for anything. What was all that about?! Jane wondered if she was all right and made a mental note to try and have a word with her some time. Not that it would do any good, she thought. Eva would probably just freeze her out as usual. Still, thanking people was not Eva's way and Jane worried when people acted out of character.

"Up. Down. Up. Down. Up. Down. Put your heels down, Simon. Up. Down. Up. Down." Jane shouted the rhythm at the little boy bouncing around on the back of a bay pony.

"Okay, Janie?" Alice said, coming up behind her in the field. "Sorry it took so long. That mare is a real headache."

"That's okay, I'll get back then." She called to the boy. "Up. Down. Up. Down. That's better. All right, halt now, Simon. Alice is here to take the rest of your lesson, so I'll see you later, I expect."

Jane kept a jar of toffees and boiled sweets on top of one of the kitchen dressers and the children would call for a sweet before leaving. It was another Chance tradition, but one that could be dated to the arrival of Jane, rather than its origins lost in the history of the farm.

* * * * *

Jane's organisational abilities had come into full play once she decided to take on the running of the farmhouse.

The first day Shirley had taken her to see Grumps, as she called him, he had glared at Jane and just said, "Well, miss, are you taking it on?"

The task seemed daunting. The chaos. The dirt. The dilapidation. The size of the place. The numbers of people.

"If it's going to be too much, say now and don't waste your and my time," Great Uncle William had said. "I can't be doing with messers." Jane saw him glance out of the window at Uncle Paul in the garden, as he added, "Whether they're relations or not."

She looked at the fierce, old man and he stared right back at her.

She looked at Shirley, who smiled and nodded encouragingly.

"I don't know," she said. "What would be my responsibilities?"

"All of it," he said, still staring at her. "Whatever needs doing. We don't operate union rules here. If it needs doing, you do it."

Jane hesitated. Just looking around the room they were in was enough to put her off. Papers everywhere. Straw on the floor. Dirty windows. Tatty curtains. Cups. Plates. And the inevitable odd boot. Total mess…and this was one small office. She looked back at Great Uncle William. He was still staring at her.

"Bit much, isn't it?" he said, in a quieter voice.

She smiled and shook her head slightly. "Well…it's…"

"I hear you got yourself in a bit of a mess," he interrupted.

Jane stiffened. Here it comes, she thought. Here comes the silent, implied criticism, the emotional blackmail. She was ready for it. She had had two years of that at home. She was a nobody. She had "thrown her life away."

She knew they were right. She was just the family's shame now and all her old confidence had disappeared under that knowledge. She realised she was stupid to think that coming to Chance may have given her a new start. Because here it comes again, she thought. He was about to put her in her place.

She lowered her head and waited for her first orders.

"Time to get yourself, and us, out of this mess," he said.

In the small silence that followed, as she took that in, she lifted her head to look at him.

"If you take this on, miss, it's your job. You do as you see fit. I hear you've got a good brain and you're a worker. The house, the food and all of that, you sort it out. No one will interfere. We're all too busy with our own work."

Jane looked at Shirley, who had moved to stand behind his chair. She said, "We'd like you here, Janie."

She looked back at her great uncle.

"Time to take control. Make some sense of the mess, eh?" he said quietly.

She nodded and took on Chance.

* * * * *

"All right, dear?" Aunt Doris said, as she poured herself another cup of tea.

Jane was preparing the pastry for the after-dinner apple pies, when her aunt appeared for elevenses.

"Anything I can do to help?"

"No, I'm fine thanks," Jane said. She knew full well that the offer of help was not meant; it was just another piece of formula chitchat. If Jane had said, "Yes please, can you prepare some carrots," or something, her aunt would have 'really loved to', but she had a senior citizen's meeting or it was her turn at the day centre.

"But you leave them, dear, and I'll do them later."

She never did, of course, and Jane and dinner could not wait. Still, she went through the motions every day, offering to help.

Uncle Paul was sitting at the big kitchen table, dipping biscuits into his tea and occasionally eating them. Most of them he held in his tea for too long, as he stared into space, deep in thought, or looked at some papers in his hand. So the biscuits disintegrated into the hot fluid and he put only the remaining corner in his mouth. At the end of every elevenses at which he appeared, Jane automatically put the sludgy contents of Uncle Paul's cup in the pig bucket, to save time unblocking the sink later.

Aunt Doris pecked a kiss on the top of his head as she passed, taking a cup of tea to her room.

"All right, dear?" she said, and didn't wait for an answer.

There wasn't one anyway.

Jane knew all of these rituals off by heart. It was only when someone didn't play their part that it impinged on her mind. Like Eva saying thanks. That wasn't part of the script. She made another mental note to speak to Eva.

Jane liked routine, liked knowing the script. It gave her time to think of other things while she gave stock answers to stock questions.

* * * * *

At four-thirty, when she got up, she would get the range going, take the dogs out, prepare early morning tea, make any sandwiches needed by those working away that day, and then start planning.

It was the planning that she enjoyed the most. She had lists for everything and a place for the lists. It was her organisational ability and self-motivation that had turned Chance farmhouse into the well maintained, well run 'business' that she considered her responsibility.

She did everything. Cooking. Cleaning. Painting. Repairing.

With eleven people in the house all the time, and more who came in for a couple of nights, or some for their meals, it was a task that continually stretched her abilities and gave her pleasure when she thought she had done it well.

She had made many mistakes at first. For example, she tried to impose town carpet standards on country tile floors and nearly driven herself daft in the process. She would sweep the floors twenty times a day, despairing at each new wisp of straw, each clump of mud. She had to sit herself down to realise that this was not just a house, but a working environment too. From then on the floors got cleaned once a day in the main rooms only, and after that, barring any major accidental mess, she ignored them.

All in all, though, it did not take long to adjust herself to Chance, nor Chance to herself. And she enjoyed it.

At first, local people thought she ought to have help. Great Uncle William was seen as "too damn mean" to get her that help. They said he was exploiting her and gossiped about why she put up with it. They knew she was a Hensham relation, so they speculated on her having a shady past, of using Chance to hide away. Or maybe she was a bit simple, not fit for much but cleaning up after others? Whatever the reason, she was being exploited, they said.

When they met Jane, she didn't fit their expectations. She wasn't downtrodden or furtive. She didn't move in a whirl of frenzied activity, trying to manage it all. She wasn't simple. She appeared to have time to chat. She seemed bright and open. They changed their expectations.

They said she wouldn't last. She wouldn't hack it. Give her a couple of winters and she would be gone. Up in that great, old barn of a place, with all those people, and her from a town?! No, she wouldn't last. The task was too great.

In the illogical way of gossip, the fact that the dilapidation of Chance didn't change overnight into a sparkling white showpiece confirmed their beliefs. She hadn't waved a magic wand. She wasn't hacking it.

Of course, they had heard that she did turn out regular meals and there was certainly more washing on the line, but nothing had changed much.

"Oh, Shirley said her bedroom had been painted and moved round, but that's just one room, isn't it? And when Mrs Arbour called for the church autumn sale donation, she said the kitchen looks cleaner, but still very dingy though…"

No, nothing much had changed.

It did change, though: slowly, room-by-room, inside and outside.

After five years people didn't talk about it any more. Jane's position was accepted and established. She was the 'domestic' one.

And Jane enjoyed it all, revelling in the occasional satisfaction of a newly painted room, in the daily satisfaction of turning out good meals and clean clothes. She set her own standards and tried hard to meet them…and nobody took much notice at all.

Jane had found her place.

* * * * *

Eva didn't appear for elevenses. She and Shirley were busy with the three Misses: Miss Marjorie Finlay, Miss Fanny Chadd and their grey filly, Miss Pittypat. These three regular clients were looked on with great fondness by all the livery stable staff, providing everyone with ongoing entertainment, from side-splitting hilarity to head-clutching despair.

Miss Marjorie and Miss Fanny lived together in a chocolate-box cottage, outside a village a few miles from Chance.

Chocolate-box cottages were quite common in this part of the county. Cottages, so quaint and attractive, that photographs of them could be seen adorning the front of calendars, or tea caddies, or chocolate boxes. Any cottage, so used earned the name of chocolate-box cottage for ever after.

Miss Marjorie and Miss Fanny were in their mid-fifties and had lived together in their cottage for as long as anyone could remember.

"A couple of lesbians," Jeff said, and he may have been right, but Jane could not imagine these two elderly spinsters engaging in the sort of sexual activity Jeff loved to describe. Both were so completely naïve and gentle, so utterly in love with their darling Miss Pittypat.

Jane remembered when Miss Fanny first phoned to ask if they would take their horse in for schooling. They wanted to enter dressage competitions with her. Shirley had invited the two Misses to come along and see the set-up at the stables and to talk terms.

The two Misses arrived, dressed in shirts and ties, tweed hacking jackets and jodhpurs, and looking alike as can be. Short, dark, greying hair. Wrinkled nut-brown faces. Soft voices and smiles. It took ages before everyone sorted out which was Miss Marjorie and which Miss Fanny.

They loved dressage competitions and had been going to see these exhibitions of balance and control for many years. Horse and rider acting as one, as they performed neat sidesteps and turns, piasse and passage, in amazing demonstrations of suppleness and obedience. The Misses loved it and, two years ago, as they had a nice paddock behind their cottage, they bought themselves a horse. They could already ride, of course – all children of their background were taught to ride – and now they wanted to do dressage. Would Shirley take in their Miss Pittypat and school her for dressage competitions?

* * * * *

When the horsebox arrived and Miss Pittypat emerged down the ramp, there was a stunned silence in the stable yard. They had expected a nice, solid old hack with the patient manners and nature of a beloved pet. What came down the ramp was a breathtakingly beautiful, grey, full-bred, Arab filly, with flaring nostrils and flowing mane and tail, stepping high with little prances into the stable yard. A Miss Pittypat it wasn't.

"Bloody hell," Eva said.

That just about said it for everyone.

Miss Fanny and Miss Marjorie cooed at it, beaming with pleasure and pride.

Shirley recovered first and took the filly to its box, leaving the Misses to settle it in, as they had requested. She said she would see them in her office, when they were ready, to arrange a schedule for schooling.

An hour or so later, the stable box now well adorned with Miss Pittypat's favourite bowl, bucket, curry-comb, rug, etc, etc, the Misses came tearfully into the office. They said they were assured of their beloved's well-being and future care, and they were very earnest in their declarations that they were leaving everything completely in Shirley's hands. Trust shone out of their eyes. They said they had tried some easy dressage exercises with Miss Pittypat, but they were not getting too much response. They 'just knew' Shirley could help them. The man they bought Miss Pittypat off said she was a good dressage type.

Shirley controlled her eyebrows from rising too high and tried to explain that Arab horses didn't really have the right conformation, the right balance, for dressage.

It didn't do any good.

It never did any good whenever Shirley repeated the statement over the following years, and she repeated it often. They were full of confidence.

And so the farce began.

Shirley always took out the new horses in for schooling first, before anyone else rode them. She would judge what was needed, and who should take on this task by this first try-out.

As was usual, everyone free came to lean against the rails and watch. New horses brought new problems, which all of them needed to learn. Furthermore, this one promised to be fun.

Shirley mounted the horse, sitting still for a moment, holding her back from walking on. Miss Pittypat tried a few small shakes of the head, a few small prancing sidesteps, then stood quietly, working out this new human.

When Shirley told her to walk on, she ignored it…until she realised Shirley wasn't going to be ignored.

When Shirley told her to trot, she realised that it had to be a trot – cantering wasn't allowed.

In fact it took Miss Pittypat very little time to understand that the firm, controlled weight on her back would tolerate no nonsense at all.

Miss Pittypat was a bright lady.

Within a very short time she was standing, walking, trotting, cantering and reining back to order.

For the audience it was all pretty boring. They couldn't imagine an Arab filly winning any major dressage competitions, but she could certainly put in a reasonable performance locally.

Eva took on the schooling and progress was quickly made. The two Misses came and watched with delight as Miss Pittypat moved around the schooling ring to order. They clapped their hands and showered compliments on Eva and Shirley and their own precious girl.

"Would you like to try now?" Shirley asked after a week had gone by.

After much polite discussion on who should go first, Miss Marjorie agreed to be the one, if Miss Fanny was really sure she didn't mind.

Miss Marjorie mounted the filly and Miss Pittypat stood quietly for her. Miss Marjorie and Miss Fanny beamed their satisfaction at each other at this display of control.

Ten minutes later and she was still standing quietly. Miss Pittypat appeared to have gone to sleep.

"You really have to be quite firm, Miss Marjorie," Shirley called for the umpteenth time, as Miss Marjorie said sweetly, "Walk on, Pitty, darling. Walk on, my baby," and tickled her back with the crop Shirley had given her.

"No! No! Give her one smart tap with the crop and say 'walk on' firmly," Shirley called. "Don't stand any nonsense, Miss Marjorie."

The other grooms were now finding it hard to control their faces as Miss Marjorie responded to Shirley's instructions by telling Miss Pittypat, very seriously, that Shirley was "cross" with her now and she was being a "naughty little horse."

Shirley suggested that Miss Marjorie get down and she would take Miss Pittypat around the paddock a couple of times to "warm her up."

"I'm going to slaughter the little sod," she muttered to the others as she smiled her way to the horse. The others were biting their lips by now and developing sudden fits of coughing to hide the laughter.

The instant Shirley got up, Miss Pittypat responded. Yes, she was a bright lady.

She went like a dream, doing everything she was asked as long as Shirley was on top.

Miss Fanny's turn was next. Shirley stood by the horse. Miss Fanny mounted. Shirley reiterated all the instructions about being firm and was ready to slap her hand down on the horse's rump if it refused to move.

Miss Pittypat was aware of Shirley standing nearby and obediently moved off straight away.

Miss Marjorie clapped.

Miss Fanny beamed.

Miss Pittypat walked until she was out of Shirley's reach and went back to sleep.

With Shirley walking behind the horse, both of the Misses managed a few circuits of the paddock non-stop. They were really pleased and praised Shirley effusively for the improvements she had made. Everyone wondered if they had actually moved on the horse at all before today. Probably not, it was decided.

Weeks on the lunging rein followed and the little darling behaved perfectly, knowing that Eva was on the other end of the rein with a long whip. As soon as she went back to free riding with the two Misses, Miss Pittypat went back to sleep.

At after dinner discussions, they tried to work out how to get the two Misses to learn to control the horse. Of course, this wasn't the first schooling they had taken where the problem lay more with the rider than the horse, but usually it was easy to show owners how to correct the fault. They decided to get the ladies riding as much as possible and increase their confidence by showing what firm control could achieve. This horse was bloody-minded, on that they all agreed. Since its normal mode of movement was excited, high-stepping prances, the fact that as soon as the Misses got up it did an imitation of a sleepy, coalman's horse had to be sheer bloody-mindedness.

It took two months to persuade the Misses to stop lying on the horse's neck with strokes and pats and, "Aren't you a good girl?" every time it took four steps forward.

It took four months to get the horse to walk around the paddock without stopping, and that was only because it realised the inevitability of someone coming up behind it to administer a sharp slap if it did.

When they progressed to trotting, Miss Pittypat showed one of her other abilities. Maths.

She could calculate, to an inch, how to trot smartly far enough away to get a good few seconds' nap before anyone could get to her.

They began using the smaller paddock, so there wasn't anywhere she could get far enough away. She then began to trot around quite nicely, going just near enough to the rails to scrape the rider's leg along the wood until the resulting pain would call a halt.

"Bring her away! Use your crop, Miss Fanny! Turn her to the centre. No! Really shout at her!"

"Naughty girl…naughty girl…" would come the sweet, hurt voice.

She might just as well be saying how good she was. The tone was exactly the same.

At dinner they debated whether they could give the Misses shouting lessons.

Shirley tried to tell them there wasn't much point in going on, tried to tell them they were wasting their money. She showed them, over and over again, how nicely the horse went for her, for Eva, even for young Jay, but all that seemed to achieve was even greater ecstasy in the Misses' minds at the thought of themselves riding Miss Pittypat like that.

"You just have to be firmer," she said to them.

They nodded and promised solemnly that they would.

True to their word, the next morning before they mounted up, they told the horse, very seriously, that she wouldn't get a carrot if she didn't behave herself.

You could tell it was serious, because they didn't smile when they said it. They did pat her, stroke her and lay their cheeks on her shining coat to explain how sorry they were about all this, but they didn't smile. It was serious.

Shirley's exasperated "Ye gods!" hissed out as she threw her arms over her head in despair, and changed to helpless laughter as they all turned away trying to control their faces.

The two Misses thought the tears rolling down Shirley's face were in sympathy with their own distress at their display of harshness. They patted Shirley's arm and said, "There, there… we know it's difficult for you too," and they understood when Shirley had to go to the house for a few minutes alone, to pull herself together.

Of course, after a time, they insisted on entering Miss Pittypat for a local horse show, in the beginner's dressage section. Everyone tried

A fleeting chance

to persuade them against this, or to let one of the grooms show the horse, but the two Misses were determined to do it themselves.

With thoughts of impending doom, Shirley and Alice loaded Miss Pittypat in the horsebox and set off to meet Miss Marjorie and Miss Fanny at the show.

The world of livery stables and horses is a small one. Everyone gets to know everyone, so Shirley knew many of her friends would be there: other owners of livery stables accompanying their own clients or riding themselves. Other potential customers would be there too. Impending doom, Shirley thought.

The arrival of Miss Pittypat attracted attention and praise. She was beautifully turned out and a credit to the stables. Shirley never was worried about that part.

When the competition started, she was sitting with a group of associates and wishing she wasn't.

It had been agreed that Miss Fanny should ride this time, Miss Marjorie declaring she was quite happy to have her turn at the next show.

Shirley's companions were prepared for some fun. Of course, they knew all about the three Misses. Horse people talk horses and the word had spread. Shirley came in for more than the usual amount of good- natured teasing, as Miss Fanny waited for her turn. Bets were made on whether she would move at all.

Shirley didn't mind all of that. What she dreaded, what all of Chance dreaded, was that the two Misses should be hurt. Everyone had grown very fond of Miss Marjorie and Miss Fanny and the thought of them being ridiculed was upsetting. No one had laughed at yesterday's 'dress rehearsal' of today's competition when Miss Pittypat walked obediently to the centre of the paddock and then put her head down and proceeded to eat the grass. Despite Miss Fanny's pleading and pulling, Miss Pittypat would not move, and the distress in Miss Fanny's eyes had quashed any amusement for the onlookers. Shirley had called the horse everything under her breath, and even more out loud, as she schooled it later.

Miss Fanny was due out after just two more competitors and Shirley couldn't stand it. In her head she threatened, she cajoled, she pleaded, she promised.

Alice was holding the horse's head, muttering at it non-stop.

Miss Marjorie was looking very apprehensive, stroking Miss Fanny's boot as much as she was stroking Miss Pittypat's side.

Miss Fanny looked set in concrete.

It was Miss Fanny's turn. Alice led them to the small ring and moved behind Miss Pittypat. Shirley closed her eyes and prayed.

The bell went for Miss Fanny to start. Alice lifted her arm as though to brush her hair from her eyes, and Miss Pittypat walked forward to the centre of the ring and halted. Miss Fanny bowed her head to the judges…then her back…then her whole body as she slid forward on the horse's neck and slowly moved off to the side, falling to the ground in a dead faint. The excitement had been too much.

In the ensuing panic, as everyone rushed to give first aid, Miss Pittypat stood quietly.

They found out later she got very good marks for her Halt and Stand. Miss Marjorie and Miss Fanny were thrilled.

Later they came to see Shirley and told her they had agreed that they had let Miss Pittypat down and, in future, maybe it would be best if someone from Chance rode her in competitions. Nevertheless, they would like to continue taking lessons themselves.

So they continued to come to Chance, once a week, to sit proudly on Miss Pittypat, whilst one of the grooms chased her round the field.

* * * * *

"Are they still with the two leses?"

Jane lifted her eyebrows ingenuously as she asked, "Which two men do you mean, Jeff?"

A fleeting chance

"You know who I mean, so you can cut out the smart arse remarks," he growled back.

"If you mean Miss Marjorie and Miss Fanny, yes, Shirley and Eva are still with them."

"The leses, yes," he smirked. "Our old lesbian friends. That's probably what your problem is: you fancy the females as much as I do. You're probably one of them yourself. Is that it, Janie? You a lesey too, eh? Fancy a bit of tit and arse, do you?"

Jane looked at him without expression or reply.

"Eh? Eh?" he pushed. "What you need is a real man. That'll soon drive all that stuff away."

She still looked at him.

"All of them little secret talks you have with the girls. Now we know what it's all about, don't we? Trying to get a feel, are yer? Eh? Wait until you've had a real man, Janie. A real man." He rubbed his hand over his crotch and pushed his hips forward.

"That's all you need. A big, hard, real man."

Jane looked him up and down slowly and said, gratefully, "Well, if I ever meet one, I'll remember your advice. Thanks a lot, Jeff."

She got up to move the pans along the range, smiled at him and added, "Oh, and by the way, can you shift your stuff. I'm doing your room next."

He was gone when she turned round.

Before Jane moved into a room to start heavy cleaning, painting and repairing, she gave the occupants plenty of warning. This gave them a chance to get ready to move out to a spare room. Of course, this didn't happen too often, as Jane only got round to painting any particular room maybe once every three or four years, but when it did happen it was looked on as exciting by some, a nuisance by others.

Aunt Doris, Shirley and Jane all had their own rooms. Sally, Alice and Jay shared one of the very big bedrooms. This was their choice and Jane thought they enjoyed the company, as well as it being a protective measure against the attentions of Jeff. He had his own room too, while Andrew and John chose to share a room. Uncle Paul slept in his study.

There were eleven good bedrooms in the house, plus three small dressing rooms off the biggest bedrooms, so moving to another room during the painting season was not a problem, unless the occupants chose to make it one.

Jeff chose.

Jane knew he would not move until the last moment and, then only because Shirley ordered it. He would complain of the disruption before and the decoration afterwards. But then, he didn't like Jane and anything was ammunition.

Jane decided to mention it to Shirley before she had to wait around for Jeff to move. She was only one wall away from finishing the girls' room, which meant she would move to the other part of the house in a day or two.

The pans were bubbling their vegetables quite nicely, so she went up to see Alice in the girls' temporary bedroom to tell her to tell the others to get ready to move back.

Alice was standing by the window when Jane walked in. This was her half-day and she hadn't gone to town as she often did, shopping or visiting. She said she had letters to write and presents to wrap for her twin sisters.

"Okay, Ali?" Jane said as she walked in.

"Hi, Janie," Alice smiled a reply. "Yes, I'm fine."

"What are you looking at?"

"Just the pony yards and that. Nothing much."

Jane moved to stand at the window with her. The windows looked down on two of the yards, which, at this time of the day, were full of activity.

As at most stables, local children – mainly young girls – loved to come and help out with the horses. They would happily fetch and carry for the grooms, just for the chance to be near these beloved animals. Most of the girls would grow out of their horse-mad years, but for a time being with horses would

A fleeting chance

be the most important thing in their lives. Jane watched too, as half a dozen girls moved around the yard, fetching hay, carrying water, stroking ponies. Sometimes the grooms would let them ride a pony out to the fields, or bring a pony in. These were moments worth waiting for and gave the opportunity to discuss the merits of this or that pony with their peers later. Each had their favourites to dream about.

Jane watched as Uncle Paul put down his spade and helped a girl up onto a tethered pony. He bent down to talk to another girl standing by his side. The girls were happy and Uncle Paul rubbed his hands over his grey hair as he said something that made them laugh. He crouched down in front of the laughing girl, hands on her arms, pulling her so she swung backwards and forwards, twisting from her waist. Then he stopped abruptly, looking past the child. The freezing movement was so sudden that Jane edged forward to peer straight down under the window, following his gaze. Jeff was there.

When she looked back, Uncle Paul was disappearing round the stable block, spade in hand. She saw him cast a nervous glance back towards Jeff.

Perhaps Uncle Paul would like to join the hit list, she thought. He could dig a hole to bury him at least.

Jeff walked towards the two girls and the one on the pony, who quickly bent forward to slither off its back. They were not smiling now, as Jeff said something to them.

"I don't like him around the pony yards," Alice said, watching Jeff walk away, going towards Shirley, who was just coming in from the schooling paddock.

"Nor me," Jane agreed. "Oh, I know a lot of what he says is for effect, to see if he can shock you, but he goes too far."

"He's been bothering Jay again, you know."

She looked at Alice. "You seem to be able to avoid him, Ali. How do you manage that?"

"Don't know. Just not his sort, maybe. Or just lucky. I don't know."

"Hasn't he ever tried it on with you?"

"Oh, the usual filthy remarks and that, but not actually had a go at me, no." She stared out of the window again. "Maybe my brothers have something to do with it." She smiled, "But I'm not exactly Miss England either, am I?"

Jane put her arm around Alice for a moment, then turned quickly to move to the door.

"Don't be daft. You're okay, you know."

The words sounded harsher than she intended – to her own ears anyway – although Alice didn't seem to notice, she continued to watch the yards.

Jane was clenching her fists in anger at the thought that Jeff had implanted in her mind. That sudden thought, as she went to comfort Ali, that this arm around her could be construed as sexual interest, and her own instinctive reaction to move away.

How dare he impart his own twisted thinking into her actions?

How could she be so stupid as to let him change her normal behaviour?

She was angrier with herself than with him. She went back to the window and put her arm around Ali again, saying, "Come and have a cup of coffee. You can teach me your Jeff-flattening techniques."

Alice was crying. Just a tear or two, trickling down her face.

"Ali?" Jane said, uncertainly.

"No." She brushed the tears away. "It's okay. I'm all right. Just being sentimental, that's all. Watching the children, you know. Reminds me of me at that age, if you know what I mean."

They looked out of the window again in companionable silence.

"I had such dreams," Ali's voice went on. "Owning the most beautiful chestnut stallion…winner at the Horse of the Year Show…adventures, when me and my horse saved the world. You know the sort of thing. I lived horses just like them. I suppose the difference is, I didn't grow out of it. I didn't find boys. Well, as I said, I'm no Miss England."

Jane looked at her. Alice was twenty-two, nearly twenty-three. Average height and heavy build. She had one of those figures that seem to be soft and shapeless, with no defined waist and large, round breasts, too far down from her shoulders. For many women, such a shape would require strong support to stop her bouncing around when riding, but, oddly, Alice never seemed to have that problem. That was her shape and it seemed to be solidly fixed where it was. She had brown, curly hair that she screwed into an elastic band at the back to hold it off her face, but tendrils of curls stuck out everywhere, refusing to be brushed into confinement. Her face was round with red cheeks and lips. If the weather was warm, or when she was working hard at something, her whole face was bright red. As she did work hard, this was the way most people saw her. 'Beetroot', they called her. That was the children's nickname. 'Beetroot'. Round and red. But the children liked her. Her twinkly blue eyes, small above her round cheeks, and her friendly smile.

"Beetroot," she said, echoing Jane's thoughts. "That's me. Beetroot." She smiled.

"You have seen my three big brothers? And my twin sisters? Yes?"

Jane nodded. Ali's brother was stunningly good-looking. Tall, dark and handsome adequately described all three. And her twin sisters were equally eye-catching, just in the full glowing beauty of nineteen years and desired by every young male in the area.

"So, how come they had me?" Ali said with a smile. "Don't seem hardly right, do it?" Her strong, rural accent emphasised the meaning behind this popular local expression.

Jane shook her head in sympathy, knowing that flattering lies would not be accepted.

"Oh, I don't mind really, you know. Not really. Horses don't go for looks, do they? We joke in our family and call me the coalman's daughter. You know…one winter when mum was a bit hard up…well, you know. It's funny, innit?" And she laughed briefly. "Anyway, it has its up-side. Saves me from Jeff, I guess. So, if you want to know my Jeff-flattening techniques, you just get born plain." And she laughed again.

Jane didn't laugh.

"Afternoon, Jane." The rich, deep tone of Sir Edmund interrupted Jane's shopping list.

"Good afternoon, Sir Edmund," she smiled at him. "Hello Lady Marguerite…Lettice…John." She greeted various members of the squire's family. They chorused their greetings back.

"I say, that looks a bit yumptious," young John said, leaning over a chocolate fudge cake that Jane had left out to set, and sticking out a testing finger.

"Get away from that, Johnnie, you disgusting child," her ladyship admonished her nephew. "Sorry, Jane, he is utterly despicable. If his nasty little fingerprint is on your cake, just let me know and I'll make him work hard for a morning to earn enough to replace the ingredients."

John skipped behind his sister and grinned ruefully at this warning. "She would too," he said.

"And serves you right," said his older sister.

Jane really loved all the county people. The old families of the area with centuries of local history behind them. The sirs and ladies. The earls and countesses. She had never met one yet who had put on any airs and graces, who was highhandedly rude, or who failed to treat every service you gave them as a great favour, despite the fact you were charging them for it. Many of the local gentry kept their hunters and breeding stock at the stables. They bought presents for everyone at Christmas, right down to the lowest groom, and made a point of thanking and praising all.

Jane thought this way of treating people must be instilled in the young from birth, a genuine concern for those who lived and worked on the land, held by their families for generations. She knew she felt like all the other villagers and would rather be a tenant of Sir Edmund's, or Lord Harcombe's, than a number on a council list.

If you lost your job or got injured, well, the squire had known your family for years and knew you were no idler, so rents would be waived and arrangements made until you were back on your feet.

If you outgrew your cottage when your wife had twins, then he would see if old Mrs Hicks would prefer the smaller Bluebell Cottage so you could take your growing family into the larger Anstey House, which she was finding difficult to manage anyway.

It was all very amicable and so much more personal than waiting for the council to act, or demand. The locals called it 'musical houses'.

Yes, Jane loved the county families, almost as much as she detested the 'New Money'. It was strange, she thought, that people whose money was only one or two generations old, so much wanted to be like county people and yet they did so much to prove they were not. Brand new cars and fashion house clothes were on display just to visit their horses. County people tended to drive old Land Rovers, or station wagons, and dressed in sensible, often tatty, clothes. But then they had nothing to prove.

It was an old Chance joke that Lady Marguerite had her rollers in under her headscarf more often than not.

"Well, I can't sleep in them you know, dear, and my damned hair will go straight before tonight's dinner anyway, unless I tame it now."

The Brydens, one generation from their toy-making millionaire ancestor, had thought Lady Marguerite was a groom at first. The subsequent grovelling when they found out the truth was amusing to watch, if Jane hadn't felt so angry at the time at their arrogant dismissal of the 'groom'. For it wasn't just the outside of the 'money' people that proclaimed their lack of local ancestry, it was their attitude. If they had worn notices saying

'I am rich, you must run round after me', it couldn't have been more obvious. They were rude, demanding, never pleased and never thankful. It seemed to take three or four generations before they felt secure enough to stop putting on a show.

Of course, there were exceptions and Mr and Mrs Jennings were one of them. They had won the pools. At least, that was what everyone guessed, for they never talked about it. They came from Birmingham and had bought a nice, old house of modest proportions, just outside Purley village. The attraction of the place was the three large fields that surrounded the house, for they enabled the Jennings to fulfil a dream. They wanted to own a couple of brood mares.

Mr and Mrs Jennings had arrived at Chance early one March morning. They asked to speak to the owner. Jane thought they might be collecting for some charity, or campaigning for a religious organisation, so she tried to find out and deal with it rather than bother Shirley, but they said they wanted to talk to her about horses.

He wore a modern suit and wide tie. She had on a neat skirt, a blouse and little jacket, and high-heeled shoes. They looked about thirty years old, nervous and excited. They didn't look like horse people.

When Shirley arrived, they explained how they had just moved here and they had asked around and found out she was the best person to give them advice about horses. They explained how they would like to breed horses "in a small way, of course" and could Shirley help them?

He was a plumber by trade and she used to be a shorthand typist until she had the two children, so they needed someone to help them choose a couple of mares and work out how to pick stallions and help with the foaling and with the breaking and schooling and with…well, just about everything really.

They spoke rapidly, in turns, as they listed out all these things. He had always liked horses "having a bet and that" and she had

A fleeting chance

dreamed of owning a horse since she was young. Oh, not to ride any more, but they were lovely things, weren't they?

Shirley agreed. They talked money and agreed that too. They were very happy. He said he would be glad to help with any plumbing problems they ever had. No charge. Jane, laughingly, advised him not to offer that as burst pipes, leaking taps and overflowing tanks were part of yearly life at Chance. The plumbing at Chance matched the house, a hodgepodge of pipes and wheels and valves that defeated the many plumbers who tried to make sense of it. So they always ended up adding some system of their own to overcome the immediate problem and, in so doing, increased the total confusion for the next plumber.

That the Jennings had money to spare was obvious. They bought the best that Shirley recommended. They holidayed abroad frequently. They never stinted on anything. The children soon had their own ponies. Local tradesmen gained from alterations and additions to this and that. They spent money freely, yet they were liked by all: genuinely nice people, never looking down on others, never assuming their right to be first.

Mr Jennings – Barry, as he insisted everyone call him – did take on the plumbing at Chance. Arriving one wintry morning to see one of their new foals, he insisted on helping with a burst pipe that was flooding a yard. Jane equally insisted he did not. She felt that a valued client shouldn't be put in such a position, but Mrs Jennings – Pauline – pleaded with her to let him do it, saying, "It'll give him something useful to do and let him keep his hand in."

As Jane was having a problem getting any plumber to come out to them, she agreed. Barry fixed it, but it took a long time. Jane wasn't surprised, but she was embarrassed. The plumbing at Chance was a mess, she knew: she had been told for years by every plumber who ever visited.

When a grubby Barry eventually returned to the kitchen, where Shirley and Pauline were having tea as they discussed the foal, he was very quiet. Jane felt even more embarrassed. She should not have let him do it.

"Sorry about that," Jane said, waving vaguely to indicate all the water problems at Chance. "It was very good of you to take the time."

He lifted his head in slight acknowledgement, but he said nothing.

He didn't smile or say anything during the rest of the visit either. His wife looked worried and puzzled, turning to him instantly they were in the car.

"You cretin!" Shirley rounded on Jane, as soon as she had waved them off. "What did you let him do that for?"

"I didn't! I tried to stop him. He insisted. Really he did."

"Oh no," Shirley moaned. "I'm sorry, Jane, but they were set to become good long-term clients. I reckon this will be their only season now."

"No, it's my fault, I know. Our plumbing defeats the best and I suppose it was an ego blow to offer to help and then be faced with something that was never in any training manual. He's obviously upset. I should have insisted. I'm sorry. They're nice people too, that's what makes it worse."

At eight-thirty the next morning their car arrived again. This was not expected and a grim-faced Barry asked if he could have a word with Shirley.

Pauline smiled at Jane, but said nothing.

"Here we go," groaned Shirley, "they're going to move their mares out."

Jane had shown Pauline and Barry into the office where they were sitting in silence.

Barry had a small leather briefcase, which he put on his lap as they entered. He looked nervous now.

"Something wrong?" Shirley asked, after the initial greetings.

Barry nodded and started to say, "Yes. Look, it's just that… well…that…"

"He's been up half the night," Pauline put in. "It's very embarrassing, you know, but…" She dried up too.

A fleeting chance

"There's something you don't like about our way of doing things? Something upsetting you? Perhaps we can talk it through." Shirley was pushing for their excuse, the better to get it over with.

Barry was looking at the floor.

Pauline was looking at him.

"Something you would like to change?" Shirley suggested.

"Yes!" he jumped in. "Yes! That's just it."

They waited, but he had gone back to floor staring.

"You're not pleased with your first foal maybe? We can discuss other studs, other sires, for next season. Or perhaps you don't want to put your mare in foal again? If…"

"No, it's nothing to do with the horses," Pauline said.

"It's not that," he added.

"One of the grooms then? Someone has done something you don't like?"

Jane felt like screaming. The reason was obvious, but they couldn't pull out because he was made to feel a fool yesterday, so what excuse would they use? Whatever they chose, she just wished they would get on with it.

"No. Look, everything is fine with the horses, it's just this place, see…"

Jane and Shirley nodded encouragement, but he was stuttering again.

"Oh, for God's sake!" his wife snapped. "Can he do your bloody plumbing?"

Jane and Shirley stared at her, the smiles of encouragement still fixed on their faces.

"He'll drive me mad if you don't let him. You don't have to pay for it, just let him do it. Apparently, he's never seen anything like it in his life."

"Pauline!" Her husband admonished her, as though she was a rude child.

"Sorry…Sorry…" he apologised to Jane and Shirley.

65

"This is to do with plumbing," Shirley said slowly, as she took it in. "Not with your horses?"

"No. The horses are fine. I told you that," he reassured them, "but your plumbing is unbelievable. I don't want to offend you, but it is you know."

"We know," Jane reassured him back. "It's the result of a couple of hundred years of alterations and additions. Then fifty years of plumbers adding their own bits because they can't understand the rest."

"Do you know, I think the back parlour sink is still fed from a spring?" Nervousness gone, his excitement now tumbled words out. "And there's miles of pipes that appear to go nowhere. Do you know there's at least fifteen tanks…"

Shirley and Jane nodded solemnly as the words became ever more enthusiastic and technical.

"Oh, God, here we go," Pauline groaned. "I've listened to this half the night."

"It'll take months to map it all out." He opened his case and pulled out a large pad of paper. "I thought, if you don't mind – and I would be very careful, of course, because I realise the historical importance of this place…well the plumbing itself is pure history, you know – I could write a book about it. No, really I could…I…"

Pauline leaned forward to the laughing Shirley and Jane. "Look, you won't be offended if he walks round with his sketch pad, will you? It'll keep him out of trouble and you can yell at him if he gets in your way. I've been doing it for years and it doesn't make any difference, but you're quite welcome to try."

"Pauline!" her husband protested, but the looks they exchanged were of fond amusement.

So, Barry and his sketchbook and his bag of tools became another feature of Chance. He didn't bother anybody. He moved around engrossed in his own business.

People suddenly came across him, sitting on a dairy shed floor, or emerging from some dubious hole in the ground. He always smiled a greeting, but was too busy for conversation. No outsider would guess he was one of Shirley's most important clients.

It was Barry that found the magazines.

It was Eva that he gave them to, his face averted and grim.

"You seen Eva?" Sally asked.

"Nope," Jane replied from up the ladder.

"Do you know where she should be?"

Jane turned her arm to look at her watch. "Damn!" she said, as the paintbrush in her hand flicked a spot of paint out. "Sorry," Sally apologised. "Shall I get a cloth?"

"Please…er…she should be back from exercising now and grooming Polly and Flip."

"She isn't," Sally said, from where she was wiping a speck of paint off a chair.

"Well I expect she will be soon. Is it important?"

"No…well…no, not really, only Sue saw her earlier and she didn't look well. Then she wasn't where I thought she'd be, so I just wondered if she was okay."

"Oh. She looked okay at breakfast." Jane rested her arm on the top of the ladder and thought. "Yes, she looked okay then. If you're worried, I'll just finish this bit and go and see."

"Thanks," Sally said and left.

Looking after all the people living and working at Chance fell to Jane. If anyone had a problem, she was the one they came to for everything from plasters to advice.

Sally was only nineteen, but she was one of the most caring people that Jane had ever known. If she had been older, it would be her that people sought out to talk to, to listen to their problems and secrets. The younger ones often did.

Sally had been at Chance since leaving school. She came from a small town, north of the county, so she lived in, going home to visit her father as often as she could. He came down to visit her too, as often as he could. He worked in a small factory unit, making boxes for various companies, and he did a lot of overtime, but any free Sunday he would drive down to see his daughter.

Jane liked Sally's father. He was a small, pleasant man, mild-mannered, but not timid. She wasn't sure if Sally's mother had died, or walked out, many years ago. Sally would say "since mum went" in conversation, without explaining the circumstances or displaying any distress about it. Jane guessed Sally had been very young when it had happened, whatever it was. Certainly father and daughter were very close, but there was no clinginess, no exclusive relationship. They were just nice people.

Sally had started as a groom almost the same time as Sue. They were of the same age and similar looks and build. Pretty with the prettiness of youth. It was clear they would either be great friends or rivals. Young girls always were one or the other, Jane thought.

Sally and Sue were friends from the start. Sue did not live at Chance, because she was one of the Batemans of Bateman's Cottage, sister of Harvey, daughter of Dave, the cause of much head shaking by Dave's wife, Eileen.

Sally and Sue may have looked alike, but they didn't dress, or act, alike. Sally was conservative in her demeanour, in her clothes, in her actions. Sue was the opposite, wearing the loudest colours, the tightest sweaters, laughing, joking, teasing, brash.

Her mother called her a "hussy". Her father said, "Now then, our Sue…" at least three times every day, but she laughed and called them worriers and old-fashioned.

Jane didn't think either girl would be at the stables in five years' time. They were the 'married with children' types, not like her, or Shirley, or poor Alice…or Eva.

Jane swilled the paintbrush until the water ran clear and decided to look for Eva in the front stalls first, just in case she got back late from exercising. Sally was probably worrying about nothing. Eva could have just got up in a bad mood…how would you tell if she had?

The sarcastic side of Jane's mind was admonished by her better side, out loud.

"Don't be nasty," she said, and went to find Eva.

She wasn't in the stalls, but Polly and Flip were…ungroomed.

Now that is odd, thought Jane. Maybe Sally was right. She stepped down from peering into the stable and Sue appeared, carrying a bucket of grooming equipment.

"Watcha," she beamed, in her usual bouncy way. "I've got to do them." She nodded at the horses.

"Why? Where's Eva?"

"Dunno. Shirley just told me to do them."

"Is she ill?"

"Dunno." She lifted the latch and went into Flip's stall. "Hello, my lovely," she said, as the big, grey gelding nosed her shoulder.

Jane went to find Shirley. She was talking to Sir Edmund and looking at the near foreleg of his grey hunter.

"Sorry to interrupt, but I'm just checking if Eva is all right." Jane smiled her apologies.

Shirley didn't look up from where she was bending over, running her hand carefully down the horse's leg. "She's fine," she said.

Jane wasn't sure if she was talking about the horse or Eva, so she went on, "Only Sally thought I ought to look at her, as she seemed a bit off at breakfast."

Shirley stood up. "She's fine," she repeated, looking Jane in the eyes. "Sally worries too much." She turned to Sir Edmund, cutting Jane out, "Well, I can't feel any heat in it, but…"

Jane walked away. Shirley was freezing her out, so something was wrong. She decided to check her chicken pies, which she had browned off earlier in the top of the range, then left to cook slowly in the low, cooler oven. Then she would go and search for Eva.

It was quite an interesting hunt really.

She caught Jay and Harvey kissing in the barn. He was supposed to be unloading hay. It was her morning off, so she was helping him.

No, they hadn't seen Eva. Jane doubted if they'd have seen a herd of charging elephants.

She found Sally, who worried even more because Jane couldn't find the cause of her original worry.

She interrupted Sue's rendition of "Ol' Man River" as she groomed an apparently tone-deaf Flip.

She watched a red-faced Alice chase Miss Pittypat round the paddock, to the obvious delight of Miss Marjorie on top and Miss Fanny leaning against the rails. She learned, as Alice ran past, that she hadn't a clue where Eva was.

She also learned six new ways to swear at the 'little darling' in front, without actually letting the doting rider hear them.

She saw young Richard, one of the farm workers, bring in another load of hay and hoped Harvey and Jay could hear the tractor, even if they couldn't hear a herd of elephants.

He said Jeff, Andrew and John were working far off, so they wouldn't have seen Eva around.

She found Barry in one of the old calf pens looking at some pipes that appeared to just rise from the floor about six inches from the wall, bend in opposite right angles and disappear through two adjacent walls.

She knew, as soon as she asked the question, that something was wrong.

Yes, he had seen her earlier, he said, and sketched more arrows and symbols on his pad. No, he didn't know where she was now.

"What's up, Barry?"

He stopped sketching and looked at his pad. There was a moment's silence, which the following "I don't know" didn't warrant.

Jane waited, but he said nothing else and got up to move to the next pen.

Okay, she decided, that was it. If they didn't want to tell her, fine, she had other things to do anyway. She strode off across the yard and back towards the house. It wasn't her problem. She had wasted enough time on it. Eva could look out for herself and, if she couldn't, well Shirley was sorting it and making it clear it wasn't anything to do with Jane. Just don't let anyone come moaning around later, asking her to sort it out, because they could forget it. She shut her mind to it and thought of dinner and vacuuming the back stairs.

The light from the granary window was wrong.

Jane knew it as soon as she approached the steps to turn the corner to the house.

If your life is completely absorbed in one small area, then three inches of grass bent the wrong way stands out as much as a missing door.

Chance was Jane's life and the light from the granary window was wrong.

She knew now where Eva was and slowed down to debate whether to go up the granary steps or not. Shirley's attitude had pointed out that it wasn't Jane's business, but Sally's concern had involved her…she didn't know what to do. Of course, she was going to talk to Eva anyway, about that peculiar thanking for helping out with Simon's lesson. That wasn't like Eva. Perhaps she was ill and it had been coming on for a long time?

She went up the stone steps of the granary. Eva was sitting on a big box at the far window. She turned when she heard Jane come in.

"Sally was worried about you," Jane started off, as she walked towards her. "Do you feel okay? What are you sitting in here for?"

Eva looked back out of the window. The view from the granary was one of Jane's favourites. Over the field that sloped down to the brook and the small woods that ran alongside it.

Then over the field that rose the other side of the brook and to distant fields and Halfpenny Hill on the skyline.

Eva was fiddling with the catch of the old window. "This is where the pigeons used to come in," she said.

"I know," Jane replied. "All those holes up there were for them." She nodded to the lines of holes set at regular intervals in the brickwork of the granary wall.

"You ever eaten pigeon pie?" Eva asked, still looking out of the window.

Jane nodded, even though Eva couldn't see it. "Yes, once or twice. It's okay. They were a major source of food in years gone by, of course." There was a pause. "Not now though," she added, to fill the silence. "What's wrong, Eva?" Jane sat on a dressing table that was part of an old cache of furniture kept at the back of the granary until it was needed, or disintegrated enough to be burnt. "What's wrong?" She put a hand on Eva's arm.

"Barry found some magazines," she answered, looking down at Jane's hand on her arm.

Jane removed her hand. "Yes?" she prompted.

There was another silence, broken by Eva's voice, sounding suddenly loud, harsh and angry. "People talk to you, don't they? People say you can be trusted, so they talk to you about things, don't they?" she demanded. "Don't they?"

"I don't know," Jane snapped back, as though defending herself against criticism, reacting to Eva's tone. Then she pulled herself back and made herself say calmly, "If you want to tell me something, I won't repeat it to anyone. Is that what you mean?"

The silence dragged longer this time. Jane wished she hadn't bothered, wished she was vacuuming the back stairs.

"The magazines." Eva's voice was quiet. "Barry found them, stuffed under the old water tank in the litter pens. You know the one?" She turned to Jane, who nodded. "They were dirty magazines, you know? Real dirty." She stared at Jane in silence again, then swung back to the window, saying angrily, "No, you don't know! You don't know!"

"Well, tell me then," Jane retorted. "I can't know if you don't tell me."

Eva stared down at her hands. "It happened to me, see. Like that. I did those things."

A small chink of light came through the slowly revolving door of Jane's puzzlement and she froze to a halt. "What things?" she asked quietly.

"The things they showed in the magazines," Eva said, then swung round and spat out, "See?!"

Jane didn't know what to say so she said nothing, her mind spinning round as she tried to take this in, and wishing even more she had left well alone.

"Shocked, are we?" Eva mocked her, turning away again to the window. "Don't want to know that sort of thing? Ha!" She made a bitter laughing sound. "Don't worry, Janie, nobody does. Believe me, nobody bloody does."

Jane could almost feel the loneliness, the desperation, coming from the figure outlined by the window light. She could also feel her own twinge of guilt that Eva was right. Her first urge was not to know, to get out of here. This wasn't her problem.

"I'm sorry, Eva." She made herself speak slowly, calmly. "Can we start again?"

Eva didn't move.

"I mean in both senses. Can we really start again?"

Eva looked down at the floor, then sideways up at Jane, who ploughed on, "We seem to be at cross purposes so much and I expect it's my fault as much as yours. What you are saying now, I don't understand. You're right, I don't understand. Can we start again?"

She waited a moment, then went on, "Are you saying that you posed for magazines? Sex magazines?"

"No, I never did that. I mean..." She stopped. Her eyes seemed to be seeking a way out, even though her body was still.

"Do you mean you've done some of the things they showed?" Jane prompted.

Eva nodded her head once, slowly.

Jane waited. But Eva said nothing.

"Things done with someone you're in love with look disgusting when you see pictures in the worst of these magazines, don't they? But these are private things, between two people. They're only disgusting when these magazines make them so."

The attempt to reassure did not work. Eva still said nothing. Jane changed tack, tried to get a dialogue going. "You say Barry found them?"

"Yes."

"I suppose anybody could have put them there. They've been printing that sort of muck for ages."

"No, these were dated recently."

Jeff, Jane thought. I told him I was going into his room, so he'd better clear it out. Bloody Jeff! Just the sort of filth he would enjoy looking at.

"They're very explicit, aren't they? Not just nude photos. I suppose they were very explicit, these ones?"

"Yes," Eva nodded. "Foreign. You couldn't understand the writing."

"Is that what upset you? That you've done these things with someone? What you do with someone you love isn't dirty, you know."

"You don't understand."

"Tell me then."

"They weren't photos of men and women. They were all photos of children doing things with men."

Jane froze inside, as realisation hit home. Eva was watching her.

"Love has nothing to do with it, Janie," she said, quietly.

"Oh, God…Oh, God, Eva…I'm sorry. I'm sorry," Jane babbled and reached for her, automatically trying to comfort, to take it all away.

Eva pulled back. "Don't touch me," she said. "Please."

"Who, Eva? Who?"

"No, it doesn't matter now. I don't want to rake it all up. It's a long time ago. It was just seeing the pictures, you know, seeing those little girls…and…"

Her eyes were desperate and she was biting her bottom lip. Jane took her hand and kept on holding it, although she tried to pull it away. "It's okay to cry, you know. I won't tell anyone. Not about anything."

The low, rasping, keening sound was not really crying and it didn't last long. Eva fought for and gained control very fast. Jane thought it would have been better for her if she hadn't. She let go of the hand as Eva pulled it away to rub over her face, wiping away non-existent tears. At least the hand had clutched back for a moment.

"Do you think it was Jeff?" she asked. "Jeff's magazines?"

"Seems likely, knowing him."

"I'm going to kill him." Eva's voice was deadpan.

Jane nodded. "We've got a list going if you want to add your name to it," she smiled. "Harvey's going to shoot him. Jay's going to use the pitchfork. I'm going to kick him to death. Uncle Paul's going to bury him. What would you like to be put down for?"

"I'm just going to kill him," Eva said. She didn't smile.

While she was hanging out more washing on the line, putting the half dry in one basket and hanging out the newly washed from another, Jane could see Jeff talking to Andrew. Andrew looked down at Jeff, who was giving instructions about something that needed doing. She saw Andrew move off towards the tractor sheds and Jeff walk slowly towards the office, hands in his pockets, head down, thinking. At least she thought he might be thinking, but with his hands in his pockets, he might not. She sent up a silent prayer that he kept his head down long enough to walk into something painful.

Eva had given the magazines to Shirley. Shirley had just said she would deal with it.

Yes, she would say that, Jane thought, but surely this time Shirley couldn't ignore it.

She started out on her familiar tracks of trying to work out why Shirley put up with him. She had nearly reached the house and got as far as if he was a cousin, when John's voice interrupted her.

"Seen Andrew, Janie?"

"He was talking to Jeff. I think he's gone to the tractor sheds now."

"Is Jeff with him?"

"No, he's in the office, I think."

"Oh, right."

John sounded and looked relieved. Jane smiled her sympathy. She thought she could add John to her list of prospective murderers with no problem at all. He came in for a lot of stick off Jeff, especially when Andrew wasn't around.

She shifted drying washing around on the pipes over the kitchen range and added more to the clotheshorse in front of it. She speculated on which method John would prefer. A bit of throat cutting might fit the bill.

* * * * *

Andrew and John shared a room at Chance. John came from the next county to the north and Andrew from a small town in the south of the county. John had arrived at Chance about a year before Andrew came and they had roomed together ever since.

Of course, Jeff made the obvious comments about this at first, but the fact that both young men seemed to be in competition to date every single female in the area rather flattened that theory.

Jane liked both men. They were not bright and witty, but they were fun in a carefree, bachelor way. They ribbed each other non-stop about their various amorous pursuits. They were the source of much amusement for everyone, as they trailed in one girl after another for tea, or dinner, or supper.

None of these romances lasted longer than a month, although each would declare the other was dying of passion before, during and after the event.

"No, don't try to get an answer out of him, Ali, he's mooning over this girl he saw at the cinema..." would change to, "Look at him! He's even off his food. This is really love, folks. Expect an announcement at any time. Start saving for the engagement present..." and end up with, "Well, I told him not to wear that sweater his Auntie Rose knitted him. It was bound to put her off. Would you like a cup of tea, son? There, there...we understand. No, don't laugh, you lot. This man is really suffering. He may never get over it..."

Yes, they were fun. Jane had a hard time trying to remember the names of the current girlfriends and, after several mistakes, which caused even more hilarity for the others, she made a point of never saying anything but hello to every newish face. There were so many new faces. Neither of the men were spectacularly good-looking, but both were single and pleasant enough to attract an apparently inexhaustible supply of temporary partners.

Jeff had been very interested at first, but his level of conversation about these young women soon alienated Andrew and John. Out for a good time they might be, but they were not going to discuss each girl's physical attributes and sexual prowess with Jeff...not on his terms anyway. So Jeff didn't get any titillation from hearing the details and, therefore, changed from enquiry to mockery. He was fond of saying that the two men wouldn't know what to do with it if it was laid in front of them begging, that all they were looking for was another teat, because their mothers had taken theirs away, that they couldn't satisfy an old maid who had given up hope...and so on.

John got the worst of it.

John was not much taller than Jane, whereas Andrew was over six foot, and Jane thought that was why Jeff was a bit more careful with him. She liked to think Jeff was a coward, although she had nothing to back it up. It was just more reason to dislike him. She was sure though that he was jealous of Andrew and John, especially when John met Penny.

Penny had been special. Everyone knew that. John had brought her to tea a couple of years ago, and right off everyone knew this was different. He was more nervous, more attentive, more excited. Different.

Of course, all the usual teasing went on, but so did the relationship. It was still Penny, long past the typical three or four dates. The teasing eased off and everyone began to look on them as an item.

She was a small, smiling girl, about the same age as John. They looked well together.

Jeff didn't ease off the teasing; he just got nastier and more offensive.

After several embarrassing incidents, John didn't bring Penny to Chance so much. Jeff's leering, "Doing all right, are yer?" said bent down into Penny's face, would cause her to draw back, feel threatened, feel dirty. It wasn't the words, it was what he made those words seem to mean.

Jane often thought no one would stay at Chance if Jeff was a constant factor, but that was one of the odd things about him. One Jeff was nearly constant, the other appeared like a wicked genie when you rubbed the lamp the wrong way. He was always around, running the farm, in the yards, working on this or that, but mostly he said nothing beyond issuing instructions. He would eat his meals in silence, or just the minimum of words. He spent a lot of time in his room. He was constantly around, but distant in a surly way. That was the usual Jeff. Then, suddenly would appear the other Jeff.

Jane used to wonder if drink was the trigger, but she thought not now. She had seen him drunk and inoffensive, sober and intimidating. She didn't know what triggered him off and she had given up trying to work it out.

She knew that John wanted to leave Chance after Penny broke up with him.

She knew that John laid the blame for this on Jeff and his little remarks that slowly eroded Penny's confidence in the relationship.

"You want to watch that boy, he's got a bad reputation."

"What have you got the others haven't, eh?"

On and on, dripped in, until she gave up.

Unfortunately, there were enough ex-girlfriends around to back up these statements, which otherwise could be seen as teasing jokes. Jane thought that if Penny had been as keen on John as he was on her, it wouldn't have mattered, but John just blamed Jeff and wanted to leave.

Andrew persuaded him to stay. Working at Chance was still a good job. They paid well. The accommodation was good. So was the food. The atmosphere was easy and pleasant, unless someone rubbed Jeff's lamp the wrong way, of course. Above all, jobs in farming were not so easy to come by now, as more machinery replaced more men, and John had never wanted any other life but farming. So, John stayed and the parade of short-term partners resumed.

* * * * *

If Jane had a hobby at all, it could be said to be her dogs.

In taking over Chance, she had inherited the dogs too. There were six of them when she came to Chance. All collies. The dogs she had now were the descendants of the original six.

When she first arrived, the dogs were friendly, but unruly. Their lifestyle lacked any structure because any attention from human residents depended on them having free time and that was not a guaranteed factor. So, basic training and playing only happened when one of the younger live-in grooms, or farm workers had nothing else to do in their time off. And, although they were fed adequately, it was done at irregular times, whenever someone had the time, usually late at night as an afterthought.

Jane had never had much to do with dogs, just the occasional pet around the houses of relations. This pack of largish, rushing, barking, barging, black, white and brown canines were a new and infuriating experience. She was forever being knocked sideways by one rushing to investigate some new sound, or falling over one lying straight across her path, or being deafened by a group barking session when a client arrived. She didn't like them and couldn't understand why they were around, or whose they were. People just said there had always been dogs and she would discover they were useful for lots of things, but they were the responsibility of no one person.

Great Uncle William just said if she thought something needed sorting, she had better sort it.

No, she did not like them, but they were an integral part of Chance, so she did it.

She approached the problem of 'sorting out the dogs' in much the same way as she approached sorting out the rest of Chance. It started with food. That was placed on the tack room floor at eleven-fifteen every morning, instead of when someone remembered.

Collies are bright. It took them no time at all to work out when eleven-fifteen was due. Then their water bowls were cleaned and refilled regularly, so they got used to walking to the back door for a drink, rather than finding a filled water bucket on its way to a stable, or going to a low cattle tank.

They were used to being fed in three large dishes, which were put down anywhere, and between which every dog rushed to and fro, seeking the best titbits, the most food. Snarling, nipping, yelping chaos.

Jane wasn't into chaos. It offended her basic sense of organisation.

One of the big problems was that although they all had individual names, if you called one, they all responded. She decided she was not having this rampaging, hairy gang running around everywhere any more. She would enforce some discipline, some order. She found six smaller, old crock dishes from the pantries and allocated one to each dog, writing their names on them in gloss paint. Then, at feeding time, she put each dish down in a separate part of the tack room, saying the dog's name firmly as she did so. She pushed, threw, kicked and shouted at all the other dogs as they rushed at each other's dishes, letting only the named dog eat from its own dish. She had bought collars for every dog and used these to drag them back to their own dish if they darted towards another one.

For a week she fought them. Anyone else venturing into the tack room during this frantic daily fifteen minutes would retreat hastily and mutter to each other about her being "off her nut" to bother. But they admired her fearlessness.

Jane didn't think about being frightened, she was just determined to win. She wasn't having this mess, she would not give up. Every day she continued to place each dish in its allotted position, the owner's name said firmly and the other dogs excluded.

After a week, at eleven-fifteen the dogs started to wait in the part of the tack room where their dish would be put down. They still ate furiously, expecting other dogs to rush their bowl at any moment. They still circled their dish and snarled if another dog's dish was being nosed too near by its owner's frantic licking. They still tried darting at other dishes, but she would yell their name and stop them.

By the beginning of the third week, eating time was still exciting, but far less competitive. They began to listen for their own name as she put the bowls down. They began to watch her. She began to watch them too. If she left the room, they would immediately restart their attempts at other dishes, so she didn't leave the room.

By the fourth week, she had worked out who was pack leader. Her name was Sam, short for Samantha, Shirley said. By now, all the dogs would keep to their own bowls, eating fast so there was nothing left for the others to try to steal. Sam would eat fast too, but started to leave a few biscuits in the bottom of her bowl. When the dogs had finished their own food, there was the usual run around each other's empty bowls to see if any scrap was left. Sam now guarded the few biscuits, growling, snarling, imposing her will on the other dogs who circled hopefully. She dared them to try and take it. This situation would go on for more than half an hour with Sam occasionally, slowly, eating one biscuit, her eyes on the other dogs all the time.

At first, Jane had just thought Sam was a slow eater and had fumed at the waste of time as she waited for her to finish. Then she realised Sam was playing a power game. Well, Jane wasn't having that, so if Sam stopped eating, getting ready to guard her bowl, Jane took the bowl away.

Without knowing it, Jane became boss and Sam got relegated to second-in-command in the pack hierarchy.

The dogs started to follow Jane around. She began to take one or two out with her each time she left the house, saying the name of the chosen dog and shutting the door on the others. She threw sticks for them, got them to sit and stay. She began to enjoy being with them, began to understand their various characters. She reared the first set of unexpected puppies and avoided any further unplanned pregnancies by separation and vigilance. She kept two of the female puppies and trained them herself.

The dogs became her entire responsibility and she accepted this, loving them without thinking she did. Shirley spoke for everyone when she said the dogs and Jane seemed to know each other's thoughts. It was true that Jane could read the dog's reactions and they, in turn, responded to her every word. From being a group of friendly nuisances, the dogs became a useful part of Chance. It was the dogs' warning barks that prevented a small barn fire spreading too far to control. It was the dogs that found escaped ponies, that saw off fox raids on the poultry houses… that now had someone who understood when they reacted to something not quite right. It was the dogs whining at the door that led Jane to where Shirley lay in the field.

* * * * *

Before the days when new horses, in for schooling, were watched on their first outings, Shirley had taken out a horse whose owner had said was, "just a bit nippy…just needs a bit of calming down, that's all."

The warning phone call from the owner of a livery stable north of the county came three hours too late. Shirley was already in hospital with five fractures of the thighs and pelvis.

The owner had paid a lot of money for the horse and he had worked his way through four livery stables, trying to get someone to stop the horse rearing high then crashing down on its own back, crushing the rider in the process. This 'fault' killed, so the owner had lied his way from stable to stable, leaving a string of serious injuries behind him. If he had told the truth, then the problem might have been tackled without riders risking their lives, but he wasn't willing to risk them refusing to take it on, and he did not know that other ways sometimes proved successful to stop a horse rolling like this. When challenged about his deceit, he said if they didn't know their job they shouldn't be doing it. So stables from Essex to Gloucester warned each other.

For Shirley it was too late. She was in hospital for some weeks and on crutches for several weeks more.

Riding lessons and all but basic stable activities were stopped while Shirley was away. Shirley had insisted on this as soon as she was conscious. Eva had tried to say that she need not worry, that they could carry on fine until she was well enough to come back, but Shirley got very agitated and insisted everything stop. She also insisted Jane send Jeff to see her immediately. Jane did not understand her urgency, nor why she should want him, of all people, but she told him.

Some good things came out of it all, as happens with most disasters. The dogs came in for a lot of praise. There were new rules for schooling unknown horses. There was time for refurbishing yards and stalls. There was time for Jane to make sure that the cause of all this never got into any other stable in the county, or any other county, for that matter.

Less than a year later, the owner's daughter was killed by the horse crashing down on her, and the horse was put down.

Everyone thought it was, and yet was not, justice, and Jane felt unreasonably guilty that maybe her warnings had caused the girl's death. Illogical, she knew, but that's how she felt. She cried in her room and the dogs put their heads on her lap in sympathy.

* * * * *

Shirley's accident was many years ago. Most of the dogs that had sounded a warning then, were long dead and buried in the orchard. Their descendants Jane had trained from puppies. It was these dogs that found Jeff's body.

* * * * *

THE CHANCES AGAINST

"What we got?"

Detective Inspector William 'Billy' Pockett opened his car door and surveyed the farm path.

"Do I need boots?" he said, before his sergeant could start reading from his notebook.

"No, sir." Sergeant Drinkwater looked at his own shoes and checked behind him to make sure the path was clear. "No, sir, looks okay to me."

Pockett put a tentative shiny shoe onto the ground and pulled himself out to look around the area. "Right," he said. "Well, what we got, Joe?"

Joseph Drinkwater tried to find his place again in the notebook as they walked towards the house followed by the young police constable, who had been stationed outside to await the inspector's arrival.

Pockett shuddered in his short, padded coat. "God, I hate all this stuff," he said, looking round. "All mud, manure and cold, old houses. It isn't healthy, if you ask me, it isn't natural."

His sergeant flashed a glance at him, but forbore to say anything. Billy Pockett saw the look, nevertheless, and smiled slightly, saying, "Oh, I know you're a country bumpkin, Drinkwater. Have to be with a daft name like that, wouldn't you? But, I don't like it. Well…" he demanded, "…come on, Joe, what have we got?"

"Sorry, sir." Joe found his place in the notebook. "Jeffrey Dickinson. Male. Mid-fifties. Farm manager. Found at eight-twenty-five by a Mrs Jane Warren."

"Where?"

"Where we're going, sir."

"In the house?"

"No, sir, round here." Joe turned and went along the kitchen side of the house, then turned the corner again. "Down here, sir. In the buildings at the back."

Inspector Pockett was carefully picking his way behind him. "Are you sure I don't need boots?" he said, his eyes on the ground.

The young constable was walking behind him, stopping frequently as Pockett stopped, to scrutinise any suspicious piece of path.

Sergeant Drinkwater didn't bother to answer.

They went through an arch that bridged from the house to one of the extensions added in some bygone age. Pockett stopped again and surveyed the area in front of them. A large yard with buildings along three sides and a gap through to, what looked like, another paved area. Joe was walking across towards the gap, avoiding some darker patches that may have been mud, manure, puddles or pits from all that Pockett could tell in the dim light from the corner lamp. "Hey!" he shouted, "come back here!"

Joe stopped and turned and, with a sigh, walked back.

"Aren't there any proper lights in this damned place?" Pockett was lifting one foot after another as though just standing there might contaminate him. "How much further is it?"

"It's just at the back of these buildings, sir. If you hang on here, I'll get the lights turned on in the sheds and you'll see better."

He pointed above the roof of the right-hand block to a glow in the sky. "Look, you can see the light from here. That's where we have to go."

"Should have brought some bloody hiking boots too," Pockett grumbled, as Joe sent the young policeman to find the lights in the surrounding sheds.

As soon as the constable disappeared into the first building, the sergeant bent down to his boss and hissed, "Will you stop your moaning, you little townie wimp! You're enough to drive anyone up the wall."

Billy Pockett beamed at him in the gloom. "Watch your mouth, Drinkwater, or I'll have you bunged down to the plods."

"Go on, do it. Please, please," his sergeant begged, in a whisper. Let me get away from your whining. Let me do traffic duty. Anything, as long as I don't have to put up with you any more. "Is that better, sir?" he added, respectfully, as the constable returned.

"It'll have to do, I suppose." Pockett sniffed and walked carefully across the yard, avoiding the grassy patches, now revealed by the lights from various sheds.

They went through the gap and into another yard. Pockett stood still again, looking around. There were stalls down the left-hand side and more sheds down the right-hand side. One of the sheds near the end of the row glowed from doorway and window, throwing a circle of light out onto the wet ground and picking out the figures of two policemen, stationed each side of the door.

Pockett leaned against the stall at the yard entrance, and took in the scene.

"Very nativity-like, if it wasn't for the uniforms. We should have come on camels, Joe." He relaxed back, only to leap forward again, holding the top of his head.

"Bloody hell! What was that?!"

The stall resident had put his head out to smell this new piece of hair, breathing and snickering onto it in the process.

"It's a horse, sir," Sergeant Drinkwater explained.

The young constable smiled and bit his lip.

"Well, I can see it's a horse, can't I?! I can see it's a horse. Just took me by surprise, that's all. I didn't expect it to be here."

"This is a stables, sir. There's a lot of horses in stables."

The constable coughed and bit his lip harder.

"Are you being sarcastic?" Pockett demanded, glaring up at the six foot three inches of his sergeant.

"No, sir, I was just explaining…"

"Huh!" Pockett walked towards the light, muttering. "Displaying your superior rural knowledge, no doubt…"

The two policemen outside the shed stood to attention as he approached.

Pockett stood in the open doorway and took in the scene. There were two rough wooden shelves running along three sides of the shed. The first shelf was about two foot from the low ceiling and the second another foot or so below that. The shelves held cardboard boxes, some tins, bags and trays. On the floor stood large, brown paper sacks, bits of string and coloured strips of paper stitched with thick cotton that pulled off the sacks to open them.

Sergeant Drinkwater had to duck to get under the doorjamb and his head nearly touched the roof of the shed inside.

"What is it?" Pockett asked.

"An old fruit store." The sergeant was trying to pick dusty cobwebs out of his hair. "They use it for general storage of fruit and veg still, plus other bits and pieces. The big sacks are potatoes. There's apples and stuff in some of the boxes." He moved to the back of the shed and pointed to some sacks. "He's here, sir."

The body was curled up, facing outwards, in the gap between the bottom shelf and the wooden slatted floor. It was hidden from the front by a row of potato sacks.

There wasn't a lot left of the top of the head. It lacked any solid shape, just a splodgy mess of darkness.

"Pronounced dead at nine forty-two, sir."

"No further info off the doc, I suppose?"

"Waiting for you, sir. The photos have been done."

"Where's the doc?"

"In the house with the rest of them. Shall I get him?"

"Yes, let's get going."

The sergeant sent the constable off to get the others. Pockett crouched down and peered over the sacks. "How big do you reckon he is, Joe?"

"Five-nine, maybe. About that. Someone had to shove him under there. He wouldn't have crawled, not with half a head he wouldn't, though we've known blokes do some amazing things, haven't we?"

"And put the sacks back in front?" Pockett shook his head. "No, I might not have laid money that he couldn't have crawled in there, but I'd bet my last penny that he didn't put the sacks back afterwards."

"Why?" Joe crouched down beside his boss and studied the curled-up figure. The legs were bent up so the knees nearly touched his chin, and the arms were rigid, lying straight down in front of the knees.

"Strewth!" Joe hissed.

Pockett nodded. "Yep, I reckon my money would be safe. Somebody's cut his hands off."

"Would you like tea or coffee?"

"Coffee, please," Pockett said. "Milk, no sugar."

"If it's not too much trouble, I'll have tea," Joe smiled.

"No trouble," she said.

"Milk. Two sugars. Thanks."

Joe watched her pour his tea from a metal teapot on the end of the kitchen range. Her hands were steady. She added the milk and sugar and put the mug in front of him. She put milk and coffee in two other mugs and poured in steaming water from one of the big kettles at the other end of the range, then sat at the table, putting one of the mugs in front of the inspector.

"Thanks," he acknowledged. "It's all been a bit of a shock, I know, but we need to ask some questions now. Okay?"

She nodded.

Joe studied her face as Pockett talked, letting his first impressions run through, then picking up anything that struck a wrong or different note. It was a system that he and Pockett always used. They would discuss Joe's thoughts later, tying in observed reactions to the questions Pockett asked.

Thirtyish, he thought. Average to good-looking. Short. Efficient. Controlled. At ease in her surroundings. At ease talking to them. Yes, very in control. She had the sort of eyes that would laugh a lot. Not now, though, of course. Now she looked tired. Not upset so much, as tired. And she was observant. Observant in the way of someone to whom observation was a habit…getting up to move a boiling kettle further along the range…open a door for a dog that Joe hadn't heard approach…move an ashtray closer as Pockett got out his lighter. Automatic reaction and observation. Efficiency. Control.

Pockett had established her name and position at the farm. Sounded like she was a general dogsbody to Joe, but her face showed no signs of inferiority as she explained what she did. She called it 'glorified housekeeper' and she seemed content with it.

She was talking about finding the body now, explaining she was going to find Shirley, the boss of the farm and stables, who she thought was in the pony yard tack room, when the dogs started worrying at the fruit shed door. She went back to them and opened the door to let them in.

No, she didn't think it was mice, or rats. She knew it was something more serious, because of the dogs.

"How do you mean?"

She said she had two dogs with her and they stood and pointed at the door, barking at her briefly to get her attention. They were still, not excited, so she knew it was something unusual.

"What happened then?"

The dogs went in and straight to the sacks at the back, where they stopped and pointed again. She looked over and there he was.

The chances against

Joe watched her face as she said this. It was set. Not hard, but devoid of expression. The hand that lifted the coffee mug was steady.

No, she hadn't touched him. She knew straight away he was dead. She had closed the door and gone back to the house to phone the police and to send one of the grooms to fetch Shirley.

No, she hadn't phoned the doctor. As she said, she knew he was dead. She sent Richard, a farm worker, to guard the door until the police arrived. She told him not to go in or touch anything.

So she guessed straight away that he'd been murdered?

Well, she didn't think he could have bashed his own head in like that, could he?

Did she notice anything unusual?

Sorry, no, she didn't, but she admitted she hadn't looked around that carefully. It was the first dead body she had ever found so that in itself was unusual enough.

There's the humour, Joe thought, and still in control.

A police constable appeared at the door, saying the doctor would like a word.

Pockett stood up and thanked her. He said he would come and speak to her later.

She said, "Okay," and started clearing the table before they left the room.

Arthur Spencer was in the large morning room. Two of the uniformed men were standing by the door.

"Hello, Billy," he grinned at Pockett, looking up from the table where he was writing on some papers. "Joe," he nodded, acknowledging the sergeant following Pockett in.

Joe smiled. "Hello, Mr Spencer."

Pockett flopped down on the long settee and reached in his pocket for his cigarettes.

Arthur Spencer already had a cigarette dangling out of his mouth as he scrawled thoughts onto the paper in front of him.

"I like this one, Billy," he said. "Very unusual."

He took the cigarette out of his mouth with one hand and put the pen in his mouth with the other. Stubbing out the cigarette in the ashtray, he leaned back in his chair and looked at Pockett.

"You realise he's got no hands?"

Pockett nodded.

"They aren't in the shed," he went on, turning the pen in his mouth, "and there isn't enough blood and brains in there either."

"So he wasn't killed there?"

"Nope. He got moved. Dead between six to eight hours, I guess. Tell you more tomorrow. Bashed with something big and flat. Hands cut off after he was dead, but only just after, I'd say. Not done with a knife, or anything very sharp. More like several blows with a broadish edge until they were severed. Lots of bone splintering and that."

"So, two different weapons?" Joe asked.

"Not necessarily," Pockett said. "Could be something like a spade."

"Well done, Billy," Spencer beamed. "That's what I thought. Find the spade and I'll tell you if you're right."

"Take some strength to do that, would it?"

"You mean can we rule out women? No, we can't. If he got knocked out with the first blow, you could take your time with the rest, couldn't you?"

"Anyway, these are pretty tough women here, sir. You've got to be strong to work with horses," Joe said.

"Shame," Pockett sighed. "Doubles the likelys."

Spencer was gathering his papers to stuff in his case. "Sorry, old son. I'll see you tomorrow, nine-ish okay? See what the P M shows up."

"Yeah, see you, Spence." Pockett lifted his hand in farewell, flopped down further in the settee, screwed up his mouth, tutted once and sighed. "Search time, Joe. Move the troops in. Let's find where he bought it and let's find the spade."

"Could be a problem that, sir. Spades are as common as horse muck around here."

Pockett eyed the two policemen standing by the door, then stared hard at Joe. "Are you being frivolous, Sergeant? Was that a joke?"

"No, sir." Joe turned to the policemen. "Go and get the search started, will you, Sergeant Walters? We're looking for the scene of crime and spades, or something similar."

"And hands," Pockett butted in, speaking over his shoulder. "Preferably two of them." Then, turning back to Joe, "Because if that was a joke, Sergeant, I do not consider…"

"No, sir. Sorry, sir," Joe was saying, as the uniforms left the room, exchanging raised eyebrows and looks of sympathy for Joe and his resigned obedience to his notorious boss. "Sorry, sir, I did not intend…you horrible, nasty, little man," he went on in the same tone, as the door shut. "One of these days your megalomania will see you carted off, or you'll have to commit suicide like your old mate, Adolf."

Pockett smiled at him. "This superior position, Joseph, has few compensations, but getting up your nose is one of them."

"Hands…preferably two of them. What sort of bloody statement is that?" Joe snorted his disapproval as he sat down in the armchair.

"Now, come on, Joe, be fair," Pockett pleaded. "It may not have been up to my usual standard, but it was spur of the moment, you know. I promise I'll get nastier next time."

Joe closed exasperated eyes.

Pockett went on, "I am trying hard, you know. Look at all the sympathy you get working for me. Everyone feels sorry for you."

"Sorry for me?! They all think I'm a nutter to put up with it."

"Well, there you are, see? It's working most of the time."

In the short silence that followed this typical exchange of acrimony, they both leaned back and closed their eyes, at ease with one another.

"What did you think of her?" Pockett's voice broke the silence. "Our Mrs Warren?"

"Very controlled."

"Cold?"

"No, she's not cold. She's got too much humour for that. Just very much in control of herself…and most everything else, I guess. She's observant too. And bright. We need to speak to her a lot more, before we speak to the others."

"Yes, I agree. Let's do it now. Let's get a picture of Mr Jeffrey Dickinson. Find out who didn't like him."

"Did he have any enemies?!" Jane's voice laughed as she repeated the question. "If you hang on a bit, I'll try and think of someone who liked him. In fact, I've been running a list of prospective murderers for years!" She stopped. "Oh dear, that's not so funny now, is it?" she added quietly. "Anyway, unless he was kicked to death, you can rule me out. I was down for kicking him to death."

The two detectives stared at her.

"Oh God, he wasn't kicked to death was he?" She stared back at them, appalled.

"No, we don't think so, Mrs Warren," the sergeant said.

She breathed out audibly.

"So, no one liked him?" Pockett asked.

"I don't think so. He really was a nasty piece of work, you know."

"In what way?"

"Oh, surly, mean, dirty-minded, you name it. Not all of the time, just when the mood took him, then he frightened most of the girls and riled most of the men, if he didn't frighten them too."

She stopped and looked at the two men. "If not speaking ill of the dead is some sort of commandment I've just shot it, haven't I?"

Pockett smiled at her. "You said you had a list of prospective murderers, can you tell me who's on it?"

Jane shook her head in agitation. "No! No! It was a joke, see? I mean, it wasn't that I thought anyone would…it was just a silly thing I used to say in my head."

"You were going to kick him to death then?" Joe smiled in sympathetic amusement.

"Yes. Sounds awful now, doesn't it?"

"Who was going to shoot him?" Joe asked, still smiling.

"Harvey," she smiled back, then hurriedly, "Not that he would or anything. That was just on my list. Just pretend."

"Who's Harvey?" Pockett asked.

"Harvey Bateman. He lives in Bateman's cottage. His father, Dave, works on the farm too, and his sister works in the stables."

"And he didn't like Jeff?"

"Well, no…but no one did, as I said."

"And what was his particular reason for getting on your list?"

"Jay. Well, Jane really. We call her Jay because I'm Jane too, see? Jane Eastham, she is. Harvey's girlfriend. She works at the stables too, and lives in here."

The men waited for her to go on as she paused, trying to choose her words.

"Jay is Harvey's girlfriend…and Jeff was having a go at her."

"Telling her off, or making advances? Which sort of 'having a go', Mrs Warren?"

"Making advances. He was your typical dirty old man. Couldn't keep his hands to himself unless they were in his trouser pockets," she flushed slightly and looked away, adding, "if you know what I mean."

Pockett and Joe exchanged glances and Pockett remarked, "Yes, keeping his hands to himself still seems to be one of his problems."

Joe raised despairing eyebrows. Jane just looked puzzled.

"Well, it's getting pretty late, Mrs Warren. I wonder if we

can just get a list of who lives here and who was around this afternoon, say from lunchtime. Then we can talk again tomorrow morning." Joe turned a fresh page of his notebook. "Before we start, when did you last see Mr Dickinson?"

"He came in for lunch about twelve-fifteen and left about one o'clock. I didn't see him after that. He never came in for tea or dinner."

"And you didn't think that unusual?"

"No. People don't often get in for every meal break. That's why I try to provide some food at regular intervals all day."

"And no one mentioned seeing him during the afternoon or evening?"

"No, not that I remember...no."

"Okay. If we can just do a list of who was around and who lives in."

Jane leaned forward to start reciting names to Joe, as Pockett added, "Perhaps we can get back to your list of murderers later."

"Yes, I think you're looking for a spade, or one of those old, heavy axes." Arthur Spencer lit up a cigarette and relaxed back in his office chair. "Or maybe both?"

"What sort of axe?" Pockett asked.

Spencer squinted as the sun from the window at the side of his office hit his eyes. "Drop that blind, will you Joe? One of those long-handled sort with a solid, flat top to the handle, where the axe is set in, and a large blade to the axe itself. Old and bluntish. That sort of thing, you know. If it is an axe, that is. Oh, and if it's a spade, it was a spade, not a shovel."

"What's the difference?"

"A shovel has a curved edge each side, sir," Joe explained. "A spade has one flat edge."

"I thought shovels were small hand tools, used for shovelling coal on a fire and that."

"Yes, sir, but you get shovels as big as spades too. Long wooden handles. Used for shovelling muck, see? And if we can eliminate them, that is very helpful because shovels are what they use in the stables and animal sheds for mucking out. Not spades usually. Shovels."

"He's a mine of information, isn't he, Arthur?" Pockett surveyed Joe with satisfaction. "Pity 'muck' isn't a subject in the police college exams." He got up and moved to the door. "Well, come on, Sergeant, let's go and tell them they can all put those shovels back. You can give them one of your informative talks on the subject at the same time. See you, Arthur," he said, as Joe opened the door for him, then let it go a little too soon as he turned to say, "Bye, Mr Spencer." The door hit Pockett in the back. "Oh, sorry, sir," Joe said loudly, opening it again and leaving the office.

Arthur Spencer smiled.

The morning room had been set up as the centre of operations. The sofa and armchairs had been pushed back to the walls and the middle of the floor had now become a busy office.

"How many we got?" Pockett asked.

The uniformed sergeant said they had four long-handled axes and eleven spades. All the shovels had been put back, he said, in a manner that also said 'and what a waste of time that was'.

Pockett ignored the tone. "Nothing else found?"

"No, sir."

"Okay. Keep looking."

Pockett turned back to the desk where Joe was looking through papers. "No sign of a body being dragged into the shed, I suppose?"

Joe shook his head. "No. Trouble is the yards are swept up two or three times a day. They were swept Thursday afternoon, about four forty-five, by one of the grooms. Those stiff yard brooms are pretty thorough, so you wouldn't see much after that. Then, of course, it rained heavily, on and off, from about two-ish until after seven-thirty."

"But forensics are looking, I suppose?"

"Yes, but no blood stains or anything obvious yet though."

"Of course, he may have been carried," Pockett mused, "and that may rule out some, if not all, the women."

"Not if he was carried in a wheelbarrow, sir."

Pockett looked at him.

"It's easier to carry heavy weights in a wheelbarrow. I'd better tell them to look at barrows too, shall I?"

Pockett raised his eyebrows. "They're going to love that. Yes, you tell them, Joe."

Joe went off to talk to the sergeant, returning in a few moments to say, "Yes, he loved that, okay."

"If you had a couple of hands you wanted to get rid of, what would you do with them?"

"Bury them? Hide them? Burn them?" Joe speculated.

"Okay. Let's start with bury them. They're digging anywhere that looks freshly dug, aren't they?"

"Yes, and they've brought the dogs in, but you've got fields of ploughed land out there, you know."

"Yes, I've noticed that, thank you, Joseph." Pockett bowed to him sarcastically and then leaned back to stare at the ceiling. "So, what about hide them?"

"Similar thing. A million places from dead tree stumps to the bottom of a slurry pit."

"What?" Pockett's chair legs returned to the ground.

"A big pit where all the wet muck is put until they use it for muck-spreading on the fields."

Pockett was still staring at him.

"What?" said Joe. "What?!"

"Tell me, Sergeant, do you have a thing about muck? Is this some new fetish I should know about?"

"It's an integral part of farming, sir. Goes with the territory, you might say. Muck is…"

"I know what muck is, I just wish you wouldn't keep talking about it."

"Anyway," Joe muttered, "they could be in the slurry pit."

Pockett cast a glance across the room to where the sergeant was talking to two of his constables. "Now they really will love that," he said, raising his eyebrows again to Joe.

"What about burn them then? That's more promising."

"Yes, basically one place only, I would say: that big kitchen oven."

Joe nodded. "The range."

"Get forensic onto it. Mrs Warren isn't going to like that, but needs must. Oh, and Joe, I suppose that has nothing to do with muck, has it? They don't burn it on the stove or something, do they?"

Detective Inspector Pockett did not like Chance Farm. He did not like all the little passages, the confusion of rooms, the number of people, the animals, and the fact it was in the country, which, as he often said, was an untidy place at the best of times.

He was stunned into silence when the incident room supervisor pointed out there was only one power point in the morning room. How could a room this size have only one power point?!

Sergeant Drinkwater told the supervisor to stop whinging, saying he was lucky they had any electricity at all.

Cables were run from other points and extension leads were everywhere.

Pockett did not like it. It was messy. It irritated him.

He was sitting at his desk, trying to work out the best way of sorting out who was around on Thursday afternoon...and he could see these cables lying all around the place.

He told Joe to swap places with him. Then he looked out of the window, instead of in the room. Trouble was, out of the window wasn't much tidier either. He didn't like the country.

"So, who was around at the time then? Who can we leave to the uniforms and who ought we to see?"

Joe was ticking a list, transferring names to a new sheet of paper.

"Shirley Hensham, owner. Eva Bartlett, head groom. Jane Warren, housekeeper. Jane Eastham, groom. Alice Cain, groom. Sally Hill, groom. Susan Bateman, groom. That's the stable staff. Then, Andrew Collins, farm worker. John Norman, farm worker. Harvey Bateman, farm worker. There are two other farm workers: David Bateman and Richard Ballinger, but they weren't around on Thursday from morning to early evening. They were at the market. So, that's the staff, if you like. Then there's Paul and Doris Hensham. He's the real owner, but he leaves it all to his daughter. They were around. And then there were some clients. Barry Jennings. He keeps his horses here, but he also works on the plumbing. Sort of hobby, you know."

"What, the horses or the plumbing?"

"Well both, but I meant the plumbing."

Pockett raised his eyebrows, but said nothing.

"And Jennings's wife called round too. Pauline Jennings."

"Pity electricity isn't her hobby," Pockett said, looking back at the cables.

"A Marjorie Finlay and a Fanny Chadd were here as well. They're clients. That's about it, as far as I can work out."

"How many does that make?"

Joe counted them up. "Sixteen."

Pockett sighed loudly. "Oh well, let's get back to our Mrs Warren and see who came in for lunch out of that lot."

"How long will it be before I can use the range?"

"We'll be as quick as we can, Mrs Warren," Joe assured her.

They were sitting in a small room off the morning room. This was used as a sort of records office usually, for storing and checking all sorts of equine information, from the details of various stallions at stud, to leaflets on the latest worming powders. It was ideally suited to be an interview room, having a small desk with four chairs, and two entrances…one through to the morning room and the other out to the hall. Its original purpose was thought to be a service room through to the larger morning room, but it had been used as a storage area for as long as anyone could remember.

Pockett stared at an old calendar on the wall by his side, showing a gleaming horse for the month of April. He lifted the page to May. It was another horse. So was June. Oh, well, each to his own, he thought.

"What are they looking for?" Jane asked.

"It's just procedure, Mrs Warren," Joe said. "Checks everywhere, you know."

Jane just stared at him. Joe knew she didn't believe him, but she was also aware it was no use pushing the point. He liked Mrs Warren.

"Right," Pockett said, "can we go through this list of people who were around yesterday lunchtime? If Sergeant Drinkwater here just reads them out, you can tell us if they came in for lunch."

Jane said nothing.

"Okay, on you go, Sergeant." Pockett leaned back in his chair.

"Shirley Hensham?" Joe looked at Jane, pen poised ready over his notebook.

"Yes, she came in."

"What time?" asked Pockett, looking at another calendar with horses on it.

"Straight away. She wanted to see the Misses about a show, so she had a quick bite and dashed off again."

"The Misses being Miss Fanny Chadd and Miss Marjorie Finlay," Pockett stated, rather than asked.

Jane nodded.

"So, she came in at…?"

"Twelve fifteen, and was gone in fifteen minutes."

"Is she on your murderers' list, Mrs Warren?" Pockett smiled the question.

"No, she's not!" Jane snapped back. "Look, it's a joke, this list. It isn't serious."

"Let me put it another way then, did she like Mr Dickinson?"

There was a small silence. The answer was quiet. "No, she didn't."

"Then, why…?"

"Why did she employ him?" Jane shook her head slowly again. "I don't know. I just don't know. He wasn't like that all the time…really nasty, I mean…he was surly, but not nasty. Maybe that was why. I don't know. Trouble was, when he started being grim, it was very grim…if you know what I mean?"

"But there must have been complaints from the others if, as you say, no one liked him. Right?"

"Yes, there were, but Shirley…well, she would talk to him… well, that was it really."

"You don't understand why she didn't sack him?"

"No, I don't."

"I understand Mr Dickinson had worked here since he was young, about thirty years or so. How long have you been here, Mrs Warren?"

"More than ten years."

"Are you related to Miss Hensham?"

"Yes, sort of second cousin type relationship."

"And what was Miss Hensham's relationship with Mr Dickinson?"

"I don't know. No family relationship. Not that I'm aware of anyway."

"You mean he may have been her illegitimate brother or something?"

Jane looked at her hands. "No, I can't see that," she said. "Maybe some more distant relationship. I don't know."

"You've thought about it though, haven't you?" Joe asked.

"Yes."

"Why?"

Jane didn't answer.

"Because it doesn't make any sense why she didn't sack him," Pockett said. It was another statement of fact.

"Mrs Warren?" Joe pushed, turning the statement into a question.

"Yes, that's it," she said. "It never made any sense."

"Did they argue at all?"

"No, but I wouldn't say they were friendly either. Just a working relationship, you know?"

The two men nodded.

"Odd that, though, when you've been living in the same house with someone all your life," Pockett mused. "Let's have the next one then, Sergeant."

Joe looked at his list. "Eva Bartlett. Was she in for lunch?"

"Er…yes, I think so. Yes, she was. At about twelve-thirty, because Shirley spoke to her as she went out."

"And when did Miss Bartlett leave?"

"About one-fifteen I think. She was looking at some papers while she was eating."

"What papers?"

"I don't know. Looked like stud records or something."

"So you didn't speak to her?"

"No. Well, hello and goodbye, sort of thing."

"And did she speak to anyone else?"

"Shirley, when she first came in. I've said that already…apart from that I think she spoke to Alice. I'm not sure."

"So, Alice Cain came in too?"

"Yes, she was in about twelve-fifteen. Left about one-thirty."

"What about Sally Hill?"

"She just grabbed a coffee about one-ish and went straight back out again. She was doing lessons, see?"

"Lessons?"

"Riding lessons. Some children come on a Thursday afternoon from a special school in the next village. They just hack around the fields for half an hour. Not really lessons, but they enjoy it. The first group ride at twelve-thirty and the second at one. Anyway, Sally was doing that with Susan."

"That's Susan Bateman?" Joe asked, referring to his list.

"Yes."

"And Sally never came in after the coffee at one-ish?"

"No. And Susan didn't come in at all. She probably went home for lunch because her mum isn't too well. Got the flu', I think. Harvey, her brother, never came in either, so he might have gone home as well."

"What about Jane Eastham? You call her Jay, don't you?"

"Yes, she was in, from about twelve forty-five to one-fifteen, I should think. She was talking to John and Andrew. They came in and left about the same time."

"That's John Norman and Andrew Collins?" Joe asked, looking up for confirmation before writing it down.

"Yes."

"Who does that leave, Sergeant?" Pockett had his head in his hands and was staring at the desk. Jane thought it made a change from leaning the chair back on two legs and staring at the ceiling. Looking at his hair was better than looking up his nose.

"Mr and Mrs Hensham?" Joe looked at Jane, pen poised, ready to write again.

"Uncle Paul never came in. Aunt Doris took some crackers and cheese and a coffee to her room. That was right at the end of lunch, one-thirty-ish."

Jane shifted in her chair and looked at her watch.

"Not many more, Mrs Warren," Joe assured her. "Barry Jennings?"

She shook her head.

"Miss Chadd and Miss Finlay?"

"No."

There was a pause while Joe checked his list.

"Is that all, Sergeant?" Pockett managed to sound bored and impatient at the same time.

"I think so, sir. Oh…Mrs Pauline Jennings, did you see her, Mrs Warren?"

"Not for lunch. She called to ask if I knew where Barry was."

"What time was that?"

"About one, I think."

Joe wrote that down. "That's it, sir," he said, lifting his list to read it out. "Er…I'll use first names to speed it up, if that's okay."

Pockett waved his hand.

"Right. In for lunch, or coffee, or whatnot, were Shirley, Eva, Alice, Sally, Jay, John, Andrew, Pauline and Mrs Hensham… er…Auntie Doris, that is…sorry…"

Pockett sighed.

"Out were Susan, Harvey, Paul, Barry, and the two Misses." He put the list down.

"Right, well thank you, Mrs Warren," Pockett smiled at her. "I expect you're anxious to get back to…er…"

Jane stood up, without filling in the 'er'.

"Oh, one more thing," he stopped her at the door, "you were in the kitchen all the time, I suppose?"

"Yes, I usually am."

"From when to when?" he asked.

Jane looked at him as she thought. "Eleven-thirty to two, maybe." She thought again.

"Yes, eleven-thirty to two o'clock," and she left the room.

"So, we can't rule out her either." Pockett leaned back again. "I wonder how long it takes to chop off a pair of hands."

Pockett turned over another month, sighed and moved to the next calendar.

"You would think they would get a few car ones, or comic ones, wouldn't you?"

He waved his hand around the room. "Look at these walls! Bloody obsessive, if you ask me."

Sue Ryland

Joe didn't look up from the desk where he was writing. "It's a stables, you little twerp," he said calmly. "These calendars are sent out by different studs, or breed societies, to advertise their stallions."

Pockett turned to him, stood to attention and saluted, his cigarette sticking out at right angles from his hand. "Sir!" he mocked.

Joe didn't look up and Pockett moved to the next calendar.

"There's too many of them," he said, studying another horse.

Joe sighed and put his pen down. "I've told you, it's an advertising…"

"No," Pockett interrupted. "Too many people in the frame. Do try and remember what we're here for, Sergeant. Someone got themselves killed. If you cast your mind back you might recall that. Try to lift your brain out of the muck, there's a good chap." Then, as he sat down, "Oh, God, I shouldn't have said 'muck', should I? Now he'll be off again, going on and on…"

Joe got up and shut the door on the two policemen, whose passing presence had triggered off this display of sarcasm. "Very funny," he said and went back to writing.

Pockett picked up a pen and flicked his thumb against it, making little tapping sounds in the silence.

"Right," said Joe, putting down his pen and picking up his pad, "if we interview the ones who came in for lunch first and find out what they were doing after that…"

"And who they saw while they were doing it…" Pockett put in.

"We might be able to clear a few out," Joe finished.

"It would be helpful if we had a place of death, spade and hands, though. There's nothing back from the lab?"

Joe shook his head.

"Okay. Who are we seeing first?"

"Shirley Hensham, the boss. Came in for lunch at twelve-fifteen. Left at twelve-thirty. Didn't like Dickinson, but never argued with him, or sacked him."

"According to our Jane," Pockett pointed out. "I know you're smitten, Joseph, but let's keep our sexual urges under control."

"You're an evil-minded little sod," Joe said, matter-of-factly.

Pockett smiled at him. "Thank you," he said.

"You came in for lunch at…?"

"About a quarter past twelve," Shirley replied. "As soon as Jane put it out. I just grabbed a sandwich and left because I had to see the two Misses about a show."

"So you saw Mr Dickinson then? At lunchtime?"

"I think so…I don't know…I mean, well it didn't register, if you know what I mean."

"Did you see him later then?"

"Yes," she said firmly. "He came to the office about half past one to check if I needed more hay moved across."

"How long was he in the office?"

"Oh, just a few minutes."

"And you didn't have any other conversation apart from the hay?"

"No, I don't think so. That was the last time I saw him."

"So you left the kitchen about twelve-thirty, went to see the two Misses…where were they, by the way?"

"By the stable where the horse is kept."

"By it, not in it?" Pockett asked.

"No, by it. Just coming along the side of the yard."

"How long did you speak to them?"

"About fifteen minutes, I suppose."

"And did you see anyone else at that time?"

"I don't remember…er…Harvey was around, I think, and my father was in the vegetable garden when I walked past to the office. I really don't remember anyone else."

"So, you got in the office about one-ish?"

"Yes and worked in there until teatime."

"That's about three-fifteen to three-thirty?"

Shirley nodded.

"What can you see from your office?" Pockett asked.

Shirley thought before answering. "The side of the pony block...part of it anyway. The top of the gardens and the orchard. Part of the small schooling ring. And the south fields, of course. But I'd have to turn round to see any of that, because I sit with my back to the window."

"So you saw no one between one and three-fifteen, except when Mr Dickinson called in at one-thirty?"

"No, no one."

"How did you get on with Mr Dickinson?" Pockett asked.

Shirley straightened herself in the chair. Joe watched her face and thought she had been waiting for this part.

"He was a good worker," she said.

"Almost one of the family, I should think, having been here most of his life?" Pockett smiled the query.

Shirley smiled back, briefly, but said nothing.

"How did he get on with the others?"

Shirley's thumb started to worry the signet ring she wore on the third finger of her right hand.

Pockett waited, still smiling.

"There were occasional problems," Shirley said at last.

"Problems?" Pockett pushed.

"He could be a bit tough on some of the men, you know. It was just his way. Not violent, or anything like that, you understand, just telling them off."

"And the girls? Did the girls complain?"

Another silence. Her left hand fingers were now turning the ring on her right hand.

"Miss Hensham?"

"Okay." She let her hands fall back to the arms of her chair. "I expect you know there were complaints about him. And I expect you know that no one could understand why I didn't sack him."

Pockett said nothing.

Shirley went on, speaking faster and becoming more defiant as she stared at him.

"He was a good worker and he ran the farm side of the business very well. My grandfather trusted him and I did too. And you're right about him being here so long as to be part of the family. No, he wasn't any blood relation, before you ask, but he was as good as."

The words were coming even faster and they could see and hear the anger.

"He looked after me when I was young. Like a big brother. Yes, the girls, some of them, would complain he was a bit pushy, but we never had anyone pregnant, or raped, did we? Jeff just never learned to control his mouth. He upset people."

She stopped and looked down. Controlling her own mouth, Joe thought.

"He was a good man," she finished, quietly.

"I understand he never learned to control his hands either," Pockett said, even more quietly.

Joe saw Shirley close her eyes momentarily, shutting out some thought.

She did not look up as she repeated, "He was a good man."

"Seems our Jane was wrong," Pockett mused, as soon as the door closed. "I think Miss Hensham did like him."

Joe nodded. "Odd, though, isn't it? She seems to know all his nasty ways, yet she almost won't admit it. I think she has to be unlikely, don't you?"

"Yes, unlikely, but stranger things, Joe, stranger things…" He leaned forward, resting his head on his hands. "What did you think of her?"

"Well, a bit like her cousin…"

"The light of your romantic aspirations…"

Joe ignored him. "…strong, controlled, but she hasn't got

Jane's sense of humour. I think she's deeper. More to her than meets the eye."

Pockett leaned back. "And, what is more, if no one saw her in the office from one to three-ish, she has no alibi."

* * * * *

Joe was not impressed with Eva. 'Sullen' was the word that sprang instantly to mind. Shirley, for all her control and toughness, had social skills that clearly Eva did not. Even her smile was brief, almost a mockery.

"You came in for lunch about twelve-thirty?"

"Yes. I'd been riding the Misses' filly and Shirley told me to stable it, then come and tell her, so she could go and catch them before they left. About the Welford Show, I think."

"Did you speak to anyone else at lunchtime?"

"Besides hello I suppose you mean?"

"Anyone."

"Alice," she said. "Just about exercising two liveries."

"Who else was in for lunch?"

"Don't know," she shrugged. "Jay, I think, and the men: Andrew and John."

"Did you see Mr Dickinson?"

"Yes."

"Did you speak to him?"

"No."

"What was your relationship with Mr Dickinson?" Pockett asked.

Eva's eyes narrowed as she said, emphatically, "I didn't have a relationship with Mr Dickinson."

Pockett smiled. "I gather from your tone you didn't like him."

Eva didn't answer.

"How long have you worked here, Miss Bartlett?"

"Since leaving school."

"What would that be…" Pockett leaned back in his chair, hands clasped behind his head, "…more than ten years?"

"Something like that." Eva's tone and expression was half mocking, half bored.

"After that time, you must have had some kind of relationship with Mr Dickinson, even if only one of nodding when you passed." Pockett leaned forward and stared at her.

"If you want me to say I didn't like him…I didn't like him. Okay?"

"Why."

"He was a dirty old man. That reason enough?" she said, flatly.

"He pestered you for sexual attentions, did he?"

She didn't answer.

"Did he frighten you, Miss Bartlett?"

"No!" she spat out. "I'm not bloody frightened of him. Dirty old sod!"

Her hands were shaking as she stabbed out a finger to emphasise the point.

Joe thought she had been very frightened of Jeff Dickinson.

"He tried it on, did he?" Pockett asked, gently.

Eva's head jerked to the side and her mouth set hard as she clenched her hands on her knees. "Yeah, he tried it on," she ground out. "Don't they all? Don't they all? Bloody men!"

She was very angry now. Joe watched her solid, muscular figure almost squirm in the chair. The tendons of her arms stood out as she brought her hands together, fist against fist. The muscles of her upper arms were bigger than Joe would have expected, even for a woman used to hard physical work.

"When did you last see him, Miss Bartlett?" Pockett's voice was calm. "Did you see him after lunchtime?"

She shook her head.

"You left the kitchen about one-fifteen, what did you do after that?"

"I didn't kill him, you know!" she half shouted. "I wish I had! He needed killing, that one. He asked for it."

Then, as suddenly as her agitation had appeared, it disappeared again, leaving her slumped in her chair. Sullen.

"What did you do after lunch?" Pockett repeated.

"Schooling." She snapped the word.

Pockett looked at Joe with raised eyebrows.

"That is training a horse to perform various moves, or stop bad habits," Joe filled in the information.

"Yeah, training," Eva repeated back in a mocking tone.

"And where was that?"

"In the big ring. I did that until about two-thirty. Then I groomed the horse until about three. Then I was exercising until about five. Then…"

"Exercising is taking a horse, or horses, out for a ride to exercise them," Joe filled in again. "You can lead two or three horses while…"

"Thank you, Sergeant," Pockett cut in, still looking at Eva. "Did you see, or talk, to anyone while you were schooling, or grooming?"

"No."

"This is a busy place, Miss Bartlett, are you sure you saw no one? Can you just go through your movements after you left the kitchen? It might jog your memory."

Eva leaned back and closed her eyes. She recited, "Left the kitchen about one-fifteen. Went to the loo…" She opened her eyes and looked at Pockett. "…I'll allow five minutes for that, shall I? Say one-twenty…"

The mockery was heavy now. Pockett just smiled at her.

"…walked to the stables to get Loll: that's a horse, a four-legged creature, about five foot high at the shoulder. I expect your sergeant will explain…"

"Did you see anyone then?" Joe tried to alter the atmosphere.

Eva thought. "Well, Andrew and John going towards the tractor sheds. I saw Mr Hensham in the garden. Sally was in the small field with the kids. That's it, I think. Oh, I saw Barry coming out of the milking shed. I didn't speak to any of them, though, and I didn't see anyone different when I was taking Loll to the ring, nor when I was schooling."

She thought some more. "When I took Loll back, Jay was messing around with Harvey again and I asked her if she'd mucked out the pony yard. She said she had nearly done it. I told her to finish it now. I saw the Misses leaving in their car..."

"That was about two-thirty, you say?" Joe asked.

"Yes...and Pauline came and asked if I'd seen Barry. I told her he was by the milking sheds, last time I saw him. I didn't know where he was now. Then I went into the stables to groom."

"Did you speak to anyone then?"

"No...I heard some shouting though. I looked over the door, but I couldn't see anyone."

"Do you know who was shouting?" Pockett asked.

"I'd have said if I had," she snapped, making clear her dislike of having to respond to him.

"Man or woman's voice?" Joe asked.

"I don't know. It was only a quick thing. Man, I think, but you can't really tell. It was just a noise."

"What time was that?"

"Just after two-thirty, I suppose."

"Could the voice have been Mr Dickinson's?" Pockett asked.

"Don't know," she said, then smiled – that mocking smile – then added, "If I'd have known someone was doing him in, I'd have gone and helped them."

She turned back to Joe, who was writing in his notebook. "Put me down for a definite suspect, Sergeant, while you're at it."

"Find out where she's from, Joe. Something has happened to her sometime. Something not nice."

Joe nodded agreement. "What do you want to bet it was rape, or some sexual assault?"

"Yes, and she was really frightened of Jeff, wasn't she? Frightened…and angry because she was frightened."

A couple of sharp taps sounded on the door leading to the morning room and Sergeant Walters' head appeared. "Okay to come in?"

"Clearly, Sergeant," said Pockett, pleasantly, "As you can see there's no one here but Sergeant Drinkwater, and I decided long ago he isn't my type."

Sergeant Walters smiled dutifully, glad Pockett seemed to be in a good mood.

"Good news," he said, "we've got both of them."

"Both of them what?"

"The spade and the hands. Leastwise we're sure they're his hands, 'cause you don't get many of them left lying around. We're having tests done on the spade."

"Where were they?" Pockett asked, getting up and taking his jacket off the back of the chair. "I thought you had eleven spades already."

"Yes, sir," Sergeant Walters was almost gloating, "but this one is more suspicious, like."

"More suspicious, like," Pockett parroted. "Really? Did you catch it trying to escape, Sergeant? Or has it got a previous record I should know about? One of the spades on the ten most wanted list, perhaps?"

Sergeant Walters flushed and looked at Joe.

"Where was it, Sergeant?" Joe asked, putting on his own jacket and glaring at Pockett as he turned to push his chair back under the table.

"In one of those big horse troughs. The one at the end of the pony yard. They've taken some of the water away for testing."

"Who found it?" Joe asked, as they went out into the hall.

Pockett went first and strode off, turning left. Joe waved the sergeant out and drew him to turn right, walking and talking to him, arm around his shoulder.

"It was one of the grooms. A Miss Sally Hill."

"And the hands?" Joe asked, smiling at the hurrying footsteps behind them.

"We found them the other side of the track, by the muck heap."

"It would be a muck heap, wouldn't it?" Pockett's slightly panting voice cut in.

"This whole bloody case is a muck heap. You should be in your element, Drinkwater."

Joe turned and smiled at him. "Oh, hello, sir. That was quick. I thought you were off to talk to someone else. So, let's look at the trough first, Sergeant. Are you coming, sir, or are you off somewhere else?"

Sergeant Walter's eyes had a definite twinkle as he led the way.

Sally was standing by the horse trough with one of the policemen. The trough was situated at the side of the end box of the pony yard.

"Well hidden, isn't it?" Pockett observed, looking at the fields behind him. "You wouldn't see it from anywhere, except if you were standing in the field."

"No point looking for tracks or anything?" Joe speculated. "Is this trough used frequently, Miss Hill?"

She nodded. "We often bring ponies here to drink if we're using them again, between lessons, you know."

"And have you brought ponies here since yesterday, apart from just now?"

"No. Well, I mean, we used the trough on Thursday at one-ish and again at one-thirty, after the children's lessons, but not since then. We're not doing lessons now. Shirley has stopped them because of…well, you know."

"So how did you come to notice the spade then?"

"Big Ears got out and was drinking from it."

"Big Ears?" Pockett's mouth was trying to keep its official severity. "That's a horse, I hope?"

"No," Sally said. "A pony."

Joe took the opportunity to launch into another irritating explanation. "A horse is about fourteen hands…"

"Don't bother, Sergeant," Pockett sighed. He turned suddenly and looked closely at Sally. "Did you see Mr Dickinson after lunch yesterday, Miss Hill?"

She went red and took an involuntary step backwards. "Er…I saw him as I was bringing the ponies in," she said quickly. "He was standing by the hay barn. That was about one forty-five, I suppose."

"What was he doing?"

"Watching Jay and Harvey. He did things like that." She muttered the last sentence.

"Things like what?"

"Watching people. He was always around the pony yards, watching the children and the grooms. I didn't like it…well, none of us did."

"Could you see Jay and Harvey then…see what they were doing, I mean?"

"I saw them as I passed the livery yard. They were just messing about, you know."

"Courting, you mean?" Joe asked.

Sally looked at him.

"Courting is an old-fashioned term for flirting, kissing and other romantic activities, Miss Hill," Pockett said, imitating Joe's explanatory tones, when enlightening him on rural matters. "You'll have to excuse Sergeant Drinkwater. He has led a sheltered life. Did you see anyone else?"

"The boss was in her office." She closed her eyes to think. "Yes, she was, because I saw her get up. And Mr Hensham was in the garden, of course. I can't remember seeing anyone else, though I might have. I wasn't really taking notice. Sorry."

"Did Mr Dickinson bother you, Miss Hill? It seems he had a reputation for harassing some of the girls."

Sally went red again. "He tried it on a couple of times, but it was mostly talk, you know? Nasty things."

The chances against

"Sexual comments?" Pockett suggested.

Sally nodded.

"No more than that?"

"Well he did try to catch me like…give us a kiss, sort of thing, but Sue sorted him out. That was ages ago. It was just words after that."

"Sue sorted him out?" Pockett raised his eyebrows. "How did she do that?"

Sally smiled. "Oh, she called him a few things and threatened him with having a nasty accident one day when no one was around…" She stopped, her hand going to her mouth as she realised the implication of her words. "Oh…Oh, dear… No, I didn't mean that. Sue wouldn't do anything. Really she wouldn't." She begged them to understand. "It was just talk. She was never frightened of him. It was just talk, you know."

Sergeant Walters opened the bag. "Hands, sir," he said to Pockett.

"Well done, Sergeant." Pockett looked in the bag. "Yes, they're definitely hands."

Joe pursed his lips and screwed his nose up at the mess in the bag, as well as Pockett's sarcasm. "Who found them?" he asked, looking round towards the house to get a better idea of their position in relation to the yards and buildings.

"Constable Wilkins and his dog. Can we move them now, sir?"

Pockett nodded and Sergeant Walters went off to get the forensic team.

Pockett looked in the shallow hole again, then turned to look at the buildings. The hole had been dug at the side of a dirt track that curved all along the back of the stable blocks, barns and sheds. It was opposite the back of the last livery yard stables and just around the corner from the pony yard horse trough.

"Dig a quick hole. Bury them. Then stick the spade in the trough?" Joe suggested.

"Looks like it," Pockett agreed. "What we want now is the place where it all happened." He looked back in the hole. "This is a bloody mess, Joe. We've got to start ruling a few of these folks out. This bloke seems to have been so unpopular we could end up with half the county as likelys. Let's get out of this horrible fresh air and sort out what we've got so far."

Joe stood by the big blackboard in the morning room, chalk in hand, and waited. Pockett pulled a chair in front of the board and lit a cigarette. "Okay, teacher, let's have it," he said. "Stick with first names. It's easier."

Joe wrote JANE on the board. He looked at his notebook. "Well, we can be pretty sure she was in the kitchen from eleven-thirty until two. People coming in and out for lunch, so she must have been there."

"No," Pockett stopped him. "Write eleven-thirty to one-thirty. We've only got her word she was there until two."

Joe rubbed out two and wrote one-thirty. He wrote SHIRLEY next.

"In to lunch at twelve-fifteen. Out at twelve-thirty. Confirmed by Jane and Eva. Spoke to the two Misses by the stables at twelve-thirty-ish until one-ish. Into her office at one. Saw Jeff at one-thirty. Stayed in office until three-thirty. Confirmed she was in office at two by Sally."

"Hang on," Pockett interrupted, "we're going the wrong way about this. We should start with Jeffrey himself. Do him over there." He pointed to the other side of the blackboard.

Joe wrote JEFF on the board and waited.

"Right. What do we know? Dead between…say…twelve-thirty and three, so how many of those hours can we knock off?"

"Lunchtime," Joe said, writing twelve-fifteen to one on the board. "Enough people saw him then, so he was alive at one."

"So, we've got him, hands intact, until one. Then, at one-thirty in Shirley's office. He must have been alive then, because

Sally saw him later, about one forty-five, watching Harvey and Jay. Even if Sally is lying, it's unlikely Shirley is too, so he was around at one-thirty at least."

"I'll put one-thirty and question one forty-five." Joe wrote it down. "Well, we've knocked off an hour. Bumped off between one-thirty and three now."

"Good." Pockett sort of smiled. "Now that doesn't rule out Shirley or Jane. What about Eva?"

Joe wrote EVA on the other side of the board and looked at his notes. "She was schooling from lunch to two-thirty-ish. Grooming until three. She heard shouting just after two-thirty when she was in the stable, grooming."

Pockett thought. "She must have been pretty visible doing this schooling, mustn't she?"

"I would have thought so."

"Okay, let's find someone who saw her. She said that Pauline asked her where Barry was then. That would confirm her being on her way back to the stables with a horse at two-thirty."

"And, talking of Pauline," Joe said, "has it struck you that, if she came into the kitchen at one, asking for her husband, why was she still asking an hour and a half later? This is a big place, but not that big."

Pockett stood up, saying loudly, "Well done, Drinkwater. I can see that all my training is beginning to pay off. Now, if you can just maintain this unusual degree of concentration, we may get this cracked for Christmas."

"Sir!" Joe snapped, standing to attention.

The other policemen looked their sympathy at him.

"Right, you go and see Pauline," Pockett said, voice projection over, as they went into the adjacent interview room. "Find out what she was doing for an hour and a half and who she saw. I'll go and see Harvey and Jay. If they confirm seeing Jeff at one forty-five, watching them, that's another fifteen minutes we've accounted for and things are looking up." He picked up some papers and went towards the hall door.

"See you later," he said. "Oh, which way is the quickest to Bateman's cottage?"

Joe told him the way. It wasn't the quickest, but he figured the walk would do young Billy Pockett good.

Pauline Jennings asked him if he would like coffee. She served it in a large mug, curling herself into a huge armchair, facing him, and holding her mug clutched in both hands. Joe could see her knickers.

"Er…yes…I went up to Chance Farm to see Barry about one, I suppose. I asked Jane where he was, but she wasn't sure. It was lunchtime, so she was busy cooking and that, of course."

Joe smiled and nodded.

"I don't know how she does it, do you?" Pauline chattered on. I've only got three of 'em and it drives me spare doing for them all. I don't know how she does it." She shook her head, making her long earrings dance, and sipped her coffee. She left a bright lipstick stain on the white rim.

"And did you find him?" Joe asked.

"Barry? Yes, eventually. It's a bloody maze that place, isn't it?" she giggled.

"What time did you find him?" Joe asked.

She twirled an earring as she thought. "I don't know. About a quarter past one, I suppose. He was in one of them sheds."

"And how long did you speak to him?"

She stopped twirling her earring and began twirling her hair at the back of her ear.

"Just for a bit, you know. It was only about was he picking up the kids from school or not, because I wanted to go to town to get me hair done." She looked up from under her lashes. "What do you think?" she said, turning her head from side to side, to give Joe the full effect of her hair-do.

"Very nice," smiled Joe and pushed on with, "And did you go straight home?"

Pauline stopped twirling and posing. "Yes," she said and sipped her coffee.

Joe didn't believe her.

"Did you see anyone after you found Barry?"

"No, I told you, I went straight home." She put the mug down on the small table by her right hand. She did not do it fast enough. Joe had seen it begin to shake.

"But did you see anyone as you left the stables?" he persisted.

She didn't answer.

"Mrs Jennings, did you see anyone after you had spoken to Barry?"

She began to cry.

"Mrs Jennings?"

"I saw Jeff," she said. "I saw bloody Jeff."

She was now crying quietly, but desperately. Tears rolled down her face, leaving dirty streaks from eye to chin as they washed her mascara away.

Joe spoke quietly. "Where did you see him, Mrs Jennings?"

She was scrabbling in her handbag on the small table beside her, eventually finding a handkerchief to wipe around her eyes, trying to remove the black smudges of make-up.

It crossed Joe's mind that it was funny how women did that. He would have blown his nose with it.

"He was by the barn, you know. He…he…" She stopped and grabbed the bag off the table, knocking over her coffee mug in the process. The coffee made brown spots all over the white, long-haired rug at her feet. She stopped fighting the tears, crying with shaking shoulders and screwed-up face, as she knelt by the rug, dabbing the handkerchief on the worst parts, and adding grey mascara spots to the brown coffee stains. The tears fell unceasingly.

Joe let her cry it out.

"Sorry," she said. "Sorry," as she regained control and her breath stopped juddering. Then, "That was bloody stupid, wasn't it?" and she flashed a smile at him.

"Shall I get a cloth?" he asked.

"No," she said. "Sod it. I've gone off the bloody thing anyway." She was back to her chirpy self and she kicked the rug aside as she sat back down.

"Bet I look a mess." She found another handkerchief in her bag and dabbed at her eyes. She found a small mirror too, exclaiming as she viewed the wreck of her make-up, "Oh, my God! Don't look while I clean up. Barry and I had a row," she went on in the same tone, so it took Joe a second to realise she was back talking about that lunchtime. "He wanted to finish some plumbing thing and I wanted him to pick the kids up. Anyway, we had a row. He wouldn't give in and neither would I. We're like that. Both of us stubborn as mules." She laughed. "I expect that's why we get on so well usually. We suit each other."

She pulled a face at herself in the mirror, sighed and gave up, dropping her mirror back in her bag and the bag on the spotted rug.

"I stormed out and turned the corner of the barn and ran into Jeff. I didn't see him there. I was mad, angry, you know. Anyway, he wouldn't let me go. Kept holding my arms. I didn't think it was anything at first. I was just apologising because I thought I hit him quite hard, asking him if he was all right, you know? I didn't realise." She stopped and shook her head. "He's a nasty piece of work, isn't he?" She stopped again. "Oh…sorry, I mean…well, he was a nasty piece of work. Dead or not, he was!"

She suddenly stared at Joe. "My Barry didn't do it," she said, glaring as if Joe had accused him. "You can get that out of your head right now!"

"Why should I think he did, Mrs Jennings?"

"Because I went and told him, that's why. He got really mad and said he was going to sort Jeff out."

She was back to twirling her hair.

"And did he?"

"No, he didn't! I've told you, Barry didn't do it." She looked indignantly at Joe.

"What time was it when you went back and told him?"

"I don't know. About two, I suppose. I don't know. I was upset. Jeff wouldn't let me go and he kept saying things." She shuddered.

"Did he do anything?" Joe asked. "Besides hold your arms, I mean?"

She thought a moment. "That's the thing about him," she said, "It's not what he does, is it? It's the feeling of what he might do. He twists what you say to mean something sexy and he touches you all the time. He frightens you, don't he?" She looked at Joe. "Oh," she remembered again, "I mean he did frighten people. I keep forgetting he's gone. Sorry."

"And what did Barry do when you told him?"

She looked uncomfortable as she answered. "He ran out to find him, but he just told him to leave me alone. He didn't hit him or anything."

"What did you do when he ran out?"

"Well, I'd been crying and that, so I tried to fix my face up a bit, then I went to find Barry."

"Did you find him?"

"I saw Eva in the stables and I asked her, but she hadn't seen him since he left the shed, but then I heard them shouting. I thought it was from the other side of the sheds, you know, but they weren't there and the shouting stopped."

"What time was that?"

"Nearly two-thirty, definitely, because I thought I'd better not look any more. I had to get the children from school, see?"

"Are you sure it was Barry and Jeff shouting?"

"Yes. Anyway, Barry was home when I got back with the kids, and he said he'd told him off."

"What time did you get back?"

"The usual, about four-ish. Say four-fifteen."

She got up. "Barry just told him to keep away from me. He didn't hurt him, I'm sure of that. Do you want another coffee?"

*

They stood in front of the blackboard and read it again.

"Well, it looks like he was killed right after the row with Barry," Joe said. "Or during it," he added.

Pockett nodded. "So we're looking to see where everyone was at two-thirty. Now, who can we take off the likely list?"

They moved into their small room, but before they could sit down, Sergeant Walters appeared with a handful of notes.

"Definitely his hands, sir," he said, putting one of the papers in front of Pockett, who had flopped down at his desk. "And definitely the spade." He put another report down on top of the first. "Traces of blood and that in the water."

"No sign of where it happened though?" Joe asked.

Sergeant Walters shook his head. "Sorry."

"When you think about it, it's odd," Pockett mused. "I mean, there would have to be blood and bone splinters and all sorts of gunge, wouldn't there? How would you cover that up? Wash it away?"

"Rain might wash some of it, I suppose," Joe suggested.

"Yes, but think about it, Sergeant. You've just bashed my head in. I'm lying on the ground. You take a spade and bring it down hard on my hand. You wouldn't chop it off in one go. The P M shows it was done with a lot of hacking, so bits of bone and that would be driven hard into the ground by the edge of the spade, wouldn't they? Rain wouldn't wash that away."

Sergeant Walters was shuffling his papers and fidgeting around, clearly anxious to get back to his 'office'.

"Okay, Sergeant, what else have you got?" Pockett said in an exasperated voice.

The sergeant put other papers in front of Pockett, listing them as he went.

"Background to Eva Bartlett... Report of interview with Eileen Bateman... Report of interview with Dr George Burgham..."

"Who's that?" Pockett interrupted.

"Local doctor, sir. Saw Mrs Bateman on the afternoon at

two-thirty and Miss Susan Bateman was with her mum when he saw her."

"Good, that's another likely out," Pockett said. Then, "Well, go on, Sergeant, we haven't got all day."

Sergeant Walters bit his lip and continued putting papers down. "Report of interview with Miss Fanny Chadd... Report of interview with Miss Marjorie Finlay. That's it for the moment."

"Well we have been busy policemen, haven't we?" Pockett smiled at him.

Sergeant Walters looked straight ahead and tried to think of his overtime.

"If that's all, sir..."

"Yes, that's all," said Pockett and the sergeant left the room, thinking of every insulting name he could and interspersing them with some colourful adjectives. The word 'bastard' seemed to predominate.

When the door closed, Pockett looked at Joe's narrowed eyes and set mouth.

"What?!" The innocence wasn't meant to be convincing. "What?!"

Joe got up and opened the morning room door, his eyes on Pockett, whose hands were raised in protestation, and whose head shake and astonished eyebrows proclaimed his amazement at Joe's attitude.

"Sergeant Walters," Joe called loudly. "Inspector Pockett wondered if you could just spare him another minute."

As Sergeant Walters appeared at the door, still held open by Joe, Pockett dropped his hands and smiled at him. Then he looked at Joe while he said, "Oh, Sergeant, I forgot to say thank you for all of these." He assumed a very serious face and intoned, "Thank you, Sergeant Walters," lay back in his chair and lit a cigarette.

Joe smiled at the bemused sergeant and closed the door. It wasn't quite shut when Pockett said loudly, "Right, let's get some real work done now."

He was raising his hands in protest again when Joe walked back to the desk.

Joe gave the corner of the sandwich to the dog sitting at his feet.

"That's not a good idea," Jane said. "You'll get inundated with dogs if they think they can cadge off you."

"Sorry," said Joe and waved his hand to shoo the dog away. The dog's head moved as it followed the hand, but the rest of him stayed exactly where it was.

"Move, Telly," Jane said quietly, without stopping her washing-up, and the dog went back to the range.

"Do you want any more?" she asked, drying her hands and waiting.

"No, no. That was grand." Joe smiled his appreciation. "Thanks very much."

She took her mug of coffee off the end of the range, and came to sit at the table opposite him.

"Yes," she resumed their conversation, "you're right thinking that I knew about Eva. I didn't know who did it, but I knew someone had. Barry found some magazines, see. Child pornography, I think they were. Foreign. It upset Eva."

"Barry gave them to Eva, did he?"

"Yes. I feel really bad about it. Eva's always been…well, difficult, you know? I thought she just hated me because I'm Shirley's cousin and she dotes on Shirley, but then that's personalising things, isn't it? I mean, she's tetchy with everyone… given her experience it's not surprising. I should have guessed there was more to it."

"Where were the magazines found?"

"Under an old water tank in the litter pens, I think it was. Barry was working there."

"And where are they now?"

"Shirley's got them, I think."

"Do you know who they belonged to?"

"No, not for sure, but I guessed Jeff. I'd told him I was about to start painting his room, so he'd better move his stuff out. I thought they were his."

"Shirley hasn't mentioned anything about them then?"

Jane shook her head.

"What did you do after lunch on Thursday?" Joe asked, getting out his notebook again. "You said you were in here until two o'clock."

"Yes, about that, then I sat down for half an hour or so in the morning room, where you lot are."

"See anyone?"

"I don't think so. I phoned to see how Eileen was, about two-thirty. I did that in the hall. But the doctor was with her, so Sue said she'd phone me back later."

"What did you do then?"

"Came back in here and started on tea. Auntie Doris was in here, swilling her cup out. She said she was off to a W I meeting at three-ish, so she was just having a coffee before she left. She wouldn't be in for tea."

"Had she just come down from her bedroom?"

"I suppose so. She was dressed up ready to go out anyway." She smiled at Joe. "Changed her suit and scarf, you know? Auntie Doris specialises in suits and scarves."

Joe thought she had a nice smile. He was glad she could be crossed off the list of likelys.

Pockett had waded through all the reports. He quite liked reading reports. Nice, orderly documents. Yes, he quite liked that, although the occasional spelling mistake grated on his nerves.

Joe was updating the blackboard. "So, unless we've got a couple of them lying for each other..." he said.

"In collusion," Pockett interrupted.

"Yes, in collusion...then we've got it down a fair bit."

"Let's go through it then, Sergeant," Pockett said officiously, aware of a couple of policemen behind them, watching the proceedings.

Joe looked at the board. "Pauline Jennings. She's out. She picked the children up from school at three-fifteen, so she must have left here at two-thirty."

"Good. That's one. Two-thirty to three is the only time we need to suss out now. Susan Bateman?"

"Definitely out, sir. With her mum and the doctor from two-thirty to three."

Pockett nodded. "Two down. Doris Hensham?"

"In the kitchen from two-thirty to three, then at a meeting. Furthermore, she was already dressed up smartly for the meeting at two-thirty. No blood or gore on her."

"I like that, Sergeant," Pockett smiled. "Gore. That's a good word. You have been practising your reading then. I told you it would pay off."

Joe said, "Thank you, sir," and made a mental note about pay-offs. He went on, "And, if she was in the kitchen, then it also confirms that Jane was with her. So that rules her out."

"Aagh…Jane. I'm very happy for you. Must be a load off your mind. So, Mrs Warren…or should I say Jane…" he smiled coyly at Joe "…looks out. That's four."

Joe made another mental note about that too. He hoped the two policemen behind finished their sandwiches quickly.

"Miss Finlay and Miss Chadd?" Pockett smiled at him through the smoke of his cigarette.

"Talked to Shirley until about twelve forty-five and…" he hesitated, "…talked to their horse until about two-thirty."

Pockett stared at him.

Joe shrugged.

"Is this another strange rural rite I should know about, Drinkwater?"

The policemen behind chuckled, but kept their heads down, scrabbling their sandwich papers together decisively, as Pockett turned to look at them.

"No, sir. They just...well, they like their horse..." Joe talked and watched the policemen getting ready for a rapid exit.

Pockett looked incredulous. "What do you talk to a horse about for two hours? Politics? Religion? The horse next door?"

They could hear the men laughing in the hall outside as the door shut behind them.

"I don't bloody know," Joe hissed, "so shut up about it. And you can stop posing: the audience has gone."

"Now then, Joseph," Pockett waved a finger at him, "temper, temper."

"Are we doing this list or not?" Joe demanded.

"Proceed, minion." Pockett gave a regal wave.

"They left here at two-thirty and were home by three. Confirmed by their neighbour. Okay?" Hissing had given way to exaggerated shouting.

"That's six," Pockett said calmly.

Joe sighed and went on, "Harvey Bateman next. You saw him and young Jay."

"Yes, and if they're not lying..."

"In collusion," Joe put in, heavy on the sarcasm.

Pockett smiled at him, "...they're out too. Harvey went to see his mum over lunch and then came back to see Jay. It was his afternoon off. He helped her do her work all afternoon and they didn't see Jeff. They remember Eva telling Jay to get on with her work. That was two-thirty-ish, Eva said, but they didn't know what time it was. Looking at the pair of them, I doubt very much if they ever know what time it is. 'Besotted' is the word that springs to mind."

"So, that's eight. Then you can add Sally. She came in from seeing to the ponies about two, and then had an hour off because she worked through lunch. She went to see a friend in the village. Biked there. Her friend confirms she was with her from about two-fifteen to two forty-five."

"Good. Good. It's looking better all the time."

"Oh, and Sally saw Eva schooling the horse as she left, so that's confirmed too."

"Right, so how many left, Joe?"

Joe checked his notebook and wrote on the board. "Shirley, Alice, John, Andrew, Paul and Barry, and I suppose Eva's still in with a chance too."

Pockett yawned and checked his watch. "I'll take John and Andrew. You talk to Alice. Tomorrow. Definitely tomorrow. We've been here too long, Joseph. The air is making me feel ill."

They were sitting in the morning room, which Pockett thought quite appropriate, as it was morning. The room was beginning to fill up with men and women coming back on duty. The two police constables, who had remained overnight, were gathering their stuff together, ready to clock off. They had nothing to report.

Sergeant Walters had already deployed some of his troops and was in the process of instructing others.

Pockett wasn't listening. He was cold and wanted a gallon of coffee to kick-start his system.

When he had arrived, at what he considered an ungodly hour, the place was already a hive of activity. People sweeping, wheeling barrows, scraping shovels, moving horses, revving tractors, doing this, doing that. They must all be mad, he thought. That was the trouble with the country. Too much inbreeding, no doubt.

Joe's appearance, with two large mugs of coffee, was the best sight he'd had since leaving the streetlights. They sipped in silence for a while, watching the others move in and out of the room.

Pockett tentatively undid the top button of his overcoat. Someone had lit the morning room fire and he stared at it.

Very Charles Dickens, he thought, but a couple of radiators would have been more homely.

He stared at an oil painting over the fireplace. Another bloody horse. He closed his eyes.

*

The chances against

"Okay, Joe," he said, sitting up straighter in his chair, sometime later, "where did we get to?"

Joe was standing by the fireplace looking at the flames, exchanging a word or two with passing uniforms.

"Sergeant!" Pockett shouted. "If you can tear yourself away from the party…"

Joe came and sat down by the desk and looked at the blackboard. The activity in the room seemed to stop as he said, "Well, we've got it down to seven likelys now. If there's no collusion, sir," he emphasised the 'collusion', "then we've eliminated nine."

"Make that ten," Sergeant Walters' voice said behind them. "We've just found the body of Mr Paul Hensham."

Pockett stood, huddled well into his coat, hands in his pockets, and looked up.

The net was swinging slightly, about eight feet off the ground, suspended from a large hook screwed into a beam of the open shed. The rope, gathering the neck of the net together, went up over the hook, then out to where it was wound around a double handle affair by the entrance of the shed.

"It's a hay net, sir," the constable said.

Pockett didn't bother to answer.

There was hay sticking out from the large holes. Bits of it dangled from the arm that was sticking out too.

"How do you know that's Mr Hensham?" he asked, watching a wisp of dark hay move gently back and forth. It seemed to be attached to the end of one finger.

The constable walked round the edge of the shed to the other side of the net, and pointed up.

The face was distorted by the ropes of the net, the mouth pulled open in a lopsided sneer, the eyebrows raised, so that one huge eye glared down at them. His nose stuck out from another hole and he looked like he had a moustache of hay. Even so, you could tell it was Paul Hensham.

Pockett surveyed the big shed. It wasn't his idea of a shed really, being open on one end and having no proper floor.

"What's it for?" he asked. "Just cover?"

Joe nodded. "Horses out to grass come in here for shelter or hay. There's a couple more like this in the other fields."

They were all speaking quietly, as if in a funeral parlour. Pockett thought it had more to do with the early hour than a show of respect. Nevertheless, he felt the death of gentle Paul was different to that of hated Jeff. This one might bring grief, and grief demanded respect. He looked out over the field. Grey mist hung by the hedges. The dawn light had nothing to do with the sun, being dull and sombre.

"I hate this bloody place," he muttered for the umpteenth time.

"This one is nearest the house," Joe said. "The path and the gardens are just behind us. You noticed the floor?"

"There isn't a floor," Pockett retorted. "If you mean have I noticed this patch of mud…" he lifted his foot, displaying the state of his shoe, "yes, I've noticed."

He followed Joe's pointing finger, looking at the dark, stained hay around one side of the shed and under the net.

"Blood?"

"Looks like it. Shall I get them in now, sir?"

"Yes, get them in." Pockett sighed. "Back to the beginning we go. I hate this bloody place."

"I thought you didn't like the country, Billy," Arthur Spencer beamed at him. "Seems you can't tear yourself away from it now."

Pockett grimaced. "Spare me the humour, Arthur. I'm miserable enough as it is. What you got then? Come on, tell me he's got no feet. Right?"

Arthur Spencer read from his notes. "Pronounced at seven thirty-five. Been dead about six hours." He glanced up. "Look between midnight and two, if I were you." He went back to his notes. "Throat cut. Not a neat straight line, more a jab and a bit of wiggling the knife about."

"Lovely," Pockett murmured.

"Hit on the head first, so he was probably out when he – or she – did it. And, you'll be pleased to know, all his appendages are intact."

"Makes a change."

"There's three interesting punctures in his belly though…"

"Oh, God…" Pockett groaned.

"…But not to worry, old son, I've worked out what they are," Spencer went on, cheerfully. "Pitchfork marks. Deffs him off, then uses a pitchfork to load him in the hay net."

"Aha! You'd have to be strong to do that, wouldn't you?" Pockett perked up at the thought that he may be able to exclude all females.

"Yes…but if you're used to using a pitchfork, they're quite handy tools for shifting heavy weights, as I expect Joe here will tell you."

Pockett subsided again. "Yes, I expect he will," he said, miserably. "I expect he will."

"Anyway, this man wasn't heavy. Ten stone or so. That's not much if you're used to humping bales of hay around."

Pockett looked more morose than ever.

"Cheer up, Billy boy, we have good news. We've got the block of wood he was hit with, the knife that cut his throat and the pitchfork that moved him. Now you couldn't want more than that."

Pockett closed his eyes and pursed his lips before saying, in a deadpan voice, "But none of them have any prints or useful identification marks. Right?"

Spencer beamed at him. "Sorry," he said.

"Yes, thank you, Arthur, that definitely cheers me up."

Pockett got up to leave, waving his hand as he went through the door.

Arthur called after him, "Oh, if you find another one, Billy, try not to do it before Monday, only I've got something on tomorrow."

Joe smiled at him.
Pockett didn't.

* * * * *

The two police constables looked nervous and tired. Joe took notes of their activities on Friday night. Sergeant Walters hovered in the background, making it very clear he blamed them entirely.

Pockett sat and listened as they described where they had patrolled, what they had checked and who they saw.

Sergeant Walters uttered enough "Huh!"s to cast doubt on every word.

They wished they had never volunteered for overtime now.

They hadn't seen anyone between twelve and two. They hadn't heard anyone. They looked in the shed about one-thirty, but they didn't notice anything. No, they hadn't looked up at the hay net. No, they hadn't noticed if it was up or down.

"Call yourselves bloody policemen!" Sergeant Walters was saying as soon as Joe dismissed them, and he and Pockett moved out to their small room.

"That's why he was strung up," Pockett said, "so no one would notice."

"Likely," Joe agreed. "And talking of likelys, we're back at the beginning, I suppose."

"Why him, Joe? What do we know about him?"

Joe sorted through the files of the first interviews. He sat down and read the Paul Hensham one. "Owner of the place, though he left the running to his daughter. Married to Doris. They seemed to get on well enough in a distant sort of way."

"What do you mean, a distant sort of way?"

"Well, both lead their own lives, you know. She's always involved in community things. He writes articles about flowers and history. Books too. They don't seem to do much together, but they don't row about it," Joe explained.

"Anything else in your little file of mostly useless information?"

"One child, Shirley. In his late fifties. Bit of a wet wick, if you know what I mean."

"A…wet…wick?" Pockett carefully enunciated the phrase, lowering his head and raising his eyebrows in a quizzical expression.

"Oh, stop doing your superior detective impression, you arrogant little sod!" Joe snapped at him, standing up to put the file back. "You know what a wet wick is. You ought to." He mimicked Pockett's voice as he minced back to the desk. "Oh! Is that nasty mud on my shoes?! Aagh! A great big horse put its nose in my hair! If I don't get out of this smelly air soon, I shall be quite ill." He clutched his chest dramatically as he sat down at his desk again, shoving his face into Pockett's and enunciating, "A…wet…wick. Right?"

"Thank you, Joseph," Pockett said, adding as Joe leaned back, "and if that was supposed to be an impression of someone, I'm sorry, I didn't recognise him."

"You want to get yourself down here with your feet in the muck like the rest of the human race," Joe muttered.

Pockett sighed. "Ah…I knew muck had to be something to do with it."

Joe gave up. "What else do we know about him?"

They thought for a few moments.

"He seemed to be always around in the garden. Virtually everyone we interviewed mentioned seeing him in the garden."

"Which means," Pockett said, taking up the idea, "he may well know more than someone likes, so they shut him up."

"How would you get him from the study, where he sleeps, to the shelter? The doc says he was certainly killed in the shelter, so how do you persuade someone to go out in the middle of the night?"

"Another good point, Joseph. Things are looking up. Perhaps, though, he was already there and someone knew he would be there."

"Why? Why would he be there? What could he do there he couldn't do in the privacy of his study?" Joe asked. Then answered himself, "Meet someone. Or to get something. Was anything else found beside the murder weapons?"

Pockett shook his head. "Nothing there but blood, mud and horse manure. Nothing on him but pencils, bits of string, half a packet of seeds, stuff like that. He doesn't seem to have put up much of a fight. Nothing under his nails but bits of hay, mud, etc. He was probably knocked out before he knew he was in danger."

There was silence again, during which Pockett flicked his thumb against his pen and Joe stared into space.

"Who can we exclude?"

"Well, if it was because he knew too much about the first murder, all those we excluded before."

"Trouble is, we don't know if that was the reason, do we? So everyone's back in the frame. Furthermore, it isn't going to be easy to exclude anyone, because there wouldn't be anyone else around to verify alibis at one in the morning. Everyone's just going to say they were asleep, and who's to say they weren't?"

After another long silence he suddenly sat up straighter. "We'll just have to pretend it hasn't happened."

"What?"

"Well, when the plods get back to their reports, everyone is going to say they were in bed asleep. We'll have nothing to go on, except it might have been because he knew who killed Jeff. See?"

"Yes, but what if…?"

"No, we'll worry about that after we get Jeff sorted."

He got up and looked out of the small window behind the desk. "Read out our list again, Joe," he said, and added, "I hate the country."

Joe smiled at his back.

This elevenses was different. No one was following the script any more and that rang alarm bells in every compartment of Jane's brain.

Yes, Jeff's death had disrupted most of the systems at Chance, but the people behaved in the way that she had expected. Nobody said, or did, anything that was out of character. But now, nobody seemed to be behaving normally. She wasn't sure if this was because of the way she was looking at them, or the way they were looking at each other.

People were polite, restrained, careful. Sudden strangers.

Everyone could understand someone killing Jeff, but who would want to kill Uncle Paul?!

It didn't make sense, unless he had seen something, knew something. Perhaps then, Jeff's killer might need to get rid of him. But that didn't make sense either. Everyone assumed Jeff was killed because he was a nasty character. Someone just couldn't take it any more and suddenly went berserk and hit back. It may not be legally correct, but it was understandable. Killing Paul wasn't. Everyone here knew he was so vague, so not-of-this-world, that the Battle of Hastings could take place the other side of the garden fence and he wouldn't have noticed.

It didn't make sense.

His death made you feel that there was a lunatic around. That, like some crime novel, they were all going to get bumped off, one after another, until the least likely suspect was left, revealed as a scheming monster.

People began to look at each other.

Jane knocked on the door and walked in, without waiting for a response.

Auntie Doris was still sitting at her dressing table. She had been sitting there when Jane first told her about Uncle Paul, early that morning. Accompanied by the inspector and the sergeant, she had knocked on the door then and waited. When they told her, Auntie Doris had sat down at her dressing table. She was still sitting there.

"I've brought you a cup of tea," Jane said.

Doris was looking at herself in the mirror.

"Auntie Doris," Jane touched her shoulder, "I've brought you a cup of tea."

The sudden animation that followed left Jane wondering if she had accidentally pressed a switch.

The smile turned on. The hand reached for her cosmetic tray. She turned her head this way and that, as though considering her hairstyle. "Thank you, dear," she beamed. "I'm late, aren't I?"

Jane started to reassure her that there was no need to hurry for anything, but Doris went on, "They're setting up at one, you know, and I said I'd open the doors."

"Sorry?"

"The jumble sale, dear. Girl Guides." She got to her feet and opened her wardrobe door, moving hangers along the rail, selecting which suit to wear.

"You don't have to do that, Auntie Doris." Jane put the cup on the dressing table and moved to take her arm. "I'll phone them. You don't have to go."

Doris turned, putting her hand on Jane's other arm. She looked into Jane's eyes and said, quietly, "Oh, I do, dear. I do."

Jane stood still, shocked, looking back into her aunt's eyes. She had always guessed that Auntie Doris used all this community activity as a way of running away from her problems... keeping herself too busy to think, or feel, but she had thought it was an instinctive reaction. It came as a shock to realise that it wasn't...that Auntie Doris was capable of creating, and maintaining a personality that she could stand back from and objectively analyse. Then the switch went over again as Doris turned and took a suit from her wardrobe.

"I daresay they will think I'm very brave, you know, but I'm not, dear. Just practical. One has to be practical, don't you think?"

She held the suit against her and looked in the mirror, head to one side, saying brightly, "Yes, this one, I think."

She was back, following the script.

Jane had tried to work out who killed Jeff and Uncle Paul too. She hadn't even considered her aunt. She did now.

The sergeant smiled as she put the two mugs of coffee on the desk in the service room.

The inspector said, "Thank you, Mrs Warren," but he didn't smile, or really look at her.

She ignored him and smiled back at the sergeant before she closed the door.

They were a weird couple, she thought, nothing like you imagined they should be. Detective novels and radio series gave you images of policemen. Tough. In control. Glamorous. Brilliant. These two obviously hadn't read the right books!

She liked the sergeant though. She supposed he was in his twenties. They both looked too young to be anything like the detectives in stories. The sergeant had fair, wavy hair, a clean complexion, twinkly eyes and a nice rural accent. He was friendly, approachable. The sort of bloke you would see at market and discuss prices with, or moan about the weather. He was very tall and she seemed to have spent the last few days saying, "Mind your head," every time she saw him. He was really too big for their little doorways. That made it even more amazing that he didn't flatten that arrogant little boy, Inspector Pockett.

Jane did not like him and, watching the interplay between him and the rest of the policemen, neither did anyone else. It wasn't just his, so often, sneering voice, with its London accent: she didn't like the way he dressed, moved…was. Nasty, she thought. And childish.

At first, she had likened the sergeant and the inspector to a sort of Watson and Holmes combination, but that didn't last long. The sergeant was no bumbling Watson and Mr Pockett was certainly no elegant, charismatic Holmes. He looked more like the kind of young man you see hanging around car parks, trying door handles, or standing outside cinemas, with a bunch of look-alikes, shouting after girls and kicking bits of paper around. Posing children.

She supposed he must be in his twenties at least, to be an inspector, but he could be any age from eighteen to thirty-five. Short jacket, styled hair, high-heeled, shiny boots, like a cowboy's, pale complexion. He had those sort of glasses that might be sunglasses, or not, and he had them pushed up to sit on the top of his head most of the time. Nearly always he seemed to be leaning back in his chair, tilting it on two legs and staring at the ceiling, and, when he ventured outside, he picked his way along, as though he was crossing a minefield.

You didn't need a degree in psychology to know that he hated the countryside, nor to see how the other policemen sympathised with the sergeant for having to work with him.

Of course, she realised there had to be more to him than the front he put on. For one thing, he must be very clever to get to the position he held. For another, having observed the sergeant, she could not imagine him tolerating the more objectionable of Pockett's comments unless their friendship was more complex than it appeared. Nevertheless, she didn't like him. Arrogant little twit!

She decided she could probably work all this out before he did. After all, she knew the place, the people, and – more importantly – she knew the original script.

At lunchtime, she listened to Andrew and John discussing the interviews they had had earlier with the two detectives. Since they had been together on Thursday, working in the tractor sheds on some basic maintenance, they were each other's alibis.

Apparently, no one had asked them what they were doing last night, or even if they heard anything. Not that they had. Both of them were dead to the world by eleven-thirty, after a night at the local and a successful darts match.

Jane watched them talking. She couldn't see anything different about either of them. They were quieter than usual, less jokes, less horseplay, but so was everyone. That was natural, Paul's death was a shock, but Jane couldn't see any constraint between them, any concern that the other may be involved. She ruled them out.

Alice came into lunch with Sally. Alice ate twice as much as she normally did. Sally ate nothing.

That was their usual response to any emotional stress and what Jane had expected. Funny thing, food and people's attitudes towards it, she thought.

Sally had been crying. Alice looked annoyed. Two more reactions that matched Jane's expectations.

They didn't talk much, not in the sense of conversation, anyway. Sally shook her head a lot and kept saying, "Oh, dear," but it was in response to the situation rather than Alice's words.

Alice said she had told the police that she had spent Thursday afternoon dozing and reading a book in-between, it being her afternoon off and all. She didn't understand why they only seemed interested in Jeff's death. They hadn't asked her anything about Mr Hensham's. Christ, who cared who bumped Jeff off?! Well rid of him, they were. But poor Mr Hensham...whatever did he do to warrant that?!

Alice was annoyed. Sally was upset. Both of them were wary of the men. They flicked glances at Andrew and John. They moved aside for Barry when he came in, smiled a very tentative greeting, and watched his back as he moved to talk to Jane. They were frightened.

Barry was uneasy. He had spent a long time with the detectives. He had told them, over and over, what he had said to Jeff and what Jeff had said to him. He hadn't laid a finger on him, though he deserved it. He'd told them that. Yes, he had!

He went over the interview again to Jane. He was worried that they seemed to think he was the last person to see Jeff alive, so they suspected him. He told Jane he had gone back to the shed to tidy up and get his tools. Then he went home, to be there when Pauline got back. They had had a row and then "that

Sue Ryland

bloody Jeff" had had a go at her. He wanted to be there when she came home. Surely they could understand that?

He had just told Jeff to keep his hands off his wife. He hadn't hit him. He just hoped someone saw him leave, or get back home.

He was worried.

Jane listened to Barry and watched his agitation.

No, not him, she thought.

After she cleared lunch she sat to write another list. She put down everyone and started making notes. She put the list in the drawer with all the other lists, flicking them through, as she always did when she opened the drawer, reminding herself of what needed doing. Grocery…urgent jobs in the house…duty rotas…menus… Now murderers?

By the end of the day, Jane had seen everyone. She had made a point of seeing everyone.

By the time she made apple pies for dinner, she had worked out who she could rule out, who wasn't around on Thursday, who was too much in the public gaze to have the opportunity. She knew what times the police were interested in, so excluding people was easy.

By the time she had cleaned the bathrooms and the outside loos, she had spoken to most of those that were left.

By the time dinner was over she had spoken to them all.

As she closed the kitchen range down for the night, she knew who had done it. She didn't know why, but she was sure she knew who.

She sat at the kitchen table and cried, surrounded by her sympathetic dogs.

Beating that nasty little inspector hadn't given her the pleasure she had imagined…she hadn't thought the exercise through properly…she hadn't thought much at all…she wished she could start the day again.

*

At the start of the day the sergeant and one of his constables stared at the blackboard.

"What does it all mean?" asked the constable.

The blackboards were now covered in names, places, arrows and asterisks. A confusion of underlining, question marks, insertion marks, and more linking lines than Clapham Junction in its heyday.

The two detectives had gone back into their small room, after a long session with the chalk.

Sergeant Walters shook his head. "Not for us to know, son," he answered, automatically dismissing the constable with his tone. But it offended him too. Police work should be systematic, methodical. They may be 'plods', but plodding persistence was the best way to get results in his opinion. He shook his head again and sat back at his table. He had worked on cases with these two before and, not only did he dislike that 'uppity' kid of an inspector, it annoyed him that they should get results from what he considered 'a bloody mess'.

He looked through his work sheets. They listed all the interviews and various activities of the last few days. Why, for instance, didn't young Master Pockett interview everyone who might be considered as a suspect? That made sense, didn't it? Why did he leap around the list of likely people, seeing that person, ignoring that one? Where was the method?

He decided it was surely more by luck than judgement that Pockett had any success at all. Yes, just luck, he decided.

He looked back at the crammed blackboards. What the hell did all that mean?

Pockett and Joe looked at each other. "It's the only thing left, isn't it?" Joe said.

"On the face of it, yes," Pockett agreed. He leaned back in his chair and blew smoke at the ceiling. "But why?" he said. "Why?"

They sat in silence again. Joe doodled a castle on the paper in front of him. Pockett closed his eyes.

The sounds of the stables penetrated the walls. Sweeping brooms. The sharp clack of a hoof stamping on a concrete floor. Shovels scraping.

Joe drew bushes around the castle wall.

Suddenly, Pockett let his chair fall back onto four legs with a clump. Reaching for the interview records, he snapped, "Come along, Joseph! You might be quite happy to stay here dreaming of your Mrs Warren, but I want to get back to normal people who don't go around bumping each other off at the slightest provocation."

Joe drew a large, heavy cross through his castle and prepared to do battle in a different setting.

"Normal people?" he sneered. "Come the apocalypse, mate, and townies like you have had it. Without your laid-on services, you wouldn't survive five minutes. Load of ruddy weaklings. Cringing at what life is really about."

"Don't tell me…blood, guts and muck!" Pockett snapped back. "Well, just because most of us have dragged ourselves out of the caves…out of the muck…I suppose we ought to be sorry for you lot who haven't got the nous to do it."

They glared at each other, the adrenalin flowing again, which Joe well knew was the point of the exercise.

There was a knock at the door.

"And what will all you superior beings do if us cave-dwellers stop feeding your fat stomachs? Not five minutes would you survive. Not five minutes!" Joe retaliated, leaning forward to jab his finger in front of Pockett.

The door opened a little, but shut again, as Sergeant Walters heard Pockett go into a long diatribe on people expecting him to work with country bumpkins whose brains had never evolved past the swamp stage.

Sergeant Walters paused, sighed, and was glad he had stayed in uniform. Then, gritting his teeth, he knocked louder and entered as Pockett yelled, "Yes!" at him.

"You wanted to know arrangements for tonight," he said.

"Well?" Pockett glared.

"Four on duty, okay?"

"Town lads, I hope?" Pockett was still glaring at him. "Got enough intelligence to stop half this lot killing the other half before morning?"

Sergeant Walters didn't answer.

"Thank you," Joe said to him as he turned to go.

After the door shut, Joe and Pockett looked at each other for a long moment.

"Doris Hensham?" Pockett asked quietly.

"Yes," Joe said. "I think so."

* * * * *

CHANCES OF SURVIVAL

He had sat with her for an hour and a half. He had been kind and held her hand as she cried. Now it was time for breakfast and he had gone.

She didn't know what to do for breakfast. She had forgotten what to do. She opened her list drawer to find the menu list and found her murderers' list. She stood staring at it.

She hadn't beaten that detective. She wasn't that clever after all.

She sat at the table screwing up the list in her hand. The dogs sat around her, heads on her knees, or her feet. Something was very wrong, for now she wasn't following the script. They fretted, trying to push their noses into her clenched hands, trying to get a normal reaction.

The police had made the arrest in the early hours of the morning.

Jane didn't know what to do now.

They had already known who had killed Jeff Dickinson before they interviewed Doris. They didn't know why, but they guessed the answer to that question would solve Paul's murder too.

Joe had watched his boss peel back the layers of scar tissue and expose the still festering sore that was the reason for everything.

It was as painful to watch, as it was to feel. Like the doctor suffering with the patient, Joe saw the bright, shallow Doris slowly broken down, dropping one protective layer after another, until all that was left was the guilt she had so successfully hidden. From herself. From others.

As the policewoman took her away, Pockett said, quietly, like reciting a mantra, "I hate the country."

Joe nodded. "Yes," he said, just as quietly, "I know."

The dogs had been restless, getting up to walk a few steps and flop down again. Jane hadn't bothered to tell them to be still. She wasn't tired anyway. Her mind was reworking her conclusions, over and over again. Lying flat on her bed, staring at the ceiling, she was really trying to come up with a different answer. The one she had reached was not acceptable.

Anyway, she thought, it's all just based on my instincts about who wasn't behaving normally, and instincts can be wrong. The trouble was, she didn't think she was wrong.

There was still a lot of activity going on in the house. Her bedroom was nearest to downstairs, the better for her not to disturb anybody when she got the day going at four-thirty. When she came up to bed, she knew they were going to talk to Auntie Doris. She had asked if they wanted tea or anything before she went up. Auntie Doris had said, "Not for me, dear, but if these gentlemen...?"

The detectives had shook their heads. The sergeant said he would get coffee if they wanted it later, and if she didn't mind him using her kitchen. She said, of course she didn't, and went to bed.

She thought the sergeant looked at her strangely, but guessed that may be because she went to bed so early by the standard of the others. Nine-thirty was early to him too, she supposed.

She hoped it wasn't because he could see she was upset... that she had worked it all out.

It was about midnight when she gave up trying to sleep. She wanted a hot drink and her own kitchen, so she put on her long, thick dressing gown and went downstairs. The dogs padded after her.

She didn't realise for a moment who the woman was. She was coming along the passage with a policewoman holding her arm. A little old woman, tottering along, head down. As they turned to go up the stairs, it was the suit that Jane recognised.

Auntie Doris?

There was a moment when her mind refused to accept this answer, almost laughed at the idea, but it was Auntie Doris. Bustling, upright, super-confident Auntie Doris. Only she wasn't like that any more. This was a stranger.

The policewoman had nodded to her but her aunt didn't look up.

Jane went into the kitchen and closed the door.

Automatic actions took over as she tried to make sense of what she had seen. She raked out the fire, risking setting fire to her dressing gown from the specks of red coke that fell on the tiles. She had forgotten she was wearing the long robe. She pushed it behind her so that it trailed like a wedding dress across the floor, then she completed the task of getting the range going.

She made a mug of coffee and stood it on the end of the range.

She washed up the mugs in the sink and left them to drain.

She took her coffee to the table and thought about doing her lists.

She looked at the kitchen clock, as she did several times every morning, when she was trying to get it all done before she needed to start breakfast.

Only she didn't need to start breakfast.

It was twelve-twenty in the morning.

It was about half past two when he found her. She was sitting on the floor, back to the wall, staring into space, surrounded by her sleeping dogs.

He hadn't expected her to be there and it made him jump.

He had come to get coffee.

The dogs lifted their heads as he came in, and she scrambled to her feet, impeded by the long dressing gown she wore.

Chances of survival

"Oh, sorry," she said. "Sorry. Did I make you jump?"

She brushed at the dressing gown, embarrassed to be seen this way and in that position. "I couldn't sleep. I was..." she gestured vaguely to the floor, "...sitting with the dogs," she finished, with an uncertain smile. "Sorry."

"That's all right," he said. "I just came to get coffee. I didn't mean to startle you."

"I'll get it for you." She moved to the sink. "Two mugs?"

"Please."

"I do daft things like that." She was still embarrassed and trying to explain it away.

"You would have thought I'd have grown out of sitting on the floor by now, wouldn't you?"

He watched her make the coffee and thought she looked very tired and sad. He didn't want to do what he had to do next.

"Actually, I was going to wake you up," he said, "if you hadn't been down here."

He saw the slight hesitation as she reached for the sugar.

"I need to talk to you."

"Right," she said, too brightly. "I'll just wait here then, shall I?"

He took one of the mugs away and was back in a minute. She was making herself a drink.

"There's been a lot going on here tonight," she said, "out there." She nodded towards the hall door. It was half a question.

"Mrs Warren...Jane...sit down." He sat at the table and motioned her to join him. She looked at him, mug in one hand, trembling cigarette in the other.

"Do I want to hear this?" she asked quietly.

He looked back at her.

"No, I don't," she answered herself, "but I have to, don't I?" She sat down.

"Jane," he began, "there's been some developments in our enquiry..."

God, that's pathetic, he thought. Police gobbledegook. Delaying tactics.

"Jane," he began again, "we've arrested Shirley."

She wasn't looking at him. She was staring into her coffee. "I know," she said. Then, as he stared at her, "I worked it out today."

The hand that moved the ashtray wasn't quite steady.

"I hoped I was wrong." A smile flickered across her face. "I wish I was."

"How did you work it out?"

She shrugged. "Just watched everyone. Seeing who was acting how I'd expect and who wasn't. Not very scientific, I'm afraid."

There was the flick of the smile again.

"Shirley should have been in control from the beginning. If you knew her, you would know that. It didn't make sense." She paused, then, "I told you it wasn't very scientific."

Her head dropped down as she muttered, "Oh, hell…hell… hell…"

"I'm sorry," he said. "Really, I'm very sorry."

The face she lifted to him was fighting to retain control. "Why?" she begged, "I don't understand why."

And he told her. He kept hold of her hand as he told her all that her aunt had said, all that Shirley had confirmed.

And she cried. She wasn't used to crying. It was painful to watch.

He told her about the years before she came to Chance, the years when Shirley was young. He said her Uncle Paul was one of those men who liked little girls. He couldn't manage a relationship with a grown woman and he couldn't keep his hands off little girls. Her aunt had known something was wrong, but even when she had seen him with their own little daughter, doing things he should not, she couldn't bring herself to face him, or the situation. She was frightened of his father, Jane's Great Uncle William, frightened of what he would do if he found out. Maybe he would disinherit Paul and send them both away. She was frightened for their position in the community, frightened of losing the respect of others, frightened of losing the life she was beginning to carve out for herself as a way of surviving her sham of a marriage. She had tried to keep Shirley away from him, but she had tried harder not to see what was going on. She couldn't face the situation.

It was Jeff that ended it all. Jeff of the dubious morals and the filthy innuendo. The one they all detested for his lewdness. The one they called the "dirty old man."

Jeff may have been all of those things, but he had his standards too, and abusing little girls wasn't allowed.

He caught Paul with Shirley when Shirley was seven. Jeff wasn't frightened of losing anything. He had no social position to maintain. He wasn't scared of Great Uncle William's anger. He didn't give a damn about consequences. He lashed out at Paul, physically and mentally. He warned him that if he ever came within a mile of Shirley again, he would make sure that the police only got what was left when he had finished with him.

Jeff took Shirley to her mother, who begged for his silence, who offered him a permanent position at Chance if he kept his mouth shut and guarded Shirley.

And so it all began.

To Shirley, Jeff was the one who gave her back her childhood, the one who made it possible to have friends to stay, to feel safe and confident. While Jeff was around, her father kept away.

As she grew older she may have needed Jeff less, except she had developed the stables, and ponies attract little girls. Jeff's guardianship had allowed her to thrive and allowed her mother to push the problem away, to forget it ever happened. Now it was Shirley who asked Jeff to keep her father away from the children...the little girls who came for riding lessons, or just to be around horses. She had seen her father's interest in them. She knew what he would do.

Jeff did his job well, but Jeff being Jeff, he didn't just watch Paul, he taunted him. Daily, he would wiggle his hands in Paul's

Sue Ryland

face, warning him to keep them to himself, or else...

Paul had hit him with a shovel and destroyed those hands. As Jeff came from his argument with Barry, he vented his frustration on Paul, and Paul took it as usual until Jeff turned to walk away. Then Paul stopped digging and hit him.

Now he vented his years of frustration on his tormentor. He kept on hitting him as he lay face down, arms stretched in front of him, hands jerking as each blow fell, those hands that had poked and pushed, taunting and denying him for so long.

Afterwards he dug the garden well, putting down lots of the blood and bonemeal fertiliser he always used for new shrubs. He trundled more sacks of potatoes to the vegetable store in his wheelbarrow. No one noticed. He was always digging and moving things, always using hosepipes and lighting bonfires. No one noticed.

Shirley knew who had killed Jeff. She also knew that, without Jeff, the world she had created was in danger. She could not watch her father. She could not ask anyone else to watch him. There was no one she could trust not to run to the police, or spread the story to others. The horse world is a small, close world. Chance would be ruined. Sooner or later he would persuade some other little girl into his shed and then...

She didn't know what to do. She sat in her office in a state of panic. Fear, long controlled and pushed down, took over from logic. Fear for others, for herself, for Chance.

She decided she had to kill him. She did it as quickly as she could, pitchforking his body into the hay net because, even now, she didn't ever want to touch him again.

She knew where he would be that night. She had seen the big, brown envelope in the post tray that morning, postmarked from Holland. His magazines. He hid them around the farm and stables, never in his own garden shed or in his study, in case they were found and he was suspected. He would read them in the shelter so no one could see him from the house. She knew that because he would take her there to look at the pictures when she was very young. She just waited for him.

She looked at his body, swinging in the hay net, and thought Chance was safe now. She could restart the riding lessons and all the normal stable activities. She didn't need to worry. She was safe. Chance was safe.

Fear had overruled logic. She hadn't reckoned on the police... hadn't thought they would look into Eva's life...tie Eva's abuse to hers...tie their friendship into similar experiences...talk to teachers about their personalities at school...how Shirley had changed when she was seven...how Eva had not asked why...

She hadn't thought about the police at all.

* * * * *

He had sat with her for an hour and a half. He had held her hand when she had cried.

When Joe left her, Jane was destroyed. Competent Jane. Controlled Jane. Jane who knew the script.

She knew nothing! Nothing! Thinking she was so clever. Thinking she knew everything that went on in her own little patch. She knew nothing!

So much made sense now. How could she have been so stupid not to know?

She beat her clenched fists against the side of her head. Thick! Thick!

She felt like smashing her kitchen to pieces. Her kitchen. Her security. The place where she swanned around acting like the fount of all wisdom. Bigheaded. Blind. Thick.

Why hadn't she worked out why Shirley needed Jeff? It was obvious, wasn't it?

Didn't Shirley stop all stable activities when she had the accident? She wanted to speak to Jeff, she had said. Obviously asking him to watch over things even more vigilantly until she was back...make sure no local children came to help out, which they would have done, even though lessons were stopped. And wasn't cancelling the riding lessons the first thing Shirley did after Jeff's death?

Jane ranted against herself for her failure to understand her own observations.

Hadn't she seen Uncle Paul's animation when he was around the children? Seen his fear of Jeff?

Didn't she know Jeff was around the pony yards far more than his job of farm manager warranted?

Oh, sure, everyone looked at Jeff and assumed he was the owner of the filthy magazines, the watcher of little girls, the dirty old man. But she should have looked harder, thought more. Didn't she pride herself on working out people? On knowing the script?

Thick! Thick!

For a long time the anger raged as she mentally tongue-lashed herself.

Now it was well past the time she should be working, but she couldn't seem to get going.

She should be in control. She should be seeing to the range, taking the dogs out, writing lists. She should be drinking coffee, getting early morning tea, planning breakfast, checking the daily rota, thinking about the day before, the day to come…but she couldn't think about anything for long. She didn't want to think about yesterday and wouldn't think about the day to come.

The dogs whined and went to the door. She looked through her fingers at them, her head in her hands. They whined again, walking to her, then back to the door.

She felt old and stiff as she got up. How long had she been sitting there?

The clock said five-thirty.

She let the dogs out, standing with the door open, hand on the latch.

After a few minutes, she realised her legs felt cold and looked down at them. It took a moment to register she was still in her dressing gown. She shut the door and walked back into the kitchen, looking at her slippered feet.

The dogs scratched at the door and she responded automatically, walking back to open it and let them in. Their feet left wet marks over the tiles and she felt cold wetness on her legs as they passed.

It's raining, she thought. That's the washing shot.

She made a coffee and stood it on the end of the range. She didn't drink any of it.

In her bedroom, she put on her trousers and top, and then remembered she hadn't washed or cleaned her teeth. She took her clothes off again.

In the bathroom the water was too hot. Why? Of course, the range had been pulling all night. She had forgotten that.

Back in the kitchen, slowly the routines clicked into place, pulling her out of the maze through which her thoughts had darted, like a rat in an experiment.

Routine brought numbness. Occupation without thought. Binary decisions with yes or no answers.

By seven, breakfast was ready and her third mug of coffee stood at the end of the range.

She waited.

It was Alice who took control. Everyone had waited for Jane to say, do this or that, but she seemed too numb with grief, or shock.

Alice sent Andrew to get Dave Bateman and arrange the work between them. They had been doing that anyway for the last few days, but they had known Shirley was around if they needed confirmation on anything.

Alice rearranged the work in the stables, allocating jobs to Sally, Sue and Jay.

Eva hadn't appeared for breakfast and said she felt too ill when Alice went to check.

The morning passed with the usual morning noises. Tractors moved around. Shovels scraped. Wheelbarrows creaked.

Jane cleaned and cooked and let the dogs in and out.
No one talked much.
No one saw Auntie Doris or Eva.
The police moved out of the morning room.
Jane smiled politely as she listened to their thanks and sympathy, then she put the vacuum on again.
In the afternoon, it started.

"Mrs Warren? Evening News. We wondered if we could just have a few words…"

"…after all, it makes sense to move the horses nearer to Rebecca's college. We'll collect them on Monday. Okay?"

"…and, of course, the Gazette would be willing to pay for an exclusive…"

"Could you have the mare ready for five o'clock? She boxes with no problem, so…"

"So sorry to hear the news, dear. Shall I come over and give you a hand with things? Give you someone to talk to…"

"…cancelling the show on…"

"…decided not to go ahead with…"

Jane shut the door and put the phone down all afternoon and evening.

She saw cars and vans turning into their lane from the main road. They parked alongside the hedges and stayed there.

People taking photographs…people trying to talk to anyone around…young Jay scurrying into the house, pursued by two men…Andrew waving angrily at a man with a camera…John blocking off the entrance to the yards with one of the jumps and more planks of wood…

At dinnertime they huddled in the kitchen as though they were in hiding. Jane left the phone off the hook. It rang every time she put it back on to try and phone for help from the police.

They thought of walking across the fields to the village and using the phone in the pub, but any appearance by any of them caused a surge of reporters and flashing cameras, so they gave up.

They sat picking at cheese and biscuits and leftovers from lunch, listening to endless knocks at various doors. Jane hadn't had time to prepare any dinner. No one wanted it anyway.

She looked round at them as she quietened the dogs again. The men were angry. The women were frightened. She was shocked.

They didn't listen to the radio or read the papers much. This whole thing had happened so fast that they hadn't realised there was any outside interest, or information, on the events of the last few days. Chance had always been a world of its own. Self-sufficient. Enclosed. Now it was being invaded.

"We should have known they would come once the police left," Alice said. "What are we going to do?"

"My dad's really worried." Sally's eyes were panicky. Her father had managed to get through on the phone earlier. He wanted to come and take her away. "It's all falling apart," she went on. "Everyone's pulling out as though we have the plague."

They jumped as someone tapped the window behind the closed curtains.

"Go away!" Andrew yelled.

Someone called something back, but they couldn't hear the words.

The dogs lifted their heads and thumped their tails on the floor.

"They know him," Jane said, looking at the dogs. She went to the window and pulled the curtains back an inch to look out. It was the sergeant and the inspector.

"Don't worry, we'll soon have them off the place." Joe accepted the offer of coffee.

"We called in as soon as we saw what was happening. I'm afraid, though, that's as much as we can do. We can't move them from the road unless they cause an obstruction, and we can't stop them phoning."

He had radioed in and the local police were there in a very short time, ejecting people from the farm and getting them back to their parked vehicles.

Those inside the farm watched all this from the dining room window. They were relieved and effusive in their praise of the quick response, but apparently the police were already on their way because Sir Edmund had phoned them earlier. He had called it a "damned disgrace" and said he would charge the lot of them with trespass if it were up to him.

It was Lettice and John who had rushed to tell him what they had seen at Chance.

"It's like a film!" John had said. They had seen it from the hill during one of their rambles. "The siege of Chance," he went on, "that's what I shall call it."

Sir Edmund had abandoned his books and confirmed with Lettice that this was not one of John's flights of exaggeration, then he phoned the police. He tried to phone Jane, but the line was constantly engaged.

"How is she?" Jane asked, when the others were settled in the lounge with coffee and biscuits. They had debated whether to listen to the radio, and voted it was better to know what people were hearing about them, but Sally had her hands over her ears, just in case it sounded too awful.

Jane had taken more drinks up to Auntie Doris and Eva, both of whom were still lying in their beds and didn't want to talk.

Inspector Pockett had suggested that Jane leave the phone off the hook for the night and then, following her and Joe into the kitchen, accepted another mug of coffee, leaning against the wall to drink it.

"How is she?" Jane repeated, after she had refilled the kettle and sat down.

She looked at Joe, but it was Pockett that answered. "Perhaps more at peace than she has been for most of her life," he said.

He pulled out a chair from the table and sat opposite Jane. "It's all over now, isn't it? She doesn't have to worry any more."

Jane raised her head, watching him trying to pick a few dog's hairs off his trousers. "Doesn't have to worry? I'd say she must be worried sick."

"No, she's not. She's spent nearly all her life with secrets. Imagine the pressure of trying to maintain that, of trying to keep the children safe, trying to find excuses to keep Jeff around, when everyone wanted him gone, of watching her father, her mother...of trying to hold Chance together, although the foundations were rotten."

Jane imagined it. "That's what it's all about, isn't it?" she said. "Chance."

Pockett nodded. "From the beginning. From the very beginning, when Doris found out. Fear of losing her position, of losing Chance, made her protect her husband. Then Shirley grew up and made Chance her life and she needed to protect that life too."

He sipped his coffee and lit a cigarette. "She doesn't have to worry now. It's all out of her hands. So I think she's more at peace than ever before."

Jane's mind repeated the phrase that had become almost a punctuation mark, after every thought...I should have known.

"You couldn't have known," Pockett said, as though she had spoken the thought out loud.

She looked at him. Was he a mind reader as well, this nasty little man?

He looked back at her. "Don't blame yourself, Mrs Warren. You really couldn't have known, because you came in when the play was half way through. It's easy to follow the action if you're there from the beginning of Act One, and it's easy to understand it all if you're there just for the final scene, when all the players drop their pretences and the whole thing becomes clear. Coming in, in the middle, you are bound to get confused. It was easier for us, we came in at the end. But you...well, you couldn't have known. You only had half the script."

Now she was really staring at him. He was even using her way of thinking about it all. People following scripts…life like a play. He must be a mind reader!

He nodded at her as though to encourage her to think about what he had said.

She knew he was trying to get her to stop feeling so guilty, to get her back on her mental feet. He may be good at reading her, but he didn't understand. Not all of it, anyway. Not what Chance meant to her.

She thought about his words. "Eva was here from the beginning," she said, "so, did she know?"

"No, I don't think she did, for two reasons. One, her own life and experiences were too traumatic for her to see beyond herself. They still are, aren't they?"

He went on, not waiting for an answer. "And two, she isn't a perceptive person anyway. Although Shirley was her idol, she only observed her in relationship to herself. Unless what affected Shirley affected that relationship too, she wouldn't register it. Maybe that's just one reason with two sides really."

He leaned back to think about that.

Joe said, "The teachers at the primary school saw them as two outsiders. They were never close. Then, when Shirley was about seven, she changed, grew more confident, and Eva just tagged along. Eva didn't have a Jeff to protect her, nor a grandfather to believe in her. By the time she came to Chance, to learn to ride, to be with Shirley, Jeff had Paul under observation. So, in a way, Eva wasn't at Chance from the beginning either."

Pockett beamed at him. "Well done, Drinkwater, now if you can just keep this level of concentration going…"

Jane went off him again. Nasty little man.

He smiled at her and stood up, stubbing out his cigarette. "We'll be in touch, Mrs Warren. There will have to be further statements and interviews, of course. Meanwhile, don't worry about that lot." He waved at the window. "In a couple of days someone else will get their attention."

Joe stood up. He took Jane's hand and said he was sorry that all this had happened, asking her to call if she needed anything.

Pockett turned at the door. "Come along, Sergeant, time we were off. The wife and kids will be wondering what's happened to you."

He grinned at Joe's scowl and turned again to speak to Jane. "Don't be so hard on yourself, Mrs Warren," he said. He looked along the hall to where the sound of the others talking could be heard. "They need you. Open the curtains and start the play again."

* * * * *

She called the dogs away from the rabbit they had decided to chase and walked on to the top of the hill. There was a small overhang of mossy rock where she liked to sit to look down over the valley. You could see a fair way across the Halfpenny Hill on a good day.

The manor house, cottages and farms. The tree-lined brook. The hedges and fields. And Chance.

She looked hard at Chance. No, it wasn't her imagination, already it looked different. It was only a few weeks from when she'd found Jeff and it looked different. The cars and vans had gone from the lane, just as the inspector had said they would. The divorce of a film star...the resignation of a cabinet minister...three people found dead in a wood in Essex. Chance was yesterday's news. New words and new pictures were needed to fill the empty pages, the empty minds.

Most of the horses had gone too.

No one had said, "I don't want to be associated with a place where murder has happened." They just made excuses, invented reasons, or suddenly realised them.

She looked down at the yards, usually so full of activity, people, horses, children. Children were kept well away. Chance was talked

161

of in the same terms as the witch's house in a fairytale. A place to be frightened of, a place of nightmares. Although the details would not be public knowledge until the trial, gossip had ensured parents knew well enough to tell their children it was 'a bad place'.

Tradesmen muttered hellos and rushed off. No more long discussions on the merits of the weather, or the crops, or Mrs Johnson's new baby.

Most of the villagers seemed to have developed blinkered eyesight, not seeing anyone unless they were directly in front of them, then suddenly remembering something they had left in the house, or forgotten at the shop. Scurrying away. And, if there was nowhere to scurry, then embarrassed awkwardness, not knowing what to do or say. They all seemed to be busy, very busy, too busy to talk.

"…must excuse me, I've just got to…"

"…oh, dear, is that the time? I'll call you…"

"…can't stop, just on the way to…"

The gossips did the opposite, putting themselves in the way, consumed with curiosity, hidden under a veneer of concern.

"…so sorry, dear. And how is Doris? It must have been…"

"…have you seen Shirley? Is she saying anything, or just too distressed? Poor thing…"

"…I was saying to Mrs Philby, I'll just pop round to Chance to see if you would like me to sit with…"

Sooner or later they all appeared at the door, clutching cakes, or flowers, and trying to glean more shocking information to share with their friends.

Jane kept them out. She knew whose gifts came with the condition that they be admitted to all the family secrets. For there were other gifts too, left on the doorstep, or thrust into her hands by the embarrassed donor.

"Just made an extra pie. Thought it might save you time. See you then."

Those gifts came with no conditions, just an acknowledgement of community membership. They found it hard to speak their sympathy, so they cooked instead. It was nice. Jane understood how they felt. They didn't need to know that so many gifts ended up feeding the hens, or the pigs. There were not enough people left at Chance to consume them all.

Sally had gone. Back home to her father. When the phone stopped ringing non-stop, she had talked to him. He had called to see her and she thought he looked ill. There was much less work in the stables and she had asked Jane if she would mind if she left. She didn't want Jane to think she was running out, deserting her at a time of crisis. She would keep in touch, come back if they needed her, but right now she thought she ought to be with her dad.

She left tearfully, taking as long saying goodbye to the horses as she did to the people. Jane did not think she would be back.

Jay had gone too, but Jane was sure she would be back.

The long hours of hand-clutching, head-touching misery...the desperate clinging as the moment approached...the promises...

Yes, thought Jane, Jay will be back one day, as Mrs Harvey Bateman.

Richard had left to work on a farm east of the county. He had never really settled at Chance and had clearly been uncomfortable with the notoriety, the media attention. It wasn't a surprise when he left.

When Eva said she was going, that was a shock. She had emerged from her room to say she was leaving immediately.

She didn't look like Eva. She seemed small, soft, paralysed, like a rabbit in the headlights of a car.

"Where?" Jane asked.

Eva had shrugged and said maybe she would take a holiday.

"So, will you be back?"

Eva nodded, but didn't say yes.

Jane tried to talk to her about Shirley, about what had happened. She tried to get a reaction off her, even if only one of anger.

Nothing worked. Nothing got through. Eva had shut off like a machine. Jane was frightened for her.

Alice came under pressure from her family. They found her another job at a stables near to them. Nevertheless, Jane did not think Alice would have taken it, except it was a higher position, as manageress, and it was a riding stables, giving lessons to children, and Alice loved children.

Children never came to Chance any more.

Then Andrew and John decided to rent a cottage on the edge of the village. The better to further their romantic aspirations... or lecherous ones, they joked. They could come and go, with or without female company, as they wanted. They were happy and excited at the prospect.

So, one morning, Jane sat down to write out her lists and realised there wasn't any point any more. It was just her and Auntie Doris now. She didn't need lists. But habit dies hard and she always wrote at this time of the morning, so she started writing down the events of the previous day in a notebook.

It was the first entry in, what she came to call, her Day Book.

By the time Shirley came to trial, there were no clients' horses at Chance. All the 'New Money' people had taken theirs away months ago.

Barry and Pauline Jennings had split up and their mares had been sold. Jane had seen them at the trial. No more closeness. No more the epitome of a 'nice couple'. It was if, in some way, they blamed themselves for what had happened, or blamed each other. They kept apart in the hall outside the court. Barry standing with the men. Pauline sitting with the women. Jane watched as they deliberately ignored each other and she was sad. She spoke to them in turns. They didn't say, "Pauline shouldn't have encouraged Jeff," or "Barry shouldn't have lost his temper," but given half a chance, she thought they might. She didn't know if that was because they really blamed each

Chances of survival

other, or if it was just another piece of ammunition in what was an older and deeper feud. After the trial was over, she never saw either of them again. They disappeared from the village and the horse scene.

Sir Edmund and Lady Marguerite, like the other established owners, reluctantly moved their horses to other stables because there was no one left at Chance to look after them. They were unhappy at breaking their long-standing agreements. They didn't like change, but what else could they do? They all worried about Jane and spent long hours discussing the situation.

The two Misses took the third Miss away. They cried when they arrived with the horsebox, and they cried when they left. They declared that Pittypat looked heartbroken and they had decided not to enter her in any more shows because it might remind her of her happy days here.

Jane thought that Miss Pittypat would find that very acceptable and would consider growing old, fat and even lazier in their paddock by the chocolate-box cottage even happier days. Yet as she saw the horsebox leave, she cried too, for those happy days, the laughter and the fun. The three Misses had been a big part of Chance.

When Jane visited Shirley, she always answered Shirley's first and only question by saying the horses were fine.

She kept on saying that until after the trial, not wanting to load Shirley with more worry, not wanting her to know there weren't any horses left now, but as the weeks went on Jane realised that the Shirley she knew had disappeared. She asked, "How are the horses?" as though it was a part of a common greeting. "How are the horses?" instead of "How do you do?" She didn't really expect an answer, didn't really listen for one.

Jane found herself babbling on about anything and everything of no importance, like visiting a sick person in hospital.

Shirley just sat and smiled.

She still just sat and smiled when Jane told her, after the trial, that all the horses had gone and the ponies had been sold off to other stables.

She nodded and smiled when Jane said she had turned Shirley's own horse, Freddie, out to grass and was that all right?

She tried to tell Shirley about Andrew running the farm now, about Sue getting a part-time job in the village post office and promising to keep an eye on Freddie and help out if needed. She was engaged to Mark Finlay, who worked on the next farm, so when they married she would still be close at hand, which would be useful, wouldn't it?

Shirley nodded and smiled.

Pockett was right. Shirley was more at peace now than she had ever been, only it wasn't the sort of peace Jane had imagined. It was the sort that went with non-existence, with death. The person Jane loved for helping her restore her own identity didn't exist any more.

Shirley Hensham. RIP.

The trial revitalised the media interest for a couple of weeks, but she had experienced that before and it didn't worry her too much.

Seeing all the people who used to live and work at Chance had been something she had almost looked forward to. Certainly, giving evidence at a trial was not the best circumstances for a reunion, nevertheless she was still pleased at the prospect of seeing them all, talking of past times, laughing together. But there was no happy swapping of memories, no recalled laughter. They had moved on, physically and emotionally. Their days at Chance were an embarrassment now, something they would rather not remember with accuracy. They had answered or avoided the questions of curious friends. They had amplified, or diminished, their own roles in the affair. They had come to terms with their own failure of awareness at the time and moved on. It was too soon for swapping happy memories.

Looking at them now, Jane found it hard to reconcile herself to the fact that they were strangers. She had known them so well, had built her whole life around knowing them and caring for them. But these people were strangers. Like actors walking off the stage, they had dropped their assumed personalities and become unrecognisable in the crowd.

Jane sat at the kitchen table and thought she had wasted years of her life. She had fooled herself into believing that she knew Chance and all of its people. She had built a house of clay as a survival technique, then failed to cope when it fell down. She was just like Auntie Doris.

* * * * *

LOST CHANCE

He had arrived two weeks after the trial was over.

Shirley had been taken to a prison where she would receive psychiatric therapy for her condition. She would be there for a long time.

Within two days the telephone had stopped ringing in the hallway of Chance and the cars had gone from the lane. Chance was yesterday's news again. So, when someone knocked on the door, Jane wasn't ready for it to be anyone but a tradesman, or a villager.

The tall, thin man with greying hair looked vaguely familiar. "Hello, Jane," he said, in a deep voice.

Jane smiled, struggling to think of his name before she had to offend him by admitting she couldn't remember it, then, in the same second, knowing who he was.

"Terry," she breathed, the smile disappearing from her face, her arm going instinctively round the back of the door, as though she would shut it in his face. For, in the same seconds, she saw fragments of her life roll past her consciousness…Elizabeth… family exclusion…snapshots of Chance…

He was saying something else about hoping she didn't mind him coming to see her, but he had heard all the news and he was worried.

She was thinking all of this was his fault. If he hadn't killed Elizabeth, she wouldn't have been here now with her life in ruins again. She hated him for what he had done to her, to her baby, to her life. She wanted to kill him. Kill him!

Lost chance

Her breath became jagged as the anger made her face set and her eyes fill with tears of frustration and loss.

Elizabeth…Shirley…Chance…mixed up in her mind and, in front of her, was the catalyst of it all.

He only saw her crying and moved to put his arm around her, glad he had come, glad to give her comfort. He held her against his chest, as her raised fists beat on his shoulders and inarticulate keening sounds came from her constricted throat.

She cried for a long time. Cried for her life turned upside down again. Cried for each part of that life…each time she had to shut a door and walk away to create a new way of surviving. Cried for all the times she couldn't cry.

Long after the need to blame someone had stopped, long after she stopped recognising him as anything but a warm, comforting place to lean, she cried.

As she calmed down, the soothing sounds he had been making became words. He was saying it was all right…he understood…she had always been the one who had to be strong for everyone…he knew how bad these months must have been…it was all right to cry now…to get it all out of her system…to let go for a few minutes…it was all right…he understood.

Sense and control returned slowly, then suddenly. She jerked away from him. This was Terry! What was she doing?!

"Oh, God!" She looked at him with horror on her face. "Oh, God!"

She was wiping her face with her hands, trying to wipe the last few minutes away.

He looked embarrassed and she found herself saying, "I'm sorry…Oh, dear…I'm sorry. I don't know what…I'm sorry."

"It's okay," he smiled. "I must have called at a bad moment. I'm the one who should be sorry."

They looked at each other, unsure what to do now. His prepared speeches thrown off track by her unexpected reaction. Her balance thrown by the same reason.

"A bad moment," she repeated, smiling tentatively at him. "Yes, I suppose you could call it that," and she grimaced.

The humour of the idea of that dramatic performance being called 'a bad moment' struck both of them. Embarrassment became shy laughter, exaggerated by relief.

She recovered first. "Come in. Please, come in." She held the door wider. She hoped she hadn't said she was going to kill him out loud, but even the idea she might have seemed funny now.

They went into the kitchen and she made coffee. Both of them were still awkward. She moved too quickly, spoke too brightly. He laughed too much. Only after they were sitting at the kitchen table, with small silences for coffee drinking and lighting cigarettes, did they both calm down.

After one small silence, he said, "I think we ought to cancel all that and start again, so...Hello, Jane. How are you?"

They talked for a long time, through more coffee and a sandwich lunch and yet more coffee. He told her what he was doing now: regional manager of an electrical wholesale business. He was on holiday and staying at a local hotel for a few days. He had read so much in the papers, heard so much on the radio, about all that had gone on here. Then he bumped into her brother at a trade show and, when he asked how she was, her brother had said okay, as far as he knew.

Jane was not surprised at that response. Throughout all of this, she had received only one phone call from the family. That was from her sister, who seemed more interested in whether Jane would inherit Chance than in how Jane was coping.

Terry said it had shocked him to realise how alienated she was from her family...a family that, to him, had always seemed so close. That was when he began to think of getting in touch with her.

By dinnertime, they had talked all day.

They had talked of their families, their working lives, their mutual acquaintances, their ambitions. They had talked of everything that could be spoken of in a polite conversational way. Neither of them had mentioned Elizabeth.

When he had gone, promising to take her out to dinner tomorrow night as thanks for her hospitality this day, she sat in the kitchen and thought about it.

She had enjoyed his company, but she wondered if she would have equally enjoyed the company of anyone at this time. From seeing to the needs of many, she had only herself and Auntie Doris to consider, and she was used to lots of varied interaction.

It was true she had always been self-sufficient, not really needing to have loads of people around her, but it had been pleasant to talk to someone not connected with the events of the last months.

He had not been pushy.

He had not wanted all the details of what had gone on at Chance.

He had not turned on the charm, as though he was trying to resume their relationship, or court her again.

And he had not had a drink.

On the one side, she considered all these things in his favour.

On the other side, he was Terry and he had killed Elizabeth.

How do you trust someone like that? How do you forgive?

Throughout the day there had been this restraint, this carefulness. Everything had been kept on a pleasant level. There were things that were not said, but wasn't that how anyone acted with someone who was a new acquaintance? A stranger? Wasn't that normal? For their history was history. Both of them had changed. Logic said that both of them had known separate environments and experiences for many more years than the short time they had shared their lives. They were strangers now.

She was still embarrassed by her reaction when she saw him at the door. Using him as her whipping boy for all her misery. Yet, the fact that she could use him that way meant that she still saw him as someone to hate, to blame; or was that just what should have happened all those years ago? Then, she had walked away from him coldly. Dead inside, as her daughter was dead in reality. Perhaps if she had cried and hit out at him then, beaten him with her fists, she would have released some of the emotions that she had so carefully locked away. She would not have had the personality change they had called a 'breakdown'. She would not have come to Chance.

And there she was, back at the beginning again. So he had arrived at a time when she was vulnerable and she attacked him, as she should have done all those years ago. She thought she understood why it had happened now, but she wasn't sure it had cleaned enough away to ever be more than polite.

Doris put back the suit she had laid on the bed, shaking her head and clicking her tongue at her own stupidity.

No, not that one. That would never do.

She moved hangers along the rail again, stopping to consider one or two others, before taking out a beige suit and laying that on the bed. Then she opened a drawer full of scarves, draping one after the other around the neck of the suit. She settled on a white one with small, geometrical wedges of brown. Into the wardrobe again to find a brown handbag. Then the shoe rack for matching brown shoes. She laid the bag by the suit and put the shoes on the floor. Gloves. She needed gloves. In the glove drawer, considering two or three different pairs. The chosen ones she draped over the handbag. Jewellery was next. She sat in front of the mirror, holding earrings against her face, turning her wrist to see the effect of this or that bracelet, putting brooches on her shoulder above her chest.

Jane walked in with the tray. She didn't knock.

She put the cocoa and biscuits on the bedside table. "Your favourite biscuits, Auntie Doris. I'll just turn the bed back, shall I?"

Her aunt smiled agreement, but didn't say anything.

Jane hung the beige suit back in the wardrobe, put away the gloves, scarf, handbag and shoes in their respective places, then turned back the bed.

"Auntie Doris?" she urged, and Doris left her dressing table to climb into bed.

"Do you want to go to the bathroom first, or have your pills first?"

Doris held out her hand for the pills and drank some cocoa to swallow them down.

"Village Hall Committee meeting tomorrow," she said. "I might go."

"Right," said Jane. "See how you feel, eh?"

She wouldn't go, of course. She would spend all day choosing her clothes, laying them out, changing her mind. Jane would put them away at bedtime.

If the weather was good, Doris might go and pick some flowers in the garden "for the church." But Jane would put these in a vase somewhere, because her aunt would decide they were not what she really wanted. She would get some different ones tomorrow. "After all, I'm not on flower arranging rota until next week."

She had been like this since shortly after Shirley was arrested. At first, she had lain in her bed, not speaking, not sleeping. Jane had the doctor in and he prescribed some sort of antidepressants. Then she started to get up, move around, say short, bright, unimportant things. Jane had thought she was bouncing back, putting on her old survival technique again. But after a few weeks she realised that the old Auntie Doris wasn't going to survive this time.

She had spoken to the doctor. He had said she should give it time. Shock worked in different ways for different people. Maybe she would slowly regain her old self and, if she didn't, well Jane could cope, couldn't she? Auntie Doris wasn't a danger to herself or anyone else. She wasn't incontinent or aggressive. Jane could cope. And, as for Doris' indecision, he suggested

Jane take over the reins for a time, and he laughed at his joke: "…reins, stables…get it?"

Jane didn't bother to point out she had always taken the reins…that Auntie Doris led in name only. Yes, she agreed, she could cope.

Nothing had changed in the following months and Jane had visions of putting back the same, increasingly ragged, suits in twenty years' time.

She had not left Auntie Doris alone in the evenings since all this happened. The doctor had said she was no danger to herself, but Jane wasn't sure. It was true she didn't leave taps running, or clothes draped over open fires, but she wasn't completely in control either.

Jane wasn't sure. She wished she had not agreed to go out to dinner with Terry. She had thought about it all day. While she cleaned the house and walked the dogs and drank coffee, she thought about it.

What was she doing going out anyway? She never went out, wasn't interested in going out in the social sense. And with Terry? Terry?! She hated Terry. Hated what he had done. What was she thinking about to agree to it in the first place?

By afternoon, she wasn't sure if she was really concerned about Auntie Doris or using her as an excuse so she didn't have to go out with Terry. A bit of both, she decided.

She ought to phone the hotel and cancel the arrangement, so why didn't she?

She tried to analyse her feelings about it. She hated him for what he had done, but that was long ago. He had changed. She had changed. But she didn't want to like him, because her feelings for Elizabeth hadn't changed.

She looked at the phone every time she went into the hall, but she looked in her wardrobe too, checking the only three dresses she owned.

She didn't know what to do. One minute she determined to phone him and say she didn't want anything to do with him. The

Lost chance

next she thought she would rather say it to his face. Tell him just what she thought about what he had done. Tell him those feelings hadn't changed even after all these years. Watch his face and see what he had to say about all that. No more polite conversation, just…what about Elizabeth?

By late afternoon she had taken her three dresses out of the wardrobe…and looked up the number of the hotel in the phone book.

She was not used to indecision and it was beginning to interfere with her day. She must choose now.

She only wore a dress for Christmas dinner, or rare occasions like Great Uncle William's funeral, so they were all old, but ageless. Black, grey and blue, that was the choice. Of medium length and basic design. She would stick on a brooch or a necklace to liven them up, if necessary. Her shoes, too, were only worn when she wore a dress, so they always needed dusting before she put them on.

She dusted the black pair and put on the black dress.

When she looked at herself in the mirror she thought she looked odd. Her legs looked too thin and she felt awkward and overdressed.

What had happened to the girl who used to act and sing in sparkling, glamorous clothes? Who used to go to work in smart suits and high heels? Now, anything other than wellies and trousers looked odd. Did your body adjust to the style of your dress over the years, so that anything out of the norm was clearly just that? Certainly tourists in the market town nearby often dressed to look the rural part, but they didn't fool anyone because they looked wrong somehow. Just like she looked wrong now.

She picked up the paper on which she had written the hotel telephone number.

In the end, she didn't have to make the decision. Auntie Doris made it for her.

When she went to tell her that she might be going out for a couple of hours, Doris stopped sorting through her wardrobe and stood still.

"Auntie Doris? Is that okay? If I just go out for a time?"

Doris didn't answer, so Jane moved to stand at her side and look at her.

"Auntie Doris?"

"Not yet, Janie. Please, not yet." Doris stared at her clothes. "I'm not ready yet."

Jane rushed to reassure her. "No, Aunt, I mean I'm going out. You don't have to come."

"I know," Doris said, moving to her bed, "but not yet, please."

She climbed into her bed, pulling the covers up to her chin.

"I get frightened, Janie. I get frightened."

Jane looked at the head on the pillows. It was the same woman she had seen coming along the hall on the night Shirley was arrested. A little old woman that Jane only recognised by her suit.

"No, don't worry," she said. "I've decided not to go anyway," and she felt relieved that she really had decided at last. "I'll go and get a cup of tea, shall I? Or do you want a nap first?"

When she spoke to Terry on the phone, she was surprised that his voice sounded so nice. She had spent all day reasoning him back into his villain's role and his voice should have reflected that. Instead, he sounded nice.

He sympathised about Auntie Doris and suggested he could bring some wine and ask the hotel to pack up a couple of dishes that they could share in the kitchen. "An out-of-season, time and place picnic," he laughingly called it.

She agreed without thinking, until she put the phone down.

Ah well, at least she could put her dresses away and wear her trousers…though with her best top, maybe.

* * * * *

The first thing she saw, when she opened her eyes, were her trousers. Draped over the arm of a chair, with one leg dangling down near her face.

It took a few seconds before she registered that they were her trousers and that they were only twelve inches from her face. How could that be possible in her bedroom?

It wasn't her bedroom.

She froze, becoming very still, in case she disturbed the owner of the breathing she could feel on her naked shoulder.

She knew who it was. She wasn't sure how it happened.

* * * * *

Terry had arrived with wine and food. He said the hotel was fine about setting him up a 'picnic'.

They sat in the kitchen and ate. She had been a bit wary when he poured himself a glass of wine, but he only sipped it and seemed to have no need to drink faster, or more.

They talked about the farm, the weather, his hotel, his job. She explained again how Auntie Doris was not quite up to being alone yet.

They laughed and smiled. They enjoyed themselves politely.

She had meant to bring up the subject of their daughter straight away. Watch his reaction. Hear his words. Tell him how it had ruined her life. But the right moment didn't seem to arrive.

She had lit a fire in the lounge, before he came, and they moved in there with their drinks, sitting on armchairs each side of the fire. She brought the coffee pot in too, and he drank more coffee than wine.

Maybe it was the tension of wanting to say what she felt, or maybe it was the uncertainty of wondering whether it would be right to rake it all up again…whatever the reason she found herself on her third glass of wine before he finished his first.

In the end, it was another decision she didn't have to make. Terry started it all. He saw her looking at his glass.

"No, I don't drink much now. After what I did…after you left…I was drunk for a long time. My sister thought I was an alcoholic. I think everyone thought that, me included, when I thought at all. I lost my job. I lived in a bedsit. I didn't want to think, so I drank. One day I woke up in a hospital. I wasn't eating, you see. It was a unit where they take alcoholics, drug addicts, that sort of thing. I would see them bring in these people. They had nothing left, you know? No dignity. No humanity. Just wrecks, waiting to die. I thought I wasn't going to die that way – not slow degradation – so I decided to jump off the hospital roof." He laughed softly. "Sounds stupid now, doesn't it?"

He leaned back in his chair and sipped the coffee.

"Did you try to jump?"

"Oh, yes, I got to the roof. I stood there and thought this is for Elizabeth. A life for a life. She had every reason to live. I didn't deserve to. Then they found me."

"Who?" Jane's voice sounded harsh in her own ears. From wanting him to talk about Elizabeth, she was full of indignation when he dared mention her name. "Who found you?"

"A doctor and a male nurse. One of the porters had seen me go through the roof door." He smiled and sipped more coffee. "Funny thing, you know, they were talking to me and I wasn't really listening to them, but I must have said something about Elizabeth because it was the porter who called me a selfish bastard, if you'll excuse the language. He said if I wanted to prove my daughter meant nothing, go ahead and jump. I heard that all right. He said if I loved her, I'd make something out of this mess that she would be proud of, because it was made in her name. Otherwise I might as well go ahead and jump and prove she was worthless like her father."

He was looking into the fire and Jane could see his eyes, so full of sadness it made her instinctively reach forward to take his hand.

"No," he said, pulling his hand away. "No, please. You're very kind, but I'm not that strong-willed," and he smiled again.

She didn't feel rejected by his refusal to be comforted, just sorry.

"Go on," she said.

"Oh, there's not much more to tell. I left the hospital. Got a job. Managed to work my way up a bit, you know. Just started again really. And I do a bit of voluntary work. That sort of thing."

"What voluntary work?"

"I help out with an organisation that works with children who are terminally ill. Playhouse, it's called, if you've heard of it."

Jane shook her head.

"Well, I do some driving and fund-raising and that. It's not much."

"And that's for Elizabeth?" Jane asked, finding that saying her daughter's name was difficult. It made her feel awkward.

"Yes," he said, briefly.

In the silence that followed, Jane didn't hate him any more. She thought of what it must have been like for him. Not just Elizabeth's death, but from the beginning. His family. His upbringing. His marriage to her. Would he have married her, if she hadn't been pregnant?

His voice broke the silence and her thoughts. "Jane, I'm sorry," he said.

He didn't refuse her hand this time, nor the long embrace that followed.

She thought he cried.

She thought she cried too. She couldn't really remember that part, because suddenly it was urgency and passion. He was saying her name, over and over.

"Jane…Jane…" His hands were in her hair, pulling her head back, kissing her face, her mouth, her neck. Then they were on the thick, sheepskin rug in front of the fire, pulling off clothes… kissing…touching…and, "…Jane…Jane…"

It wasn't all over in a few minutes, as one might have expected. Yes, the first desperate thrusting was quickly brought to a shuddering, grasping halt as he arched his back, head raised upwards in a climax of sensation, but within seconds he was kissing her again, rolling to her side to touch and lick and probe.

* * * * *

Lying on the rug now, rethinking all that, she thought it was strange how she had reacted. She had always thought she wasn't a person with strong sexual needs. Over all the years, since they were separated, she had never considered taking any other man to provide her with fulfilment. She had never had that much of an urge. Sex hadn't figured that much in her life when she was married to him, let alone since. Maybe once a year or so she might think of sex, maybe even masturbate if the small ache became a nuisance, distracting her from more important things, but she never fantasised when she did it. It was just a purely functional procedure, over quickly and not thought about afterwards. Yet she had gone berserk with him last night! That was the only way she could think about it. Time and time again she had felt the waves of sensation as she clutched at him, begging him not to stop.

She screwed up her eyes, burying her head in her arm to shut out the embarrassment she felt now.

God, she must have been mad!

That moaning, sweating creature could not have been her. Unthinking, only feeling.

Out of control. She must have been mad!

She flung back the rug that was covering them and jumped to her feet, trying to shut out this image of herself. She grabbed her trousers and other clothes that were scattered around the floor, and rushed to the door.

Lost chance

She pretended not to hear him say, "What's the matter?" She just had to get out of there...out of this mess.

She locked the bathroom door and didn't look in the mirror as she ran a shallow bath. She lay on her back in the water, then turned onto her stomach. She put her head under the water and squeezed the water out of her hair as she stood up to get out. The whole bath had taken no longer than five minutes.

She put on the clothes that she had dropped into the washing basket yesterday. She thought only about the kitchen range and the dogs.

By the time she appeared in the kitchen she was in control again.

He said, "Okay to use the bathroom?" and she answered, "Yes," as she shut the tack room door and went out with the dogs.

When she got back from feeding the hens and ducks, he was standing at the kitchen window, watching the rain.

She said, "Do you want coffee?" and clumped past him to put the early eggs in the larder.

He turned to watch her, waiting for her to come back before he answered, "Yes, please, if you're having one."

"Oh, I'm on my second," she said, turning to face him, knowing that she looked nothing like the person who answered the door to him last night, and glad that she didn't.

Farm coat, full of small tears and paint stains and worse, Wellingtons, no make-up, wet hair, flat on her head. She looked at him defiantly. She wanted to say, "See, this is me. Not that other person. Not that dressed-up, tarty person. This is me. I milk cows and muck out horses. I pluck chickens and clean loos. I don't wear glamorous, smart clothes and sing songs for the punters. That person you knew is dead. This is me! Go back to your city and leave me alone. I don't belong in your world. With you. Leave me alone."

He moved towards her. She bent to take the ashcan out of the range bottom, standing up with the flat tray of hot ash held out in front of her. "Just got to empty the ashes," she smiled and walked out to the yard. She felt annoyed that he was in her way.

"Now, your coffee," she said, after she put the tray back.

He was still standing, watching her. "What's wrong, Jane?"

"Nothing." She shook her head vigorously and smiled.

She made his coffee while he watched.

"Sit down with me," he said, taking his coffee to the table.

She was making another coffee. "I've got to see to Auntie Doris now."

"Please." He took her arm as she passed. "Please."

She sat down and reached for a cigarette. He lit it for her. She was glad her hands were not shaking.

"I'm sorry about last night, if that's what the trouble is," he said. "I'm not sorry it happened, but I'm sorry if it upset you."

She saw herself, head thrown back, mouth open, the sinews of her neck standing out, as she moaned with the intensity of the feeling. She tried to blank out the image. If he said he thought she had enjoyed it, she would set the dogs on him.

"No, I'm okay." She wanted him to go away. "Look, last night was a mistake. I think I'm not used to that much wine." She got up. "I really do have to see to Auntie Doris now."

Her mind had leapt on the excuse her mouth had just given her. Of course! It was the wine! She should have realised that before. Now it made sense.

"I'll wait," he said.

Go away, she thought.

"Then I have to check other things too...the farm...the work...and..." She struggled to think of things she had to do, only there weren't any any more. "...things like that," she finished, lamely.

"If you don't mind, I'll wait. Can't we just talk for a few moments?"

She sat down again. Better to get it over with. Get him out of the house. Out of her life.

"I'm sorry," he said. "I wouldn't have let that happen if I had realised. You didn't seem to be drunk at all. Not even merry, you know?"

Because I wasn't, she thought, with a sinking feeling as the excuse disintegrated.

"Well, I was," she said, "and I'm sorry, too, if you got all the wrong messages from that."

He looked at his coffee. She got up to get hers from the end of the range.

He stared at her as she sat back down as if trying to judge her words.

"I expect it was another of those bad moments," he smiled.

She smiled back, saying lightly, "Yes, we do seem to get a lot of those."

Their smiles faded as their words took on a deeper meaning than she had intended.

He stood up. "I'd better be going. I'm back at work tomorrow."

"Yes, of course." She busied herself, making sure all the 'picnic' things were repacked. "This was very nice, wasn't it?" She indicated the basket.

"Yes, very good. That salmon especially, I thought."

She nodded agreement.

"Well, I think I have everything," he went on, checking around the kitchen.

They were back on their friendly, polite terms.

"Phone me sometime, won't you?" she said.

He took her hand and said he would, of course. He thanked her for her hospitality and she waved at him as he disappeared around the corner to his car. She thought he was probably as glad to get out of there, as she was to see him go. Certainly it was one of the fastest exits she had ever seen. Perhaps that was because they were both trying so hard to make it so…to get over it. She shut the door and went back to the kitchen.

She kept herself busy all day.

She did some of the cleaning that she didn't bother with usually, now the house was empty. Polishing furniture, cleaning windows in empty rooms.

She talked brightly to Auntie Doris.

She had a long discussion with Andrew about the state of the winter wheat.

She threw those trousers and her best top on the bonfire.

Every day she wrote in her Day Book. She had intended to write just what had happened each day. Short notes on the weather and any particular event of national or county importance. Something she could look back on later and say, Oh yes, that was the year of the big storm…or the Queen's celebrations… or whatever.

It had started that way, but soon she was writing down her thoughts on the storm, or the celebrations. Then it became her thoughts on most everything and, soon after that, it became a lifeline, the only place where she could be herself, where writing out her fears, or anger, helped to sort them into action, or acceptance. From a couple of lines a day, to sometimes four or five pages.

Her Day Book became several Day Books, as time passed. She dated them on the outside and stored them in an old box on the top of her wardrobe. She made a vow to herself that she would burn the lot when she felt that she was getting old. They were not for anyone else to read.

She wrote about Terry in her Day Book. Sitting at the kitchen table, words scrawling fast onto the paper, oblivious to all other sounds and needs, as she exorcised the incident from her mind. Only after that was done could she really close the door and walk away.

The doctor called to see Auntie Doris and cheerfully announced he thought she looked very well. He gave Jane more tablets and told her to keep up the good work.

Sally phoned to ask how things were going. Jane lied that they were fine.

Alice phoned, happy in her new job. She said she would come and see Jane as soon as possible. Jane said she would look forward to that.

The Batemans called at Chance regularly to see if she needed anything. Harvey was phoning Jay every chance he got and they were writing long letters.

Sir Edmund and Lady Marguerite called regularly too. "Just checking everything's okay," they said.

Andrew and John called in, mainly to tell her about any particular project or problem to do with the farm.

Perhaps a whole half hour, every third day, was taken up with such visitors or phone calls.

She giggled as she recorded this 'hectic social life' in her Day Book.

The dogs did well out of this change of lifestyle. Jane wasn't someone who could drift through a day. She had to have routines, or projects. They gave her a purpose, stopped her thinking too much, and she had always believed that having too much time to think was the cause of many people's problems.

Walking, training, playing with the dogs, was something they – and she – enjoyed. With less people the dogs got more time. Coming down the back lane with them, throwing sticks, smiling at their antics, she felt happy. She stood and looked across the fields, back to the house. It was one of those moments when she appreciated how lucky she was to live in such a beautiful setting.

That was when she noticed the garden wasn't a garden any more. All those rows and patches of flowers and vegetables had disappeared. She now had a fenced-in patch of tall weeds. As she walked round the buildings back to the house, she really looked at the yards, the stables, the sheds. There were weeds growing out of every available crack in the concrete. She closed her eyes to recall when the yards were full of activity, swept clean twice a day, not even a wisp of straw allowed to remain, let alone a clump of nettles. Now green patches dotted the ground and crept up to obscure the lines of walls and buildings. She ought to try and pull them up before Chance disappeared, like the castle of Sleeping Beauty, hidden under a mass of greenery. She didn't hold out much hope of a prince arriving to do a bit of forest hacking, so she ought to do it herself. It would give her another project. She quite looked forward to starting.

The Day Book entry for Thursday the 16th had only three words: I am pregnant.

* * * * *

Jane had started work to weed the yards. She spent part of every day, when the weather allowed, trying to pull up nettles, grub out daisies and excavate docks.

It was quite satisfying to stand back and see the cleared area afterwards. She thought she might try her hand at a bit of real gardening later. She liked being outside, liked the idea of growing things. You had a lot of time to think when you were pulling up weeds, but it was painless thinking, practical thinking: what to get for dinner…what yard to start next. It was as if the need for physical exertion didn't leave time for mental stress.

She was on her knees trying to get a dandelion from a crevice in the middle of the yard, and thinking she must check her weekly shopping list again when she got back to the house. There was something she had forgotten, she was sure. She kept a notebook of things that were needed, or that were getting low, and checked that each time she wrote out her shopping list. She did not write staple items in this notebook, such as coffee, tea or bread, as she automatically wrote those on her shopping list if they were needed; but things such as toothpaste or light bulbs, she jotted down.

This morning she was sure she had forgotten to write something on her list. It nagged in her mind, as any failure in her systems did, so she was going over the most likely things in her head while her hands worried at the dandelion.

Toilet rolls…no…toothpaste…sanitary towels…soap…

And she stopped.

When did she last buy sanitary towels? Months ago.

Her hands became still and she sat back on her heels. There was a sudden flutter of fear inside her. No! That wasn't possible! It was the shock of all that had happened, or perhaps she was in an early change. She must have had a period last month and she had forgotten, that's all. She made a decision to write it down from now on. Sally always used to write down her dates, to be sure she had some protection with her if she started when she was going out somewhere. The other girls did too. Jane thought she really must start doing that. But, even as she thought it, she remembered being sick a couple of months back…she remembered waking in the night with aching breasts and thinking she must have been dreaming about that time with Terry…she remembered she was annoyed with herself for thinking of him, even subconsciously.

That time with Terry.

She knew she was pregnant.

* * * * *

She woke up and smelt the vomit. For a few moments she couldn't remember what had happened. Then she did. She dragged herself up on her elbows, opening her legs to stare down at the bed in between. Nothing.

Nothing.

The dogs were whining downstairs, scratching at the kitchen door, and her head felt as if it was swollen to three times its size.

She looked at the clock. Seven.

She looked around the room. She had been sick everywhere. The bed. The wall. The floor. The whole place stank of it.

The gin bottle was still on her bedside cabinet, lid off, empty. She hated the taste of gin, but had desperately hoped it would work. People said it did.

She dragged herself off the bed, through the mess, and staggered to the bathroom. She had to do the next part. It had to work.

She ran the bath so hot her fingers went red instantly she put them in. She stood on one leg and put in a foot, snatching it out as the steaming water burnt her. Her hand went to the cold tap, but she stopped herself. No, she had to do this.

She dabbed her foot in again and again, until the heat was tolerable. Then she lowered the foot further, inch by painful inch.

It took a very long time before she was lying in the bath. Then she waited, willing her body to eject its unwanted load, willing the water to turn red.

Nothing happened.

She let out some of the water, adding more hot, until she was burning again.

She did that several times.

Nothing.

She dried her bright red legs, cursing under her breath. She cursed herself and every old wife whose tale she had tried. Now what could she do?

She had decided by the evening that she couldn't stay here. She would go to one of those homes for unmarried mothers. She would have the baby adopted and then try to get a job and a bedsit. She could see herself ending her days in some dingy room in the middle of town. Unknown. Dead. And who cared?

She berated herself for her self-pity. She had brought the whole situation on herself, hadn't she? She knew Terry. God, she of all people knew Terry! Knew how clever he was, how glib, how manipulative, how much a liar. Yet she had learned nothing from the experience. So stupid that as soon as he appeared, she repeated the whole process just like before.

Had he got some sort of antenna that picked up her moments of greatest vulnerability? Or her greatest fertility? Or both?

She had done it again. She had been charmed by him…felt sorry for him…leaned on him…lay with him. She had learned nothing.

Well, he wasn't going to know about this, on that she was determined. Here was where the repetition stopped. Tomorrow she would find a place to go. She would arrange for Auntie Doris to be looked after. She would leave Chance.

Terry had phoned several times since that evening. She was glad now that she had maintained her distant attitude. It was clearly having the desired effect, for his calls were becoming more infrequent.

What she did not want was for Terry to find out where she had gone when she left.

The only way she could be sure of that was to invent a cover story to tell Auntie Doris, the Batemans and Andrew. That exercised her mind all through the next few days.

She had found the address of an unmarried mothers' home in a big city to the north. She had made enquiries at the Social Services department of the council and fended off any personal questions by pretending it was for a friend.

She checked how much money she had and knew it wasn't enough to live on for very long.

She made plans on what she should take and began to throw away what she could not carry.

The excuse was the problem. The story she must tell the others.

And the dogs. What to do with the dogs?

She was sitting on the kitchen floor with the dogs when the tack room door opened.

Eva was in the kitchen and staring down at her before Jane had time to get to her feet.

"…so there wasn't anywhere else to go," Eva finished.

Jane had made her tea and eggs and bacon and listened to Eva's story of trying to settle in the town. She had taken a factory job when her money ran out, but she couldn't stand the place, or some people, or the town. She wanted to come back and she wanted to see Shirley.

Jane thought she looked thin and sad, rather than surly, which was the way she usually thought of Eva.

Eva thought Jane looked desperate, which wasn't the way she usually thought of Jane.

Jane had told her how she thought Shirley seemed so different when she visited her, told her about Auntie Doris, about Andrew and John. She brought her up to date on what news she had of Sally, Alice, Jay and the Batemans.

The more they talked the more they realised that the other had changed dramatically.

Jane listened to Eva talk…actually talk. Not short, begrudged replies to questions, but interest in the conversation. She filled the silent gaps with descriptions of her own experiences in the town. She asked questions to stimulate a response off Jane. She seemed older. Jane thought she had been wrong to worry how Eva would survive without Shirley. But then she was often wrong, wasn't she?

Eva was shocked by the change in Jane. That something was badly wrong was obvious. Where had the humour gone? The control? Eva found herself having to carry the conversation, as Jane seemed to slip into daydreaming. Yet this was the person who always had time to listen to everyone, who was the one you could rely on to lead the way or lean against if you got lost. She seemed really lost now, and only perked up when Eva asked if it was okay for her to stay here. Chance was her real home and, if Jane didn't mind, she wanted to come back.

Jane didn't mind.

"Can you take that up to Auntie Doris?" Jane gave the tray to Eva.

Lost chance

She knew what she was doing was devious, but she closed her mind to that aspect of it. Eva's arrival had given her the answer to her main problems: what to do about Auntie Doris and the dogs. This grown-up, more amenable Eva could take her place. After all, she reasoned, Eva had been at Chance longer than she had. She had as much right to be here as Jane, and she wanted to be here. Jane wanted to go. So, from the first day of Eva's arrival, she had deliberately promoted the relationship between Auntie Doris and Eva. She had made sure everyone knew about Eva 'coming home'. She got Eva to take, or give, messages to Andrew regarding the farm, using the excuse of being a bit 'off colour' herself, or being too busy with something else to see him. She successfully encouraged Eva to take over her role at Chance and, though people were wary at first, they soon accepted this new, pleasant Eva.

Everyone was pleased that Jane had company now. It meant that they didn't have to worry about her too much. The more thoughtful of them wondered what had brought about this change in Eva. They didn't see much of Jane, so they didn't notice the change in her.

* * * * *

When Eva had left Chance, she intended to commit suicide. She planned to jump off the bridge in the nearby town. There wasn't any point in life when her life was locked in with Shirley's, for Shirley's life was over.

She had taken a room in a boarding house. A bed and a wardrobe, shared bathroom, breakfast and evening meal. It was the first boarding house she saw with a 'Vacancies' sign.

She wasn't interested in all the information the landlady reeled off about house rules and meal times. She wasn't interested in eating anyway.

As soon as the landlady shut the door, Eva sat on the bed and found her writing paper and biro from a side pocket in her haversack. She wanted to write to Shirley one last time. She wanted to say all those things she had failed to say over the years...how Shirley had changed her life, kept her from worse harm...how she loved her and wanted to thank her...how she understood what Shirley had gone through when she was young because she had been abused too. It seemed important that Shirley should understand all these things.

When it grew light, behind the faded curtains, Eva was still alive and still sitting on the bed with her writing pad.

There wasn't anything written on it.

Some time during the night, as she sought for words to say, the panic that had engulfed her since Shirley was arrested changed to guilt. If she loved Shirley so much, how come she never realised what was going on? Why didn't Shirley talk to her about it?

She stood outside herself and saw pictures of Chance. She saw herself as others saw her.

She saw Shirley laughing with Jane. Shirley never laughed with her.

She saw her smiling at Alice and Jay, talking with the Misses, making fun of Andrew and John...and, at the edge of these pictures was this scowling, lurking figure...the jealous child who resented anyone taking their mother's time and attention. She saw herself.

The landlady knocked the door when she didn't appear for breakfast. She made it clear that breakfast was now over and she could not supply food out of set times.

She looked at Eva's unpacked bags and worried that she might have one of those queer people on her hands.

Eva made the excuse that she was so tired she had fallen asleep straight away.

The landlady raised her eyebrows and sniffed; then she left, re-iterating the time of the evening meal in a firm, accusatory tone.

She would certainly have to keep an eye on this one.

Eva sat in a café drinking tea.

She walked around the town.

She sat on a bench in the park.

She went to the bridge over the river and looked down.

She walked away from the river and bought herself fish and chips.

Everything she did, what she saw, what she tasted, seemed new. It was as if she had never done any of these things before.

She watched people hurrying by. She watched the birds in the trees, the ducks on the water. She looked in shop windows and thought things were nice, or not.

She stepped out of Shirley's shadow and walked on her own.

Over the next few weeks she changed slowly. It was not a sudden, miraculous personality swing, but she learned to relate to people in a more effective way.

She had to learn to smile to get a job. She had to learn to listen to understand her duties. She had to learn to share to be accepted in the bedsit community. She had to learn to say 'please', 'thank you' and 'sorry' without resentment, without feeling she was losing face.

She grew up.

Now she wanted to see Shirley to support her, to be there for her, and she wanted to be back at Chance, because it was her home.

The town had been an excellent school, but she was a country girl. She needed space.

It was a measure of her success that she left with so many promises to keep in touch, her writing pad full of addresses and phone numbers.

* * * * *

Jane told Eva she was thinking of leaving, rushing on before Eva's shocked expression could find voice, to say that she hadn't been away from Chance in years. She needed a break; felt that a long holiday, perhaps touring around, may do her good. She wondered if Eva wouldn't mind holding the fort for a while?

Eva said she didn't mind, but how long was Jane thinking of going away? And where?

Jane said she hadn't really planned that. Just touring, you know? Perhaps six months or so. She could phone Eva from wherever she was.

Eva said fine, okay…but it wasn't okay, she knew that. Something was wrong.

* * * * *

You could see it now. Jane looked at herself sideways in the mirror. It was a good thing that she would be gone in a couple of days, because you could see it. Worse than that, she could feel it too.

It was while she was on the phone to Terry that she realised at first. Ironical that, she thought. He was saying that he was coming down to see her and she had told him she was going on holiday, so there was no point. Then it moved. She had felt the fluttering before, but had never stopped to think about it. This was a stronger movement and she realised what it was.

As she stared at herself in the mirror, she heard feet running across the landing. The dogs raised their heads. Eva burst through the door and Jane drew her blouse over her figure.

Eva's voice was urgent. "Auntie Doris! Come on, quick, something's wrong with Auntie Doris!"

* * * * *

The doctor said she was doing fine. Jane thought she would have put a bet on him saying that.

Doris lay on the bed, holding Jane's hand, and smiled at him.

Eva saw him out.

To be fair to the doctor, Auntie Doris did look a bit better, more at ease anyway.

Jane had spent a few frantic days living at the hospital whilst her aunt was in Intensive Care, then another couple of weeks visiting regularly until she was well enough to come home. Now she needed complete bed rest for a few weeks, they said, then if all went well, gentle exercise.

"Cup of tea?" Jane asked.

"In a minute, love." Doris smiled at her, still holding her hand. "There's something I want to show you. Look in the drawer." She pointed to her bedside cabinet.

Jane opened the drawer. There was a long, brown envelope at the top.

"Yes, that's it," Doris nodded as Jane took it out. "Read it."

Jane took the papers from the envelope. She knew what it was, but she wasn't ready for what it said.

"I've left it all to you, Janie. Chance. You've put more work into here than anyone else and I don't think anyone would quarrel with it being yours by right. When I die, it would be my sister's, but she's not interested. She has her own life in Australia. So it's yours."

Jane knew she was making a will. She had asked to see a solicitor when she came out of hospital. Eva and Jane had tried to say it could wait, but she had shown a rare determination.

"Don't leave, Janie," she said, taking Jane's hand again. "Please. Eva told me you were going on a long holiday. Please delay it for a few weeks. I feel more comfortable when you are here."

She looked at Jane, pleading with her eyes and a small shake of her hand. Then she said, brightly, "I might even get up tomorrow. Do you think I should wear my blue suit, the one with the velvet collar? Or I could try that dark green..." She paused and begged again. "Don't leave, Janie."

*

Eva had taken the call while Jane was out with the dogs. She had told Terry that Jane hadn't gone on holiday yet, due to her aunt's heart attack, and Terry said he was coming down that day.

Jane rushed into the hall to phone him back, tell him she was ill, or had to go out. She cursed as she tried to find his phone number. He had given it to her on the back of a business card and she had thrown it into the telephone desk drawer.

When she found it at last, there was no answer to her persistent ringing.

Eva stood watching this frantic response to her message. She was standing in the hall as Jane put the phone down again and let out a sigh of defeat. "Is he the father?" she asked.

Jane's head shot up to look at her. Then she realised what she meant and relaxed.

"Yes, he was Elizabeth's father."

"I mean is he the father of the child you're carrying now?"

Jane started to deny it, shaking her head.

"It's pretty obvious," Eva said. "Sorry, Jane, but it is."

"Oh, God." Jane closed her eyes in despair. "What am I going to do, Eva?"

"You can't tell him?"

"No."

"Why not?"

"I don't want to." Then, in the silence, "I don't like him."

Eva's eyes widened. "He didn't rape you, did he?"

Jane saw herself again, lying on the sheepskin rug with Terry. "No! No, he came to visit…I don't know…It was just madness. I think I was just vulnerable at the time, you know? Feeling lonely or something. He always seemed to pick his moments," she added, bitterly.

"What are you going to do?"

Jane exploded with anger and frustration. "How the hell do I know?! I was going to go away and have it adopted, but then Auntie Doris got ill and…well…I don't know. I don't know!"

She got up and walked into the kitchen. She made coffee, slamming the kettle back on the range, spilling coffee grains all over the table.

Eva followed her in. Jane stopped and looked at her. "Oh, God, Eva, what am I going to do?"

"There's no chance you could make a go of it with him?"

"No. He makes out he's changed. Maybe he has, I don't know, but he always was a con merchant and, anyway, I can't forget Elizabeth. I don't want another baby by him. I must have been mad."

"And you don't want him to know? Well, if you wear a loose top, he won't see it."

"You saw it!" Jane spat the words out.

"Yes, but I'm with you all day. It's different. If you sit down, he won't notice. When is it due?"

Jane shrugged her shoulders.

"Haven't you been to the doctors?"

"No."

"Well, you can work it out when you…you know. Work it out," Eva urged.

"I'm not keeping it, so it doesn't matter."

They sat and stared into space, Eva thinking hard, Jane trying not to think at all.

"I can't stay here with it, Eva, you know that. I don't want Terry's baby and Chance has taken enough away."

"What do you mean, 'Chance has taken enough'?"

"Child molesters. Murderers. We don't exactly qualify as a nice place to be any more, do we?"

"Who cares?" Eva said. "Since when do we have to care what the neighbours think? Oh, come on, Jane, that's rubbish."

"We may not care," Jane nodded down at her stomach, "but that one might. Can you imagine growing up with the reputation of this place around your neck?"

"But by the time it's grown up people will have forgotten, won't they?"

Jane looked at her.

Eva's hands, that had been held out to emphasise the point, dropped down. "No, they won't," she answered herself. "You're right. They still date things from events in the First World War here. You're right."

"And by the time the story has been round a few times this will be Jeff's baby, or Uncle Paul's. You know what they're like. What makes it worse, if they do bother to work out the dates right, so they know it can't be Jeff's or Paul's, the witch-hunt will start. Everyone knows I haven't left here, so whose baby is it? I don't want them to know it's Terry's, because, sooner or later, that will get back to him and I don't want him having a lever to apply some emotional blackmail. Anyway, whoever they decide is the father, it will be a Hensham baby, won't it? And what else would you expect from one of those Henshams?"

She pulled a face, parodying the gossips of the village.

After a few minutes of silent coffee drinking, she added, "I want to go away, Eva, but Auntie Doris won't let me."

"She can't stop you," Eva pointed out.

"No, I know she can't really, but…well, she gets upset… and…"

"You've always been too soft, Janie. Underneath all that efficiency and strong exterior, you're too soft."

"Do you know she's leaving me Chance in her will?"

Eva nodded. "Quite right, too," she said. "What were you saying about emotional blackmail before?"

They smiled at each other. Eva got up and put her arms around Jane. "Go and put on a loose top. Let me do the talking. We'll get rid of him and then we'll have a serious think."

Eva didn't like him either. She couldn't quite put her finger on the reason, but it was more than just the fact that she was Jane's friend. Something to do with him being too glib, too smarmy, she thought. He gave an impression of quiet bravery in the way he had overcome his problems, atoned for his faults. Trouble

Lost chance

was, he did it too well...mentions of his charity work...small silences after talking about some family member...sad eyes when they touched on some incident in their mutual past. Poor Terry, you thought. Poor Terry.

Jane sat down and Eva waited on them with coffee and cakes. She didn't leave them alone and Terry's quick glances at her every time she got up to pour another cup, or fetch a cake, were obvious. He wanted her gone.

She also noticed his deep, meaningful looks at Jane, which Jane carefully avoided noticing.

He suggested Jane have a "little break" and come out to dinner with him.

She said she had to stay in for a few weeks because of Auntie Doris.

He looked at Eva and she said, "Auntie Doris relies on Jane, you know," before he could ask her to take over for the evening.

He stayed for two hours and Eva saw him out, with Jane walking behind her.

She stood behind Eva to wave him off at the door too.

He said he would phone and come again soon, as he realised Jane couldn't get away at the moment. He sent his regards to Auntie Doris.

"Well, that's the end of Part One," Eva said, as she shut the door. "Now let's work on Part Two."

"You've got to see the doctor."

"No. Even if he keeps his mouth shut, Mrs Parkes won't and she will have all the details to put on my file, you know that."

Mrs Parkes was the head receptionist for the local doctor and an unfailing source of information on every patient. The village knew the results of Miss Benson's blood test before Miss Benson did; not that they hadn't 'guessed it all along', and everyone started extra knitting for Mrs Allen before the doctor held her hand and confirmed it was twins again.

"Go to the clinic in the town then," Eva suggested, admitting that the local doctor was out if they wanted to keep it a secret. "It's moving now, isn't it? Soon even loose tops won't hide the fact."

"Whichever way you look at it, Eva, I have to get away. What about when it's born? I'll have to leave then, won't I? Get somewhere where they'll let me stay for a couple of weeks and then take the baby…"

When Jane said 'the baby', she hesitated, "…for adoption," she finished the sentence. She always thought of it as 'it'. Saying 'the baby' made it seem different, gave it identity. She put her hand on her stomach.

"What are you thinking?" Eva asked, watching her.

"I don't know." Jane looked down at herself. "I never thought of it as a baby really. I always…" She stopped again.

"It may not be so easy to give up?" Eva realised what was happening.

Jane shook her head firmly. "No, it's Terry's. I want nothing to do with Terry."

"Elizabeth was Terry's too," Eva pointed out. "You had better think about it, Jane, before we make any more plans."

Over the next two days they tended Auntie Doris, talked to Andrew and answered the phone to Terry twice. In between they talked about what to do. Both were aware that each day made the problem more urgent. Eva was also aware that Jane's attitude was changing.

At the end of the second day, they decided.

"She's bound to be better in a couple of months, or she'll be…you know…so either way, you can take a couple of weeks away."

Jane nodded. The Auntie Doris problem wasn't so bad when you stopped panicking and realised that it wasn't tomorrow, or the end of the week, that was under discussion. They had some time yet before the birth.

"She's a bit brighter, don't you think?" Jane asked, seeking reassurance that in thinking of the alternative they were not being callous.

"Yes, I suppose so." Eva didn't sound reassuring.

Jane had tried to talk to the doctor, but never got past his "doing very well" line.

Eva had taken over the doctor's visits now, just in case he noticed Jane's increasing girth. She, too, had no luck in getting more information out of him.

They had agreed that Jane should go to the maternity clinic in the town. They had agreed that she should use Eva's name and old address in the bedsit area. That way there wouldn't be any note from the clinic to the doctor telling him – and, more importantly, Mrs Parkes – that one of his patients was pregnant. Jane could have her check-ups and give birth in their unit, then tell Social Services at the clinic that she wanted the baby adopted.

There was a steady stream of young women in the town without backgrounds or permanent addresses or apparent family, who had 'got into trouble'. The clinic staff were used to the situation, used to them arriving to leave their baby, then disappearing again. They might think Jane was a bit old to have got herself in this mess, but they wouldn't question it too closely.

As for the months preceding the time, Jane and Eva agreed that it was lucky that winter was coming. Farm coats were always several sizes too large, the better to accommodate thick sweaters underneath and still allow free movement for the wearer. Figures trudging around in boots and large shapeless jackets were the norm. What Jane had to do was the reverse of what they had done when Terry arrived. If she could not let Eva take over the task, she had to see people standing up, outside.

It was all settled. They knew what they had to do. Eva answered all the phone calls, fending off Terry with excuses that Jane was out, or had not been well, or they were very busy with the Christmas lambing. Jane spoke to him sometimes, just so that he didn't get suspicious.

Everything was going to plan. Eva took over nearly all Jane's work. She visited Shirley and was dismayed at how Jane was right. Her Shirley wasn't there any more.

Eva looked after Auntie Doris too, with Jane sticking her head round the door for a quick chat every now and then.

During the last days of pregnancy, Jane "got the flu" and wasn't in evidence to anyone.

The doctor said there was a lot of it about.

When the contractions started, it was two o'clock in the morning. They agreed that even that was lucky, for no one noticed the taxi arriving from the town.

They had phoned the moment they had timed three contractions, ensuring Jane had lots of time to get there without any drama on the way. Eva put Jane's bags in the car and told her not to worry. She would not be phoning the clinic to see how Jane was as that would ruin Jane's 'no family, no background' cover.

Auntie Doris was used to Jane's absence now, as the doctor had said she had best keep away. This 'flu' was very catching.

Everything had gone to plan.

It was six days later, on Christmas Eve, at lunchtime, when the tack room door opened and Jane walked in.

"Sorry," she said and looked down at the baby in her arms.

Eva wasn't really that surprised. She had sensed Jane was changing her attitude for some time. She had thought, when push came to shove – a quite appropriate phrase to use in the circumstances – Jane would not find it that easy to give the baby away. So when Jane appeared in the kitchen, she just said, "Boy or girl?"

* * * * *

The birth hadn't been particularly easy, but it wasn't the terrifying experience that Jane remembered so vividly from when

Elizabeth was born. She had done it before. She knew what to expect.

They talked of her being "an elderly mother," which she found amusing, and they carefully monitored her and the baby throughout the delivery.

"It's a girl," they said and put it in her arms.

She wasn't going to look at it, but they were beaming at her, expecting her to feel proud and happy. So she looked and pretended.

That was it really.

After that, the plan went out of the window. Logic battled against instinct and instinct won. It wasn't much of a fight.

When the health visitor came, Jane said she hadn't picked a name yet, so the visitor wrote Baby Bartlett on her notes. Jane nearly said, "No, Baby Warren," but stopped herself in time. The health visitor said she would be coming to see Jane and her baby at the bedsit address in six weeks' time.

(She was not surprised when Jane wasn't there, nor when she was told Eva had left some time ago. It happened a lot in this area of the town. She just noted it, checked it off her list and went off to the next new mother.)

* * * * *

"We've got to make another plan, haven't we?" Eva said, smiling at Jane. "Don't worry, we'll work something out."

Jane just kept saying, "Sorry."

Thirty minutes after Jane walked in, the tack room door opened again. Terry said, "Surprise! Couldn't not come and wish you all a happy Christmas…" before he stopped and stared at the baby in Jane's arms.

Eva recovered first. "Hello, Terry," she said, and then turning to Jane, "Come on, give her back. I have to feed her soon."

Sue Ryland

She took the baby from the frozen Jane.

Terry watched her as she sat down in the corner chair, wrapping the shawl around the baby. "I didn't know you were..." he began, looking from her to Jane and back again.

Eva felt awkward picking up the baby, awkward holding it. She tried a confident smile.

Jane was stunned, not knowing what to do.

"What's its name?" Terry asked.

"Jenny," Eva replied. It was the name of a horse on the calendar behind Terry's head. 'Spinning Jenny', the caption read, above a picture of a bay mare, famous for being the mother of several racing winners.

"How old is she?"

"About a week, aren't you, Jenny?" Eva stroked the sleeping baby's head.

"Well, you're a dark horse, all right," Terry teased her. But they could see he was puzzled.

"We were a bit worried when she arrived early, but she's fine," Eva explained, her mind working ten to the dozen. "Do you want coffee?"

The baby was stirring, adding to her feeling of awkwardness.

"No, you sit down," he protested, looking at Jane.

Jane knew she was in trouble in more ways than one. She had planned to feed the baby as soon as she arrived at Chance, but the baby had slept on longer than usual, soothed by the sway of the taxi. Her swollen breasts were aching, leaking milk, making wet patches that showed against the pale blue sweater she was wearing. If she stood up, unfolded her arms from the table, Terry would notice. He wasn't stupid. He would know.

She was about to say, "Look, this is my baby," and take the inevitable consequences, when Eva stood up, putting the baby back in her arms. "No," she said, moving to the range, "I have to keep active. It's the new thing, you know. They say it helps recover your muscle tone faster if you keep active."

She had read that in some magazine when she was visiting Shirley.

"Anyway, Jane's getting over the flu." She still looks peaky, don't you think?"

Terry looked at Jane and agreed she did.

The baby was now nuzzling at Jane's breasts, head moving urgently from side to side, seeking the nipple and hiding the stains.

"She wants feeding," Terry pointed out.

Jane cursed her betraying body, which responded to the baby's needs rather than her own. She felt as if her breasts were streaming milk now.

As Eva gave Terry his coffee, Jane cast an agonised glance at her over Terry's head, holding the baby out from her breasts for a moment. Eva looked and saw the patches on Jane's sweater by the baby's head. "Jane," she responded, "will you just go and show Auntie Doris the baby again? It will be better if you do it. I'll feed her then."

She turned to Terry, explaining, "Auntie Doris relies on Jane and she seems a bit brighter today, so we have to pick our moment. If she hears the baby cry, she panics sometimes. She gets confused, you know? You don't mind, do you, Jane?"

Jane mumbled something and escaped the room.

Sitting on her bed, the baby suckling with little sniffs and sighs, she decided to tell Terry. This feeling of panic that had swamped her since the moment he had set foot in the door was intolerable. She wanted back her control. She would rather fight him, chase him away, make it clear that the baby was nothing to do with him and he had no rights. But she knew the baby was to do with him and he would seek those rights.

She laid the sleeping baby on the bed and changed her bra and sweater. She chose a baggy, black sweater for two reasons: to hide any further seepages and to make sure Terry didn't think she was dressing up for him. She would invent some tale of spilling a drop of tea that Auntie Doris had left, on the other sweater.

She didn't want to be alone with Terry, but Eva had to go off and pretend to feed the baby.

As soon as Eva had left, he turned to Jane, pulling her towards him. "You smell of the baby," he muttered, rubbing his face in her hair.

She kept her hands in front of her, flat on his chest. "Don't, Terry, please," she said, trying to push him away.

He pulled her closer. "Jane, I keep thinking of that night. You said it was a mistake and I tried to accept that, but when I think of how you were, it couldn't have been a mistake. I've tried to talk to you on the phone about it. Please, Janie, let's try again. We were good together, weren't we? You couldn't have pretended all that. Please, Janie."

She shook her head and yanked away from him, feeling dizzy as she stumbled backwards. She grasped the back of the chair to steady herself.

He was all concern. "God, I'm sorry! I forgot how ill you've been." He helped her sit down, crouching in front of her, holding her hand. "Won't you think about it, please? Let's try again."

She froze as he said, "That could have been our baby, you know," nodding to the door through which Eva had gone.

He looked at her immobility, felt the sudden jerk of her hand, and she thought she had given herself away, but she relaxed as he misinterpreted the signs, saying, "You're thinking of Elizabeth, aren't you? That was long ago, Janie. I've changed." He pushed her bag aside to pull out a chair and sit facing her.

Her bag! The overnight bag with baby's clothes stuffed in the open side pockets, with her initialled handbag looped through the handles. He knew that bag, because it was one of the few articles she had retained from the old days. The initials were obscure enough to be safe in the clinic, but Terry would remember… and it was at his side.

"Can you get me a drink, Terry? I don't feel too good," she said.

He got up to comply and she pushed the bag further under

the table with her foot, as Eva walked back in. Jane nodded urgently at the bag and Eva bent to pick it up, saying, "Sorry, I forgot the nappies." She was walking out with it before Terry turned round.

They managed the rest of the afternoon and early evening by using Auntie Doris as an excuse for Jane's disappearances when the baby needed feeding.

Jane refused to go out with Terry, claiming she was still unwell and Auntie Doris needed her.

Eva paraded the baby around every now and then, after Terry made a joke about it disappearing upstairs, never to be seen again.

During one such display, Mrs Bateman called in with some Christmas presents. Then they both knew the arrival of Jenny Bartlett would be known to everyone in the village before the church bells rang next morning.

They could hear the coke shifting and cracking behind the range door in the silence of the house after Terry left. They dropped the latch on the tack room door, to prevent any other unexpected visitors, and they stared at each other with huge eyes, shocked by the enormity of what they had done.

"I'll go and tell Mrs Bateman," Jane said.

"No, I'll go. You've only just come home. It's too far to walk."

"You'll have to tell her everything. Who Terry is. Everything."

Eva nodded. "I know."

They had introduced Terry as an old family friend. Eileen Bateman had assumed the baby was his, cooing over it, as she made the usual comments about 'seeing the resemblance'. She had assumed that Terry's wife was upstairs, visiting Auntie Doris, or in the bathroom.

Terry had laughingly declared it was nothing to do with him, so Eva had to say it was hers.

Eileen looked at them with puzzled eyes. Those eyes widened a fraction, though, as that information sunk in, and she left soon afterwards, to spread the word, no doubt.

Eva put on her boots and coat, turning to where Jane was standing in the kitchen doorway. "Sorry, Jane, I just said it because I knew you didn't want Terry to know. I never thought it would get this complicated."

"I went along with it too, so don't apologise. I should be thanking you. If Terry knew…well, he wouldn't let go, you know? I don't want him in my life again. I know he may have changed like you said, but I don't trust him."

Eva didn't know if she ought to mention Terry's behaviour each time Jane left the room to "see to Auntie Doris." She thought not, but she agreed with Jane's judgement completely now. It wasn't that he actually did anything, or said anything, that couldn't be taken in a nice way, but the expression on his face and in his voice wasn't pleasant. "Been having a good time then?" as she explained she had been living in the town for a while. "Teaches you a lot, doesn't it, living in the town? Lets you get around for a bit."

Innocent words, belied by his leers and the way he stressed the words.

No, Eva didn't trust him either.

"We do have to tell Mrs Bateman, I suppose?" She looked up at Jane. "Yes, of course we do," she went on before Jane answered. "There have been enough lies at Chance. I'll explain about Terry. Ask her not to spread it around, because we don't want him to know."

"It's not going to work, is it?" Jane said quietly. "She won't keep it to herself."

"No, she won't. She might have worked it out, though." Eva's voice quickened as she went on. "After all, you're the one that's been out of sight for some time. You're the one we said had the flu. I mean, she's seen me around, or the men have anyway. I haven't actually seen her for some time." Her words slowed down again. "And I suppose the men won't remember when they saw me really. They're hopeless at things like that."

She opened the door. "I'll go and tell her."

Eileen Bateman had already told her family, old Mrs Jacks at the cottage on the way home, and Mr Carson, the village postman, who she met bringing a Christmas tree back from the estate.

She wasn't surprised, she said. Well, that Eva had always been a strange one. Gone off, got herself into trouble and brought it back to Chance. No, she wasn't surprised. She hadn't been fooled by all the smiling and sweet words. Some people might have thought she had changed, but people are what people are, and that Eva Bartlett had always been a strange one.

When Eva arrived at Bateman's Cottage, an embarrassed Dave avoided her eyes as he said his wife was out, delivering presents to other people.

No, he didn't know where exactly.

He was glad to shut the door, after muttering, "Merry Christmas," in response to Eva's good wishes. He didn't want to be involved in any of these 'women's things'. It was too complicated for him.

Eva stood in the freezing gloom of the winter evening and debated touring round the village, but she knew it was too late really. The damage would have been done.

She went home.

"I think it's the only way, Jane," Eva said.

"Well, it's true: you can deny it until the cows come home, but no one will believe you."

"I know," Eva agreed. "Tell you something else too: Mrs Parkes will be on to the clinic in the town like a shot, using some excuse to find out if the baby was born there…and they will confirm a Miss Eva Bartlett gave birth to a girl. We have really mucked this up, haven't we?"

"I have. You've done nothing wrong, Eva."

Eva didn't answer, just patted Jane's hand. "So what now?" she asked.

"Well, believe it or not, I'm still going to tell everyone she's mine."

"If you do, you know what they'll say, don't you?"

"I don't care what they say. It's the truth."

"They'll say that Jane is a saint, taking on Eva's mistake like that. Well, we all know who the real mother is… And I'll be her mother, as far as everyone here is concerned, if not in law. Oh well, at least she won't have to put up with all the extra flak she'd get if they thought she was a Hensham. You don't deserve that, do you baby?" She stroked the baby's head.

Jane's eyes widened. "The birth certificate!" she exclaimed. "We've got to register the birth. That will prove I'm the mother. We can show people the certificate."

Eva's mouth turned down in an ironical smile. "All that will prove is what a saint you are. No one will believe it. What are you going to call her anyway? What goes well with Warren? We had better make sure Terry never hears her surname, because I don't know how we would explain that when he expects a Bartlett. How about Diane Warren? Sheila? Christine? I like Christine. Christine Warren. What do you think?"

Jane looked down at the baby and thought about it. Maybe it would be like adoption, without actually losing the baby.

"Jenny Bartlett?" she asked. "If you're really sure that's okay?"

Eva nodded.

* * * * *

SECOND CHANCE

"Mum! Mum! Can I go out with Lizzie?"

Jenny burst into the kitchen. "Please, Mum. She's got a new pony. Please!"

"Dinner in half an hour," Jane said, without looking up from the peas she was shelling.

Jenny pulled a face behind Jane's back. "Please, Mum," she begged.

"Go on then," Eva said, "but be back by eight."

Jenny ran out before Eva could change her mind.

Jane glared at Eva. "I don't like her messing around with horses. You shouldn't have let her."

Eva looked down at the greying head bent over the peas. "We can't stop her, Jane. She's horse mad, you know that. She's been begging for a pony of her own again."

"No!"

"We can afford it. It's what she wants."

"No." Jane shook her head once to emphasise her determination.

"I'm going to get her one," Eva said, quietly.

Jane's head shot back. "You are not!" She hissed the words between set teeth.

"No!"

Eva sat down. "I'm going to get her a pony. You can't stop me, or her, Jane. She's ten years old. She's pony mad."

"She'll grow out of it."

"Probably, but until then she has to be allowed to have what most of her friends have, and she has to be encouraged to pursue her interests. I'm getting her a pony."

Jane earthed up the potatoes, drawing soil around them so the rows assumed the shape of a corrugated tin roof.

Jenny called her garden 'the allotment'. Jane didn't grow flowers, just vegetables and fruit, in a large square of ground that would have been the centre of the old garden. She liked growing things, useful things. She grew too much for the needs of three people, giving the rest away to those who wanted it, or selling it at the local W I market. Well, to be precise, she didn't give it, or sell it; Eva did. She just grew it. She centred her life on this square of soil. Planning, acting, and reacting. It was her place. It was where she felt at home, in control. She came here to think, or escape from thinking.

Jenny didn't like her. She had known that from the first time the toddling Jenny had fallen and cut her knee, struggling out of Jane's concerned grasp and crying, "Mummy!" until Eva arrived to comfort her.

That was natural, she knew. Jenny thought Eva was her mother, so it was natural. Only Jane wasn't ready for the hurt she felt, the rejection, the loss.

She wasn't ready for not being a central part of Jenny's growing up either. Having doctors and teachers ignore her, telling Eva that Jenny needed to drink plenty of fluids, or practise her spelling more. It was not that Eva usurped her role, it just happened naturally.

Eva baked for the Brownies' fete.

Eva joined the PTA.

Eva took her to dancing class.

So Eva became her mother. She grew into the role, as the expectations of society pushed her to conform. Jane became the tagger-on: going along, but outside the circle.

She knew that Jenny saw her as old-fashioned and grumpy. Why did she seem to be the one who always said No?

She pulled some dead leaves off the currant bushes and thought about that.

Fear, it was fear. She didn't want Jenny making the mistakes she had made. She wanted her to be sensible, to be safe, and to not have times of madness when you could throw your life away in a moment.

That was part of the reason. She knew what the rest was, but thinking about it made it more real, so she tried not to let her mind accept the fact that Jenny reminded her of Shirley. The older she got, the more she looked like her, acted like her. When she mentioned it to Eva a couple of years ago, Eva said she was imagining it. She said perhaps it was Jenny's young, fanatical interest in all things equine that made Jane think she was like Shirley.

Jane wrote down Eva's answer in her Day Book, but she added that Eva was wrong. You didn't notice it so much when Jenny was running around, smiling, frowning, animated. Then she smiled and pulled expressions that were all Eva. But when she was still, staring out of the window at the rain, thinking about some school work, then it showed. She looked like a Hensham.

Jane sat down on the grass by the side of a lettuce row and stared at the ground between her feet. It wasn't logical thought. After all, she herself was only part Hensham and looked nothing like Shirley. And Terry...well, Jenny had some features that were like him, but not enough for him to have noticed. No, it wasn't logical. Perhaps she was imagining it.

Eva looked out of the window at the figure on the grass. It looked small and strange, sitting out in this square of cultivation, surrounded by green foliage on all sides. Out of place. Strange.

She turned to finish putting away Jenny's laundered clothes. They would have to buy her a new uniform soon, for she was going up to secondary school this autumn.

As she hung up a pinafore dress, she saw her own hands, really looked at them. Smooth. Clean. A housewife's hands. In and out of water all day. She turned them over. Clean nails, of reasonable length. Not bitten, broken, or jagged. It seemed to her they symbolised all that had changed.

She moved to a full-length mirror on Jenny's wardrobe door. There she stared at this neat, pinafored woman. Brushed hair in a sensible style. Pleasant expression.

Confident in her purpose and position. You could meet thirty of them, waiting outside school, any afternoon.

She walked back to the window and looked again at the figure on the grass.

"Are you taking those up to the churchyard?"

Jane nodded. It was the anniversary of Auntie Doris' death. Jane always remembered it, carefully choosing flowers from the meadows and hedgerows, and taking a pair of garden shears to tidy up the grave before she arranged the flowers in a small holder at the base of the stone.

Auntie Doris had died before Jenny was one year old. Jane had taken her up her tea one morning, and she was gone.

She did not think she would be as upset as she was, but, sitting on the bed, looking at the small face above the blankets, she felt a great loss. It was the end of another era, changing the environment, changing the structure of life, as did every family death.

Jane had grieved for this sad old woman. She had taken a long time clearing away all those suits and scarves, packing them in cardboard boxes to send to a charity shop in the town. She had taken a long time too, choosing which suit Auntie Doris should wear for her final appearance. She hoped she would approve.

There were letters, cards, photographs, to be collected up; all the memorabilia of life.

She cried as she looked at images of young Shirley: smiling and waving from up on a fat pony, head to the side, as she grinned at the camera, arms around a horse's neck…holding a handful of rosettes, trophies from some show…standing beside

Second chance

a sign which read 'Chance Livery Stables', looking proud and confident...

She cried for her own past, and because this girl was nothing to do with the shuffling, vacant figure she visited once a year at a hospital unit, in a northern city. Empty eyes. Empty smile. Nothing in common but their name. Shirley Hensham.

She burnt all the letters and cards. Most of the letters were to do with Auntie Doris' various charities, or the odd family letter. There weren't any from Uncle Paul, or any photographs of him.

There was one old creased photo of a smiling young man, but it wasn't Uncle Paul. He was holding a pitchfork and dressed in farm worker's clothes. It just said 'Cliff' on the back.

"She's beginning to ask questions."

"So answer them."

"Not just questions about what happened here, questions about her father."

"What did you tell her?"

"He was someone I met and had a brief romance with, and then he disappeared before she was born. I said his name was John."

"Did she accept that?"

"I think so. I don't know."

Jenny sat on the stone step of one of the old stables, watching a caterpillar crawl under the stems of a clump of weeds at her feet. She wished her mum would tell her more details of the murders. The girls at school seemed to know more than she did! That wasn't fair when she was living at the actual scene of the crime.

She liked living here, being able to act tough when they shuddered and said it would scare them. She had described the shed to one of the girls from another village and she talked about the strange noises from the back of the garden. Of course, it was all a load of rubbish. She didn't know in which shed the man was supposed to have been killed, and the garden was only Aunt Jane's 'allotment'. Not very spooky at all. Well, rows of cabbages weren't very frightening, were they? So she made it up.

Her mother seemed more embarrassed when she asked about her father than the murders. Of course, it was a great sin in those days, she supposed, years ago. They had done that in social science. Unmarried mothers being treated like criminals. Stacks of her friends came from one-parent families now. She wondered if that was why the miserable old cow treated her mum so bad. She wished her mum would tell her to get stuffed sometimes. Oh, she knew her mum was employed by her, sort of housekeeper and that, but that didn't give Aunt Jane the right to interfere in things the way she did. Miserable old cow...moaning if Jenny was late in from the youth club disco...saying she ought not to be allowed to stay over at Lizzie's...criticising her clothes... What the hell had it got to do with her?! She never seemed to say anything nice. She messed around with that bit of land all day and grunted out a few words every evening, most of them beginning with 'don't'. Her friends said she was probably mad, because she was a Hensham, wasn't she?

Jenny wished she knew more about the murders.

The caterpillar was making tiny, semi-circular fills around the edge of the leaf when she heard the voices.

"God, it's a bit of a dump, isn't it?"

There was a murmur of agreement.

Jenny's head swung round, looking for the owners of the voices. Then she realised they must be in the lane, behind the stables. She sat still, the better to hear what they were saying.

"I thought Dad said it was a classy place."

"Classic. Not classy. Well, whatever he said, it's a dump."

Jenny looked round the yard at the stables and sheds, trying to see it with their eyes. Tiles missing. Doors hanging off with great holes in them. She supposed it might look a dump to others. She had never noticed it before.

The voices moved past the yard where she was sitting, out of range of her hearing. She ran round the yard entrance and into the next yard to hear more of what they were saying. She flattened herself against the end stall, listening hard.

"...we've come this far, we might as well."

"It looks deserted to me. Where are all the horses and people? It must be closed down. I don't think anyone lives here now. We could go and explore a bit."

"No, knock the door first. If someone's there, we'll get done for trespass, or something."

"We won't. We're sort of relations, aren't we? Anyway, I don't think anyone's here."

Jenny stepped out from behind the wall, enjoying the way the three people jumped when she appeared. She felt vaguely annoyed that they were on her patch and talking about her place as though she didn't exist.

"Can I help you?"

There were two young men and a girl, dressed in walker's clothes, rucksacks on their backs. The men were in their late teens, early twenties. The girl was about Jenny's age.

The dark man recovered first. "Oh, sorry," he said, "we were just wondering about the house, you know. If anyone lives here... and that," he finished, lamely.

"I do." Jenny spoke shortly. She had no intention of making things easy for them.

"Right," he smiled. "Right."

"Are you one of the Henshams?" asked the girl.

"No."

"Oh, right." Her smile vanished, faced with Jenny's obvious hostility.

The older man said, "Do the Henshams still live here? Only we're relations of a sort and we thought it would be nice to meet them."

Jenny thought they wouldn't want to meet Aunt Jane if they knew her, and Aunt Jane wouldn't want to meet them, as she didn't like visitors.

That decided her. She smiled her sweetest smile and told them to follow her. Let the old bat have a bit of her own interference back for a change!

They followed Jenny, exchanging glances behind her back, up a side path and through some weed-covered yards, until they saw the house. It was big and a bit tatty, crumbling red bricks showing through the whitewashed walls.

The girl and the older man pursed their lips and looked at each other.

The younger man just looked. "Wow!" he whistled.

Jenny turned, waving her arm. "The central part of the dump. Hope it lives down to your expectations."

The girl flushed and looked away, but the younger man ignored the sarcasm. "It's great!" he said.

Jenny turned to see if he was being sarcastic in turn, but he was looking at the house with admiration. "I love all the angles, you know, all the different bits, sort of added on. Great!"

Jenny opened the tack room door and held it open for them to walk in. The dogs rushed around the new people, barking and barging. It pleased Jenny that the older man and the girl drew back, intimidated by this canine crowd. It pleased her, too, that the younger man wasn't intimidated at all, bending down to pat and talk.

"Aunt Jane!" she called. "Visitors!" and walked into the kitchen.

Her mother was at the sink. Her aunt at the table. The three young people hovered in the doorway, looking from Jane to Eva.

"They say they are relations," Jenny said.

Jane and Eva looked at them. The older boy asked, "Mrs Hensham?" He spoke to Jane.

"No," said Jane. "I'm Mrs Warren." As they turned to Eva, she added, "But I'm from the Hensham family. This is Mrs Bartlett."

Second chance

Eva smiled a greeting.

Jane was trying to work out which of her brothers, or sisters, were the parents of these children, or whether they came from some part of Auntie Doris' family.

The older one moved forward and held out his hand. "Hello." His handshake was firm. "I think we're sort of cousins or something. I hope you don't mind us visiting, but we heard so much about Chance Farm when we were young, and we're touring around this area, so we thought we would try and find you."

Jane smiled politely and, encouraged by this, he went on, "I'm Allan. This is my brother, Steven, and my sister, Lisa. I think we must come from the same branch of the family as you, because we're all Warrens too."

His excited voice slowed as he saw the woman become pale and still, the pen slowly dropping from her fingers onto the writing pad below.

He spoke hesitantly, trying to reassure without knowing why. "Our father was Terry Warren, you know? Terry Warren?"

After Jenny was born, Terry phoned regularly. He visited a couple of times too, but Eva and Jane stuck together, blocking out any attempt to renew his relationship with Jane.

By the time Auntie Doris died, they thought he was giving up. He didn't visit and phone calls were infrequent, just polite chats. Then they stopped. They hadn't heard from him at all in years.

How could these people be his children? How could they claim a relationship with the Henshams?

Eva had covered the moment by offering tea and cakes, giving Jane time to get over the shock.

Jenny could see, and sense, her mother's agitation. She could see her aunt was in real distress. She felt guilty and wished she had never done this thing – whatever it was she had done – because the whole thing puzzled her. Nevertheless, she was sure it was her fault.

Eva told Jenny to show them into the lounge and she would bring tea and cakes through. Jane got up to help Eva.

As soon as they were out of the hall door, and out of hearing, Eva whispered, "How can they be Terry's?"

Jane shook her head.

"Do you have any other relations called Terry?"

"No, anyway they wouldn't be Warrens, would they? That's Terry's name."

They were putting tea and cakes onto two trays, working fast, their hands responding to their racing thoughts.

"We'll find out," Eva said, as they went through the door. "Don't worry." She looked at Jane. "Okay?"

Jenny was giving them a tour of the house. "…from there, you go into what we call the morning room…don't ask me why… then you can go through one of two doors…"

She was trying to be nice, trying to cover up the uneasiness she felt about the adults' reaction. She had expected Aunt Jane to be annoyed. She had not expected her to be…well, almost frightened.

Over tea and cakes, her mother did most of the talking. They found out that Allan was twenty and worked in an office. He was taking evening classes to gain extra qualifications. Steven was eighteen, nearly nineteen, and he was at agricultural school. It was him that had been really keen on finding Chance. Lisa was still at school. She wanted to go into medicine, she thought, if she could get the right examination results.

Jane watched them as they talked. She thought she could see Terry in their faces, especially the girl, who not only had many of his features, but his way of smiling and raising his eyebrows at the same time.

"And how are your mother and father?" Eva was asking.

The three young people looked at her. They realised that this branch of the family was not close to them, but they had assumed they would know some of the things about their history.

Second chance

Jane picked up their puzzled expressions. "I'm sorry," she said, "we really are out of touch here."

"Of course," Allan nodded his understanding. "Well, Dad died some years ago. He was killed in a car crash."

Eva and Jane murmured condolences.

"He was a sort of cousin, wasn't he?" Steven asked. "He talked about Chance a lot, you know, when he got back from visits. He liked to tell us all about the place."

"We would have invited you to the funeral and that, but Mum didn't know where you were exactly. I know Mum talked about it, because he didn't have any other relations, did he?" Allan waited for an answer. When none was forthcoming, he went on, "It would have been nice to have some of his family there."

"And is your mother well?"

Jenny noticed that Lisa had bitten her lip and looked down at her hands since they started talking about her father. Now she saw a tear glittering on her eyelashes.

"Well, she was in the car too, you know. She never really recovered from that." He put his hand out to Lisa's as he went on, "She was in a wheelchair until she died, last year."

"Oh, I'm very sorry," Jane said. "It must have been an awful time for you."

"Anyway," Allen smiled, "that's how we found out where you were. Mum must have forgotten, or…" He stopped, his face flushed.

"We found newspaper cuttings," Lisa explained, "when we were sorting out everything?"

"Ah…" Jane nodded, realising the source of Allan's embarrassment.

"But all that was a long time ago," Allan ploughed on.

Jenny knew the cuttings must be about the murders. Even these three knew more than she did. It wasn't fair.

Steven changed the atmosphere by asking if he could see around the farm, if they didn't mind, that is.

221

Jenny jumped at the chance of getting him on his own, for three reasons: one, she could pump him for details of the murders, and two, she thought he liked the place. So she could show off a bit… The third reason was more to do with having a new male face on which to try her flirtation techniques. Of course, she didn't consciously admit the last two reasons to herself, but they were as real as the first for all that.

She tried to figure out an excuse to phone Lizzie before they left the house. It would be much more fun if Lizzie was here too, and it would give them lots to talk about afterwards.

She was just about to say she would be back in a minute, making an excuse about needing her watch, when Aunt Jane got to her feet and said she would walk around the farm with them. Even her mother looked surprised at that. And Jenny was "pig sick," as she told Lizzie later.

They left after the tour, exchanging phone numbers and promising to keep in touch. Jenny hadn't had one second alone with them. She went to tell Lizzie about it.

Jane flopped into the kitchen chair, feeling all of her years.

"What did you do that for, you daft woman?" Eva remonstrated. "You needn't have walked all that way."

"It's not just the walking; it's the whole messy situation. Anyway, didn't you notice our Jenny flashing her eyes at that Steven? If that's Terry's son, she's his sister, isn't she?"

"Oh, God." Eva sat down as that fact sank in. "What a mess. I was trying to add it up when you were talking to them. If they're his children, he must have been married when…you know."

"Yes, I know. Sounds like the Terry I knew and didn't love all right. And did you notice that bit about him having no other relations? Rubbish. He came from a big family. Not a very nice lot, but they were a lot. He's lied to them like he did to us."

"I suppose he said you were a relation to make himself sound more important…relations in the country, at the family house. I

Second chance

can just imagine him showing off. Makes it easier to come and visit you too. Well, we'll just have to cut them out, like we did their father. We don't have to see them again."

They turned up at ten o'clock the next morning.

Eva and Jane hinted that they had to go out, sent Jenny on errands that could have waited, and tried not to be hospitable.

Steven said he didn't mind just wandering around by himself, if they didn't mind him doing that. The others explained it was Steven who had nagged them to stay another day in the area. He was 'into' all this farming thing and it would be his last chance to look around until the next holidays.

That thought cheered Jane and Eva up a bit, so they crossed their fingers and let the day go on.

It took Jenny and Lizzie a long time to find Steven.

Jenny could have screamed at her mother when she was sent to Bateman's with some book that Eva said she had promised old Mrs Bateman.

Then she had to go to the village for some grocery stuff, which her mother had to have now. (At least she managed to pick up Lizzie while she was doing that.)

Then Aunt Jane made them take the dogs out for a run in the bottom meadow.

Then it was lunchtime and they said she and Lizzie must eat.

Jenny could have screamed.

Surprisingly, though, over lunch, they asked if Lizzie would like to stay the night.

That was unusual and an opportunity jumped at by both gleeful girls. Lizzie's mother was phoned and agreed to the arrangement. Of course, then Eva insisted they go and get some clothes and so on from Lizzie's house. They ran there, intending to grab some stuff and run back, but they got into a long discussion about what Lizzie should wear and it was teatime before they got back

223

After tea, they dressed in their most attractive 'casual' gear and went to find Steven.

Steven sat on the rocky outcrop, overlooking the farm. The sun was behind him and the house glowed in the deep green of a summer evening. It was a magic sight. He could see the cows moving slowly in a far field, birds circling lazily overhead. It was like some painting of an idealised rural fairyland. The skies were a deep, almost violet blue. The green was a colour that existed only in this special moment: a shimmering, warm, emerald light. The cornfields splashed a bright yellow. The house, a shiny white. The chimneys, dark red. Even the cows stood out, like black and white china figures.

Every colour was enhanced and deepened. Every movement seemed in slow motion. A magic sight.

Steven had seen this happen once before, on a late summer evening. They were on holiday somewhere and he was about nine. He remembered standing, suddenly still, fascinated by this new world.

When he called to Allan to come and look, it was gone. It was just a dusty summer evening again. Allan said it was probably to do with atmosphere, or air pressure, or something. Allan was keen on science. Steven preferred the magic theory.

Sitting on a hilltop, watching the glow, Steven determined that this was where he was going to stay. He didn't know how, but this was home.

The girl's voice interrupted him. It was the housekeeper's daughter and another girl, coming up the path at the side of the hill. He felt irritated that they were intruding on his space.

His space? He smiled to himself.

"Steven! Steven! Are you coming in? The others are looking for you."

Allan and Lisa had gone off, after polite greetings, to walk around the neighbourhood, leaving Steven to look around the farm. Now they were waiting for him.

The two girls stood in front of him, smiling and talking.

Second chance

"This is my friend, Lizzie. She lives in the village."

Steven smiled at Lizzie and said hello.

Lizzie smiled back and bit the corner of her lip as she looked down, not meeting his eyes and trying to control the urge to giggle.

"I was just looking at it all," he said. "You're lucky to live here."

Jenny ignored that. Lizzie looked out over the farm and agreed, saying, "Yes, it's nice, isn't it?" in a quiet voice.

Jenny was annoyed at Steven's look of approval at Lizzie. She wished she had never asked Lizzie to come now. To regain his attention she launched into a long description of the places he could see, naming the cottages and their residents, pointing out the brook, turning to show him Cap Hill and Halfpenny Hill.

He nodded and smiled, but he didn't seem that interested in the guided tour.

"Well I'd better be getting back," he said, when Jenny ran out of words. "Can you see your house from here?" he asked Lizzie as they turned to go, talking to her, walking by her, down the path back to the farmhouse.

Jenny was furious. The sly cat had probably been making eyes at him behind her back all the time she was telling him about places. She wished she had never asked Lizzie to come.

They were all in the lounge, being polite and remaking promises to keep in touch, Allan and Lisa sitting on the settee, Eva and Jane on the two armchairs either side of the fireplace.

Jane was worrying that Jenny was still out there somewhere with that young man. She wished they would come in and get it all over...get them gone. At least Lizzie was with them. That should cut out any serious stuff. She wanted these people away from Chance. The fear and tension was like a physical pain.

"Where is Steven?" Allan said, looking at his watch again. "It doesn't take this long to say goodbyes, does it?" He smiled, trying to turn his obvious impatience into a joke.

Steven had been back at the house and gone out again to find Andrew. He said he wanted to thank Mr Collins for letting him spend the day around the farm. He had really enjoyed watching all the different activities and seeing how it worked.

Jenny and Lizzie said they would go with him to show him where Andrew lived. They had been gone over an hour now.

The conversation in the lounge was painfully stilted by the time Steven and the girls reappeared. Allan and Lisa leapt to their feet at the sight of him and barely controlled the rush to the door, words of thanks tumbling out through the sudden increase in activity and noise.

"You're right, he's really nice." Lizzie stared at herself in the mirror. "Is that another spot?" she moaned, leaning forward and lifting the hair off her forehead.

Jenny was sulking.

"Oh God, it is!" Lizzie groaned louder. "Grim. Absolutely grim."

She tried squeezing the offending lump.

"Have you tried the new lotion you were going to get?" She looked through the mirror at Jenny's figure lying on the bed. Jenny turned her head to the wall.

"What's the matter?" Lizzie turned round.

"You know what's the matter." Jenny didn't turn round.

"It's not my fault, Jen! I didn't do it on purpose."

"He was visiting us."

"I know. I know. Anyway nothing happened, did it? He was only talking to me. Jen? Jen…" Lizzie pleaded for a return to friendship. "The other one liked you, didn't he? The older one. He didn't even say hello to me." Lizzie tried a new tack.

Jenny sniffed loudly.

"I'll go home, shall I?" Lizzie said in a small voice.

"It's bloody ten o'clock, you can't go home."

"I'll phone Mum. She'll come and get me."

There was a silence, then Jenny turned over and looked at her. "Do you think the older one really liked me?" she asked.

Lizzie nodded enthusiastically. "And he's better looking, isn't he?"

Friendship resumed.

* * * * *

Steven did keep in touch. He phoned once or twice in the following year. He spoke to Jane, updating her on Allan's progress, telling her the results of Lisa's exams, keeping her in touch with major news.

He phoned Andrew too.

They sent cards at Christmas and Steven said how he regretted he couldn't get away to visit them. Jane wasn't that upset.

She didn't know what to say when he said he was coming for two weeks in the summer. She knew she ought to offer for him to stay with them. Big house. Lots of rooms. Member of the family. It was obvious she ought to ask. It would seem peculiar if she didn't.

What she said was, "Well, I'd offer for you to stay here, but I don't think you'd enjoy it with just us two old women. And Jenny's never around much. Always out with her boyfriend, you know…"

He jumped at the chance.

Jenny had got a boyfriend. She always had a boyfriend, a different one every other week.

Having a boyfriend was a status symbol and, although these relationships never went beyond the original agreement to 'go out' with someone, it was enough to keep face with her friends.

They, too, had boyfriends in name only. They understood the game.

"Do you want to go out with me?"

"Okay then."

And that was it. You might kiss them a couple of times coming home from school, but you didn't actually go out anywhere.

A few of the girls were 'serious'. They really went out with their boys and made plans for the future. Once this happened they were not part of the group any more. They were not considered as rivals, or close friends. They were 'serious'.

The news that Steven was coming to stay created tremors in the young female population. It gave Jenny a chance to air her knowledge on the background and attributes of this new potential romantic interest.

Eva and Jane had discussed ways of removing Jenny from the scene for a couple of weeks, eventually deciding that Eva should take her on holiday.

Jenny was torn between her desire to be here, to parade this young man around her friends, and the excitement of a holiday.

She had never been on a proper holiday. There had been occasional day trips to places with her mother, or the school, but they had never stayed overnight.

She argued for the holiday date to be set some other time, trying to have her cake and eat it, but her mother was adamant it had to be these two weeks. She said it was a special deal that the holiday company was offering. She said it was the last chance they would have before Jenny was locked into all the extra studying she would have to do to get her examination levels. She reeled out many small reasons why it had to be these two weeks, take it or leave it.

Jenny took it.

They left early on Saturday morning to get to the pick-up point in the local town in plenty of time.

Jenny and Lizzie had been in a fever of activity for weeks, trying to decide what clothes Jenny should take with her. It was a touring holiday, so she was only allowed one suitcase.

Second chance

Eva had taken her shopping in the town, buying her clothes for the holiday. She had a "fantastic" day, she told Lizzie as they reviewed her selection.

Eva bought herself a swimsuit and a pair of sandals. She thought she could fish out enough stuff from her wardrobe to get through without buying anything else.

She wasn't looking forward to being away from Chance. She never felt safe anywhere else.

Jane was pleased to notice that Steven didn't seem that upset that Jenny wasn't around.

During the first week he was at Chance she saw very little of him. He spent his time around the farm with Andrew or down the village pub with Harvey and John.

He visited Bateman's Cottage quite a lot, taking meals with Harvey and Jay and their three children.

He visited John's house in the village too. John had married one of the Thomas girls. They had no children, but they were reported to be quite content with the situation.

Jane was in bed by the time Steven came home at nights and she was out in the garden, or working in the house, when he left in the morning.

Eva and Jenny sent her a postcard from Bournemouth, where they were staying for two nights, and a postcard from somewhere in Cornwall arrived a few days later. Jenny wrote the words and they were full of bright comments on the 'great beaches' and 'terrific shops', the 'super' this and the 'fabulous' that.

It rained long and hard at the beginning of the second week of Steven's visit. Parallel lines of water hitting the ground, sending up splashes from every small puddle. Soon the yards were flooding with fast small streams, pouring from overflowing dips into the next gathering point, only to overflow again seeking yet lower land. Steven stayed in and Jane was obliged to talk to him.

It was during these conversations that Jane found out that Steven and Allan had taken the name of Warren when their mother married Terry. They were not blood relations at all.

Jane lay in bed that night relieved that any relationship that developed between Steven and Jenny would not be morally wrong, but still unsure what the legal position was about such things.

Steven and Allan's real father had never married their mother, but they had been together for some years until one day he just left. Steven had only been a baby at the time and he didn't know exactly what went wrong.

Terry had moved in with them not long after that and Steven had always thought of him as their father.

There had been a marriage after Lisa was born and that was when Allan and Steven became Warrens. He didn't know if they had been legally adopted, or whether they had just taken the name.

Jane was annoyed with herself, annoyed that she had panicked at the thought of explaining to Jenny why she couldn't go out with Steven. She should have asked questions first, found out all these things, but she had been so determined to keep her distance, fearing that asking questions would have shown interest and encouraged more contact.

She wrote it all in her Day Book.

Maybe Eva need never have gone on holiday if she hadn't panicked. She felt guilty about that, because she knew Eva didn't want to go and Eva had been so good to her. She let her mind slide back to the angry sullen young woman that used to be Eva. Who would have thought then that she would become Jane's only friend? The only person she trusted completely?

Eva had taken Jane's role at Chance and Jane was glad of it.

Eva had become the one who saw to things, who talked to neighbours, who was the front person. She had allowed Jane to curl up in her own corner and lick her wounds. She had allowed her to work through the shame she felt at her failure to understand and control. She had allowed Jane to hide.

Jane wished she could tell Eva it wasn't as bad as they thought...that Jenny need not have been kept away from this boy.

* * * * *

Eva wished she could get Jenny away from this boy, but on a coach tour you were with the same group of people from start to finish.

She looked across the room at the top of Jenny's head. That was all she could see of her because her face was buried in his chest and his arms were around her shoulders. Each time the light flashed past them, she could see Jenny's hair.

Every evening there was a dance at whichever hotel they were at for the night. Apparently that was what was meant to be 'entertainment included'.

Eva did not find these dances entertaining. Music pounding much too loud. Lights flashing in the darkness. It wasn't dancing.

Jenny tried to get her to do whatever was the alternative offer, usually bingo, and Eva did go to one or two sessions at first, but that was before this boy latched on to Jenny.

The lights flashed past again and Eva could see Jenny's face, white in the glare, lifted up to him.

"Don't worry so much. It's just one of those holiday romances," Bill said. "I've been watching you and you worry too much. They'll write to each other a couple of times maybe, when this is over, and that will be that."

"If he can write at all," Eva retorted.

Bill laughed. Eva smiled back at him. "Sorry," she said, "I suppose I am a worry-guts."

She liked Bill Hallett. He was easy to talk to and they had spent most of the holiday doing just that.

Nearly everyone on the coach had soon formed into groups: eating together, sitting together, making strong friendships that usually only lasted as long as the holiday.

Having someone to walk with on sightseeing tours, or to talk to during the long coach trips between hotels, made people feel less awkward, especially those who were on holiday alone.

Eva liked him straight away, liked his old-fashioned manners: opening doors, pulling chairs out, walking on the outside down the street. She liked his neat appearance and his quiet accented voice. She thought of him as a gentleman and a gentle man. She was comfortable with him. She thought she understood why he picked her to share the holiday. It was because she was quiet and safe, not someone threatening his still painful widower status.

There were lots of other women on the tour, in their forties or fifties. They formed the largest group. Most had arrived in pairs and those that came alone soon teamed up with others.

Eva had watched them at the central collecting point. Sophisticated women with coiffured hairstyles and skilful make-up. They talked loudly and laughed a lot. They wore coordinated casual clothes with scarves and shiny jewellery, looking and sounding smart and confident.

Eva was dowdy by comparison. A country mouse. She thought that Bill, taking his first tentative steps alone, would choose someone like her to accompany him. She would have done the same in his position.

When he first spoke to her she froze him out. It was Jenny that chattered back, Jenny that broke the ice.

Eva wasn't good with men. As a sex, she avoided them if possible. Over the years she had run from any attempt by locals to get beyond passing pleasantries. And overt sexual overtures of any kind, from wolf-whistles to leering "Hello, darling! Looking for some fun?" shouted from building sites, or pub doorways in the town caused a flutter of panic in her stomach.

That was one of the things she liked about Bill. He never, by look or word, appeared to have any interest in sex at all.

*

The three young men in the coach made it clear from day one that sex was their main interest and objective. They were shouting at Jenny from the moment they sat down.

"Come and sit with us, love! Hey Blondie! Come up here!"

Eva tried to stop Jenny shouting back, but Jenny told her not to be a killjoy. It was only a bit of fun.

The other people in the coach laughed as Jenny called out things like "Now, be quiet, you lot. Read your comics and stop disturbing the grown-ups..." or "I'll set my mother on you if you don't start behaving yourselves!"

Eva blushed, embarrassed by the laughter. Secretly she wished she had Jenny's confidence.

Bill said it was natural that Jenny should want to be with the only other young people on the tour, and he sat by Eva when Jenny eventually went to sit with the young men.

By the second day everyone was swapping seats to be with their chosen companions, so it seemed quite the accepted thing to do.

It was the fourth or fifth day that Eva noticed that Jenny and the darker young man had sort of split off from the other two. They walked around together on tours. They lay on the beach, talking rather than running around playing games, or splashing in and out of the sea, shouting at the top of their voices.

Jenny was quieter too, in their room at night. She didn't chatter about what to wear at dinner, or should she buy that top she saw in town?

When Eva asked her if she was okay, if she was enjoying the holiday, she smiled and said it was great, but she didn't accompany the word by twirling round, or falling backwards on the bed, or practising a new dance gyration. She just said it quietly and continued putting on her make-up.

She suddenly seemed ten years older to Eva.

*

The young man's name was Scott, Scott Creese. He was nineteen and lived in the city. He worked in some sort of factory. That was all Eva managed to find out about him.

She didn't like him. The way he kept his arm around Jenny while he said a short hello to Eva…the way he walked holding Jenny's hand, touching her as they stopped to look at this and that…the way he danced with her…the way he was with her…as though he owned her…his property. Her thoughts worried on.

She tried to tell Jenny to be careful, but she didn't know how to start the conversation beyond saying those actual words each time Jenny went off to shop, or dance.

"Be careful."

During the second week of the holiday, Eva wrote the postcards home.

If she hadn't had Bill to talk to she thought she would have gone mad with worry. Bill understood her concerns, but he was also logical about them. What could she do? He pointed out that Jenny was seventeen. Eva couldn't force her to stay in. There was nothing she could do but hope everything would be all right and be there for Jenny if it wasn't. He said he had worried the same way about his children. It was natural for parents to worry.

Eva wondered what Jane would say.

On the last day of the tour Eva didn't see Jenny from breakfast until two o'clock in the morning.

The other two men were around the beach when she walked with Bill to look at the sunset. There were a lot of young people on the beach having a sort of party with radios blaring out music and loud laughter, but she couldn't see Jenny.

Even with her cardigan wrapped around her she began to shiver in the breeze blowing in from the sea, so Bill suggested they go and watch the sunset from the big window in the hotel lounge. She thought she should find Jenny, but he said that could prove an impossible task so she should come in before she got too cold. They could watch from the window.

Second chance

He got them a drink from the bar and they sat looking at the sea.

It got dark very quickly. The warm golden water disappeared, leaving the shimmer of white moonlight on the tips of the waves.

On the sands the beach disco – they had seen the advertisement for it as they came in – was in full swing. Black figures dancing around a huge orange bonfire.

"Reminds me of November," Bill said.

You couldn't tell one figure from another now, so Eva gave up looking for Jenny.

Bill insisted they did the last waltz. The hotel was holding a ballroom dance inside for the older people. Many of the hotels had ballroom dancing sessions in between the disco sessions, and Bill had encouraged Eva to try out some of the dances. She learned the Old Time dancing quite fast. It was easy just to repeat the same patterns over and over again, but quicksteps and foxtrots were different. She had just about mastered the waltz, letting Bill take the lead, responding to his guidance, but the quickstep always ended with her tripping over his feet, or her own. Nevertheless, once she got past the stage of thinking everyone was looking at her, she did enjoy dancing.

After the last waltz, they went back to their window seats. Bill sipped his pint of beer, watching another group exchange addresses and phone numbers, promising to keep in touch.

"I'll give you my number," he said. "You can let me know how all this turns out...Jenny I mean. Don't worry." He bent sideways to reach in his coat pocket, bringing out a small paper bag. "I nearly forgot this. This is just to say thank you for making this holiday so much more than I expected." He put the bag in her lap.

It was a bracelet set with different coloured stones. 'Beach Stone Souvenirs', the card read in the shop where they had stopped to admire them. Jewellery and little ornaments, set with stones you were supposed to be able to find on beaches. Eva had said how pretty they were, inexpensive too, and thought about buying an ornament for Jane. She didn't though. She had chosen a wooden telephone jotter instead, a little pad and a pen set in a holder with a lighthouse on the side.

"Oh, you shouldn't have. Thank you. It's lovely." She slipped it on her wrist.

They exchanged addresses and telephone numbers and agreed it had been a lovely holiday. Weren't they lucky with the weather? Only a couple of rainy days. They said goodnight and went to their rooms at eleven-thirty.

Eva dozed on and off until Jenny came in at about two. She pretended to be asleep then, actually falling to sleep not long after.

* * * * *

Steven had gone by the time they got back to Chance.

Jenny walked into the kitchen, muttered hello to Jane, and went straight to her room. She was out of the door before Jane finished, "Did you have a good time?"

Eva had watched the desperate kissing and clinging at the collection point.

The boy's local coach had left the station first. Jenny watched it until it turned a corner out of sight. She was still waving, even though the boy had turned, smiling, to talk to his friends after one quick thumbs-up to Jenny.

Eva found her crying in the women's toilets when it was time for their coach to leave. She didn't answer any of Eva's questions, or attempts to comfort her. She didn't talk all the way home.

Eva couldn't wait to get home, peering out of the taxi window, looking for the first glimpse of the hill, the first chimney of Chance. She was more excited at getting back than she had been throughout the entire holiday.

*

Second chance

"What's up with her?"

"She met a boy."

Jane told Eva about Steven. Eva told Jane about Scott.

"She'll get over it. I'll take her up a cup of tea."

Jenny said thank you for the tea and she had a headache, so she was going to bed early.

Eva was tired too after all the travelling that day. Everyone was in bed by nine o'clock.

They decided later that Jenny must have left in the night, because her bed hadn't been slept in. Eva took her a drink at ten the next morning and she was gone.

They had phoned the police, who said they would look into it, but Mrs Bartlett should realise that Jenny was over the age when they could take any action, unless it could be shown that she was actually missing, or in danger.

"But she is missing!"

"Not in the sense of failing to arrive at her destination," they pointed out.

"We don't know her destination!"

They tried to reassure her... lots of young girls ran away and most of them were back in a couple of days. Had there been a row? Had she got a new boyfriend? Don't worry. They would look into it.

Eva gave them the only details she knew about Scott... Scott Creese, aged nineteen, worked in a factory, lived in the city, met him on a coach tour.

They would look into it.

"They will get his address off the coach company. She will be there and we can go and get her."

"What if she won't come?"

"I'm sorry, Jane. God, I'm sorry."

*

Bill phoned in the afternoon to see if they got home all right.

"Who's Bill?" Jane asked, handing the phone to Eva.

Eva didn't even try not to tell him, she just poured it all out the moment he said, "Everything okay?"

He offered to do everything he could to help, feeling guilty, thinking of all the times he had told her it would be all right. He said if they had Scott's address, he could go there. After all, he was nearer to the city than they were and he had time on his hands.

They phoned the police again, but there was no news yet. They would be 'in touch' as soon as they knew anything.

The night was spent drinking coffee, going over the same points again and again, dozing on the large settee in turns, waiting for the phone to ring.

They phoned the police the moment the clock hit nine.

No news.

When Bill phoned, they scrambled to answer it.

The waiting was awful. Conversation died completely as they sat on…waiting.

* * * * *

Jenny had walked to the village and phoned for a taxi from the callbox there. She gave the address of a cottage, just by the pub, saying she had to get a train urgently to town as her grandmother had been taken ill. She told the taxi company that she would walk to the main road, by the junction, to save them having to come down into the village. It would speed things up, she said.

At the station in the town, she had to wait nearly two hours for the next train to the city. She sat on a bench by the platform, ignoring the calls of a trio of drunken young men, and just turning her back on a shambling smelly figure, who sat on the bench by her and tried to start a conversation. When he touched her arm, she looked at him as though she hadn't realised he was there. Then she got up to sit on another bench, opposite the man

Second chance

behind the glass in the ticket office. The tramp stretched out on the vacant bench and went to sleep.

She didn't really notice him, or the man in the ticket office, because her mind was full of the need to be with Scott. From the moment they said goodbye at the coach station, the emptiness had started.

Yes, they had promised to phone and write and see each other as soon as possible, but she had college and he had work. It could be months before they could be together. She could not live that way. He was the most marvellous thing that had ever happened to her. She wanted to be with him always, every second of every day.

As the taxi had taken her home from the holiday, she knew she couldn't survive without him. This empty screaming need was intolerable. She loved him. Loved him.

In the train, going towards the city, she smiled at her reflection in the black windows, as she imagined his surprise when he opened the door.

The city station was huge, an empty echoing cavern at that time in the morning. She asked at the information desk about taxis and followed the signs that they pointed out.

Excitement ran through her at the thought of just a few more minutes and she would be in his arms. Everything would be all right.

She did not notice the empty streets...not much traffic, not many people.

"Okay here?" the driver asked.

She looked out at a terrace of tall Edwardian houses, checking the number on the paper in her hand.

Fifty-four.

The driver took her cases out of the boot and she paid him, looking up again at the windows, looking for Scott. She half expected him to be looking out for her, knowing by some sort of telepathy that she would be there.

All the curtains were closed.

She left her cases at the bottom of the wide grey steps and climbed to the porch of the house. There was a box with numbered red buttons and slips of paper slotted into little metal holders underneath each one. The names of the tenants, she guessed, but she couldn't read most of them. Faded ink or pencil. Scrawled letters. Some of them didn't have a slip of paper at all. Her own piece of paper just said fifty-four. It didn't say any other number.

She looked around the porch. The tiled floor was littered with cigarette ends, bits of paper, a cardboard box full of empty bottles and screwed-up sweet packets. The door had two half panels of patterned glass. There was a crack running across one corner, which someone had held together with wide brown parcel tape.

She tried the door handle and it opened into a large hall with the same chequered tile floor as the porch. A wide staircase went off to one side, a passageway to the other side. There were closed doors everywhere. Some of them had numbers on, but no names.

She didn't know what to do, a small feeling of panic flattening her excitement. He hadn't said he lived in a flat.

She went back to the porch and studied the name slips harder, trying to make out the word Creese on one of them. No good.

She walked down the steps and looked up at the windows.

Should she wait until someone came out of the door, then ask for Scott, or should she ring a bell?

As she stood back in the porch, trying to decide, she heard a baby cry. It echoed loudly in the hallway. She tiptoed to each door, listening until she identified the source as from the door right at the end of the passageway, by the stairs. Number five.

She debated whether to go back and press the number five red button, or just knock the door.

The baby was still crying, but she couldn't hear any other sound from inside.

She knocked the door quietly, more tapping than knocking. The crying went on. She knocked again.

"Bugger off!" a voice shouted from inside, making her jerk her head away from the door.

She put her lips to the crack where the door met the frame and called in a whisper. "Please, I'm looking for Scott Creese. Could you…"

There was no response, so she called louder, trying to get above the cries of the baby.

The door opened a couple of inches. "What do you want?" An eye looked her up and down. "I'm trying to keep the little sod quiet, so just shove off will you?"

"No! No!" Jenny interrupted the owner of the eyes. "I'm looking for Scott Creese. Do you know him?"

"Bloody hell!" The door swung open wider, revealing the rest of the angry face, hair tangled up in a mat, eyes smudged with black mascara underneath, dressed in a short nightshirt with a large teddy bear motif on the front. 'Love Me. Love My Bear' it said in big red letters.

"Scott Creese?" Jenny asked tentatively.

"It's seven o'clock on Sunday morning. You've got a bloody nerve!" The eyes glared on. "Moaning at me about the baby and knocking people up at seven o'clock."

"No, I wasn't moaning about the baby. I was looking for Scott Creese."

The girl moved back into the room, returning with a baby held over her shoulder, patting its back as its crying changed into occasional sniffs.

"What?" she said. "Who?"

"Creese. Scott Creese."

"It's seven o'clock!" The girl looked at Jenny as if she was mad.

"I know. I just arrived, you see. If you could tell me where…?"

"Scott Creese?"

"Yes."

"He isn't here. They've gone away on holiday or something."

Jenny's excitement returned in full flood at this confirmation that this was her Scott that the girl was talking about. "No, he's back now," she said, smiling at the girl. "He came back yesterday."

"Well I haven't seen him." The girl went to shut the door, but Jenny put her hand out to stop it.

"Please can you tell me which number is his flat?"

The girl looked at her. Curiosity took over as sleep receded. "Top floor. Door at the end, on the right," she said and watched Jenny run up the stairs.

Jenny knocked the door for a long time. Knocking and waiting and knocking again. At last she heard noises from inside the flat and the door opened.

She recognised the young man in the T-shirt and shorts as Martin, one of the other two boys on the holiday. He didn't seem to recognise her.

"Is Scott in?" she asked.

"Christ!" Martin's half-opened eyes shut in disbelieving exasperation and he retreated into the flat, leaving the door open behind him.

Jenny put her foot in the doorway in case it swung shut on her.

She heard Martin yell, "Scott! Come on, get up! Some bird wants you…"

Jenny moved into the flat, shutting the door behind her, worried the yelling might attract the attention of the other residents.

She waited. Any moment now they would be together. Any moment now.

There was a bed in the middle of the room, its covers thrown back. Martin had gone into another room. She heard him say, "Get up, you lazy git!"

She couldn't hear the mumbled words that followed, but she heard Martin's, "Christ, I don't know!"

Second chance

When Scott appeared from the doorway at the side of the room, Jenny flung herself at him.

He retreated, pushing her away as though he was being attacked.

Martin said, "Christ!" again and flopped back into the sofa bed in the centre of the room, pulling the bedspread over his head.

Scott held Jenny at arm's length, not hearing her babbling words about being with him forever, about loving him. He was just trying to wake up enough to work out what was happening.

"What are you doing?!" His face was appalled as, at last, he worked out who it was and where she was. "What are you doing?!" He pushed her further away.

The expression of horror in his tone and on his face stopped her excited explanations, her attempts to be close to him. He was not happy and excited. He was shocked and horrified.

She started to cry. "I thought you would be pleased." The tears were brimming out of her eyes and the words were shaky.

Scott turned away, picking up his jeans from the corner of the room. He glanced at her as he put one long thin leg into the jeans, hopping to keep his balance. He looked around for his T-shirt, still casting quick glances at her.

"How did you get here?"

"On the train." She was watching him, pleading with her eyes. "I thought you would be pleased."

"Yeah…well I am. Of course I am."

There was a muffled laugh from the sofa bed.

"It was just the shock, you know," he excused himself.

He had his T-shirt on now and was smoothing back his hair with his hands.

"Does your mum know you're here?"

She shook her head.

They stood looking at each other. She was frightened. He was in a quandary, his mind working ten to the dozen as he tried to think what to do next.

"She'll be worrying," he said.

Jenny just looked at him.

"Do you want a cup of coffee?"

She didn't answer. None of this had gone right. He should have held her and said he would never let her go again. He should have been happy and excited.

The great big empty feeling was back.

"I'll make you a coffee." He moved to the back of the room and filled a kettle from a tap over a small sink. He laid out mugs from a cupboard that was underneath the table-top electric plate. "Here, sit down." He indicated a chair at the table.

She sat, staring down at the bright yellow Formica top. The empty feeling was getting worse, rising like the noise from the kettle.

"Do you want something to eat?"

She shook her head again.

"What's the racket?" The other boy appeared in the bedroom doorway. He stood, holding the frame with one hand and rubbing his head with the other.

"Nothing," Scott said. "Go back to bed, Andy." He stirred the coffee, not looking up.

"What's she doing here?" Andy said, focussing on Jenny.

"Sod off, Andy," Scott muttered to him.

"What's she doing here?" he repeated.

Martin's voice sounded gleeful as it sang out from under the bedspread, "Scotty's got a problem…Scotty's got a problem."

"Shove it, Martin!" Scott snapped at the lump in the bed.

"Here, drink this." He put the mug in front of Jenny. "Go on. Drink it." He put her hands around the mug, urging her to lift it up. She grabbed his hands with both of hers, spilling the coffee. "Please, Scott, please. I want to stay with you."

"'Please, Scott, please,'" the voice mimicked from under the bedspread.

"I told you to shove it, Martin, you prat!" Scott snarled at the figure. "You can't stay here, love." He pulled his hand free, putting his own mug of coffee in front of her. "Drink that." He mopped up the spilt coffee with what looked like an old facecloth and made himself another mug. "You just can't stay here. There's no room, see? Andy and me share the bedroom and Loudmouth over there kips down in here. There's no room. Anyway..." She was crying loudly now. "...you ought to be at home. Your mum will be doing her nut. There's no room for you here."

The empty feeling had grown like a bubble inside her. It burst into panic. She almost screamed, "I'm not leaving! I'm not! I'm not! I want to be with you. You said we would be together one day. We can be together now for always. I'm not leaving. I don't want to go home. Don't make me go home."

He put his arms around her, trying to stop her, trying to shut her up.

"Get her out of here," Andy said from the doorway. "Get her out of here before there's trouble."

"Do you know anyone you can stay with in the city?" Scott was desperate. "Christ, Jen, you can see you can't stay here!"

She stared at him, eyes and nose streaming, racked with great sobs of fear.

He shook her, holding her arms. "Do you know anyone you could stay with here?"

She screamed. They couldn't understand the words she was trying to say, it just sounded like screaming.

"Shut her up, for God's sake!" Andy yelled, panic in his face.

Scott tightened his arms around her.

"What the hell's going on here?!" A little figure darted into the room, straight to the table, standing, hands on hips. "What are you doing, Scott Creese?"

She pulled him away from where he was trying to muffle Jenny's cries against his chest.

"What are you doing, you toerag?!" She knelt in front of the shaking, wailing Jenny, looking hard into her face. Then she stood up and hit her across the cheek, immediately gathering

245

the stunned Jenny into her arms and cuddling her against the big red bear with the words 'Love Me. Love My Bear'.

"There, there, love… That's better… That's better…" She swayed back and forth, crooning to the quiet, shaking girl in her arms.

Scott's words tumbled out, trying to explain it wasn't his fault, she just turned up and wanted to stay…it wasn't his fault.

Andy and Martin, now emerged from the bedspread, fell over themselves to back up Scott's statements. "It wasn't his fault, Trish, really…"

"Well, you must know her. How do you know her?" Trish kept rocking the girl as she glared, above Jenny's head, at the three boys.

"We met her on holiday," Scott said.

"Oh…you couldn't keep it in your trousers again, eh?"

"No, Trish, no. It wasn't my fault."

"Not your fault? What's the matter? Is it so small it keeps getting out without you knowing?"

The two other boys giggled. Scott went red and tried to think up some scathing answer…or indeed any answer.

"You're pathetic, Scott Creese. You and your playmates," she sneered at them. The other two stopped giggling. "She's nothing but a child."

"She's about the same age as you, Trish," Scott protested.

"We're not talking about the number of years, as you damn well know. You should be ashamed of yourself, Scott Creese. You should all be bloody ashamed of yourselves."

She knelt in front of Jenny. "Okay now, love? Where do you come from? We've got to get you home."

Jenny shook her head. She felt humiliated. She wished she was dead. Scott didn't want her. Scott didn't love her. They would laugh at her when she was gone.

"Don't you want to go home?"

"I don't know," she said. She kept looking at the girl with the teddy bear on her shirt. She couldn't look at Scott, or the other boys, fearing what she would see. His annoyance at this unwanted visitor. The mockery in their eyes.

"You'd better come with me," the girl said, taking her arm to pull her up from the chair and leading her out. "She can stay with me today until we sort this out." She spoke over her shoulder at the three boys. "Where's her stuff?"

The boys looked around the room and shrugged.

"Bloody useless, the lot of you," she said, leading Jenny out and down to her room.

She gave Jenny tea and insisted she eat some biscuits to help her get over the upset. She said her name was Tricia Saunder, Trish for short, and the baby was James. She chattered on and on, while Jenny shook and tried to nibble the biscuits. She put on her transistor radio and talked about the different groups that were in the charts at the moment... She gossiped about the occupants of the flats, the woman at the new supermarket, her teacher at school... She chattered about the price of everything and how she had to feed her electricity meter as though it had worms... She talked about her uncle, who wouldn't use the 'electricals' in his house during the war, in case it attracted the bombs... "Oh, he was a case, he was!"

She didn't stop talking until Jenny smiled, then she made another cup of tea and said, "What are you going to do then, love?"

"I don't know. I just thought I'd be with Scott, you know? I didn't think..."

"Bloody men," Trish said, looking at the baby in her arms, sucking happily away at his bottle. "Good for bloody nothing, men." She stroked the baby's head. "Good for bloody nothing," and she smiled at the baby. "Do you want to go home? Best place really, you know. There's nothing here for you...nothing for anyone, unless you've got money."

Jenny thought of home, going back and explaining. Her mother and sour old Aunt Jane... Oh, Aunt Jane would have a field day! And, if she went home, her friends would laugh at her...

247

"You got any money?"

"About forty pounds," Jenny said.

"That won't get you far, will it?"

"I don't want to go home." A large part of her mind was already planning again, saying, if she stayed, soon Scott would get interested again…would remember how they were.

"Don't think about him, love," Trish read her thoughts. "He's not worth it." She put the baby over her shoulder and rubbed its back. "Got anywhere to stay, if you stay that is?"

"No."

"What will you live on?"

"I could get a job."

"What as?"

"Anything."

"Not that easy, love. It's hard here. You'd be better off at home."

"You manage," Jenny said.

Trish laughed. "I survive. I don't know whether you'd class that as managing. You've got enough to get home, haven't you? Only I couldn't lend you any…"

"Yes I've got enough, but I don't want to go."

"Are you sure of that? You could get a taxi back to the station, collect your cases and go."

Jenny stared at her.

"What's the matter?" Trish stared back.

Jenny ran to the door. "My cases! I left them on the steps!"

Trish followed her to the porch. The cases were gone. "Ah well," she said, "that's decided it. You'll have to stay with me. We're about the same size, so my clothes should fit…and you'd look a bit stupid in Scott's gear…"

* * * * *

The police lady said that they had seen Jenny and she was not in any danger. She was not living with a boy. She did not want to

Second chance

return, nor would she agree that they could tell her mother where she was. They were very sorry, but there was nothing else they could do. Mrs Bartlett should try not to worry too much. Jenny would probably come back sooner or later. They usually did.

* * * * *

A year went past and, although they thought of the possibility some time during every day, she didn't come back.

The three of them sat around, moved around, worked around, each one consumed with a gnawing guilt.

There were three of them, because Bill was a regular visitor now, staying in the house for weeks at a time. He blamed himself for dismissing Eva's worries, for encouraging her to ignore the situation between Jenny and Scott. He tried to be around, to help out, to make up for what he had done.

Eva blamed herself for letting this happen. She should have looked after Jenny better than she had. She had lost Jane's child and she owed so much to Jane…the person who had helped her to learn to be part of society…the person who had stepped down so that Eva could step up.

Eva clung to Bill's company for comfort, wanting so much to tell him everything.

Jane blamed herself for everything. The whole mess. She couldn't talk to Eva about it, because she could see any mention of Jenny hurt her. The person who had been her only confidante became the person whose eyes she couldn't meet. She thought she had destroyed Eva's life with her selfish need to hide away, to keep people at a distance, to lose herself on one mad night with Terry.

She wrote in her Day Book that she was glad when Eva announced she was going away with Bill. Glad for Eva. Glad for herself. It was another escape from the pressure of the constrained atmosphere that surrounded Chance.

* * * * *

Andrew thought Jane would be pleased when he employed Steven. Many men had applied for the vacancy, but he could honestly say that Steven was the best applicant. He had been to college. He was a good worker. He could live at Chance. It all tied in nicely.

Jane wasn't pleased as such, but she didn't mind.

The village thought that Steven was a relation of Jane's –he thought he was too – so he moved into Chance and Eva took the opportunity to move out.

"I'm sorry, Jane," were the last words Eva said when she left.

"No, it's all been my fault," Jane answered. "He's a good man, your Bill. Be happy. And thank you for…well everything," she finished, conscious of Bill standing by Eva's side.

She shut the door. Yet another door. Life was full of such doors.

* * * * *

NEW CHANCE

After three years Jane didn't think of Jenny several times a day, but once or twice, every now and then, she would lean on her spade, or stare into her coffee, and wonder where she was, what she looked like, what she did.

After five years she thought of her on special days most of all. When it would have been her birthday, or at Christmas time.

Eva wrote to Jane frequently, enclosing photographs of her new family. She was very involved with Bill's children and grandchildren. The tone of her letters was busy and comfortable...going to a nativity play at a primary school...doing a bookstall for the Women's Guild fete...describing Victoria's 'lovely engagement party'.

Jane studied the photos of Eva and Bill with various members of their family. It was funny, she thought, that Eva reminded her so much of Auntie Doris now.

Occasionally Eva phoned. It was pleasant and polite. They never mentioned Jenny.

Steven married Lizzie, Jenny's best friend, and they went to live with Lizzie's widowed mother. He had only lived at Chance for a few months and Jane didn't miss his company when he moved out.

Now it was just her and the dogs pottering around the big old house, but Steven felt a responsibility towards her and would call in to check everything was okay, doing any urgent repairs, bringing her logs, asking her to Christmas dinner. She never went.

The children of the village made jokes and pretended she was a witch. They dared each other to go to the house on Halloween. But it was only fun, only pretend, because Steven's position in the village was soon accepted as important, and he couldn't possibly have a witch for an aunt.

"Don't be daft! That's Mr Warren's auntie!"

Furthermore, as Steven and Lizzie's two children grew up, they played around the crumbling buildings in the yards of Chance. The opportunities to create dens and special clubs, playhouses and adventure trails, were just too attractive for other children to resist, so, although they pretended to hide in terror when Jane passed by, they were always hoping the Warren children would ask them to play there. Still, none of them went into the house. They had grown up with legends, even if they didn't really understand them.

Steven talked to Lizzie, in the early years, of using the buildings at Chance to extend the farming work, raise more pigs, or start a poultry unit, but he never got round to suggesting this to Andrew. He was kept busy on the set farm work during the day and busy during his off-duty hours taking on various roles in the village community. He helped with the Cubs, eventually becoming the pack leader. He coached at the football club. He became a PTA member. He was treasurer of the angling club. He was at home in the community, as he always knew he would be, from the first time he sat on the hill above Chance.

One day he intended to do something about Chance.

Jane stopped growing vegetables. There wasn't any point, because there wasn't anyone to eat them, or to give them away to, or to sell them to. She still spent most of her time, on good days, pottering around outside, nurturing the few rose bushes that remained in the old garden, pulling up a few weeds. The rest of the time she spent walking, or training, her dogs, or writing in her Day Book.

Her Day Book became her one form of communication, the one place she could express herself without reserve. She wrote in it as though she was talking to somebody, to her best friend… to her gran.

There were two big boxes in the small room off the morning room where those policemen used to be. They were full of her Day Books. She had nearly filled a third box too. She was going to burn them all when the time came that she was finding it hard to get about any more. No one must ever read them.

She felt twinges of aching stiffness in her hip and knee, but, all in all, she was pretty fit and judged she had plenty of time yet.

She threw an old curtain over the boxes to hide them. Steven might have to go into the room for something, so the curtain was just in case. Better safe than sorry.

Sometimes, she lowered herself onto the floor by the boxes and read some of the old days. It made her sad and it made her happy. Little incidents she had long forgotten. Big incidents she would rather forget. What amazed her most of all was all that feeling, all that passion. Words describing long-dead emotions. She would frown, or smile, or shake her head as she sat reading them.

She didn't feel anything now. She existed in a robotic state, finding little pain or pleasure in anything. She just functioned.

* * * * *

Jane opened the door and there was this woman with two children: a boy of about ten and a girl a couple of years younger. She didn't recognise the woman, but from the way she was dressed – one of those short mini skirts and high-heeled little boots – Jane guessed she was one of the women from the patch of new houses on the far side of the village. Selling cosmetics, or wanting her to sign a petition to get a lower speed limit on the main road by the village? Probably.

Jane was prepared to close the door, saying she wasn't interested, thank you, when the woman said, "Mrs Bartlett?"

Well, whoever she got her information off, she was well out of date!

"She doesn't live here any more." The woman pulled at the short top she was wearing, that didn't quite reach her skirt, leaving an inch of bare flesh showing at her waist. She smiled and fiddled with the buttons of the jacket she was carrying. It was made of the same stuff as jeans.

Jane thought she hadn't heard, so she repeated, "Mrs Bartlett doesn't live here any more."

The smile on the woman's face dropped and she looked more upset than that information should have warranted. Jane stopped in the action of closing the door. No, that wasn't the right reaction at all. The woman should have turned away and ticked off the name on a sheet of paper, or something like that. Instead she stood there, looking very young and bewildered.

"What do you want her for?"

The smile half-returned, highlighting the pretty oval-shaped face again. Pity about all that make-up, Jane thought.

"Oh…are you Aunt Jane?"

Now Jane really stared at her, trying to place who she could be, where she had seen her before.

"I'm Jane Warren…yes."

"Can I come in and talk to you for a moment?"

"What about?"

The girl looked around as though someone might be listening.

"About Jenny," she said.

* * * * *

Jane's stomach had turned over when she said, "about Jenny." Now she sat in the morning room, looking at the young woman and the two children perched on the edge of the settee opposite her, and tried to take in what had been said.

She wasn't used to shocks, wasn't used to feeling much of anything. The woman's words had made her heart beat too fast, made her legs tremble and weaken, made her hands shake. She felt ill.

"I'll get you a cup of tea," the young woman said, getting to her feet. "You two stay here," she ordered the children.

She put her hand on Jane's, bending down to ask where the kitchen was and saying never mind, she'd find it, while Jane just looked back at her silently.

"Sip this. Go on, sip this," the woman said, pushing it towards Jane's mouth. "I'm sorry. I didn't realise it would be such a shock. Me and my big mouth."

She held the mug, her hands over Jane's, crouching in front of her until Jane took some tea.

"Sorry I was so long. It's a bloody maze out there, innit?"

Jane hadn't realised she had gone.

The sweet tea worked. Whether it was the sugar or the act of drinking, Jane's body calmed down.

The woman was chattering about the dogs. How they had followed her everywhere until she found the kitchen, and followed her back with the tea.

The children were stroking the dogs now. The settee was surrounded by wagging tails vying for attention.

Jane stared at the children.

The woman sat back on the settee between them, putting her arm around the little girl. "This is Katie," she said, smiling at the children.

The child looked at Jane, head down, smiling politely.

Jane smiled back at her grandchild.

* * * * *

Jenny had stayed with Trish in the bedsit for nearly a year. She had got a job in a cake shop on the High Street. There was a card in the window and she just walked into the job.

Trish was pleased at Jenny's luck in getting work so fast and pleased at the extra income it brought into their 'family'. Jenny didn't get paid much, but every little helped.

Trish wasn't so pleased at Jenny's continuing pursuit of Scott. She knew they were using the bedsits to get together every time she took James to the health clinic, or when the other two boys were out. It worried Trish, who looked on Jenny as a younger sister to be protected. Although they were about the same age, Trish thought she was experienced in the ways of men and the city. Jenny was not. They had rows about the situation, ending in hours of sulking and silence, but the room was too small for isolation and they made up in the end.

"Just be careful," Trish pleaded.

"You sound like my mum," Jenny laughed.

Having Jenny around to babysit allowed Trish more freedom to go out, but she seldom stayed out late. It wasn't just that she didn't trust Jenny or Scott not to take advantage of the situation, although the thought always crossed her mind, it was because she didn't have anywhere she wanted to go really. No family to visit, because she was raised in a children's home. No real friends, because you didn't make real friends there, ones who stayed around once they were free to leave the home.

There wasn't anywhere to go.

* * * * *

After Trish left the home she went into a bedsit. She got a job in a local factory – well the social worker got it really –and she went out dancing and dating, enjoying the money and the freedom. She went around with a group of young people, a gang of ever-changing membership. None of them had families they talked about. None of them stayed long at one address. They drifted from place to place, town to town, always teaming up with those in a similar situation until they moved on again.

New chance

Trish didn't know who fathered James. She didn't really care. During that year she had slept with many boys. Everyone slept around. Most of the girls got pregnant.

Most of them had babies who would be adopted, or eventually taken into care, as their mother's lifestyle was deemed unfit for effective parenting. Trish guessed her own mother would have been one of these vagrant groups many years ago.

Oh, Trish knew her mother had probably meant to keep her; most of the girls had the intention of keeping the baby, starting their own little family, creating some security, but soon most of them would be back out with the gang. The pull of the streets was strong: it's hard to sit in a small room and be a mother when you're sixteen or seventeen and feel your life is over.

Trish had looked at James and thought she had someone who was hers now. Just hers. She would make a real home. She would not let this baby be taken away from her. She would not be like Bonnie, or Sarah, nineteen-year-olds and on their third pregnancy, two babies gone and one more coming along for someone else to rear. Social Service fodder. She sat and thought of the past year. It was like trying to see through fog. Images of wild laughter, lights, alcohol, music, drugs...faces of boys whose names she couldn't remember...places that spun from flashing discos to rooms in derelict houses. Streets, lots of streets...huddled in clothes too trendy to be warm...standing in groups kicking cans across the road, acting as if it was fun... being tough...having street cred...waking up and not knowing where you were, frightened.

This baby would always know where it was. Trish was determined. She would be different from Bonnie and Sarah...and her mother.

She found a bedsit that would let her keep the baby with her. Some of the old gang turned up now and then and she was pleased to see them, but she resisted all their urgings to come out to this or that club, this or that party. Above all, she resisted their attempts to add her bedsit to their 'dossing' places.

Soon they stopped coming, most of them leaving for other areas.

She didn't know many of the new intakes of members.

Social Security money was tight, but she managed, just about, and she would rather struggle than leave her baby with anyone else.

The other people in the house of bedsits got used to her being around all the time and soon came to rely on her to look after things, take messages, to be a mother figure. She gave others advice and sympathy. She shouted at those that needed shouting at and encouraged those that needed help.

She was eighteen and they nicknamed her 'Mum'.

The loneliness was the worst thing. The residents at the bedsits changed fairly frequently. Relationships were short. The advent of Jenny proved a blessing in more ways than one. Extra money, someone else to care for and, above all, a companion.

* * * * *

Jenny did well at the cake shop job. It wasn't only the fact that she stayed there, while other girls came and went in a few weeks, sometimes days, it was that Jenny was good at what she did. Customers liked her pleasant willing manner, so different from the begrudged service of many other girls.

The shop was clean. The bread and cakes well presented. The wastage cut to a minimum. All of this was Jenny's doing. For the manageress of the shop was astute enough to realise that she had someone who could take over much of her work, and was happy enough to be given just a few extra cakes for her effort.

Mrs Pindar was in her early fifties. A nice comfortable woman cruising along in a nice comfortable job. She had been with C P Cakes since she left school, rising to the position of manageress by dint of long service and reliability, rather than talent. She knew everyone in the firm and they knew her. It was all very comfortable.

New chance

There were Mrs Pindars in branches of C P Cakes all over the country. Reliable, middle-aged women managing products and business that hadn't changed much in thirty years.

Mrs Pindar didn't see Jenny as a threat to her position, just the opposite in fact. Staff turnover was high in a job that paid little, that offered small chance of promotion, that was 'boring', as most girls said when they left.

Jenny didn't leave and the various visiting area and district managers began to notice her, to think they ought to remember her name.

Mrs Pindar told them Jenny had 'promise' and she was grooming her to take over when she retired.

She told the same things to Jenny, using that carrot to keep her in the shop; doing work she should have done herself. But when Jenny came up with ideas that meant change, Mrs Pindar dismissed them. She didn't want change. Change wasn't comfortable.

Jenny had been at the shop about a year and a half when C P Cakes was taken over by a multinational food group. Changes were inevitable and Mrs Pindar decided to retire. Jenny was offered the position of manageress, thus justifying all Mrs Pindar's promises, and letting her prepare for retirement well satisfied with the success of her protégée. Any twinges of conscience she may have felt abut Jenny's willingness to ease her own load vanished in self-congratulation. Well, hadn't she always said she was grooming Jenny to take over?

She stood behind her counter, smiling and nodding, as Mr Simpson, promoted under the new regime to southern area manager, thanked her, praised here and begged her to "hold the fort" while Jenny was away on a six months' training course. The course was mandatory now for all management staff, he said.

Mrs Pindar was glad she didn't have to go away on a training course. The decision to retire was certainly the right one. Everything had turned out very well. Nice and comfortable.

Sue Ryland

When Jenny returned six months later, Mrs P enjoyed her retirement party and the speeches of thanks. She took her presentation clock and bouquet of flowers and departed happily for her cosy fireside, leaving Jenny to take over the reins...and Trish to become nanny to Jenny's new baby.

* * * * *

Clifford Simpson was twenty-eight. He had been district manager at C P Cakes for three years, joining them from a soft drinks company where he had been a salesman.

C P Cakes was a step up for him and moving up the executive ladder was the main aim of his life.

After three years he had started looking around for another position to attain – checking the job ads...talking to business colleagues – when C P Cakes was taken over by Britel Foods. He was promoted to southern area manager. Another step up, without the trouble of changing companies. He was well pleased with life and himself. In Britel he could just keep going up. And he would. He knew he would. He had all that was necessary to get to the top. Brains. Looks. Background. An attractive wife, whose social skills were beyond doubt, two pretty children to give the desired aura of domestic and emotional stability. A good house in a good area. The right friends and the right leisure activities.

He also had AIDS, but he didn't know that.

* * * * *

Travelling around as district manager, Clifford Simpson would visit two or three cake shops in his area every day. Every cake shop would have at least two young girls working as assistants; it was essentially a female occupation. Furthermore, as the turnover of staff was very high, there would be different young girls on nearly every visit.

New chance

Clifford Simpson liked young girls. He considered their availability to be one of the perks of his job. He was commended by his superiors for the way he always took extra care to visit shops where the manageress was on leave, or ill, making sure everything was "ticking over okay." His boss recorded him as a conscientious worker. And conscientious he was, ringing the dates of arranged holidays on his office calendar, with the address of the shop in brackets at the side, planning his visits there on those weeks, responding immediately to any unexpected sick leave of the managerial staff. Yes, you could guarantee he would spend a lot of time visiting any such shop.

'Nookey time', he called it in his head. Time for a bit on the side. He would pick a girl, flatter her, take her out and have a night or two of hotel room passion. It was all very safe, very easy. No middle-aged manageress to watch his approach and maybe report back on him. Safe. Easy. And the next time he visited that shop, his erstwhile bed partner had usually moved on. No comeback. No ties. Easy.

He targeted Jenny the first time he saw her. Pretty, fresh and bright. Maybe a bit too bright for his usual choice, but there was an aura of innocence about her that was very appealing. He was used to girls who knew exactly what he meant from the first private word whispered over the counter. Girls who were happy to spend a night with him in a 'posh' hotel with free food and drinks. Fair exchange. They knew the score.

Jenny wasn't like that. She was intelligent, but naïve. He had to romance her and he quite enjoyed it. It was different. A challenge. It took time to get her to come out with him, but once he had, he got her into bed the same night. She was just as susceptible to flattery as any of them, but she needed to think she was loved too.

He wasn't too upset when Jenny didn't move on. He began to think of her as his permanent mistress. He still picked different girls from shops in other areas, but Jenny would go out with him every time he came to her shop.

They passed notes over the counter behind Mrs Pindar's back. They smiled and pretended. It all added to the excitement.

Jenny didn't tell him she was pregnant until she was five months gone. He was a bit annoyed that she was not on the Pill as he had assumed, but it wasn't a big problem. Britel had recently taken over C P Cakes and it was easy to sort out the situation. Yes, everything was going right for Clifford Simpson.

Trish was pleased when Jenny lost interest in Scott. She knew Jenny had met someone at work. She expected Jenny to bring him to the bedsit to meet her soon.

"He's married, isn't he?"

Trish stood, hands on hips, and demanded an answer. It hadn't taken her long to work out that if Jenny was starry-eyed about some new boyfriend, yet only went out with him once a month, there had to be something wrong. She expected Jenny to sleep with her boyfriend, that was natural, but only once a month?

"So what if he is?"

"You're a fool to get involved, that's 'what if he is'." Trish sighed her exasperation.

"I suppose he says his wife doesn't understand him, or is crippled with some disease. God, Jen, you are a prat!"

"No, he doesn't actually," Jenny snapped back. "You wouldn't understand."

"Trouble is, I understand too well. What does he say then? Come on, let's hear the brilliant excuse."

Jenny thought about what Cliff had said about his wife having problems. He hadn't exactly said what, because he seemed too upset to talk about it, but Jenny knew they couldn't sleep together and that it was something that was getting worse.

"You don't understand," she said and started to cry.

Trish looked down at her and wished she had said nothing. She turned to put the kettle on. "Ah well, it's your life," she said and told herself to stop being such an interfering old sod.

Years later those five words came back to haunt her and she flayed herself for not interfering more.

*****

Jenny kept the secret very well. She quite enjoyed the idea of knowing something that only she and Cliff shared. She would laugh inside when Mrs Pindar said what a nice young man Mr Simpson was, or when one of the girls said he was very dishy.

Andy had moved out of Scott's bedsit to one of his own in another part of the city, and Martin was due to move out soon as well. They had stayed together longer than most.

Jenny was puzzled when she met a smiling Scott in the hallway one evening. He had been hanging around waiting to see her when she came in from work. He wanted to ask her to move in with him.

For a moment Jenny wondered what on earth he was talking about. When she realised what he meant, she almost laughed in his face. What, for crying out loud, had she ever seen in this scruffy, awkward boy?!

She had been meeting Cliff for over a year when she realised she was pregnant. They met two more times before she told him, because she wasn't sure how he would take the news. It wasn't that she thought he would be angry, or stop seeing her – they loved each other too much for that – it was just that she didn't want to add to his problems. His job was very demanding and he had all the worry about his wife too. "Like an oasis in the desert," he called the time he spent with her. It made her want to cry for him.

When she did tell him, he said he thought she was on the Pill, and she should have told him sooner, when something could be done about it. He seemed annoyed about that for a moment, but then he had his arms around her, telling her not to worry, he'd sort it out.

She thought she was about five or six months pregnant.

Once Clifford knew, things happened very fast.

He told her she was to be manageress of the shop when Mrs Pindar retired.

He found her an unfurnished flat in a better part of the city. Jenny thought it was beautiful. A sitting room, kitchen, bathroom and three bedrooms.

Three bedrooms and her own bathroom! The height of luxury.

He said she was officially away on a management training course. She would have the baby, get a nanny and return to C P Cakes in a few months' time. With her higher salary and help from him, to set up the flat, she would well be able to afford it.

Clifford, in his new position as southern area manager, would still be able to see her now and then, though perhaps not as often as before.

That was the only miserable part.

When she took Trish to see the flat, Trish was open-mouthed.

"Who are you going with...Rockefeller?"

She agreed to be Jenny's nanny for the new baby and they moved in as soon as the basic furniture was installed.

If Trish was a homemaker by nature, Jenny was a businesswoman.

With the encouragement of the Britel management, Jenny transformed C P Cakes.

She started to sell sandwiches and baps, experimenting with various fillings, building a new clientele from all the factories and offices around the area. She got heated cabinets and new ovens and started selling hot pies and pastries.

New chance

People liked food they could eat out of a bag, sitting in the park, or still working at their desks. It made a change from fish and chips and was easier to handle.

Jenny added new lines regularly, maintaining customer interest and drawing in more people to her 'Lunch Bar'.

Coffee and tea in plastic cups with lids. Slices of the new pizza. Baguettes. Individual slices of cake. Small pots of curry and casseroles, with plastic cutlery. She responded to every new eating fashion and created ways to offer the latest food in a convenient way.

Jenny was a success.

Britel sent her to train other prospective manageresses.

They sent her to look at the products offered by food wholesalers all over the country.

They sent her to meetings and trade fairs, conferences and seminars.

She wasn't often at home.

Trish and the two children would watch out of the bay window when Jenny phoned to say she would be home for the evening. The children would jump up and down and tap the window at the sight of the red car pulling onto the forecourt of the flats, but when Jenny walked through the door, they would be shy.

Looking for a red car was exciting. Talking to strangers was not.

If the children found that having her around was uncomfortable, well, Jenny felt just the same about them...and Trish.

She was used to hotel rooms and facilities now, used to service and civility. The flat seemed small and crowded, the food dull and tasteless, the children distracting and demanding. And Trish...well, Trish was common.

Jenny felt guilty about that, but every "bloody" every loud laugh, grated on her nerves.

Going home became a duty rather than a pleasure.

Sue Ryland

She tried to explain her feelings to Cliff and he said it was natural to feel that way. She had grown in experience. They had not.

Jenny still met up and slept with Clifford every now and then, although it wasn't just in local hotels now, but wherever they chanced to be together.

On Jenny's part it was more out of habit than anything else. She had outgrown him too.

She had the flu'. Then she had the flu' again. Then bronchitis. Then more flu'. Then she collapsed and they took her to hospital with pneumonia.

"Do you have any relatives near, Miss Bartlett?"
She shook her head.
"Friends?"
"Trish," she said.

Trish nursed her for seven months. One bedroom of the flat became like a mini hospital, full of medicines and packages, visiting nurses and doctors.

The children were kept out.

Trish sat for hours, holding her hand and talking. She would go in when the children were off to school and stay most of the day. Then, after they were in bed at night, she would come back and talk some more. She did housework and cooking while Jenny slept. She slept herself in small naps, jerking awake at any sound.

It was during this time that Jenny talked of Chance. That was her main topic of conversation, as though all the years in between had never happened. Chance was home, happiness and safety. Jenny wanted to go home.

She kept saying she was sorry to Trish, but Trish didn't know what she was sorry about.

The last month they took Jenny to a hospice and she died there on September 14th.

Trish looked down at the figure they called Jenny Bartlett. This figure bore no resemblance to her friend. Her only friend. She didn't cry. She had done all that long ago.

"I'll take Katie home, Jen," she promised.

* * * * *

"And is the child all right?" Jane asked, watching the boy and girl outside in the yard, playing with the dogs.

"Yes, they tested her for HIV as soon as Jenny was diagnosed. She's okay. The father must have picked it up from someone else after Katie was born. The doctors said they were getting more and more cases now."

"Who was he, this father?"

"Someone she worked with. She never told me about him properly, but she had to tell the doctors because of passing the disease on and that. The doctor told me he was seriously ill too. He's probably gone now."

Trish looked at the old woman standing by the window. Her face was stern and disapproving. "Sour old Aunt Jane" Jenny had called her, saying she always thought the worst of everything Jenny did.

"Don't think Jenny was one of those girls who slept around, because she wasn't," Trish tried to defend her friend. "She just had this one bloke…may he rot in hell…she never bothered with no one else. She was a businesswoman, travelling everywhere for the company she worked for. She never had time for messing around. Jenny was my best friend and I miss her."

Jane turned to look at the defiant little figure perched on the edge of the settee.

"She was lucky to have you," she said, and busied herself clearing the tea cups, embarrassed by the astonished look Trish flashed at her.

"Can you tell Jenny's mother about Kate?" Trish asked. "Do you know where Mrs Bartlett is?"

Jane said she would try and get in touch with her right now, if Trish wanted to go out and supervise the children, only there were some dangerous bits of machinery around out there and, if they weren't used to farms…

Jane felt numb. She thought she ought to be crying and grieving, but she didn't feel anything except a vague feeling of irritation at this intrusion into her ordered life. As soon as she recognised that this was what she felt, irritation turned to guilt. Had she become so removed from life, from people and feelings, that the death of her only child was just an irritation?! She stopped in the act of picking up the phone to dial Eva's number, appalled at herself. What, in God's name, had she become?!

She put the phone back down again and sat on the chair by the little table. There was a long mirror opposite her. She stared at herself. An elderly woman, grey-haired and etched-faced, dressed in her usual overall and working trousers, the same sort of clothes she had worn daily for the last twenty-five to thirty years.

People used to come to her for comfort and help.

She saw mind-pictures of herself, painting these walls, rushing to and fro with food, dusters, lists. Busy, always busy. And smiling. When did she last smile? Really smile?

Her daughter was dead. She ought to feel something.

What was she doing? Sitting here, waiting to die, or to be turned off like the machine she had become?

She couldn't even picture Jenny's face in her mind.

She sat on and on, thoughts flashing through the years, until she heard Trish calling.

"Mrs Warren? Mrs Warren?"

She got up as Trish appeared in the hall, the two children behind her, the dogs milling round, panting from their games.

New chance

"I couldn't get through," she lied. "If you want to make the children a drink and get some biscuits or something..." she waved towards the kitchen, "...help yourself. I'll try again.

"What are you going to do?" Eva's voice was anxious. "I mean, I would come down, you know that, but Bill hasn't been too well and I have to look after Alison while Laurence and Betty are away. I told you they were in America for six weeks, didn't I? Then there's the problem with..."

Jane listened to Eva, not really hearing the words she was saying, but sensing the panic.

For one irrational moment, Jane was angry as she listened to the excuses. She nearly yelled, "Come on! This is your problem! You sort it out. It's your daughter..." Only it wasn't, she thought, as she bit back the words. It wasn't Eva's problem and it wasn't Eva's daughter.

"Don't worry, I'll sort something out," she said, cutting in on Eva's words. "Don't worry."

There was a pause at the other end of the line, then, "Are you sure?"

"Yes, don't worry."

"I'm sorry, Jane, it's just that..."

"Yes I know. It's all right. I'll speak to you later."

Poor Eva, she thought, as she put down the phone. She had built herself a new life. Katie would have been a complication.

So now what?

She had to send them away. Yes, that's what. She went into the kitchen.

"Any luck?" Trish asked. "I've made you a cup of tea," she went on, before Jane could answer.

Jane sat at the kitchen table. "Mrs Bartlett can't come down," she said, trying to get the words right, trying to think of some plausible lie or half-truth. "Her husband is ill."

"Oh." Trish frowned as she took this in. "Can I take Katie to her then?"

269

Sue Ryland

"No, no. He's very ill. It wouldn't do."

Trish said, "Oh" again and stared at Jane. "I expect it was a shock, was it? About Jenny and Katie?"

"Yes."

"Does she want me to phone her?"

"She didn't say."

"Oh."

Jane tried to think of something to say. "She'll probably come down, when she can."

"Yes." Trish got up and put her mug in the sink, collecting the squash glasses from in front of the children and closing the lid on the biscuit tub. "I'm sorry to have taken your time," she said. "Go and get your coats on, kids," she directed the children, and they went down the hall to the lounge.

"I'm sorry." Jane couldn't think of anything to say but that. She felt guilty and strangely sad.

The young woman's unhappiness and uncertainty was clearly written on her face. Still, she smiled at Jane briefly with, "It's not your fault."

Jane had to make herself not think about that.

Trish went on, "Only I would have liked to have seen Katie settled here, you know? Might break my heart to lose her, and all that, but I sort of promised Jenny…at the end. This place was all she talked about." She smiled at Jane again, shaking off her sadness, bouncing back to say, "Well, there you go. It wouldn't have worked, would it? What with Jenny's mum not living here any more and that. Thanks for your time, Mrs Warren. I've written my address and phone number on this." She put a piece of paper on the table in front of Jane. "If Mrs Bartlett can get away, tell her she'll be more than welcome."

"What will you do now?" Jane asked, watching her put her arms around the two children.

"It's back to the flat for us, innit kids? Say thank you to Mrs Warren and go and get in the car."

The children intoned their thanks and ran out.

New chance

"Don't worry, Mrs Warren, we'll be all right. Jenny left me some money and we manage."

Jane sat at the kitchen table for a long time.

She wrote it all down in her Day Book, then closed it firmly, put it all out of her mind and went to bed.

It wasn't any good. She couldn't sleep. She went down to the kitchen again at two-ish and made herself a drink.

At five o'clock she was sitting on the kitchen floor, surrounded by her sleeping dogs.

Her knees had creaked when she got down. Everything screamed in protest when she got back up. She was so stiff, so staggering, towards the kitchen range that the thought of what she must look like made her smile in her head. Silly old fool! Still, she had liked sitting on the floor with the dogs. It was comforting. It reminded her of other days. Her gran would have understood.

She was still feeling the gentle pleasure of doing something different when she picked up the phone. She wasn't dead yet. She could still make something of the next years. She could still put things right. It was time to stop waiting to die. If she could sit on the floor with the dogs, she could do anything!

This time, the smile reached her eyes.

"So, I'd like you to think about it."

"Bloody hell," Trish muttered, for the fourth time.

Jane felt an odd bubbling in her throat, as Trish "bloody hell"ed again. It took a couple of seconds to realise it was laughter.

"What, all of it?" Trish's head moved around to indicate the whole place.

Jane nodded.

"Bloody hell."

This time the bubble exploded in a harsh, quickly stifled, guttural sound, as Jane laughed.

Trish looked at her and laughed politely too, though she wasn't sure what at.

"Are you kidding me?" she asked.

Jane shook her head.

Trish opened her mouth and Jane cut in with, "Bloody hell?"

This time, Trish really laughed.

"It's what I used to be here, you know, a sort of housekeeper. Only, as you can see, I haven't done much keeping of any sort for years."

"I thought you were one of the family. The Henshaws or whatever."

"Henshams," Jane corrected her. "Yes I was…am…but I was a sort of minor branch. Here I was the housekeeper. When this was the stables I did a bit of everything really. General dogsbody, I used to think. Oh well, that was long ago and another story."

She watched Trish, who had moved to the window to check on the children.

"What do you think? Would the children like it?"

Trish laughed as she came back to sit down. "Like it? They've never stopped talking about it since we first came. It's having all this space, innit? Like going to a park."

"What about your own family? Would you mind being away from them?"

"I haven't got any," Trish said, still smiling. Then the smile faded as she fiddled with the teaspoon in the sugar bowl. "Thing is, though, I don't know if I'd sort of fit in around here." She looked up at Jane. "I mean I'm not…well…I mean, like…I know I used to get up Jenny's nose sometimes. Me and my loud mouth, you know." She nodded solemnly to emphasise the point. "Common as muck, me."

That made Jane start to laugh again, until she saw Trish's eyes.

"If Jenny ever thought that, she was wrong." Jane spoke directly at her to also emphasis the point. "You were Jenny's best friend and

New chance

I'm sure she valued that far more than you believe. You don't have to be a certain type to fit in here, or anywhere. If people don't like you as you are, that's their problem, not yours. If you are honest and caring and people reject you because you don't speak, or dress, the way they do, then they are not worth the bother. Little people with little minds. You are worth more than them."

Jane stopped, suddenly realising that she hadn't strung that many words together in years and feeling embarrassed at this unusual eloquence. Laughing and talking felt strange.

"Anyway," she went on, hastily resuming her gruff attitude, "you will think about it? Let me know if you want to take in on."

Trish was thinking that Jenny had got it wrong. She wasn't so bad, 'sour old Aunt Jane'. Quite soft underneath all that glowering.

"And I see to the house? Cleaning and cooking and that?"

"Yes."

"Anything else?"

"Whatever needs doing? It's your job, you do whatever you see fit."

Jane had the sudden feeling of being here before, saying these words, doing these things.

Then she remembered Great Uncle William glaring up at her with, "Well, Miss, are you taking it on?"

History repeating itself, she thought. Just substitute Old Aunt Jane for Great Uncle William and Chance moves into another era.

She froze as, unbidden, her mind added: both of them built on a lie.

* * * * *

"Well, who are they anyway?"

Lizzie followed her husband around the cottage as he looked for his 'Farmer's Life' magazine. This edition had an article on pigs that he wanted to discuss with Andrew.

"I've told you, I'm not sure. Aunt Jane was very vague about it. I think the woman was a friend of Eva's."

"Not a relation then?"

Steven rounded on his wife. "For crying out loud, Lizzie, I don't know! Will you stop going on about it. I'm glad Aunt Jane has someone there with her. Takes the pressure off me."

"Yes and might take Chance off you too, if it's a relation!" Lizzie shouted back. "Chance is yours by right, Steve. You're the one who's looked after her all these years. I'm not having some common little tart walk in and take what's yours."

"For God's sake, let it be, will you?" Steve groaned.

"But you've got plans for there, Steve, you know you have. Chance should be ours."

"But I don't like it." Katie's muffled voice shook as she buried her head deeper in Trish's nightshirt. "I can hear things."

"What things?" Trish stroked her curly blonde hair.

"I don't like it either, Mum." James leaned on Trish's arm, solemn-faced.

"What's the matter?" Jane's voice came from the doorway.

"They're frightened," Trish explained. Then, to the children, "Just leave the big light on if you like. That's okay, isn't it?" she asked Jane.

The children had slept heavily since they came to Chance, exhausted by all the excitement of a new place and the freedom of running around all day, but this had been their first day at their new school. They were less physically tired, because they had to sit still at their desks. They were more mentally alert, because of playtime information on the 'terrible' history of Chance.

Of course, they acted as though they didn't care in front of the other children but, at bedtime, they had lain looking up at their rooms. Not nice square boxes with white wardrobes and bare, shadow-free spaces. These rooms had ceilings that pointed upwards into an unknown gloom. Black beams everywhere and odd little recesses making dark corners. There were big blocks

New chance

of solid furniture with carved tops, causing strange shapes on the walls. Above all, the rooms were large…and you couldn't hear any cars.

"What are you frightened of?" Jane asked.

The children just clung tighter to Trish.

"Answer then." Trish shook their arms to encourage them.

"I heard a noise," Katie said.

"What like?"

"A ghost noise."

"Like this?" Jane hooted softly. "Whoo-oo."

James looked at her and Katie nodded dubiously.

Trish opened her mouth in amazement. "Hey! I heard that! I wondered what the hell it was."

The children smiled at her obvious pleasure in having confirmation of the noise she had heard.

"That's a tawny owl. A bird. It's not very big and it calls at night sometimes. See?"

"It sounds like a ghost anyway," Katie persisted.

"I told you it wasn't." James spoke from his superior ten years.

"No you didn't!"

"Yes I did."

"You didn't! You were frightened too."

"No I wasn't!"

Trish broke in. "Cut it out, you two. It's only a bird. An owl, that's all."

"I don't like howls.' Katie clutched Trish again as she went to get up.

"Owls, not howls," James said.

"I don't like it. I want to go home."

Jane came into the room. "There's nothing that can hurt you, Katie. Do you know why?"

Katie shook her head.

"Because of these." Jane pointed to her dogs, standing around her.

Katie lifted her head off Trish's chest, peering sideways to look down at the dogs.

"They are guards, you see. If anyone, or anything, that shouldn't be here came round, they would bark and chase them away. That's their job and they're good at it."

Jane looked at the three faces, all staring down at the dogs. Over the last two days, one of the things that had provided them with amazed fascination was Jane's ability to get the dogs to do anything she said. She would tell one to stay and they would run away with the other dogs, all around the buildings, and it would still be there when they got back. She would tell one not to accept food, and it wouldn't take the offered biscuit until she made another signal. She would tell one to corner one particular duck, with a bad wing, and it would without hurting it.

The dogs were magic. All three of them believed that.

"Barn owls are supposed to be here too, and you just wait until you hear the noise they make!"

"What? Do it. Do the noises," James begged.

"I can't," Jane smiled at them. "They sound as if they're being strangled; screeching enough to think someone's being murdered." She put her hands round her throat, stuck her tongue out and pretended to strangle herself. They all laughed. "But the dogs know it's just a barn owl, so they take no notice, see?"

"But the dogs are with you," James said. "They can't hear in our rooms."

Trish jumped in at that. "Of course they can. You know those dogs can hear all over the place."

The children nodded agreement, remembering all the games of Hide and Seek that the dogs won with astonishing speed.

Jane looked at the children stroking the dogs. Katie smiled up at her and Jane's heart bumped, as she put a name to the child's features at last. She had been watching and trying to see Jenny in her face…perhaps recall her daughter that way.

Katie and James used the facial expressions of Trish, which was only natural, as she had reared them both from babies. They smiled like her, opened their eyes wide and pulled down their mouths at any new thing. That was all Trish. But you could tell James belonged to his mother. The same mid-brown hair, thin, straight build, brown eyes that drooped at the corners and smiled a lot. Katie was blonde, curly-haired with big blue eyes and a pointed, heart-shaped face. She wasn't tall and thin, she was short and stocky. Jane could not see much of Jenny in her, or of herself, except maybe the build, and she was pleased that Terry's features didn't show in her face. Yet Katie reminded her of someone.

Now, seeing the child in the light of the small lamp, she knew. Her gran. Her beloved gran. The best friend of her childhood. To Jane it felt like a bonus.

"Would you like a dog in your room?" she asked.

"What?! All night?" Katie's eyes opened wide. "Can I have this one?" She clutched the head of the dog she was stroking.

"No. I will say which one." Jane's voice was firm. She almost regretted making the offer now. These were her dogs, her companions. But this was her grandchild...and she looked like her gran. "That is Scamp and he is an old dog. He wouldn't like it if I didn't keep him with me. You can have Em." She pointed to a young bitch. "All right?"

Katie was speechless with delight, reaching for the dog Jane had indicated.

"But, no letting her lie on the bed, when she's just in from the yards. Okay?"

Katie nodded. "Thank you... Thank you..." her face against the dog's neck.

"Can I have a dog?" James asked tentatively.

Katie cried, "You are frightened! I knew you were frightened. See!"

"No, I'm not. I..."

"Shut up, Katie," Trish cut in, before it got into another shouting session.

Jane pointed to another dog. "You can have Ben. This one. But both of you mark this well, I am lending them to you to keep you company at nights. You are not to favour them above the other dogs, because all the dogs are mine and must be treated fairly. Perhaps, when you are older, I'll teach you to train your own puppy."

The children exchanged excited glances and said they understood about being fair to all the dogs.

"Come on then, James, let's go to your room," Jane said, signalling Em to stay with Katie.

When James was settled, with Ben lying by his bed, Jane said goodnight to Trish and turned to go down the landing, followed by the rest of her dogs.

"Mrs Warren…" Trish's whispered voice stopped her. "Could I have one of them?"

Jane turned to look at her. Trish smiled in self-mockery. "To tell the truth, I'm more bloody frightened than they are."

It took time for Trish to get used to so many new things. For instance, saying good morning to everyone she met, rather than hurrying past, lost in a crowd.

When you are walking towards someone coming along a lane and you are the only two people around, it would be very odd to put your head down and pass in silence. Some sort of communication – conversation – was expected.

Then there was not dressing up the children to go out. She always used to make sure they were smart and well dressed before she left the flat, even if they were only going to the shops. It took a lot of extra washing before she realised she was only making a rod for her own back, and theirs.

Wellies, old sweaters, T-shirts and trousers. Farm clothes, whether you were going to the village or not. Good clothes for town visits only.

Once they were out of those 'town clothes' the children didn't stand out as different.

Trish abandoned mini skirts and high heels very quickly too. She needed old trousers and tops to explore the house and area.

She did a lot more cooking than was actually put on the table. Most of it ended up feeding the hens, because she was in the middle of a no-holds-barred war with the kitchen range. She swore at it. She pleaded with it. She was deliriously happy when it did something right.

At first, she tried to defer to Jane for instruction on what she wanted done, or confirmation that something she had done was all right, but Jane just said "as you see fit" and left her to it. Sometimes Trish felt like yelling at her that she ought to give advice. But after she tried changing the furniture arrangement in the lounge, and Jane simply said, "This is nice," as she sat down after dinner, and after a couple of successful dishes from the kitchen range, she began to grow in confidence and really go it alone.

Jane enjoyed watching the children play. She enjoyed reading to them, helping with their schoolwork, taking them for walks.

The other village children got used to seeing her around more and she lost much of her 'witch' image.

Katie and James started calling her Aunt Jane, copying Steven and Lizzie's children, who still came to play at Chance nearly every day. Trish called her Aunt Jane too. It just happened as a result of using the title when talking to the children.

"Ask Aunt Jane if she wants some more tea."

"Aunt Jane! Katie says can she feed the hens?"

The weeks went on and the children thrived.

So did Jane.

All her mothering instincts, so carefully hidden from her daughter, now flourished as she cared for her grandchild and James. She couldn't keep up with all their running around, swinging from trees, climbing up hay bales, but watching them was fun, and she was always there when the inevitable bumps, bruises and cuts needed tears wiped away and ointments and plasters applied.

Katie was a daredevil, taking as many risks as the older children. At bath time, her stocky little body always looked as if she had been 'thrown through a hedge backwards'. Trish would shake her head in mock despair. Scratches and bruises dotted her skin, but Katie didn't care. Any tears were long forgotten by then.

Jamie was very protective of her. It was usually him that brought her in to have her latest accident treated, but it was often him that had caused it. For, if Katie was agile and deft, James was clumsy and uncontrolled. It was his foot that had knocked her off a branch…his arm that had flailed out and thrown her to the ground. His brown eyes would be full of distress, as he picked her up yet again, ushering her into the house for more nursing.

On rainy days, Jane would sit with them and read, or paint, or make models. Their latest artistic creations were displayed, stuck on the kitchen wall, or standing on the kitchen dresser.

Katie would splash colour on paper, declaring in five minutes that it was finished and it was a picture of a pony and a pig.

Jane was hard pressed to work out which was which.

Her modelling skills were equally hopeless. She had little patience or interest in indoor activities. So, while James produced the most intricate, yet solid, structures, which could stand displayed for weeks, Katie's efforts disintegrated the first time anyone breathed on them.

Trish was thriving too.

She started going into rooms that had been unused for years.

She started a bit of painting and decorating.

"Just tarting the place up," she told Jane.

She went to the mobile library, when it came to the village, and got DIY books, which she studied for hours.

New chance

She had stopped asking whether Katie's mother was going to contact them. Jane's evasive answers and short descriptions of Eva's new life made it clear that Katie was an unwanted problem.

Trish could understand that, even if she didn't agree with it.

At first, people were willing to believe Lizzie's assessment of the new housekeeper at Chance. They were wary of her, perhaps even more restrained than their usual reticence with strangers. But children are great door-openers and communication between mothers, waiting for their children to finish talking to each other, just happened.

Soon the gossips had worked out Trish's place in the scheme of things, and worked out Lizzie's antipathy too. Well, everyone knew she had her eyes set on Chance and, let's face it, old Doris Hensham had left Chance to someone who was really just a housekeeper, hadn't she? Oh yes, she was a Hensham relation, but only a minor branch. You could understand Lizzie being worried.

And Lizzie was worried, but not just about Trish taking Chance, more about Trish taking her husband.

* * * * *

Lizzie Warren had planned out her life at a very early age. She always wanted to be 'Queen of the castle' and that was what she would be.

She wasn't especially pretty, but she worked hard at enhancing all her good features: dressing well, carrying herself with confidence, so that people thought her as attractive.

She took the lead in school plays.

She was the Spring Princess at the village May Festival.

She had her photograph in the local paper, presenting a bouquet to the Countess of Purley at the school leaver's assembly.

Her mother was very proud of her.

There was never any question in Lizzie's mind that she would marry well. If she could she would have set her sights on one of the county families, but they had no suitable unattached males, so she had to scale down her dreams. If she couldn't be one of the local aristocracies, she would aim to be one of their associates.

The advent of Steven was a godsend. She had grown up with stories of Chance in its heyday. She knew the local squires were friendly with the Henshams. Chance, and the owners of Chance, had status; so she dreamed of restoring it to its former position and imagined herself at the centre of this revived social circle.

She married Steven with high hopes.

At first she had gone to visit 'Aunt Jane' regularly, but the old lady didn't respond to her overtures of friendship, her claims of family relationship, her attempts to be part of Chance, so the visits stopped and she bided her time instead. Meanwhile she encouraged Steven to take an even larger role in community affairs and thereby increase her own profile.

* * * * *

Steven still called to see Aunt Jane. He felt quite justified in calling less now that she had a housekeeper in situ, but he still did call, especially when Andrew had a message about some farm business.

It was during one such visit that Jane asked him to help Trish with some of the outside decorating, or could he ask Andrew to get one of the lads to come and paint the high bits, if Steven was too busy?

It wasn't until Jane mentioned this that Steven understood why he felt Chance looked a bit different. There was a sort of brightness to the place. He had noticed it coming down the lane. Not a startling difference, but as though someone had picked it up and given it a good dusting.

Inside was different too. Sparkling windows. Clean flowery curtains. Furniture moved around. And everywhere the smell of paint.

New chance

Jane explained that Trish had started painting the rooms upstairs, intending to get slowly round the whole house. She knew that it would take several painting seasons, so she would like help to get the outside walls repaired and painted this summer. Then she could potter on with the inside over the next few years, until the outside needed doing again.

Jane sent James to find Trish to explain better what she needed doing.

Steven was anxious to get away. He had a pile of work to do, but he listened and waited politely through Jane's introduction and the young woman's explanation that she could do the low bits outside, but she was hopeless up big ladders.

Steven smiled, saying, "Right... Right..." at intervals, not really listening, thinking that Andrew wouldn't be too happy losing one of his lads to do the painting. They were busy on the farm. Still, Aunt Jane was the owner, so...

"...and some of the brickwork's really naff. Pointless me painting inside until that's done."

Steven realised she had stopped talking, so he stuck in another, "Right..."

In the silence that followed, he realised that she really had stopped talking. "Oh right, I'll tell Andrew," he said and turned to leave.

It wasn't until that evening, after dinner, when Lizzie asked him what he thought of the new housekeeper, that he realised something else: he hadn't really looked at her.

"I don't know. I was so busy trying to get away to get those forms done for the Min of Ag, I never noticed."

"You're hopeless, Steven Warren," she laughed and smacked his arm with her tea towel.

Trish said, "Sorry," for the umpteenth time. It was pretty clear to her that Steven was here under protest.

He had arrived in the farm kitchen to say that Andrew had said it would be better if he did the painting. If one of the lads was sent to do it, they may string it out as long as possible, so Steven had better clear it away himself. After all, it was his aunt. Should he need any help, Andrew would send a lad down to him, which should stop any skiving around, but Andrew thought it would be done quicker if Steven worked alone.

"I can do all the windows downstairs and up to the height just above them, but anything higher than that, I've had it."

Steven wished she would just shut up and go away so he could get on with it. It was several days' work, what with the pointing repairs to the brickwork and all the painting.

Why Aunt Jane couldn't employ a painter, he didn't know. Of course it was traditional that people did their own decorating around here, and the farm was expected to provide any service to the house, but he could have done without this.

"Sorry…" she said again.

She looked at him, mixing cement, moving the ladder, getting this and that, set-mouthed and obviously annoyed. Oh, sod it, she thought. She tried to be nice to him.

"Look," she snapped, "I get giddy standing on a bloody house brick, otherwise I'd do it myself. Okay?"

He looked down at her from a couple of rungs up the ladder. She glared back at him and walked off.

She appeared twice again that morning, just yelled, "Tea!" put down a mug and stalked off again.

At lunchtime he felt an outsider.

The children were not at school and the kitchen was full of noise and action. Aunt Jane was in the thick of it too, which surprised him. When did she get so animated? She looked twenty years younger. He thought, ruefully, that Lizzie wouldn't like that!

He watched the young woman move around, putting some dish on the table, pretend fighting with the boy, bending over with laughter at something the girl said. Mostly, though, they laughed at her.

New chance

She was funny. The way she came out with things in that accent of hers. The expression on her face as she talked, describing how she had fallen over in the hen yard, or found a new recipe book in the morning room bookcase.

"What's this, Mum?" the lad asked, as he tasted some dish.

"God knows, love," she answered, without looking up from the sink.

Steven joined in the laughter as she said, "What? What?" in feigned amazement.

The next day he asked her was there any order she would like the walls done, as he knew she was doing some inside painting too.

She said no and walked away.

She answered his "Morning." She answered his "Bye." She said to help himself to water, wood, whatever, but she didn't talk to him again.

Up the ladder, he could hear her talking and laughing, singing to the music coming from the little radio that she carried into any room where she was working. He would see her running around with the children. He noticed when his own children, Robert and Tim, mentioned her name at home.

"Trish said we…"

"Trish hid in the barn and…"

He started thinking about her too much.

Trish was avoiding him, he knew that, but he was wrong about the reason.

Trish was avoiding him because she knew she would tense up at the sound of his voice, or the sight of him in the kitchen doorway. She didn't agree with getting involved with married men and she was angry with the half of herself that refused to obey this basic rule.

She was glad when he finished painting.

Out of sight. Out of mind.

So why did she start to attend all the PTA meetings where he was chairman?

Why volunteer to help with the school fete?

Why accept the lift home? Why were they sitting in his car, parked in the lane, kissing? What the hell did she think she was doing?

Each time they met, she would vow it was the last time.

She would stamp around the farm, furious with herself.

She would glare at him, if their paths crossed.

She would treat him with total disdain.

She would fall into his arms the moment he said her name.

Katie and James and Steven's two boys, Robert and Tim, went everywhere together. From the first day of their meeting, from their first game of Hide and Seek, their first shared den, their first Secret Society, they were a team. They called themselves the Chance Gang.

Katie was the youngest, but her exploits were as daring as any of the boys' and none of them thought of her as anything but one of the gang.

Other children came and went from the group, but the four stayed together.

After consultation with Steven and Trish, Jane bought ponies for them all. Their parents made it clear that they were responsible for restoring four of the stables at Chance and for keeping the yard tidy and repaired. The children were deliriously happy and worked with a will.

The sight of them on their ponies, cantering over the fields, or standing outlined on the hill, became part of the village scene.

The Chance Gang.

* * * * *

"This is my best bit," Katie said. "The lights from the farm shining on the snow. Like a Christmas card."

"Nah...summer's best." Tim hopped up and down, smacking his mittened hands together to knock off some of the snow. "You can do more in summer."

He gave up trying to get the snow off and put on more instead by scooping up another handful to pack into a snowball. As he chucked it at Robert's back, he added, "and it's warmer."

"Pack it in, Tim!" Robert rounded on him. "We said pax, didn't we? The fight's over."

"Come on; let's push it down now, before it gets too dark." James was rolling a huge ball of snow to the edge of the hill. "We won't see it if we don't do it now."

They all hurried to help push the ball to the steepest part of Chance Hill.

"Ready? One...Two...Three...Go!"

They cheered as the ball rolled over the edge and down the slope. It hit a small shrub and disintegrated, having only rolled a few yards. "Total waste of time." Tim stared over the edge at the mound of snow, in disgust.

Robert laughed. "I told you we should have used the usual path."

"Shut up, Rob," Tim said and kicked some snow at him. "Big head! 'I told you we should have used the usual path,'" he mimicked Robert's voice.

"If you had any brains, Tim, you'd be dangerous."

Tim pulled a face at him.

"I'm going home," Katie said and walked away, with the boys trailing after her.

"When Aunt Jane dies, we're going to live at Chance," Tim said, as they started down the hill, running to slide down the icy paths they had made earlier.

James stopped and turned to Tim. "Who said so?"

"Mum," Tim shouted, as he slid past, arms out straight to keep his balance.

"Hang on." James reached out to catch him, causing him to fall over on his backside. "Why are you going to live with us?"

Tim shook James' hands off his coat. "Get off! I don't know! That's what Mum said."

"Rob?" James turned to Robert. "Is that right?"

"That's what she says. Dad's our Aunt Jane's relative, so I suppose we'll inherit Chance."

"What does inherit mean?" Katie asked.

"Move in with you, Titch." Tim pushed Katie and ran up the hill to slide down again. "It'll be great, won't it? We can all share one of the big bedrooms and turn it into our own private den."

That idea pleased Katie, who yelled, "Yippee!" and took off down the slide after Tim.

"No, we can't!" James yelled after them.

"Why not? Why can't we?" Tim and Katie looked up at James and Robert from the bottom of the slide, as the two older boys trudged down to them.

"You two are such children." Robert shook his head in superior despair. "Katie is a girl. We can't all sleep in the same room."

"No, she's not!" Tim exclaimed. Then, as the other boys laughed, "Well, she is…but not one of those wimpy girls like them at school."

"It wouldn't be allowed."

"Why not?"

"We've told you why not, so shut up about it," James said. "Anyway, I haven't heard you're going to live with us."

"Our cousins, Emma and Dean, share a room, don't they, Rob? Don't they?" Tim appealed to his brother. "And Emma's a girl, isn't she?"

"That's different. They're only little."

Tim kicked some more snow. "It's not fair," he moaned. "It's not fair. Just because Katie's got a chest growing. It's not fair."

New chance

"Shut up, Tim," James and Robert said together and ran to slide down the next path. Tim charged after them, leaving Katie looking down at her chest.

Katie took off her pyjama top and stared at herself in the mirror.

Tim was right. Somehow she hadn't noticed the lumps before…and it wasn't fair.

She sat on her bed with her head on her knees and cried. She didn't really know why she was crying, except she had this feeling, like when one of the old dogs died, like she had just lost something important.

Jane studied one of her Day Books from twenty years ago. She didn't read the words, she looked at the writing. She was surprised at how her writing had changed over the years. The strong rushed lines of those days were very different from the carefully formed words she was writing now.

Her writing then was deeply indented, with straighter uprights and clear curves. Now the writing looked shaky and fainter.

So, even writing ages, she thought.

She had shut herself in her room. The big blanket box where she stored her Day Books was open. When the children were small she had bought the chest, using the excuse that she could keep her valuable papers in it, safe from little hands. The chest had two strong locks and she kept the keys in her handbag.

Trish never questioned it. "Good idea," she said. "The little sods get in to everything."

Jane did keep a few papers in there, but mostly it was full of her Day Books, patiently transferred from their boxes in the morning room annexe.

She put in the old book, and the current one she had just written, and locked the chest. She sat heavily back on the bed, tuning in on herself…her aching hip and knee, her pattering heart. She wondered if it was time to start burning them.

She would take one pad at a time to the kitchen range. Start with the oldest ones. The ones no one must know.

It was also time to sort out Chance. She must make a will. That was the problem, because she knew Steven expected to inherit Chance.

Steven...Steven and Trish... They thought she didn't know. Trouble was, she and these books knew all the secrets.

* * * * *

"Oh God, Trish!" His hand moved over her naked body as she lay beside him, her skin glistening from the heat of their lovemaking. He reached around her waist and pulled her back to him, holding her tightly, as if he wanted to force her inside him, groaning as he slowly moved his body against hers. "Oh, Trish...please...please..." She became still, then pulled away from him.

He closed his eyes and cursed himself with a sigh of exasperation. Every meeting ended this way and every time he swore to himself it would not happen again.

She was out of bed, pulling on her pants and trousers, reaching for her bra.

He sat up and swung his legs off the bed, his head drooping down in despair. "Sorry." He ground the word out again.

She looked at him as she put on her sweater. "Do you want a cup of tea?" She smiled politely as he looked up at her.

"Fine." He smiled politely in return, reaching for his clothes.

The mood was gone. The intimacy. The ecstasy. The total surrender of mind and body. Gone.

She waited for him to dress, then checked outside the door, before they went down to the kitchen.

* * * * *

New chance

They met each other often at various village functions, or passing each other in the shop, or on the road.

They waved and talked. They were friendly and at ease. Just part of the village scene. No one would think of them as more than that, they thought. The village was small. Everyone met everyone often.

About once a month, if they were lucky, they were lovers. In quiet meadows, or deserted bars, when the weather was warm. Sometimes in her room at Chance, in the wintertime, but these meetings were rare and difficult to arrange.

Winter was a cold lonely time.

He wanted to marry her. She would have none of it.

He didn't care about the social implications of divorce. He knew the village would take sides, half with him, half with Lizzie. He knew it would be a source of endless speculation and gossip, an event by which to date future events, but it wouldn't be the first divorce in the village and it wouldn't affect his job, or his status, because his integration into village life was accepted.

Trish feared the same would not be said of her. Even after all these years, she feared that they would condemn her, blame her for misleading him. They would remember she was the one from the city, the one with the strange accent and ways. The days were long gone when she couldn't have cared less what they thought. By the time he was begging her to marry him, she had carved out a new life for herself. A new personality. Not the common little slut from the city slums, but the bright and cheerful, hard-working woman, who was the housekeeper at Chance: always willing to help out at church jumble sales and school fetes...baking cakes for the Senior Citizen's Tea... collecting Mrs Taverner's groceries when her arthritis got too bad. Yes, a nice woman...and hadn't she done wonders with the old farmhouse?

Trish had made a place for herself. In her own mind, she had pulled herself up in the world and found her home. Nothing must ever drag her down again.

She wouldn't listen to his pleas. Sexual satisfaction was very nice, but it didn't compare to the feeling of security.

* * * * *

Lizzie guessed Steve was with some other woman and she guessed who it was. It didn't really bother her that he should be sleeping with someone else, except that Steve was her possession and the woman he was sleeping with lived in her house. She thought of Chance as her house, her land. She had resented Trish being there from the first moment she heard the news. She imagined Trish wheedling herself into Aunt Jane's affections, stealing the property that rightfully should be Steven's and hers.

She had waited so long to take up her proper place in society. When she married Steven, she hadn't realised it would mean years and years of waiting.

She had grown bitter, felt cheated.

She had waged a verbal war against Trish from the start, taking every opportunity to revile her to her friends, to seek information on her activities and to diminish her attainments and her personality.

"Common little tart," she called her.

But, slowly, her friends had fallen away. Put off by her obsession. Feeling guilty because they found Trish amenable. Now, only one or two people called at her cottage, and they did so more out of a sense of community duty than a desire for friendship.

She still sought to belittle Trish to them, but she didn't tell them Steven was having an affair with her…that "common little tart." She feared that, if the village knew, they would laugh at her. So she kept it secret and planned the vengeance she would take one day.

* * * * *

New chance

Katie sat on her stone and looked down at Chance.

The white house gleamed in the low sun of late afternoon. She picked out the pony yard, with its neat stable block and well-brushed area. Her doing; and the boys, of course. They had repaired, painted and weeded it years ago, to keep their own first ponies. They had done the whole block, making plans to get other ponies when they were older. They were going to have a whole string of ponies to enter in local gymkhanas. They were going to be Pony Club champions of the world.

Only they didn't: they grew up instead. Too big to ride their ponies. Too busy to think about them much any more.

James was away at agricultural college. Robert was at university. Tim had already got a job. He worked at the big supermarket in the local town.

She smiled to herself as she thought of Tim as a shop assistant.

"Trainee manager, if you don't mind!"

The Chance Gang.

Good days. Fun.

Now she looked after the yard and the ponies on her own, including the larger pony she had for her thirteenth birthday. Aunt Jane had promised her a horse for this birthday, but she wanted more than that, and today she was going to ask.

She had tried to ask many times over the past year. It was the thought of refusal that stopped her, because that would be the end of all her plans, all her dreams. But she had reached the time when she had to take the risk. It had to be now.

"But don't you need qualifications these days?"

"Not just for that. Not just for locals."

"But you wouldn't make enough to live on just from locals," Jane pointed out.

"I know."

Jane looked at Katie's curly blonde hair. She couldn't see her face, because she was looking down at her hands.

293

What was wrong with her? This wasn't like Katie at all. Direct. Open. Tough. Katie wasn't good at hiding her feelings, or at subtle approaches.

"Well?" demanded Jane.

"I wasn't thinking of just doing riding lessons. I want to start the livery stables again." She peeped up at Jane from under her lashes, trying to judge her reaction, waiting for the put-down. Then, rushing out more words, before Jane could open her mouth and end it all. "We have the ponies and we could do lessons with them, just locally at first, and I could do up the other yards. The Belmont's said they would like to have their hunters back here, so that would be a start. I could employ a groom for the lessons and concentrate on the liveries myself. I know it would take money to get going – do the yards back up – but I could pay you back. And I know it wouldn't make much at first, but if the word spreads...after all Chance used to be a big name and..." Katie's voice trailed off as she stared at Jane. "I'm good at it. You can ask Lodge Hill."

You could touch the silence that followed.

Shirley, Jane thought. This is about Shirley. Katie knows the history of the place and she thinks I won't want to be reminded of Shirley.

"You're only young," she said, and thought that Shirley ran the place effectively when she was even younger.

"I've been going to Lodge Hill for years. I'm good at this... really," Katie urged. "And by the time we've got it up and running, I'll be older."

Katie spent all her free time at Lodge Hill Livery Stables. She had been to stay there every school holiday for years, preferring that to a holiday by the sea, or abroad. Lodge Hill was in the north of the county, forty miles away, and Trish had spent a lot of time ferrying Katie there for weekends, or longer breaks.

"So you want to start the stables up again and you want me to pay for it?"

Katie looked at her.

New chance

"But what about those qualifications? If you expand past local business, surely you have to get those?"

"We could employ a groom with BHS qualifications for the lessons. Schooling and livery are more by success and word-of-mouth recommendation."

"And how would you pay this groom?"

"Well, that wouldn't be straight away. I mean, none of this would. I just want to know if I can start building it up again. It will take years, I know that, but I can do it, Aunt Jane, I can. It's what I'm good at."

"What does Trish think about all this?"

Katie flushed and bit the corner of her lip. She pictured Trish demanding that she be sensible, think about someone else rather than herself. "You know how your Aunt Jane suffered after all that business, when this was a stables before. Don't you upset her again. She's been good to us."

"She said it was up to you," Katie slightly twisted Trish's last words, carefully omitting her earlier admonitions. "I'll be careful, Aunt Jane. I won't do anything to hurt you, or Chance."

Jane knew what Trish had said, just by the look on Katie's face. Katie was not Shirley. You could never tell much from Shirley's expression. Katie was as open as Shirley had been closed.

"I'll think about it and let you know," she said.

Jane sat at the window in the morning room and thought about it.

She didn't doubt Katie's ability with horses. Whether the stables would be successful or not was not the problem. Katie would work until it was. That was something she got from her Hensham blood. Determination. The sort of determination that sets targets and reaches them by plodding forwards, rather than leaping over obstacles, risking life and limb. Single-minded, steady progress. It was a Hensham trait.

She thought of herself, years ago, slowly transforming the mess that was Chance into a well-run, well-maintained unit.

Plodding progress and delight in each small achievement. A newly painted room. A better working rota. Organisation.

Her daughter must have had a similar ability, rising high in her company's structure before she died.

Oh yes, ability mattered, and flair…seeing an opportunity and grasping it. But many had ability and only the few the determination to carry on when the inevitable setbacks occurred. That was the Hensham trait. Dogged determination. Not just about work, about everything: Great uncle William, despising his son, Paul, but keeping him at Chance for the sake of his grandchild… Shirley, doing a similar thing with Jeff, despite years of pleas, despite years of fears.

Determination to protect Chance. Some even killed for that.

Jane sighed, moving her position on the window seat as the nagging ache in her hip demanded attention.

Starting up the livery stables again? Repeating the history of Chance?

Perhaps life did repeat itself over again, but if that was the case, did she want it?

As the sky darkened outside, she stared at her reflection in the glass of the window. She was an old woman. Did it matter what she wanted? But at the back of her mind was this uneasy feeling that stopped her from just agreeing, from just taking pleasure in Katie's pleasure.

She loved Katie more than she ever believed she could love anyone. More that she loved her own daughter. She felt some guilt about that.

Her Katie. She thought of her as 'her Katie'.

She looked around the room. Up to the beams crossing the ceiling. Across to the large fireplace with its brick surround. She looked at the panelled doors, the alcoves, the red flag tiles, with rugs placed in front of the settee and the fire.

She loved Chance too. It was her hiding place, her healing place. Every nook and cranny held memories. She would leave this to Katie, because she loved Katie and Katie loved Chance.

Yet the uneasy feeling persisted. History repeating itself?

It was funny that she couldn't remember clearly why she denied her daughter, why she had let Eva assume her role. The feelings that had let that happen were long gone and now it all seemed so stupid. Why didn't she just tell the world that Jenny had been her daughter and claim Katie as her grandchild? She didn't care what people thought now, so why not?

Because she cared what Katie thought, she answered herself.

Open, honest Katie. Jane didn't think she could stand it if Katie rejected her. And she might. She might be appalled at the lie that Jane had made of her life and her sense of identity.

No, she couldn't risk telling her.

Katie and Trish had long ago accepted that Eva didn't want any contact with the illegitimate child of her younger days. Jane had never said that, but as years passed, they worked it out for themselves. They assumed that Eva had made a new life and needed to cut her ties to the past. Trish could understand that, and explained it to Katie, when she started asking questions.

There had never been any hint that Eva was not Katie's grandmother and it had been many years now since Jane had had any contact with Eva. So it was safe, wasn't it? Let Katie start up the stables. No one need ever know that history was repeating itself…that it was built on yet another lie.

Jane got up to go and find Katie. She anticipated Katie's excitement and smiled at the thought.

It would be all right, wouldn't it?

She refused to attend to the uneasy feeling that danced at the back of her mind.

It would be all right. Nothing could go wrong this time.

* * * * *

Detective Inspector Pockett looked at the blood spattered up the kitchen units, smeared down the white front of an electric stove and pooled across the floor.

"What a bloody mess," he said.

The uniformed constable looked at him, unsure whether this was a joke or not. It wasn't.

Sergeant Joseph Drinkwater put his rubber-gloved hand out, using the top of a unit to pull himself up from where he had been crouching to study the lump of mangled bone and flesh that used to be a head.

"Tell me, Joseph; is this another of your weird rural syndromes?" Pockett asked, as he peered round Joe's shoulder at the body on the floor.

The kitchen was narrow and long. Matching beige units, the sink, the stove and a washing machine lined each wall, making the space only wide enough for two slim people to stand side by side.

Joe Drinkwater wasn't slim any more. He turned his head to look down at Pockett's face, peering round his upper arm. "Sir?"

Pockett leaned back on the washing machine, talking as he studied the kitchen from ceiling to floor. "Well, how come the only crime that happens here is murder? Not even a bicycle stolen, or the odd bit of vandalism. Only the occasional murder. I just wondered if it was one of those local traditions. Like it's okay to kill your neighbour, but 'mind you don't go trampling on me 'olly 'ocks.'" He mimicked Joe's accent.

The constable stared quickly at the floor to hide his smile, while Joe stared at Pockett, who smiled back at him. "Or did they get one of those encyclopaedias from the library? 'Crimes of the World' or something like that. Only no one could ever read it fast enough to get past Chapter One, 'Murder', then it had to go back in case they got a fine for being overdue? Eh? Is that it?" He lowered his head, pretending to whisper sideways to Joe's upper arm, as he assumed a 'county' accent. "Did you hear old Bloggs got a library fine? It's shocking. Really shocking. The thin edge of the wedge, old boy. Total breakdown of law and order. You won't be able to walk down the lane soon without some hooligan throwing a crisp packet on the ground. 'Sorry, can't stop, though, only I promised to murder the wife tonight.' Is that it?" he asked resuming his own voice and looking up into Joe's blank face.

"Go and watch the gate, Constable," Joe said to the young man, who was biting his lip and trying to memorise all this to tell his mates later in the staff canteen. He scurried out and Joe turned to stare at Pockett.

"What?" Pockett protested, opening his hands in wide-eyed innocence.

"Shut up, you stupid old man," Joe hissed at him. "They've heard it all a million times, so you can stop playing to the crowds."

"What crowds?" Pockett protested, with even more innocence.

"You know what I mean," Joe growled at him. "For God's sake, grow up."

A uniformed sergeant appeared at the door on the far side of the kitchen.

"Have you identified the victim, Sergeant?" Pockett did his best Sherlock Holmes impression: hands behind his back...voice cold and efficient. "Is that better?" he added, looking sideways at Joe, who was trying not to laugh.

"Is what better, sir?" the sergeant asked from the doorway.

"Who's the victim, Sergeant?" Joe encouraged him.

"Oh, a Mrs Eliza Warren, sir. Found by her neighbour, a Mrs Jane Bateman, who recognised her clothes. She's in the other room with the doctor. Shock, and that."

"Where's Mr Warren?"

"At the market, sir. They're trying to get hold of him."

"Okay. Thank you. Go and ask the doctor if we can talk to Mrs Bateman."

Sue Ryland

"Sir." The sergeant disappeared through the door that led to the rest of the house.

"Have we got a murder weapon, Joe? Can't see anything obvious, can you?"

"No. When forensic have finished we can have a better look. There's quite a few places I can't see from here." Joe craned his head, trying to see down the gaps between the units and the machines. "There's a rubbish bin over there too."

"Anything in the rest of the house?"

"Not obvious, no, according to the uniforms. All the action seems to have been in here. No sign of burglary."

"A domestic, most likely. See what the husband has to say. Let's go and talk to this woman. Which way do we go?"

"Back out and round to the front door." Joe pointed the way. "Left out of this door."

They passed the forensic team going in as they walked along the gravel path, around the cottage and to the front door.

"Very Ye Olde English," Pockett remarked, looking at the well-kept garden with its rows of vegetables and banks of flowers.

There was a cast iron pump over a brownstone sink by the side of the front path of the cottage. Pockett gave it a couple of experimental pushes up and down as they passed. When a trickle of water dribbled out, he stopped and turned back to pump the handle a few more times.

"Hey! Look at that!" He was delighted as gushes of water pushed out in response to his actions.

"It's called a pump. You move the handle up and down and water comes out."

"Okay, thank you, Joseph. You can cut the sarcasm now. Only a lot of them are fake these days, aren't they?"

The constable appeared in the doorway of the cottage. He stood in the small porch, watching his superiors, hoping for some more gems to pass on to his mates. All the force knew it was an act, enjoyed by the two participants as much as the onlookers,

New chance

but that didn't mean that working with them wasn't a sure way of livening up the staff room. He hoped to hear a lot of the famed 'Billy and Joe' cripplers.

Pockett didn't disappoint him. As soon as he noticed the constable, he walked on, saying loudly, "Come along, Sergeant. We haven't got all day for you to play in the water."

Jay Bateman sat on the sofa, staring into the glass door of a chunky black log-burning stove.

There was a big churning gap where her mind should be, as though she was standing in a doorway, looking down into a huge precipice with clouds swirling along the bottom. She knew she ought to step back into safety, but everything seemed to be frozen, except the feeling of fear.

"I've given her something, but it will take a few minutes yet."

The doctor sat by her, encouraging her to drink the tea that a constable had borrowed from the next cottage along the lane. The bright yellow cup from the top of the thermos flask looked out of place in the room. The colour reflected on Jay's face as she sipped the drink.

"That's it...that's it..." the doctor encouraged. We've sent young Allan to find your Harvey. He'll be here soon. Just you try and relax."

Pockett and Joe stood by the door, waiting. "That's the young woman from last time, isn't it?" Pockett whispered.

Joe nodded. "She was one of the grooms at the stables. Went out with one of the farm workers, if I remember right."

They both stumbled as the door was pushed open, knocking them to the side.

Harvey Bateman fairly ran into the room. He went straight to Jay, looking closely at her face, then gathering her in his arms. "What the bloody hell's going on here?" he demanded. He glared accusation at the men in her room, ready to flatten anyone who had upset his Jay.

Despite three children and many years of marriage, Jay Bateman was still a small slim woman, no bigger than when she'd worked at Chance. Her frame looked lost in Harvey's arms, for he had filled out. The gangling youth that Pockett and Joe had interviewed was now a solid six-foot block of protective muscles. Pockett felt quite relieved that it wasn't him that had upset Mrs Bateman.

"It's all right, Harvey," the doctor soothed. "Jay's had a bit of a shock. There's been an accident. Lizzie Warren's been killed and Jay found her."

Harvey pulled his head back to look at Jay's face. He lifted her chin from where it was buried in the folds of his shirt. She was crying now. The familiarity of the touch and smell and sound of her husband had released all those frozen emotions. She was safe again. She could feel again.

"You all right, love?" He scanned her face for signs of injury. "You're not hurt?"

She shook her head and stroked his face to reassure him. She could feel his shaking body relax as he realised she was not in danger or pain.

Joe looked at the floor, embarrassed to witness this display of affection.

Pockett stared at them and tried to analyse his feelings. He was quite surprised to realise he was curious. He had never felt that way about anyone and he was certain no one cared that much for him. Plus, you didn't see a lot of overt affection in this job. He was reluctant to disturb this insight into a life he had never known, or witnessed. It was interesting. Still, needs must…

"Mrs Bateman, I don't know if you remember me. It was thirty odd years ago. I'm Inspector Pockett."

Jay smiled at him from Harvey's chest.

"I'm sorry to bother you now, but we need to ask a few questions."

Jay sat up, rubbing her face with the back of one hand and holding Harvey's hand with the other. "Yes," she said, "of course."

"Can you describe how you found Mrs Warren?"

"We were going to the village together. There's a book fair at the village hall and we thought we might get some books for presents and that, you know?"

She stopped, her face reflecting the memory of the last time her friend had spoken and seeing the horror of the kitchen again. Her body shook and she stared wild-eyed at Pockett.

Harvey put his arm around her, rubbing her shoulder. "All right, love," he said. "All right."

"Take your time, Mrs Bateman," Joe murmured.

"Sorry…sorry." She shook her head and bit her lip, then went on, "so we arranged that I would call for her at eleven and we'd go down together. I was a bit late, so I must have got here about twenty past." She stopped again, taking large breaths to calm herself. "I walked in…"

"The door was open?"

"No, not open, if you mean wide, but it wasn't locked or anything. We don't usually lock our back doors. I lifted the latch and called to say it was only me…and…"

"You saw Mrs Warren on the floor," Joe finished for her.

"No…well, yes…but I didn't think she was dead at first. I sort of came in backwards, you see. I was pulling my shopping trolley through and I sort of saw her feet just to the side of me…" She stopped again, looking desperately at Harvey. "I thought the washing machine had broken again. I don't know why. I thought she was lying on the floor trying to fix it. It doesn't make sense, does it? I don't know why I thought that."

Jay was talking fast, clinging to Harvey's hand, trying to make him understand, trying to make herself understand.

"It's all right, love," he murmured. "Steady now. It's all right."

"Anyway, I said something like, 'It's not broken again, is it?' And then I sort of realised her feet weren't moving and I turned to look at her… It is Lizzie, isn't it?"

Pockett said there had been no formal identification yet, but with her clothes being recognised, they must assume it was.

Sue Ryland

They were trying to locate Mrs Warren's husband.

"Oh God, Steven!" Jay looked at Harvey again. "You had better go and get Andrew, love. When Steven finds out, he'll..."

"He's at market. Steve's at market. Shall I go and get Andrew?" he asked Pockett.

"Andrew would be...?"

"He's the farm manager and Steve's best friend."

"We'll send someone to fetch him," Joe said. "You stay with your wife, Mr Bateman."

Jay leaned back against Harvey, eyes closed. The doctor stood up and looked at her. "If it's okay with you, I think Harvey should take her home now. The sedative I gave her will make her tired for a time."

"Yes, take her home, Mr Bateman. We'll be in touch later," Pockett agreed.

Harvey half carried Jay to the door.

"He never asked how she died," Pockett mused, as the door closed behind them.

Trish sat on the stairs and felt sick. The news of Lizzie's death had sped around the village faster than any telephone system could have operated. People said she had been murdered.

Murdered!

Trish thought of the times she had wished Lizzie gone... wished she and Steve could be together always. She felt guilty. She felt sick. Steve wouldn't do that, would he? No matter how desperate he was, he wouldn't do that, but the police were bound to suspect him. Hadn't she read somewhere that most murders were done by family members? Husbands were the first suspects. But Steve wouldn't do that, would he?

She pictured him pleading with her the last time they met. Pleading with her to marry him. She saw herself saying she would not even think about it while Lizzie was alive...while Lizzie was alive...Oh God! Oh God!

She felt sick.

Jane was frightened. It was happening again. The police would find out things...all the secrets...and then Katie would know.

Pockett and Joe studied Steven. He was sitting where Jay had sat earlier on the small settee. The police had found him at the market and brought him home in a police car. They said there had been an accident, but they didn't know any more details. Now Pockett had just told him that Lizzie was dead and it looked like murder.

Reactions were funny things, Pockett thought. He had seen everything from instant faints to unfaltering hospitality, as the recipient of the news bustled around offering tea and biscuits, apparently unable to hear, or comprehend, or accept, or admit, that any tragedy had befallen them.

Steven was somewhere between the two extremes. He looked more puzzled than horrified, more numbed than grief-stricken. He answered their questions in the same tone of voice he would use to say his telephone number. Automatic, unemotional response.

He went to the farm at seven-fifteen. He went to the market at eight. He always went to Thursday market. He took calves, or pigs, or lambs, to sell. He bought whatever was planned, or a bargain, if he saw one. He came back to the farm at four. He came home about six, unless there was something extra on, like calving, or lambing.

No, today hadn't been different. He was in the auction ring area when the police found him at about two-thirty.

He had his lunch in the market café about one o'clock.

Yes, he had sat with some farmer friends there. He gave them some names.

He said he would contact his sons, Robert and Timothy. Robert was at university. Timothy was lodging in town.

He said he would stay at his manager's house tonight.

Yes, he would be at Andrew's house when they wanted him.

Yes, he knew he had to identify her.

Automatic. Unemotional.

Pockett watched him leave with Andrew's arm around his shoulders. "He never asked how she died either," he said.

"What we got?"

"Beaten to death, basically. Massive skull and facial fractures. Fractures of the lower right hand and arm, probably defensive injuries. Done by a piece of wood. Rough. Round. About twenty centimetres wide."

"What's that in English?"

"What?" The young pathologist looked up.

"How many inches is that?" Joe explained.

"Oh, about eight, but that's just the width of the impact area. The circumference of the implement would, therefore, be double that. Say forty centimetres…er…sixteen in English."

"Round piece of wood. Sixteen inches. Got it. How about a log for the fire?"

"Yes, that would do. We're having the splinters analysed so we can tell you what sort of wood soon."

"Anything else?"

"No sign of sexual interference or assault and she was about eleven to twelve weeks pregnant. Time of death between nine-thirty and eleven, give or take a bit."

Pockett and Joe were drinking coffee.

"We drink too much coffee," Pockett said.

They drank on in silent agreement.

"Did you get them to check the woodpile by the back door, as well as the log box in the lounge?"

"Yes. Nothing. Probably burnt it straight away in that wood-burning stove. It heats the water, so it's going most of the time. Open the door. Shove it in. Evidence gone."

They drank some more.

"Get a tape measure."

Joe rifled through one of the drawers in his desk, producing a frayed green tape measure held in a coil by a press-stud at the end. The first numbers were indecipherable, rubbed off by age and use."

"Can you read sixteen inches on that still? You really ought to look after your equipment, Joseph. Departmental property, you know." Pockett leaned back in his chair, tutting in mock disapproval.

"Equipment? One naff tape measure. Just about sums this department up. Tell you what, I'll fill in a form to get another one and you sign it. That'll make them buggers in finance sweat a bit. I mean, a new one could cost all of seventy-five pence."

He held part of the measure between his hands in a straight line. "Sixteen inches."

"Curl it round."

Pockett leaned forward to see the result laid out on the desk. "Put your hands round it."

Joe did so.

"Do you think it would be comfortable holding that one-handed?"

"Who said it was one handed?" Joe asked, studying his hand encircling the measure. "Anyway, not too bad, but maybe a bit smaller would be better."

"And you have great peasant mitts," Pockett leaned forward to circle the tape with his hand, "whereas I have the smaller refined hands of a true intellectual and, as you can see, one hand barely covers half the circle. Not comfortable at all for bashing someone's head in…"

"If your little girl's hand was strong enough to pick up the log in the first place…"

"…so does that mean we can rule out ladies?"

"Or weedy little men?"

Pockett glared at him.

"Sorry, I meant refined intellectual old men," he smiled a dubious apology, "unless they did it two-handed." He went to his desk and rolled up a piece of paper, announcing a darts match in the staff canteen next Thursday, and taped it in position so that the end matched the sixteen-inch circle on the desk. "Try that."

Pockett put his hands around the tube. "Not likely," he said, "although you could get more grip from the rough surface of a log than this. Still, it's not balanced, if you know what I mean."

Joe put his hands around the tube then held it with one hand.

"Yes, more likely," Pockett observed. "So, unless we've got a piece of wood with a much narrower end, we want someone with big hands. Time to talk to Mr Warren again, do you think?"

The formal identification of Lizzie was done by the birthmark on her back.

"It's shaped like a little shoe," Steve said, "with a high heel."

He was right.

Joe looked at Mr Warren's hands as he answered Pockett's questions. A bit bigger than average, he decided. Farm worker's hands.

The forensic team had identified the wood and confirmed the house log theory. They were now trying to fit the remaining logs together to get the dimensions of the murder weapon. If the missing log was not much narrower at one end, then it would be an unlikely weapon for small hands. Pockett always wanted to eliminate people off the blackboard as soon as possible... always wanted to get the list of 'likelys' down to the minimum, so he put pressure on.

"No sign of disruption in the rest of the house and nothing stolen then?" Pockett was asking.

Steve shook his head. "I don't think so."

"I'm sorry to have to ask some of these questions, Mr Warren, but the sooner it's done, the sooner we can move on to other possibilities."

Steve said he understood.

"Now, we have confirmed you arrived at the market about eight-fifteen. You booked in the calves and unloaded into a pen. We have also confirmed you had lunch in the market café at one. What we need to know is where you were and who you saw between these two times. Let's say between nine and one."

Steve didn't answer. He was staring into the fire and appeared not to have heard.

"Mr Warren?"

"I didn't kill her," Steve said, still looking at the fire.

It was a quiet statement. No panic or fear.

"Between nine and one then?"

"I don't know. I looked around the pens. Watched a bit of the sheep sales. Went to the calf ring…you came then, though, so that was after lunch…I don't know…"

"Did you go around with anyone in the morning or talk to anyone?"

"I don't know. Probably." He suddenly remembered something and looked up at Pockett. "I went to the M F to see about some new bits for the milking machines. Barry would remember. I talked to him there and he got some catalogues out. We were comparing prices."

"The M F?"

"One of the market shops, sir," Joe explained. "Farming equipment and so on."

"And what time was that?"

"Before lunch. About twelve, say. I was there a good half hour. Barry takes his time, you know?" He huffed a small laugh, then looked back into the fire. "Barry would remember," he said.

"What about between nine and twelve then? Can you think of anyone else who might remember seeing you?"

"No."

"Well, you think about it and let us know if you do, okay?" Joe sounded kind and reassuring.

"Thank you. Yes, I will."

"Do you know of anyone who might have a grievance against your wife, Mr Warren? Real or imagined?" Pockett's voice sounded cold by comparison.

Steve shook his head. "She had no face, did she?" He was still looking at the fire.

"You wouldn't have asked about any other marks if she had."

"I'm sorry, Mr Warren." Pockett's tone confirmed Steve's reasoning. "Can you think of anyone?"

"No."

Joe watched the figure on the settee. Numbed immobility, he thought, refusing to let himself think, or feel…or was it the frozen panic of guilt or fear, like a lazy student now faced with an incomprehensible exam paper? Whichever way, he wasn't coping with the questions.

"Did you know your wife was pregnant?"

"No, she wasn't."

"How do you know she wasn't, Mr Warren?"

"Because…"

"Yes?"

"Because I've had a vasectomy…and…"

"They've been known to go wrong," Joe said. "You could have a test."

"No. No…we haven't anyway…you know…not for a long time."

"You haven't had any sexual relationship with your wife for a long time? How long?"

"Some years." He shook his head. "She can't have been pregnant."

"So the marriage wasn't all cream cakes and honeysuckle?"

They put their mugs of coffee on the table.

"And she was seeing someone else." Pockett tapped his biro on the mug. "The question is: who? And, if she had a lover to satisfy her needs, who was sorting her husband out?"

New chance

* * * * *

Trish put the phone hard against her ear, in case someone else might hear the voice on the other end.

"No!" She breathed the word urgently into the mouthpiece, her eyes checking the hall and stairs. "No."

"Please, Trish, I've got to talk to you. Please, listen. I know we can't meet anywhere, but please listen."

Katie came into the end of the hall, smiling at Trish, as she passed into the kitchen.

Trish smiled back, pressing the phone harder against her, trying to hide the "Trish?!...Trish?!" sounds of panic he was making at her silence.

"Yes?" she said, loudly, to shut him up.

Katie disappeared into the kitchen. Trish hissed into the phone, "You shouldn't do this. I don't want to talk to you. Please don't do this."

There was silence at the other end. Then, "Do you think I killed her?"

Trish screwed up her face and pushed the hair back off her forehead as she tried to sort out her feelings.

"You do, don't you?" he accused.

Half of her wanted to say, no, she didn't. She loved him. She knew he wouldn't do that. But the other half was frightened, remembered his desperation, remembered her own words of refusal: "not while Lizzie is alive."

"You didn't, did you?" she begged.

Jane stood on the landing and closed her eyes, waiting to hear the tone in Trish's voice when the question was answered. But she heard nothing more, because Steve put the phone down.

"Do you think I should go over?" Katie asked Trish.

Robert and Tim were back, living in an estate cottage, looking after their father, who had left Andrew's house as soon as Sir Edmund offered a temporary place.

"What do you think, Aunt Jane?" Katie turned to her after Trish's apparently disinterested shrug.

"If you want to. Take James with you."

James was watching his mother. "What?" he said, hearing his name.

"Do you want to come with me to see Robert and Tim? We ought to show our faces, show we care, hadn't we?"

James agreed.

"Have you seen much of Uncle Steve?"

They were walking to the village along the lane and cutting through fields and footpaths only used by local people.

"What, before or after?" Katie asked. "No one has seen him since it happened. I can't believe it. I really can't. Makes you start looking over your shoulder, doesn't it? Makes you nervous."

When James didn't answer, she said, sulkily, "Well it does me, anyway."

"So you haven't seen him?" James persisted.

"No, why?"

"I just wondered, that's all."

They trudged on in silence for a while, then he said, "Who do you think did it?"

"Some passing nutter. That's what most people think. Though you've got the usual nasty minded gossip, you know. The usual lot who've got nothing better to do with their time."

"What do they say?"

"That Uncle Steve did it because he was having an affair with someone else. Or that Aunt Lizzie was having it off with someone and they did it. The usual sick stuff."

They didn't say anything else all the way to the village.

Trish stood at the sink and wondered if she could risk phoning Andrew, asking him if there was a phone at the estate cottage.

She could say she just wanted to offer her sympathy and any help to Steve and his sons. But then, what would she say if she spoke to Steve? He had put the phone down on her. He might do that again. Even if she said she believed he wouldn't hurt anyone, would he know she wasn't really sure? Because if he had done it, she was to blame.

"Do you want any help with dinner?" Jane's voice, from the table, interrupted her thoughts.

"No."

How could she have said not while Lizzie was alive?! But then, she wasn't to know Lizzie would be killed. No one could have known that.

"Do you want to talk about it?" Jane interrupting again.

"No!" she snapped.

Who could have known that? It wasn't her fault, so why did she feel so guilty? She couldn't talk about it to anyone, not anyone, because…

Her thoughts stopped, as the meaning of Jane's words penetrated through the mess of her mind. She turned to look at the elderly woman sitting at the table. "Sorry, what did you say?"

"I said, do you want to talk about it?"

"About what?" Trish tried for her usual bright tone as she splashed a plate around in the sink.

"Steven and you," Jane said.

Hot blood flushed into Trish's face, which she kept turned to the sink, fighting the urge to look at Jane now. How could she know? No one knew. Nosey old biddy. Spying and listening around! Her hand squeezed the scourer in the water, anger turning to fear. If she knew, who else knew too?

"I don't know what you mean," she croaked out.

Did all the village know? Were they a local joke, to be whispered about in the shop, nudged about in the pub?

"Steve's bit on the side…" Nudge, nudge.

Oh God…God…

"I know, Trish. I've known for years," Jane said. "I haven't told anyone else and, if you want to talk about it now, I won't tell anyone that either. Sit and talk about it."

Trish looked at her and believed her. She swung from fear to relief. Relief that no one else knew. Relief at the idea of being able to talk about it. She rubbed her hands down the side of her overall. "How do you know?" The back of her nose and eyes were smarting and filling. She didn't want to cry.

Jane shrugged her shoulders. "I don't know. It's to do with plays and scripts, I always used to think. People behave in a certain way and, when they act out of character, you sort of notice the script change." She put her hand out to Trish as she moved to sit opposite her at the table. "I wasn't spying on you, or anything. Sorry."

Trish cried quietly for a few moments. Jane patted her hand.

"What is worrying you? It's not just the fear that everyone feels at the thought of some lunatic going around, is it?"

"No."

"What then?"

Trish stared at her, unwilling or unable to put it into words.

"You think Steve might have done it?"

"No! Yes...I don't know..." The tears rolled down again.

"Why?"

"Because I said I wouldn't marry him while Lizzie was alive."

Jane had to strain to hear the words.

Trish looked at Jane's face to see what reaction that had, to judge herself through Jane's response. She didn't see anything but sympathy. No withdrawal or accusation.

"But you didn't tell him to kill Lizzie, did you? He knew what you meant. And, more importantly, you knew what you meant. So you are not guilty."

"I know, but I wish I hadn't said it. He was really desperate, you know, but I didn't want to be involved in divorce and that. Now I wish I had, because...well, because..."

"You're frightened he might have done it," Jane finished the sentence for her. "Does he know how you feel?"

"Yes. I wish he didn't. I keep thinking I ought to phone him and tell him I'm sorry. Tell him I know he wouldn't do anything like that. But, well, it's too late, isn't it? He knows and I can't take that back. I should have agreed to the divorce. I should have."

The words came tumbling out now. "I just love it here at Chance, you know. I'm a different person here. This is my home. I couldn't risk losing all this. It's where I belong. You can't understand, but this is my whole life really…"

Jane listened to the words, to the short raw phrases and emotions.

Chance, she thought. It's all for Chance again.

"Well, now, it's a small world, isn't it?"

Pockett leaned back in the passenger seat to look past Joe's head to the white house among the trees. "It's a bit ramshackle, isn't it? Well, the yards are; the house looks the same."

"The stables packed in after the other business. Disused, I suppose. Looks like that bit's been done up though. That was the pony yards, wasn't it?"

"Yes, I think so."

They looked around in silence for a couple of minutes. Pockett sighed. "Ah, well, we were young and keen then, never giving a thought to our pensions." He sighed again. "Come on, Joseph, enough of all our yesterdays, to work we go." He opened the car door and swung his legs round to get out, freezing before his feet touched the ground. "Hell's bells, I'd forgotten about the mud," he muttered in disgust. "Or is it muck? Because you're an expert on that now, I remember."

He turned to smile at Joe, who ground out a sentence about people who never grow up, never give things a rest.

"Sour grapes, Joseph. I don't want to say 'I told you so', but you will have noticed that the 'muck' expertise, while no doubt useful, has not been a strong aid to your promotion. I think I more or less predicted that."

Jane watched from the landing window. She knew them instantly, despite the years that had gone by. They were heavier, greyer – but she knew them – and their approach made her nervous. She decided to stay in her room, play ostrich with her head buried under the bedclothes. She was too old for this. She didn't want to know.

The woman who opened the nail-studded door was slim, attractive and frightened. Without taking a step into the red-tiled hall, Pockett knew the gossips were right. This was Steven Warren's mistress. And since the forensic team had come up with the dimensions of the missing log, proving it had been narrower at the end that had reduced Lizzie Warren's head to a pulp, women were back in the frame. So Pockett smiled and said good morning to this definite 'likely'.

Joe thought it odd how quickly he remembered his way around the house. He knew she was leading them to the morning room before she opened the door, saying, "We can go in here." He looked across to the door on the far side of the room. That had been their 'office' during the other business. He could still see this room in his mind, full of desks, paperwork and blackboards…and the small room full of horse calendars. How many years ago was that?

"Billy Pockett and Joe Drinkwater. They are a legend in the Midlands force."

Joe had overheard a sergeant say that to two young constables once. It was funny how all the uniformed constables these days looked like they were playing truant from school. He thought it probably worked the other way round, too. Anyone over the age of fifty must look ancient to them. And any pair who had been together as long as he and Pockett had, may well seem to be pieces of history. Legends.

He made out to others that the only reason he was still with Pockett was because the bosses knew no one else would put up with him. It wasn't true, of course. Over the years they had fended off any scheme that would see one promoted and the partnership split up. They had stood, separately and together, and listened to officialdom ordering one or the other to move on. They had sat and listened to the same thing being advised in cosy office chats. But they had resisted, holding up their success rate as a shield against change. And eventually the system stopped trying to drag them into line. Now they were left alone, to coast along into retirement, which wasn't that long away… to become legends.

Pockett had gone through the formalities by the time Joe brought his mind back to the present. He had done this quickly and was now asking what was her relationship to Steven Warren?

Shock tactics. And they worked. The woman was stunned. She made no attempt at denial when Pockett suggested an intimate relationship; she just stared at him in dismay.

"Miss Saunder? How long have you been intimately associated with Mr Warren?" Pockett repeated the question. "Miss Saunder?"

It wasn't any good. The woman seemed paralysed with fear.

"Get her a cup of coffee or tea, Sergeant," Pockett said. "Do you want coffee or tea?" he asked her, trying to break through the frozen immobility by making her talk of normal things, safe things. "Miss Saunder? Coffee or tea?" he insisted, demanding a response.

"Coffee."

"Sugar?" Joe asked.

"Two." Her eyes were blinking again and her hands were beginning to move as she rubbed her little fingers on her palms. She went to get up, saying, "I'll make it," but Pockett waved her back.

"It's okay. Sergeant Drinkwater knows where everything is."

"But no one knows," she said, "except Aunt Jane."

For a moment Pockett thought she was talking of the whereabouts of the coffee.

"Jane Warren?"

"She didn't tell you, did she?"

"No."

"Then how do you know? We were so careful. How..." Her eyes widened as she thought of who it must have been. "Steve?"

"How long have you been seeing Steve, Miss Saunder?" Pockett asked, evading answering her question.

Actually there wouldn't have been one answer to give. It was the usual story of hints and innuendos: "Mrs White said...," "Mrs Black saw...," "Well you know what men are like...," "Poor Lizzie, you could tell how upset she was...," "...and that one up the farm is no better than she ought to be...."

Lizzie hadn't kept quiet about her dislike of Trish and lots of prying eyes had looked for anything to fuel the drama, to give them a bit of vicarious excitement.

Joe was pouring water into the mugs when Jane walked into the kitchen.

"Oh, I thought you were gone," she said.

She had heard someone moving around in the kitchen and assumed it was Trish. She cursed herself for being a stupid old woman, because if she had thought it through, she could have checked out of the window for the car. Anyway, it was too soon for them to be gone.

"How have you been?" Joe asked, thinking that the answer was she had been getting old. He supposed she could say the same about him.

"Fine. Yourself?"

"Fine."

"Still know your way around, I see."

She sat at the kitchen table.

"Oh…yes…yes…" He felt embarrassed, as if he'd been caught stealing. "I'm just getting coffee for Miss Saunder. I hope you don't mind."

"Help yourself."

She sat still, watching him. Her voice was flat, maybe mildly sarcastic. There didn't seem to be any humour left in her. He wondered if all that other business had done that, or whatever life had brought since.

"I'll just take this in." He excused himself, glad to leave the room. He couldn't think of any more polite chit-chat.

"Is she all right?"

He didn't know how to answer that.

"Trish, is she all right?"

"Yes. I'll just take her this coffee. I expect I'll see you later."

He got out.

Pockett was wiping his shoes on the grass verge, carefully tilting his foot from side to side.

"What have we got on her, Joe?" he said, as he jumped into the passenger seat, trying to avoid walking on the mud between the verge and the car.

The papers in Joe's hands jumped into the air as the car rocked under the weight of Pockett's collapse.

"For God's sake! It's mud. It's not going to kill you."

He picked up the papers and tried to arrange them back into order.

"Temper, temper. Well, come on, what have we got?"

"A bit of shoplifting, drugs, prostitution, vandalism, dossing. A bit of a lot of things, but not since she had the child. Straight since then. No family. Reared in a children's home. No known father of the child."

"So, how did she get here?"

"I thought you were going to suss that."

"Yes, but she was in full flow and I didn't want to break the rhythm. Well, you saw that."

"What do you think of him doing it, but she wouldn't have him until the wife was out of the way?"

"Puts him in the frame and lets her out; unless, of course, she's playing it really clever. Pretending all the guilt is his because of what she said, when really she did encourage him to kill his wife."

"Or murdered her herself," Joe cut in.

"Put them both on the blackboard, Joseph."

* * * * *

"He's not the father. Find me who you think it is and I'll prove it for you." The pathologist leaned back and smiled at Pockett. "But Steven Warren certainly was not. DNA doesn't fit."

"Is that more reason to suspect him or not?" Pockett mused. "Perhaps he found out she had been putting it around and killed her in a fit of jealousy. But since he wanted a divorce anyway, it seems a bit of a pointless exercise." He stood up and thanked the young doctor. "I think it's back to the village gossips for us," he said.

Joe raised his eyebrows. "Us? What do you mean, 'us'?"

"But we can't, can we? The Civil Rights lot would be spitting fire if we tried it."

"Not if we ask for voluntary blood samples."

"They won't wear it. Oh come on, you know they won't."

Pockett threw his chalk at the blackboard, slamming his desk drawer shut with his foot, as his chair returned all four legs to the floor. "Do they want us to solve this bloody murder or not?! I mean, what's it going to take? There's only half a dozen people daft enough to live out here in this godforsaken muck heap!"

"The population of the actual village is about 350. Then you've got the outlying houses…"

Joe's attempt at reason was cut short by Pockett's, "See what I mean? Half a dozen people. Hardly a street's worth in civilisation."

He stubbed his cigarette out in the ashtray, reducing it to a shred in the process. "I suppose it wouldn't do any good anyway," he sulked. "They're probably all related. So much inbreeding, you wouldn't be able to tell one from the other. God, I hate…"

"Shut up," Joe said.

Lizzie may have talked freely about her dislike of Trish, but she had certainly been close-mouthed about her own affair.

Joe drank enough tea to float a battleship, but learned nothing about Lizzie's love life.

Unfortunately, as Pockett pointed out later, he did learn enough to start filling up the blackboard.

It soon became apparent that Lizzie thought Steven would inherit Chance because Steven was a relation of Jane Warren. Furthermore, Lizzie's two sons, Robert and Timothy, also thought they would soon be living on the farm.

Although Lizzie's lads and Katie and James were very close, when Jane gave permission for Katie to start up the stables again, Lizzie was very angry. She thought her sons would lose their rightful inheritance. After all, who was this Katie Bartlett – just a by-blow – and Eva used to be just a groom at the stables years ago.

No, no one had seen Eva around for years, so why Jane Warren should give this girl so much was beyond comprehension.

The first blackboard began to look crowded.

Trish and Steven, together or singly…ridding themselves of the just impediment to their alliance?

Robert and Timothy…believing they would inherit Chance; perhaps they found out about their mother's affair, about her pregnancy? Perhaps they sided with their father and Trish? Perhaps they thought their mother threatened their friends?

Katie...defending herself and her right to the stables?

James...defending his mother, or Katie?

Eva...defending her grandchild's rights? (Who was Katie's father? Where was Katie's mother?)

Lizzie's lover...fearful of Lizzie making known their relationship?

Jane...defending Trish? Or Katie? Or...?

"Swap Trish, Steve and the lover on to the other board," Pockett said. "Definite likelys. The rest, well we'll have to do some fishing about. It's too messy. I don't like it."

They both stared at the board in silence.

"Funny how it's all down to Chance again." Pockett laughed at his own unintended double meaning. "Down to Chance. Hey, that's good, isn't it?"

"Very good," Joe said, laconically.

"You had better go and see our Jane. She seems in the thick of it again. Makes you wonder if it's the place or her that attracts all this aggro. She knew about Trish and Steve and she owns Chance. Go and see her. You always did get on well, didn't you? And she's probably the one with all the answers, unless she's lost her marbles a bit."

"Who's your money on?" Joe was still studying the board.

Pockett squinted at the board through the smoke of his cigarette. "It ought to be Mr Steven Warren," he said, waving at the second board, "but I'm not laying down anything until we've sorted that lot out." He peered at the first board again. "Too messy. I don't like it."

Joe wished he had a pound for every time he had heard that.

* * * * *

"...and when Jenny died, Trish brought Katie here," Jane answered the sergeant's question.

"Why? Why did she think Eva lived here?"

"Jenny was brought up at Chance and, during her illness, she had told Trish about it."

"So Eva lived here with her daughter?"

"Yes."

"Since her daughter was born?"

"Yes."

Joe had got used to the garrulous gossips: ask one question and you get two hours of non-stop chat. Jane was hard work by comparison.

"So, let me get this straight. After the other business, Eva left. She got pregnant and she came back here with her child, Jenny." He looked at Jane for confirmation.

"Yes."

"What did Eva do here? I thought the stables were closed."

"Housekeeper."

"Right." Joe wrote that down. "Then Jenny ran away. She lived with Trish, had a baby by a married man, contracted AIDS and died."

"Yes."

Trish brought the child back here to find Eva, but Eva had gone?"

"Yes. Married and left."

"Do you still keep in touch?"

"We used to, but I haven't heard from her in a long time."

"Can you give me her address?"

Jane got up and went into the hall, returning with an address book. She opened it at the appropriate page and put it in front of Joe. "I don't know if she's still there," she said.

"Right. Then you offered Trish a job here?"

"Yes."

"So Trish stayed with her son, James, and Eva's grandchild, Katie?"

"Yes."

"And Eva didn't ever come to see her granddaughter?" Joe struggled on.

"No. She had a new life."

"Right. How long have you known about Trish and Steve?"

"Since the beginning."

"What relation is Steve to you?"

"It's complicated. Just say a distant relation," she answered vaguely.

Joe made a note in his book: 'Distant Relation'.

He made a note in his mind to find out exactly what sort of distant relation. Jane Warren was never vague.

"Would I be right in assuming that he would be likely to believe he would inherit Chance?"

"I'm not dead yet, but he might assume it."

Joe waited, but she didn't elaborate on the statement.

"Right," he said again. "Right."

Like getting blood out of a stone," he reported to Pockett later. "I may have got on okay with her years ago, but this woman bears no resemblance to that one then…no relation at all. And, talking of relations, that all seemed a bit…oh, I don't know…wrong somehow. Messy, like you say. I think she's hiding a lot."

"Is Steven in line to inherit Chance?"

"'He might assume so', is what she said. He's a distant relation, but she didn't say how he was related. I think we have to fish a bit."

"Right."

They studied the boards for a while. "Oh, by the way," Pockett muttered, "I think we can rub out Robert. He was sitting some sort of exam."

"Right," Joe muttered back, equally absorbed in thought.

The sounds of the police station filled the silence: footsteps, voices, doors, telephones.

New chance

The tap on their door made them both stir. Joe put his feet on the floor, leaning forward to his desk. Pockett lay further back in his chair, his feet resting on an open drawer, his eyes glued to the blackboards.

"Message, sir." The constable held out a piece of paper.

"Well, rub it off, Sergeant, rub it off," Pockett said irritably. "I told you Robert's out of the frame."

"Sorry?" The constable looked from Pockett to Joe.

Pockett turned his head. "Have you been promoted, Constable?"

"No, sir."

"Then if I say 'sergeant,' why are you listening, let alone answering?" He looked back at Joe. "Rub it off, Sergeant," he enunciated.

Joe took the message paper off the constable, who stood frozen to the spot, unsure what to do.

"Okay, off you go."

The young man escaped, shutting the door loudly behind him. He would have been hard put himself to say whether that was nerves, or belated defiance.

"Did I say he could go?" Pockett demanded, banging the door shut with his foot and leaning forward to glare at Joe. "That message might require an answer from someone in authority. It might need an intelligent response, a quick reaction, some mature consideration."

"Well, that lets you out on all three," Joe snapped back, "especially the 'mature' bit."

"Watch yourself, Sergeant. The trouble with you is you're so mature the inside of your head is going as grey as the outside. What I need is a younger, quick-thinking man. So you just watch yourself, Drinkwater."

"Getting rid of me again, are you? Come on then, do it, you pathetic little neurotic. Do it. Make my day."

They glared into each other's faces, while their unseen audience gathered outside the door and smiled at each other.

325

Sue Ryland

It was almost a station tradition, these shouting matches from within.

"Make my day?!" They heard Pockett's voice whoop with laughter. "Make my day? You've been watching those grown-up American movies again, haven't you? I've told you you're too impressionable for that sort of thing. We don't go up to some little toerag in Woolworths, with his thieving hand on a tube of Smarties, balance a truncheon on his head and say, 'are you feeling lucky, punk?' It doesn't work that way here. You shouldn't watch these things. It gives you the wrong impression and it gives the public the wrong impression. We have to appear as sober solid citizens. Impressions count."

"Oh God, look who's talking! The original piece of tart trying to look like new crumpet. Gives the wrong impression? Take a look in the mirror, sunshine. Preferably one without the rose tints around it."

They stopped, face to face, over the desk.

"It's Eva, isn't it?" Pocket said.

Joe blinked agreement. "Yes. We won't get anywhere until we find out all about Eva."

"That's nearly the title of another film," Pockett said, as they got up to go, ignoring the scurrying sounds from behind the door. "Too many films, that's your problem. Just too many films."

"Oh, by the way," Joe was looking at the message paper, still in his hand, "they want to know if we want our names down for the Christmas dinner in the canteen. I'll leave you to make an intelligent, quick, mature response, shall I?"

The house was select.

Pockett thought that would be an estate agent's choice of adjective.

A detached residence in a select area.

Four bedrooms, separate loo and a nice bit of garden. That probably qualified as a select residence. He wondered how you defined a select area. Not too much traffic, not many children, and trees planted on the pavement? Likely.

The doorbell was one of those that went ding-dong and played a tune.

Pockett didn't like doorbells that went ding-dong, let alone played a tune. He was just finishing tutting in disgust, when the door opened.

"Good evening, sir. I am Sergeant Drinkwater and this is Inspector Pockett, Bradshore CID."

Joe showed his identification card and Pockett moved his hand vaguely towards his jacket pocket, but he couldn't be bothered to get out his own card. Anyone who owned a bell that went ding-dong didn't need to see a card.

"Does a Mrs Eva Hallett live here?"

'No, I'm sorry, she doesn't. She died some years ago. Sorry."

"Oh, are you a relative of hers, sir?"

"Her stepson. My father's dead too. We live here now. Why, what's wrong?"

"Nothing to worry about," Joe reassured the middle-aged man. "Could we just come in and have a word?"

"Yes...yes." The man held the door wider, pushing his spectacles back up again. "Please..." he invited.

They sat in the lounge on the beige settee. The carpet was beige. The curtains were beige. Even the picture frames looked beige.

The TV was turned off as they walked in and his wife went to get coffee, which was served in matching cups and saucers on a floral patterned tray. It wasn't beige, so Pockett lost that mental bet.

Pockett thought they suited each other very well, this couple. Middle-aged, comfortable, polite. They were the sort of people who apologised when someone else crashed into their trolley at the supermarket. He would bet that these two had never seen so much as a parking ticket in real life, thought they probably

327

watched one or two soaps and a police series on TV. That was quite enough drama for them.

Pockett couldn't imagine the Eva he knew fitting in here at all.

The man said his father had died long ago. Heart attack. Eva had died a few years afterwards. Cancer. They had nursed her at home for nearly two years. It was all very sad.

They showed photographs of their father and Eva. Together. Alone. With themselves. With various children. The smiling, confident woman in the photographs was nothing like the sullen angry girl they had known. Mr and Mrs Hallett called her "a marvellous person," said how the children loved her and everyone really missed her still. Mrs Hallett's eyes filled with tears and she had to excuse herself to get a tissue. She was sorry for being so silly.

What did they know of Eva's life before she met their father?

Well, she had lived on a farm and worked with horses. She had taught their children to ride. They didn't think she had a very happy life, which made her cheerfulness all the more amazing, didn't it? A marvellous woman.

"Why do you think she didn't have a very happy life?" Pockett asked.

They weren't sure. Just little things that their father or Eva would say.

"Like what?"

Mr and Mrs Hallett looked at each other, reluctant to talk of things that weren't quite nice, reluctant to say anything that might besmirch their stepmother in any way.

"We thought she may have had a child herself, at one time, but it seems we were wrong."

"What made you think that?"

Mr Hallett said, "When they first met – Dad and Mum…Eva, that is…sorry, we called her Mum, you know – there was some problem about a girl running away. We thought that was Eva's

New chance

daughter. Dad used to go away for days to be with Eva at the farm. Anyway, shortly after that they got married and no one mentioned anything about it again, so we were wrong, see."

Joe asked if Eva kept in contact with any of her old friends, and they said she had occasional letters from the south, but that stopped when she became ill. Mrs Hallett thought they stopped before she became ill, actually. After she died, they had not found any letters in her belongings, or they would have written to inform the people, of course.

Pockett noted that they didn't seem to have any idea that Eva lived at Chance and had been involved in a major murder enquiry, which, after all, was a matter of headline newspaper reports for some time. But then, he thought, looking at Eva's photo on the sideboard, that person was nothing like Eva.

On their way back to Bradshore, Joe said, "To use our old friend's way of thinking, she wasn't only not following the script, she was appearing in a whole new production."

Pockett appreciated the reference to Jane's way of likening life to a play. "Yes, but when did she change? That's what interests me. After all, this man she married, if you judge him by his family, was a solid citizen. He would be very unlikely to be attracted by the old Eva, so she must have assumed a new identity before she met him. Put it all in chronological order, Joe. She leaves Chance after the Shirley affair. Gets pregnant. Comes back with the child. Rears it. Meets a man. Child leaves. She leaves. Marries the man and ignores her grandchild. Right?"

"Yes."

"Okay, why? The man knew about her daughter, so why should she ignore her granddaughter?"

"Protect her position in the family?"

"Maybe, but she had already risked keeping her daughter when she was unmarried, so she had already faced public condemnation. She must have felt strongly about it, or she would have had the baby adopted. Surely a grandchild would be less of a stigma, especially in these more liberated days. People may change their appearance, move into a different social circle, but rarely do people change strongly held beliefs. Yet she abandoned her grandchild. No recognition. No support. That doesn't make sense. As you say, it's like she changed roles completely."

"Like Jane," Joe said. "That person isn't the Jane we knew either. Dour, not much humour, sort of locked in on herself…well, with me, anyway. Maybe it's just age, but she's not like the old Jane."

Pockett looked at him. "No, she's not," he said. "Fancy a cup of tea, Joe?"

"Okay. Look out for a place."

"No, I don't want to stop now. I was thinking more of you revisiting your tea-drinking friends in the village. Let's see what they say about Eva and Jane."

Joe sighed and offered up prayers for more patience and increased bladder control.

Pockett leaned his head back and closed his eyes. "Wake me up when we get there. Oh, and by the way, Joseph, I'm very impressed with all this intuition. Those Phyllosan seem to be doing you a lot of good."

Joe renewed the prayers for patience.

Jane watched Katie wheeling a barrow of rubble across the yard. The weather was cold, but Jane could see the glistening on Katie's face, see the knotted muscles and tendons in her forearms.

She was renovating the livery yards, working with the determination that Jane had expected. Her single-mindedness was admirable and she seemed the least affected by Lizzie's death. Rebuilding Chance was her whole objective. Jane just had this niggling worry that, anyone who was that tunnel visioned, really didn't give any consideration to anything, or anyone, in their way.

She turned her eyes to look at the entrance to the yard. The still figure, half-hidden by the wall and the shadows, was watching Katie too.

She couldn't see his face properly, but she knew James often stood and watched Katie.

She smiled as she wondered how much longer before he declared his feelings for her.

* * * * *

"A lot of people saw him at the market, but none of them could pin down a time."

They were sitting in front of the blackboards again. Eva's name had been rubbed out. So had 'Katie's mother' and 'Katie's father'. All dead. Tim's name had gone too. He was definitely in the supermarket that morning.

Jane, Katie, James and Unknown were left on Board Two. Board One still read Steven, Trish and Lover.

"I think Unknown's unlikely," Joe said. "No burglary. No sexual assault. So, if Unknown exists, why do her in?"

"For an unknown reason. That's the whole point, isn't it? We know she was pregnant, so the motive could have been to do with that. Jealousy or fear of her telling, or some such. We know the ownership of Chance is another motive. Stop someone else inheriting, or help them. Greed, fear and sex. Three motives. But Unknown may have had another one."

"Like what?"

"I don't know. Revenge?"

Joe thought. "Maybe the lover's wife? Or someone Lizzie narked in the past? Yes, I see what you mean. Unknown has to stay. What about Jane then? Surely she's unlikely to bash Lizzie's head in to protect the inheritance of her own property? She just had to rewrite her will, that's all."

"But she may do it to protect someone else. Steven, for instance. He's her relation, isn't he? Or Trish?"

"How does killing Lizzie protect either of them? Shut her up about the affair? I can't imagine Jane would care much about other people's opinions."

"Maybe the old Jane wouldn't but, as we said, this isn't the old Jane…which brings us back to your tea-drinking cronies. So, they are saying Eva changed after she came back to Chance?"

"Yes. After the other murders she left. Well, most of them left, you know that. All of the grooms and some of the men. Jane and her Aunt Doris were here on their own for a time. When Eva came back, she had changed, they say. Pleasant and more mature. She took over a lot of Jane's responsibilities, even looked after Aunt Doris."

"So what was Jane doing then?"

"Nothing much. They say she never recovered from that business with Shirley. Shut herself away, if you like."

"Became a recluse?" Pockett suggested.

"Sort of. Let Eva take over anyway, but they think now that Eva was feathering her own nest in preparation for dropping her illegitimate child."

"Didn't any of them know she was pregnant then, when she came back? I wouldn't have thought that would have escaped them."

"Well they all say they guessed as much. But it still seemed to have caused a shockwave running through the gossips of the village, when Eva appeared with a baby, so maybe they didn't."

"So what happened then?"

"Nothing, as far as I can tell. Eva still seemed to run Chance. Jane was in the background. Then Jenny, Eva's daughter, left, and Eva not long after that. Jane did become a recluse then, as you said. Kept very much to herself until Trish arrived with Katie and James. Trish seemed to have taken over where Eva left off."

"Maybe the change in Jane is just age and bad experience. After all, a lot's happened and she's getting on now." Pockett waited while Joe thought that through. Then he added, "Remember how that other business hit her harder than anyone. A bit of a self-control freak, our Jane. She thought she had the world sussed and she couldn't cope with the fact that she had failed to understand part of the script. Perhaps it's just that still."

"No," Joe said after a while, "it's more than that. Have you seen her with Trish and the youngsters? But she pulls down the shutters as soon as I appear. She's hiding something. Maybe to do with her relationship with Steven."

"But doesn't he seem as vague about that as she does?"

"Yes, but it's an honest sort of vagueness, if you know what I mean. He says his father was some sort of cousin. Jane just evades the question."

"Well, we'll see what the lads come up with when they have a fish around. Meanwhile we've still got six on the board and that includes your Jane."

"Plus Unknown," Joe added.

He lay on his back, suddenly turning onto his side, hips jerking and stifling a groan, as he pushed through his hands.

Bitch! Bitch! He hated himself and he hated her.

His hands dropped to his side and he rolled over onto his stomach, feeling the wet patch on the sheet underneath him.

Bitch! Bitch!

His fist beat the pillow in time to his thought.

Katie added more sand, turning over the grey sludge with her spade, cutting the sand into the mixture.

Her wrists ached. Her back ached. She kept turning and cutting. She knew she shouldn't have made up another batch of concrete, knew it was getting too late, too dark. She had to keep working, though, because if she stopped, she would have to go back inside the house.

She thought of all the times she had wished she knew more about the murders long ago, wished she could ask Aunt Jane about them, but Trish would never let her. Trish said that was in her grandmother's time. Best forgotten, she said. But Katie wished she could have known more, especially when she was

Sue Ryland

at school. The other children ended up pumping their parents and grandparents for information to pass on to Katie. She had thought it wasn't fair.

Now she wished she wasn't involved in any murder. It wasn't glamorous and something to boast about to your friends. It was frightening.

People you thought you knew started acting like strangers. The atmosphere in the kitchen felt on the edge of screaming. Everyone was tiptoeing around everyone else, as though one false move would bring the whole house crashing down.

The edge of screaming.

Katie thought she was better off with the concrete. She scraped the heap back together, turning and cutting.

Policemen, going everywhere, taking notes, looking at things.

Those two men, those detectives, asking questions. Questions, questions.

She added more water and turned again.

She didn't like Aunt Lizzie...Mrs Warren...hadn't liked her, she corrected herself. The way she looked down her nose at Trish. The way she always called James "the housekeeper's son"... "Oh hello, boys, I see you've brought the housekeeper's son to play." The way she said, "So you're Katie. Well, I knew your mother," and sort of sniffed her disapproval.

That was the first thing she ever said to her, though she told her many times after that how lucky she was that Aunt Jane took her in.

The last few years had been the worst. She seemed to freak out at the sight of James and Katie. Talking, talking, and talking...all little smiles, probing for information on what was going on at Chance...

"How's your mother, dear? I hear she's going on the PTA committee... Was that the doctor that called on Tuesday? How's Aunt Jane? Of course she isn't really your Aunt Jane... Was that the solicitor...?"

On and on, sticking her long nose into everything. Nasty woman…nasty words…

"Oh yes, she's a very busy woman, your mother, too busy for her own good… No, I shouldn't get too keen on the horses idea, young lady. You don't want to be disappointed, do you? Do you think you'll go back to the city? I do think it best to be with your own kind, don't you?"

Sticking her long nose in. Opening her poisonous mouth.

Katie could see her face in front of her. She stabbed at the concrete, her spade hitting the ground underneath, as she cut it and cut it…

"So, Steven is the stepson of your ex-husband, Terry Warren?"

"Yes."

"There's no blood relationship really?"

"No."

Pockett was finding this hard work too.

"Is Steven aware of that?"

"Of what?"

"That his stepfather was your husband."

"No."

Joe's voice cut in and she turned her head slightly to look at him. "Why didn't you tell him?"

"There was no need," she said.

Pockett resumed the questions. "What was your relationship with Lizzie Warren?"

Jane just looked at him and he was annoyed with himself for rushing to expand the question. "I mean, did you get on well?"

"We got on all right."

"But you weren't friends?"

"No."

"Did you like her?"

"Not particularly."

"Why?"

Jane shrugged. "Not my type," she said, with a small smile.

"In what way?" Pockett pushed. "In what way?"

"Too pushy," Jane said and smiled at him again. He smiled back at her as he acknowledged the point in this verbal tennis match. Love-fifteen. Joe was wrong about her sense of humour. She was still sharp, even if she kept it well hidden.

"You were here that Thursday morning, say between nine and twelve?"

"Yes."

"Did you see anyone else?"

"No."

"No visitors?"

"No."

"Who else was here?"

"Trish, Katie, James."

"You saw all of them?"

"At breakfast."

"What about after breakfast?"

"I don't remember. They were around, I suppose."

"But you can't remember actually seeing them?"

"No."

"And would it be unusual not to see them?"

"No. It's a big place."

"Where would they most likely be?"

"Trish in the house. Katie and James outside."

Joe watched her closely as he asked, "Katie is starting up the stables again, is that right?"

"Something like that," she said, and picked up her mug of coffee, looking at him over the rim.

"Were Steven and Lizzie in agreement with that?"

"Not their business."

Pockett tapped his finger on the top of his mug. "Let me put it another way: would they have agreed to Katie carrying on with the stables if they inherited Chance?"

"After I'm dead?" she said and stared at him.

He stared back, responding to the challenge. "After you're dead," he said, and could have sworn her eyes laughed in acknowledgement of the picked up gauntlet.

"I don't know." The monotone quashed his burgeoning hopes of getting more response. It crossed his mind that she was probably better at the game than he was.

"Where were you on Thursday morning?"

"Working in the livery yards," Katie answered. "I'm doing them up...the yards and the stables."

"What were you doing?"

"Weeding the yard."

"How long were you out there?"

"I don't know. Until lunchtime, I suppose."

Katie didn't like the way the little man stared at her. She tried not to look at him, in case he could read that in her eyes. She looked at the carpet, or her own hands.

"Did you see anyone between nine and twelve?"

"Not that I can remember. No visitors or anything."

"What about Aunt Jane? Did you see her?"

"After breakfast? I don't think so, but she was in the house."

"What about Trish?"

"She was in the house too. James was around. I waved to him. He was messing around with an old tractor in the barn. I saw him a few times."

"Did you get on with Lizzie Warren?"

"She was all right."

From the sudden stiffening of the figure on the settee, it was clear to Joe and Pockett that Lizzie Warren was not 'all right'.

"Did you see much of her?"

"Only when we went there with Rob and Tim. Not so much since they went away."

"What about their father, Steven?"

"He comes here more often," she was relaxing again now, "to see Aunt Jane and that, you know."

"He's a relation of hers, isn't he?"

"Yes."

"Does he think the stables are a good idea?"

She took time to answer, looking at her hands. "I don't know. He never said." Then she was defiant, lifting her head to add, "Anyway, it's nothing to do with him."

"If he inherits the farm from Aunt Jane, it would be," Pockett said quietly.

Joe could see the muscles moving in her forearms as she clenched her fists.

"I was trying to get the old tractor in the barn going," James smiled at them. "Just messing around with it really. I don't think it will ever actually get working again, but I like old machinery and Andrew doesn't mind."

"So you saw Katie outside?"

He frowned. "No, she wasn't…" He looked at Pockett without really seeing him, as he thought. "That is, she might have been. I don't really remember. Yes…" he nodded his head decisively, "…she was outside. I remember now. She's doing the place up, you know."

"Where did you see her?"

"Oh, by the barn and the yards and that. She was painting, I think."

"You could see her painting?"

"Yes."

"What was she painting?"

"The barge boards along the store shed roof, I think."

"Up a ladder then?"

"Yes, that's why I saw her. I saw her most of the morning, on and off."

"What else did you do on Thursday morning, apart from weeding the livery yards?"

Katie looked puzzled. "What do you mean?"

"Well, did you do any other work on the outside yards or buildings?"

"No. Weeding the yard, preparing it for re-concreting, took all morning and some of the afternoon too."

"Can you see the tractor barn from the yard?"

"No, unless you go round the corner to the pony yard."

"So where did you see James?"

"I don't know...passing the yard entrance, I suppose...or the store sheds entrance. Anyway, passing the entrances a couple of times."

"Back-breaking work, weeding," Joe sympathised. "I don't know that I could have stuck it out that long."

"Needs must..." she smiled at him.

"...when the devil drives," Pockett finished for her.

She looked at the carpet again.

"You say you were trying to get the old tractor in the barn going on Thursday morning?"

James nodded.

"Did you leave the barn at all, to go and get some tools, for instance?"

"No, I wouldn't need to. They're already in the barn."

Joe leaned forward to emphasise the question as he said, "Think hard, James, you didn't leave the barn for any reason?"

"No." James looked puzzled. "Not until lunchtime. No."

"But you could see Katie up the ladder?"

"Yes, definitely, yes. She was there all morning. Why? What's the matter? She did say she saw me, didn't she?"

"Yes, but she said she was weeding," Pockett said, as he turned to look at some papers.

"Well she may have been...I mean, I didn't stare at her non-stop." James was clearly struggling with all this. "I was working on the tractor, so she was probably weeding as well."

"When was the last time you saw Lizzie Warren?" Pockett snapped the words at him.

"I don't know…er…when Tim was home the other weekend, I think. We called back in for him to pick up some tickets he wanted. Yes, that was it, I think. Tim will tell you. Ask Tim."

"Was Katie with you?"

"No."

"Does Katie go to the Warren's cottage much?"

"No more than I do. I mean, neither of us go unless it's with Rob or Tim."

"Why not?"

"I don't know. We just don't."

"You're not friends with Steven and Lizzie then?"

"Not friends, but…"

"Does Katie like them, Steven and Lizzie?"

"I think so…I don't know."

"If Steven inherits the farm, he might not let Katie run her stables here. That's right, isn't it?"

"I suppose so."

Joe's kind voice cut in on Pockett's quick cold questions. "It must be a worry for her."

"Yes it is," James responded to his friendliness. "She's really worried about it. She says she won't…" He stopped, the smile fading, as he caught Pockett's eye.

"What does she say, James?" Pockett asked.

"She worries a bit, that's all," he said.

"He's lying to protect her, or she's lying to protect him. Which?"

"More importantly, Joe, why?" Pockett's feet were on the open drawer of the desk again. "Because, if one of them is lying, it means that one of them suspects the other did it."

Joe doodled flowers over the open notepad on his desk. Pockett tried to blow smoke rings.

The silence was broken by Pockett. "To speak in your vernacular, Joseph, "it don't seem hardly right, do it?"

"What?"

New chance

Pockett lifted one leg, bending it towards him to take off his shoe. "Look at this." He leaned forward to wave the small fashionable boot under Joe's nose.

"Do I have to?" Joe protested, retreating backwards.

"It's ruined. Ruined. Seventy pound and ruined. One shouldn't have to walk in mud and muck in seventy-pound shoes."

"Well, put wellies on then."

"You miss the point, Joseph. One shouldn't have to walk in mud and muck. This is the late twentieth century. Civilisation has arrived. Everyone knows mud and muck are unhealthy, so why the hell are they still littering the countryside?"

Joe sighed and doodled two caterpillars climbing up the flower stalk.

Pockett sighed louder and more dramatically, returning the 'ruined' shoe to his foot. "No, it don't seem hardly right," he said again.

"What doesn't? A bit of mud on your dainty footwear, or what?"

"Well, look at them, Joe!"

Joe raised his head obediently to look at Pockett's shoes.

"No!" Pockett swung his feet under the desk. "Not my shoes! Look at those two. They're young, attractive, bright. Children like that shouldn't be going around smashing people's face to a pulp. Children like that shouldn't have..." he stopped struggling for a word "...that darkness inside them, should they? Do you know what I mean?"

Joe knew what he meant.

* * * * *

FINAL CHANCE

Jane sat at the kitchen table, absentmindedly stroking the head of one of the dogs. It was happening again. The cold taste of fear in her mouth, the empty quivering in her stomach.

They had been interviewing Katie all day.

She was frightened. She had had this feeling before, but she couldn't quite remember when.

She looked at the head on her lap. The soft brown eyes looked back at her, the dog's tail slowly thumping on the floor; she automatically stroked its head.

Sitting at the table...with the dogs.

She watched the tail...thump...thump...thump...

In the evening, at this table...frightened, because she knew...

The hand stopped its movement and the dog nosed her palm, urging more attention.

Shirley.

Shirley... She had worked it out, worked out who had killed Uncle Paul, and she sat here, at this table, feeling the cold fear and wishing it wasn't true.

Shirley. And Katie. Shirley and Katie. It was happening again. She had wanted to beat that detective, get the answer before he did. She was so sure she could. But the answer was Shirley. And her whole life fell apart. She hadn't even beaten him, because, the next morning, Shirley was gone. What happened then?

She looked inside herself, seeing her whole life roll round in front of her, like one of those Victorian peep-show toys. Put your eye to the hole and spin the wheel and the dog, or goat – or woman – came alive, sitting, standing, or jumping, as the wheel spins round. Stand up. Sit down. Stand up. Sit down...

She saw herself, young and confident, striding forward, reading the signs, knowing the way...then her Gran died and there was Terry and Elizabeth...confidence gone, as she hid in the family, sitting in shadows...then Chance, and control returns, running the house, forging ahead, knowing the script...then Shirley...and Terry again...hiding behind Eva, letting her lead, confidence lost, huddled in a corner...then Trish and Katie, love and contentment...and she wants to stand up, begins to move, but the wheel seems stuck, jammed by fear, snagged by secrets...

So, is this where her life stops?

She stared at the dog, seeing the wheel turn again and again to the sticking point.

"Life is for learning," she would say to the children. She didn't seem to have learned much.

Katie was suspected of murdering Lizzie. Would they take her away like Shirley? And would she just sit here, never moving again, until the wheel stopped turning forever?

She stood up.

"How is he?"

Robert closed the door behind her, speaking in an undertone, "Bearing up." He walked through the small hall into the living room. "Aunt Jane to see you, Dad," he announced to the figure in the armchair.

Steven looked grey. That was Jane's first impression. He always seemed a man full of life, glowing with health and activity. Now he looked grey.

He stood up, smiling. "Aunt Jane, you shouldn't have come." He ushered her to the chair where he had been sitting. "Would you like a cup of tea or coffee?"

She smiled. "Either. That would be lovely."

"I'll get it," Robert said and left them to it.

"How are you? Bearing up, Rob says."

"Yes, I'm fine thanks, fine."

They settled down, going through all the usual polite conversational gambits about the weather, the cottage, his new phone number, Tim's job, the state of the farm.

Robert left the coffee and said he'd just take the opportunity to pop down to see a friend in the village. There was more polite conversation, in case Jane had left when he got back.

"So, how are you really?" she asked, when they settled themselves down again.

"Oh, you know…you know. It's not been easy."

"No, I can imagine it hasn't." She leaned forward to pat his hand.

"I expect they're saying I did it, are they?" He nodded to indicate the outside world.

"Well, I expect the Mrs Parkes of this world are, but there's only a handful of them, so I shouldn't let that worry you."

"What does Trish say?" He looked at her closely. The answer mattered.

"Why don't you ask her yourself?"

He shook his head. "No, she doesn't want to speak to me. I tried to tell her, but….you know about me and Trish?"

"Yes, love, I know."

"I guessed you did. I expect the whole village knows now. I didn't kill Lizzie. I bloody well felt like it, but I didn't do it."

He spat the last sentence out, then relaxed in his chair, letting the anger go. Jane guessed he had learned a lot about futility.

"She was a mean woman, Aunt Jane, but I didn't kill her."

"Do the police think you did?"

He shrugged. "I don't know. They come and ask questions. Then come again. More questions."

Jane tutted sympathetically.

"Did you know she was pregnant?" he asked.

"No, I hadn't heard that."

"I expect they're not spreading it around yet. Well she was, and it wasn't mine. They took a blood test and it wasn't mine. I told them it wasn't."

"Do you know who…I mean, can you guess?"

"I wish I did. I've thought and thought, but she never gave a hint of it. She'd just smile in a nasty way sometimes, when she thought I'd seen Trish, and say I should watch it, because what was sauce for the gander…but I thought she was just threatening me. I didn't think she was actually seeing someone. I wish to God we knew who it was…"

* * * * *

"Would you like a biscuit?"

Jay fussed around Jane, pleased and surprised at her visit.

"Well I wouldn't say no," Jane smiled back, "but don't go to the trouble of laying them on a plate. I'll just have a fish in the biscuit tub, if that's okay?"

They smiled at each other, happy to re-establish a friendship that needed no niceties.

"Do you remember Miss Pittypat and those digestives?" Jane asked, as she chose two biscuits from the tub.

Jay exploded with laughter at the memory, her hands to her face and her head thrown back. "Oh God!" she spluttered. "Oh God! And there we were trying to explain to the two Misses that she didn't need her stomach pumped…"

"And they were crying and crying…" Jane joined in.

"And all because the bloody thing had eaten a packet of digestives out of their shopping bag…"

"And Alice said, 'Pity it wasn't a can of baked beans, because that might have given her a bit more forward motion.'"

They whooped with laughter and Jay wiped her eyes with her apron.

"Good days," she said. "Oh, good days."

"It seems like yesterday sometimes, and other times… well…" Jane sighed.

Jay nodded agreement, picking up her mug of tea.

Jane dipped her biscuit in her tea, nibbling at the hot moist end, and they sat with their thoughts for a few moments of companionable silence.

"We've been thinking about central heating," Jay said, staring round the sitting room.

Jane pursed her lips. "Well, your place is like ours, isn't it? Nice and cool in summer, but hard to heat in winter."

"On a smaller scale, though," Jay smiled.

"Yes, but the same sort of thing. What kind of heating then?"

"Oil or solid fuel seems the best bet. We've got some leaflets…"

They sat and discussed the merits of various heating systems, looked at leaflets, walked around the cottage and tried to consider where radiators would best be sited.

They were on their second mug of tea before Jane said, "I'm sorry about Lizzie. Do you miss her very much?"

Jay leaned back. "It was the shock, you know, more than anything. Just finding her like that." She shuddered. "I keep getting pictures in my mind."

"Well, you're bound to, aren't you? Enough to frighten anyone rigid."

Jay flashed a smile at her. "I wasn't that close to her, you know. I mean, we went out sometimes, to the village and that, and we had coffee, but I wasn't that close. She didn't have many friends and I used to pass her place on the way to the village and, well, I just used to pop in some days."

"I remember when she was younger," Jane said. "She seemed a nice friendly girl."

"Yes…" Jay stared into her tea. "She changed a lot, you know. Got very bitter about things."

"Really?"

"Yes. She didn't make any secret of it either. I think that's what put folks off."

"Well, I know she didn't like Trish. That stuck out a mile on the odd occasion I've seen them together. That was to do with Steven, wasn't it?"

Jay looked uncomfortable, so Jane went on, "I guessed ages ago they were having a bit of a thing, Trish and Steven. From what I hear now, seems I was right."

Jay relaxed again, as she realised Jane knew about the gossip. "Well I didn't know about that," she said. "Not then anyway. I just thought she hated Trish because she thought she threatened her prospects of inheriting all this." She waved her hand. "The house and the estate, you know."

"Couldn't wait for me to pop off, eh?" Jane smiled.

"She thought you might leave it to Trish for some reason."

"Why?"

Jay looked uncomfortable again. "I don't know. Said it had been done before. Stupid really, because Aunt Doris was your aunt, wasn't she?"

"Yes, but some folks still think of me as the housekeeper. Well that's right really. I was the housekeeper, wasn't I? Plus a few other jobs."

Jane laughed and Jay looked at her with a questioning face.

"Sorry," Jane said, "I was just thinking of the two Misses again and some of the things we all got up to."

Jay grinned back at her.

"Mind you," Jane went on, "it must have been bad for Lizzie, if she knew about Trish and Steven."

"Yes, it must. She would get very angry sometimes, you know, but, as I said, I thought that was about Chance. She said Trish would get a nasty shock one of these days, said she would put her in her place right and proper."

"What did she mean by that, I wonder?"

"I don't know," Jay said, "sack her if she came into Chance I suppose, but when I said to her that Trish would leave anyway,

Sue Ryland

when she wasn't needed to keep house, she said 'tit for tat.' I don't know what she meant, but she laughed when she said it."

"Did she?" Jane frowned. "Did she? It's a wonder she never took up with anyone herself. I mean, you think after all those years of knowing her husband was off with another woman, wouldn't you feel like flying your own kite, just to get your own back, if nothing else?"

"Yes, I suppose so. That would be 'tit for tat', wouldn't it? You could be right, but she never hinted to me she was having an affair with anyone. Jay leaned back to think. "No, no, I never saw any bloke around her, apart from Steven and Andrew. There was the washing machine bloke and the man who put a new electric point in the kitchen. Tradesmen, you know. But you can't count those."

"Talking of tradesmen," Jane said, "who were you thinking of to do the central heating?"

The subject of central heating was resumed for fifteen minutes, then Jane said she ought to be getting back.

Jay was pleased she had come. She waved her off and went back to cooking and cleaning, happy to see Jane about again and wondering if she was right about having the radiator at the far end of the sitting room. Maybe the alcove by the window would be better...

Jane walked down the lane from Bateman's Cottage to Chance.

The high banks of the winding lane created a still trail through the landscape. As she turned the corner, the low late-afternoon sun dappled a light through the hedgerow of the left bank, illuminating the undergrowth on the right bank to a glowing colourful clarity, and leaving the left bank itself dark and featureless by contrast, already turned off for the night.

Two totally different settings in one lane, like the dark and light of people's characters, Jane thought

She decided the early morning was the best time to see Andrew.

"Oh, do you want to see me?" Jane stopped in the act of closing the door and waited for the two detectives to come up the path.

"Morning, Mrs Warren," Pockett said, looking into her eyes with puzzlement in his own.

"No, we wanted to speak to Miss Saunder. Is she in?"

"She's in the kitchen." Jane pushed the door back open, calling Trish, "Trish! Police!"

She left them in the doorway, without saying anything more.

"I wonder where she's off to," Joe muttered, watching the little figure go down the path.

"Wrong interrogative pronoun again, Joseph. What you should be asking is when and why."

"When and why what?"

Pockett finished wiping his shoes on the grass by the door. "When she decided to make a new entrance and why she's stayed behind the scenes so long."

"So, all in all, we thought we'd just dig our heels in and wait."

They were discussing the latest farming crisis.

"Everyone's in trouble, but we are luckier than some because of diversification. Nevertheless, we will lose out too."

"Of course," she said. "And are you managing with one man short? I expect in some ways all this trouble means less profit to pay someone else anyway. Have you been to see Steven much?"

Andrew put down his biro. "I try to call in every day."

"I've been to see him once. He looked very down, what with the police and the gossip; well he's bound to, isn't he? What do you think about all this?"

"I don't think about it, Jane, if I can help it. It's just too much like something on the telly, not quite real, you know? Steve didn't kill Lizzie, I know that. There's no way he would. Oh, I know they had their rows and that, but they were never violent. Lizzie had a tongue on her, didn't she? That was the trouble."

"Well, I never got out to see her much," Jane admitted, "but that's what I've been told. Had a bee in her bonnet about inheriting this place, didn't she?"

"Yes. Sometimes she would hint to me about the changes they would make. She had this way of sort of sneering, I suppose. When I would go to talk to Steve about something to do with the farm, she would be…well, odd, sometimes. Swanning around and sort of smiling at me in a nasty way, as if she knew something I didn't. She was a weird woman. I think Steve had a lot to put up with."

"Did you know about him and Trish?"

"I think I sort of guessed it was something like that. Don't blame him." He shifted in his seat. "And not my business," he said, shortly.

"No, you're quite right." Jane eased any tension with nods of agreement. "It's just a pity that it all came out now. Makes things look black for them to outsiders. I know Steve would never do anything like that. Well, we both do, don't we? He's a nice man."

"The police had a go at me, did you know?"

Jane shook her head in amazement. "What about, for goodness sake?"

"Well, boiled down, I think they were trying to find out if I resented Lizzie because I might get sacked when Steve inherited Chance, or whether I fancied her." He laughed at the idea. "Fancied her?! Ye Gods! And as for worrying about my job here, well Steve always said we worked well together." His face looked sad, as he added, "And we did. We did."

"It's not my business," Katie snapped. "I'm sorry for everyone involved, but what Trish and Steven do is not my business."

She was sitting in the tack room, saddle-soaping the reins, the head collars, and all the leather straps and saddles which hung from nails, or sat astride thick wooden beams. In a bucket, at her feet, several metal bits lay soaking in warm water. Jane watched as she expertly reassembled odd pieces of leather and metal, until the bridles were reformed, ready to hang back on the wall.

"But James is feeling pretty badly about it, isn't he?"

Katie's face flushed and concentrated on the straps in her hand. She didn't answer.

"How are Robert and Tim? You went to see them, didn't you?"

"Looking grim. Especially poor old Tim."

"At least it seems the police aren't bothering them now. Did you see Steven?"

"Just briefly."

"Poor man," Jane sighed. "I don't believe he or Trish had anything to do with this. I just wish I'd seen Trish that morning. Then she would have an alibi, wouldn't she?"

"Trish had nothing to do with killing Lizzie Warren," Katie said, bluntly.

"I agree, but it would have been easier if I'd seen her. I mean, you and James saw each other, didn't you?"

Katie nodded. "But that doesn't seem to have made things any easier," she said. "They still keep asking the same questions. What time? Where? I don't know what time." Exasperation showed in her face and voice. "I was weeding. I mean, you don't time yourself weeding, do you?"

"But you definitely saw James, didn't you, so why do they keep on?"

"You tell me, Aunt Jane! James crossed the entrance a couple of times. I saw him. Which entrance, they keep saying? What time? I don't know, for crying out loud! But I do know James didn't kill Lizzie Warren. You can't bash someone's head in by accident and that's the only way he might kill someone."

They smiled at each other, the atmosphere easing in remembering him and his two left feet, arms, legs, and any other apparently uncontrollable piece of anatomy that represented the child

James. His clumsiness was a family joke. A walking disaster for everyone around him.

"I'm sorry, Aunt Jane," Katie acknowledged her harsh attitude earlier, "but I'm sick of people going on about Trish and Steven. I wish it was all sorted and over, but it seems some folks have nothing better to do. It's their business, isn't it? If they want to be together, they should go for it and to hell with anyone else."

Jane watched the strong deft hands assemble another bridle.

Honest Katie. Direct Katie. Katie wanted the stables – wanted them more than anything – so who would she send to hell to get them?

"How's it coming then?"

"Well…" He looked up at her and smiled.

"Not ready for display at the show yet?" she laughed at him.

"One day…one day." He wagged his finger at her, patting the old tractor as though it was a favourite carthorse.

"Well, it looks good, even if it won't move," she said, trying to sound encouraging.

"Oh don't give up on it, or me, yet, Aunt Jane. We'll be in the Vintage Engines section at the Three Counties Show one day."

"I believe you! I believe you!" she protested, still laughing. "Of course, you've been saying that since you were thirteen, but I still believe you."

His brown eyes surveyed her laughing face as he leaned back to wipe his hands on a piece of old towel.

"You're very chirpy today," he smiled.

She let her face fall for a moment. "I'm trying to do my best, lad. It's bad times for everyone these last days."

They kept a respectful few seconds of silence.

"It must be hard for you too, James. I mean you and Katie, Robert and Tim. The Chance Gang. Well, you all go back a long way, don't you? How were they, the boys, when you went to see them?"

"Pretty cut up, like you'd expect. Tim, especially."

Jane sat down on a crate by the wall. "Poor Tim…poor Tim," she murmured. "What about Steven?"

James turned to put the rag down in a toolbox by the wheel of the tractor.

"I only saw him for a moment," he said.

Even with his back to her, Jane could feel the antagonism.

"Have you spoken to your mum about it?"

He slid down on the earth floor with his back against the wheel. She thought he looked as if he was about to cry. He picked up a handful of dry soil, turning his hand over to let it run through the curve of his little finger.

"Didn't you know?"

"About Steven and mum having it off?" he spat out harshly. "Do you know something, Aunt Jane, I don't bloody know if I knew or not. That's good, isn't it? I mean, I used to watch her: doing her face, putting her good clothes on, laughing and giggling, and then he would come. But I don't know if I ever thought it was to do with him. Not then anyway. And sometimes she would treat him like trash, you know? Glare at him and slam doors when he was around. Like she hated him. But I didn't know then. Love and hate…it's two sides of the same coin, isn't it? I didn't know that then."

"Do you think he's to blame for Lizzie's death?"

He shrugged but said nothing, back to filtering dry soil with his hand.

"Well, you don't think your mother had anything to do with it, do you?"

"No!" He threw the soil down. "No, of course she didn't. She's not to blame for anything. I think he was just using her, you know. His bit on the side."

"What makes you think that, for heaven's sake?" Jane looked horrified.

"Well, he was sleeping with his wife, wasn't he?" James defended himself.

"Of course he wasn't." Jane shook her head. "He loved your mother. He…"

"He was! He was!" James' agitation interrupted her indignation.

"No, not Steven…" Jane refused to believe it.

"Well, they said Lizzie was pregnant, didn't they? How do you think that happened?"

Jane looked shocked. "I can't believe it. No, no, I don't think Steven or your mother had anything to do with it. I just wish we were all together that day, so we could give each other alibis, you know?"

"Steve said he was at the market. And we were all here."

"Yes, but we never saw each other, did we? I expect the police asked you that."

"No, we never saw each other, but…"

Jane cut in, "No, you saw Katie, didn't you?"

The hesitation was barely perceptible. "Yes, I saw her; two or three times and places. Well, I don't know exact times. I mean, you don't keep looking at your watch, do you? But I told them I saw her. I really did. Lots of times."

"Painting," Jane said."

"Yes," he nodded emphatically. "Painting and weeding."

No, thought Jane. No. Katie's painting coat was in the tack room all morning. She had moved it to get her own coat when she took the dogs out at ten, and she moved it back again at eleven when she went to feed the cats.

She looked at the earnest young face in front of her. He had always loved Katie, she thought sadly.

Two sides of the same coin.

Trish wasn't Trish any more. All the animation, all the spirit was gone. She still put the music on her radio all day, but now it seemed to echo around the house.

No one sang to it, or danced little steps. No one shouted over it. It wasn't even comfortable background music. It filled the house with a noise no one heard.

"What did they want?"

"Oh the usual stuff."

"More questions?"

Trish nodded. "Mostly the same questions," she said.

Jane watched as Trish rolled some pastry out, turning and rolling until the rough circle was the size of the tin plate on the table.

The music thumped a happy beat and high young voices sang about taking some girl to the pictures.

"I'm leaving when this is sorted out." Trish's face was expressionless. Her voice a monotone.

"Where are you going?"

"Back to the city."

"What about James?"

"He's old enough to make his own mind up."

"But he wants to work in farming though."

Trish crimped the pastry edge with her thumb and forefinger. She shrugged.

"He might feel he has to go with you," Jane pointed out.

"No, he won't. He's been going his own way for some time. He's not a child."

She spooned mincemeat from a jar into the pasty case, levelling the surface.

"What about Steven?"

The spoon jerked, then smoothed the dip it had made in the surface.

"That's over."

"I've been to see him, Trish. He's desperate."

Trish brought a pan of stewed apple from the stove and began to spoon it over the mincemeat.

"Trish?" Jane urged. "Trish?" She watched the set face, looking down at the apple, smoothing the surface. "Don't do it, Trish," she pleaded. "Don't do what I did."

The spoon stilled on the apple and Trish looked at her.

"Don't run away." Jane reached for her hand, pulling her down to sit at the table.

"Do what you did," Trish repeated. "But you've always been here. You never ran away."

"You don't actually have to leave a place to run away. You can just disappear inside yourself. That's what I did and I was wrong. You have to stay and see the play through. If you and Steven are finished, then say it to each other. Make it clear, so you can shut the door and get on with your lives. Don't dodge the issue, or you'll waste so much time looking back."

"He put the phone down on me."

"Because he thought you thought he might have killed Lizzie. Is that what you believe, or was it just a knee-jerk reaction to your own feelings of guilt about saying you wouldn't marry him while Lizzie was alive?"

"Does it matter which? The effect is the same."

"Yes, it does matter. Look, you might feel a bit jealous if your partner smiles at another woman, but does that mean you believe he will jump into bed with her at the first opportunity? Of course it doesn't, because you recognise it as a knee-jerk reaction, and so does he if you tell him to keep his eyes off her. You smile at each other, because such feelings reaffirm your relationship. You don't go around worrying yourself sick that he's going to start an affair unless he's got a track record of that in the past. And Steven hasn't got a track record of killing his wives, has he?"

Trish smiled.

"No, he hasn't," Jane answered herself. "So, either you believe he did this, or you just overreacted. Whichever it was, you need to tell him. Phone him, Trish."

"He didn't kill Lizzie," Trish said.

"Then phone him. Tell him you believe that. Tell him you got stuck in reacting to your own feelings of guilt. He'll understand that. His new phone number is in the telephone drawer."

Trish stared at her.

Jane shook her hands. "Go on, do it. Do it. You need each other now."

Trish squeezed her hand and left to make the call.

Jane closed her eyes, head drooping down. Oh God, let me be wrong, she thought. Let me be wrong because if I'm not, they really do need each other now.

Jane wondered if they kept details of murders in the County Archives too. Had the story of Shirley and Jeff and Paul been added to the boxes about Chance? Were they going to start a new file now? The murder of Lizzie Warren.

She sat in the window seat in the morning room and looked in: to the fireplace, to the beams. What was it about this place? Maybe it was evil. Taking in life's waifs and strays, giving them purpose and confidence, then snatching it all away again.

She stood up and walked into the long hall, standing by the doorway, looking up and down the passage. She tried to see it like a stranger, really notice the old red flagstone floor, the wood panelling, the wealth of beams, some arranged regularly across the ceiling, some just appearing from the middle of nothing in particular, to disappear again, going nowhere in particular.

When she had cleaned and painted all around the house, she spent a lot of time trying to work out what disused window or doorway, what boundary or level, was signified by these haphazard appearances. Sometimes you could tell it was where a doorway used to be, or a cupboard, or something, but mostly they defied explanation.

She looked at the white walls, dotted everywhere with paintings and plaques, old candle-snuffers, key holders, pieces of poetic script with flowery borders. Everything from watercolours in carved antique mahogany frames, to bright beige pine thermometers, held by a smiling girl in a swimsuit, with 'Present from Brighton' scrawled in black on a flag across the top.

She looked at the thermometer, but she couldn't read the

temperature. She never had been able to see the tiny red line in the middle of the glass unless she took it to a window light.

She smiled as she looked at the uneven walls, thinking of little Katie, long ago, saying they needed ironing.

Yes that was long ago. City Katie, used to city houses. Straight lines and bare, uncluttered sterility. There wasn't any magic in buildings like that. There wasn't any emotion. Any continuance. Any life.

Katie. Katie and Chance.

No. Chance wasn't evil. Yet people would kill for it because they wanted to keep it, or because they wanted to take it.

She reached the telephone table and lifted the receiver.

She put the phone back, having said just five words to Mr Pockett.

Pockett put the phone down. "She knows," he said.

Joe looked at the blackboards, covered with names and lines, like a family tree.

"Why are you messing with all this? It's really got nothing to do with it."

"Yes it has. If you go back to why they were here in the first place, it has."

"Let's just go and finish it now. She could be in danger."

"She has the dogs. I told her to stay close to them. Don't worry."

"Finish it. Do it now," Joe said, but neither of them moved.

"How will she survive this time?" Pockett murmured, almost to himself.

They both sat, staring at the blackboards. The name at the top read 'Jane'.

They had their murderer, signed and sealed.

When they came to make the arrest, Jane had opened the door and Pockett had looked her in the face and made a small bow, as he said, "Mrs Warren."

It wasn't mockery. It was respect.

Now they were back to talk to the family. They were all there: Steven and Trish, close together on the settee, hands clutching hands, Katie, white-faced, on the hearth seat. Pockett and Joe sat in the armchairs. Jane went to the window seat.

"I'm sorry, Miss Saunder. Very sorry," Pockett said.

"Why?" Trish's face echoed the anguish in her voice.

"Jealousy. Possessiveness. He really loved you, you know. To him it was a way of getting rid of everyone who took your attention away from him. It all seemed so neat. Not at the time, you understand, not when he killed Lizzie, but afterwards. That Lizzie seduced him is beyond doubt. He went to see her to try to get her to keep her husband, Steven, away from you. Once he realised that you and Steven were meeting, and what that meant, he was frantic and angry. Angry because he thought he should have guessed years ago. Frantic to stop it now. He was young. He thought Lizzie could just order it to stop and it would. Lizzie knew better, but Lizzie saw a way to exact a perfect revenge. You had taken her husband. She would take your son."

"Tit for tat," Jane said. "What's sauce for the gander..."

"Yes, I believe those were the sayings she used to her friend. Young men are easy to seduce. A heady mixture of sexuality and romanticism. A few tears, leaning against his chest. A few confidences, muttered in a helpless voice. And it is done. Later on, when the need for her was strong, he planned his life around her. Go into farming. Take a cottage together. He almost forgot about Steven and you. But Lizzie didn't. Getting pregnant was an accident. Lizzie didn't want that. It wasn't part of the plan. She wanted to slowly poison his mind against you, and she wanted to hold on to Steven. So that one day she could go into Chance and kick you out, knowing your son would reject you, knowing she held a trump card over him for the rest of his life. A baby would destroy that dream. She was angry about it and she made the mistake of telling him she was pregnant. He was over the moon, wanting to make plans to get a house, talking of their 'family' and their future. She laughed at him, told him she had to get rid of it. It would spoil everything. She didn't want to live in a poky little cottage with him. She wanted Chance. The more he tried to say, but they loved each other, didn't they?, the more she spurted out the truth. Surely he realised that she was only getting back at Trish and Steven? Surely that's what he was doing too? He must be mad to think that she would give up Chance for him. Why this might even be Steven's baby, she lied, trying to put him off. So he cried and hit her, and kept on hitting her, to shut up the words he didn't want to hear. When he calmed down, he burnt the log on the fire and went back to Chance. He was still angry. Angry at seeing his dreams disappear. Angry at being used. All his life people had used him, put him second. He went back to Chance and Katie waved at him as he passed the store shed entrance. It was bad timing, for there was the very person he hated most in the world: Katie. Taking his mother's time. Taking his friends' attention. Taking the stables. He had always hated her, right from childhood."

"Too many accidents," Jane said. "Too many times when Katie was hurt."

"Yes," Pockett agreed, "he was clever. Pretending to look after her. Earning his mother's praise. But he hated her. Now he planned to pin Lizzie's murder on her. He went back to the house to check who was around. Katie saw him pass the livery yard entrance. She saw him pass again a short time later. When the questions began, he started to drip in the poison. Little hesitations, then obvious covering up for her. Hints about her hatred of Lizzie and her ambition for the stables. He was setting her up. Things were working out very well. His mother had ceased contact with Steven and he was getting rid of Katie. At last it would be as it should be. Just him and you, Miss Saunder. No more the second fiddle."

Steven had his arm around Trish and she was crying on his chest.

"Don't blame yourself, Trish," Jane said. "You never did treat him as second fiddle. That's just the way he twisted it in his mind. I think he needs help, love. I think he's needed it for a long time."

"I'm sorry, Trish." Katie's voice made everyone turn. She looked very young, huddled on the hearth seat.

"No, love, no." Trish's voice sounded cracked. "It wasn't your fault. Steve and I have had all night to talk and think. Somewhere in me, I always knew he wasn't right. He was good with his hands, even when he was young. Remember those really delicate models he used to make? Mending things. Making things. He was good. All that clumsiness when he was with you, it never seemed right. All the times he hurt you because his hand slipped, or his foot slipped. It never seemed right." She turned to Jane. "You guessed, didn't you? That's why you said we needed each other now."

"Yes I guessed. The accidents never seemed right to me either, but it was his own words that really made me think. He said he never realised that love and hate were two sides of the same coin. I just wondered why he realised it now. I thought he was talking about his feelings for Lizzie at first, but I think he meant Katie. He had hated her, been jealous of her, for so long. Then he grew older, started his affair with Lizzie, became sexually aware and the hated person became the desirable person too. He loved and hated Katie. And he couldn't cope with that."

Joe spoke to them of arrangements about visits and interviews and Jane got up to see them to the door.

"Goodbye, Jane." Joe held her hand longer than the handshake needed. "I'm sorry about all this. Thanks for letting us know he knew Lizzie was pregnant."

Jane smiled at him, but spoke to Pockett. "Seems you had already worked it out anyway."

Pockett bowed his head to her, smiling agreement.

Sue Ryland

"I won't be seeing you here again, Mr Pockett," she said. "I think it's time to really clean out the stables, don't you?"

Pockett took her hand. "You're a brave woman, Jane Warren. You would make a great psychologist, or a detective. You missed your vocation, you know."

"Too late now, Mr Pockett," she smiled. "Anyway, I never could abide policemen."

Pockett finished scraping his shoes on the grass verge, while Joe sat in the car, tapping his fingers on the steering wheel.

At last, Pockett heaved himself into the passenger seat. "I'd like to know how that turns out," he said, looking at the lighted windows of the farmhouse.

"She going to tell them, isn't she?" Joe followed his gaze.

"Yes. She's a brave woman. I think she will be all right. She's on her feet now and, once the shockwave passes, I think it will be all right. We could do her for fraud, you know. Falsifying birth documents…"

Joe fastened his seat belt.

"…and wasting police time…"

"But you won't," Joe said, "because not only do you like her, you're very like her as well."

"What?!" Pocket got ready to explode.

"Oh come off it, you know you are. As soon as that stepson and his wife said they were wrong about Eva having a child, you started worrying at it. Just like her, you are. Picking up little words, odd statements, and watching people."

"Are you calling me an old woman, Joseph?"

"I've been calling you that for years. I'm glad you noticed at last."

Joe started the engine. Pockett fastened his seat belt, choosing to ignore the last muttered statement.

"Right," he said. "Home, Joseph, and don't spare the horses…" He leaned his head back on the rest, "…because I've had enough of bloody horses to last me a lifetime."

There was silence in the morning room. A long stunned silence.

Steve was looking at his hands, occasionally lifting one to brush the hair back from his eyes.

Trish stared at Jane, her face frowning, her eyes questioning.

Katie looked as if she had been turned to stone.

Jane watched them and waited.

She had told them all of it...looking at Steve, as she spoke of Terry...looking at Trish, when she described how Eva had taken the role of Jenny's mother...looking at Katie, as she claimed her as her grandchild...looking at them all, as she apologised for her cowardice.

The dogs stood up and flopped down again.

Logs moved on the fire.

The clock ticked on.

No one spoke. The silence dragged.

"I've made a new will," Jane said, at last, "leaving the house and farm to you, Katie, to take over control when you are twenty-one. I've made an allowance to Trish and Steven to hold the place in hand until then. I know you will want them to continue in the house and farm after that too."

She got up and moved to the doorway. "I'm sorry to spring this on you now, Trish, on top of everything else, but there have been too many lies and secrets at Chance for too long. I just wanted it all clear. And I'm sorry about taking so long to get the guts to do it."

"I don't want the place." Katie's voice rang out clearly, as Jane reached the door.

Jane felt her stomach turn. It was the answer she was dreading.

"That's your choice," she said, turning to face her. "It will go to Steve and Trish then."

"Oh God, Jane." Trish found her voice, holding out her hand to her friend.

Jane could feel her heart working like on old pump in thick oil. She hadn't thought of Trish deserting her. She turned now to Trish, prepared to beg if necessary. But Trish didn't even appear to have registered Jane's last statement; she was still locked in trying to absorb and adjust to all this change, trying to understand how it happened.

She drew Jane to her. "You must have been through hell. Why didn't you tell me before? Jenny and I often talked about how hard it was in the old days to have an illegitimate child. Then to have lost a child before, due to the drunkenness of a man who…" She stopped, turning to Steve. "Oh God, Steve, I'm sorry. He was your father, wasn't he? I…."

Jane said sadly, "You see what I mean about complications…"

Steve shook his head. "No, he wasn't my father and he was a drunk. His driving killed him and crippled my mother. So don't worry, Trish, you won't offend me by sympathising with Jane." He put his hands on top of their two clasped hands. "I understand, too, Jane."

"I'm sorry, Aunt Jane," Katie responded to the clear bond of affection and support between the three older people…and to the look of disappointment she had seen Trish flash at her. "I'm sorry if I seem rude," she flushed, then with a rueful glance at Trish, went on, "But I don't want the farm just because of our…er… relationship. I want to build the stables on my own merit."

Jane looked at her and Katie stared back, lifting her head defiantly.

The direct blue eyes. The heart-shaped face. So like Jane's own grandmother. With Katie in charge, there wouldn't be any more secrets. She wanted this girl to love her, to be her friend, but for now it was enough if she just stayed around.

So she fought down her emotions and stared back into those eyes, saying sharply, "And who said anything about the stables? This is a farm. A farm that is now, and will be in the future, run well by Steven and Andrew. And this is a farmhouse, which is

Final chance

run by Trish. If you want the stables, you'll have to work at it, as your great aunt did before you."

They glared at each other, both heads held high.

"And it will be the best damned stables in the county," Katie snapped.

"It had better be," Jane snapped back, and for a moment their eyes twinkled at each other.

Jane sat at the kitchen table. Tomorrow she would start to face the world with nothing to hide.

She took the key out of her dressing gown pocket, the key to her chest of Day Books. Tomorrow she would burn them. The world may know the facts, but the feelings were her own. Tomorrow she would burn them.

She stroked the dog's head on her lap and thought about tomorrow. She sipped her mug of coffee and thought.

It was two-thirty in the morning. She hadn't been able to sleep, feeling a little sick and uneasy after the tensions of the day. So she came down with the dogs to her old place at the table.

Trish and Steven had gone to bed at midnight. She had heard them go up together. Together. No need for subterfuge. That was good. They would need all their strength for the months ahead. The court case would revive press interest, but Steven had had a little of that already, not as much as before, when the press surrounded Chance, but enough to be ready.

Jane thought back over those times. It seemed she remembered all the incidents, good and bad. Shirley and Eva and all the girls. The Misses and the Jennings. It was odd, because she had forgotten so much that had happened since. Perhaps she was really alive then. Vividly alive.

She hoped that Trish would feel that way when Katie got it all going again, because Katie would succeed and, this time, there would be no undercurrents waiting to pull anyone down.

Good times. Yes, they were good times. And Chance would see those days again. That made her feel good too.

Chance needed people – lots of people – to come alive again. Good days.

She stood up, wondering if she ought to get the range going, or was it too early yet?

She was so tired now. The sickness had passed. She wanted to sleep, but the stairs seemed so far away and she felt a bit giddy.

She was sitting with her dogs on the floor again.

She couldn't remember how she got there, but it was all right.

The dogs put their heads on her lap and whined softly as she closed her eyes.

She was smiling, thinking of all the old days at Chance. She could almost see them all, hanging over the schooling paddock fence, laughing as Shirley pushed a reluctant Miss Pittypat around the field.

She wasn't sure why Great Uncle William was there, or her Gran, but she was happy to see her. She could take her up the hill now to show her Chance, all laid out before her…

She was sitting on her rock, looking down.

This was her land, her life. There was nowhere else she wanted to be. She looked to Halfpenny Hill and then, nearer, to Cap Hill. She let her eyes fall slowly downwards…across the fields…across the brook…to the green and brown tiles of the granary…and then to Chance. That black and white structure that was the centre of it all.

No defined pattern.

No architectural grandeur.

Just Chance.

Home.

Heart.

"Look, Gran…" she said, as she held out her hand to her.

* * * * *